# Attack Hitler's Bunker!

## Lazlo Ferran

# Attack Hitler's Bunker!

## The RAF secret mission that never happened – probably.

Lazlo Ferran

Acknowledgments

Thanks to Ash and Derek, for their help bring this book to publication. A special thankyou goes out to Max Williams from the Stirling Aircraft Project for checking the technical accuracy of this book.

This book is dedicated to the actor and Academy Award Winner Cliff Robertson, who inspired me so much in my youth and, with whom I shared a passion for aircraft.

# Chapter One

--.,---,---,-..,-..,..-,-.-.,-.-,-..,---,.-.,..-.,--.,-,-.,-.,-.,...,--.,---,.-.,..,-
.,--.

At precisely 4.15pm, Michael eased back on the throttle and let his Bf 109E settle on her cushion of air. The silver ribbon of the Thames Estuary opened up below and ahead of him, as they emerged from below the cloud that had concealed the three aircraft for the last few miles while crossing the English Channel.

As planned, in the distance ahead of he could see the tiny bursts of flame and drifting smoke of the diversionary attack on West London by Heinkel He 111s. Everything seemed to be going to plan. Above him the glorious afternoon sun beat down in an almost clear blue sky on the Perspex of the cockpit. He twisted in his seat, first to his left and then right, to check Gustav and Joachim were in position behind him. Joachim, to his right waved once and stuck his thumb up, grinning. Michael turned back to look ahead and then took a deep breath.

'This is it!' he thought.

From 24,000 feet, he pushed the nose gently forward. As Gunther, his chief-mechanic had warned him, Daisy felt a little sluggish, loaded with 850 kilogrammes of the latest explosive, W-salz, packed in behind the pilot and fuel-tank. To compensate, rather than remove the heavy 20mm engine-cannon as well, they had left it in place. He heard the Daimler-Benz engine revs climb as the shaking needle on the airspeed indicator indicated 480 Km/h, 500, 520 … .

As the roaring slipstream started to shake the compact fighter the little Donald Duck Anna had given to him before the War started swinging violently from side to side, until its head started hitting the bullet-proof windscreen. He had to reach up and steady it to satisfy some strange inner urge. He pushed away the image of Oxford's old University buildings framing Anna's beautiful face, which came into his head unbidden, and focused instead on the image of all three aircraft flying smoothly between the span of Tower Bridge. He lined up the yellow nose of his beloved 109 Emile on the centre span and led the three Messerschmitt's, screaming, down to just ten feet above the choppy brown waves. Ack ack fire burned hot slices in the air all around them as they dove, but they were quickly too low for the desperate aim of the gunners.

***

Just before dawn on the 12th July, 1943, Oberleutnant Michael Dorfmann had swished aside the dewy grass with his leather boots as he walked up to the yellow nose of his Messerschmitt. Today would be the day of the attack and the first time he had seen Daisy since she had emerged modified from the Jagdgeschwader (JG) 26's workshops at Vendeville. The other two modified 109 Es, called affectionately Emiles, squatted menacingly in the grass either side, but both their pilots were still in their beds.

Michael reached up and patted the yellow spinner and then ran his left hand down one of the black propeller blades lovingly. His hand left the blade and flew through the air to land on the yellow-painted lower cowl of the engine. He patted her as if patting a lover's chin. Then he ran his hand along the leading edge of the port wing as far as the leading-edge slats. As his fingers passed over them, he ran his index finger around the glued patches over the machine gun ports. Although he hated war war, it seemed an injury that his aircraft had had her guns removed. She had been designed for one thing and one thing only; shooting down other aircraft, one of the things he didn't like about her. But love is able to accept a flaw.

She looked beautiful. She had also turned out to be the last 109 E in JG 26. Michael's old III Group had been using them when he had been posted to the Eastern front to command a new Group for the Russian invasion but then re-equipped with Focke Wulf 190As while he had been away. Out of all groups, the III's pilots had been least happy with the 190s and switched back to 109s, to the new 109 Gs by the time he had been posted back for this one, special operation. Somehow, Michael had been able to cut through red tape at every turn to keep Daisy. Being an ace had helped.

She came with the model's unique configuration of three cannons, two on top of the nose and one between the two banks of engine cylinder; a configuration, along with the 109's great manoeuvrability that Michael thought gave him the edge in battle.

He ducked under the wing and kicked the port tyre gently. Her stalky, splayed undercarriage made her look as awkward as a heron on the ground, but in the air, she performed like a swallow. Only the British Spitfire could be compared for beauty.

Gunther stood by the cockpit, cleaning oil from his ham hands with a blue rag.

"Taking her up, then Oberleutnant?" asked Gunther, his red-haired mechanic.

"A-ha. I bet she's a mess inside, but she still looks great! You did a good job. Thank you."

"She *will* be sluggish, especially in turns. Anyway, I think it the right decision to keep the cannon, but even with this and only half a tank of fuel, she will still tend to be tail-heavy, especially as you get low on fuel. You have about sixty kilos less fuel than the others, but as you say … you won't need it." Michael looked at his mechanic's piercing grey eyes, and both faces broke into wry, boyish grins. "Still, your take-off will be longer, so watch out for that. And don't tell anybody I left the cannon in. I will be court-marshalled, and Heidi will have my guts in a sausage!"

Michael loved Gunther's pithy remarks. Though he tried, he could never match them. "*If* … I survive."

"You will," mumbled the mechanic, turning his back on the young pilot and walking away. "Don't be late for breakfast. Schnapps!"

Michael turned and stared down the length of his aircraft's yellow nose, past the gothic black 'S' insignia of JG 26, to the yellow spinner and beyond to the horizon where the red streak of dawn's first light cut the sky like a gash.

"Red sky in the morning … ," he said idly, forgetting the rest of the English saying. He took one more glance to the rear, past the yellow '1' on the rear fuselage indicating his rank, to the tail and then climbed onto the low wing and into the cramped cockpit. Gunther always checked Daisy over thoroughly. Normally Michael would go right around the aircraft, checking everything, but his stomach felt like the Gordian knot. He could not unclench his abdominal muscles. Not having slept for fear of the day's mission, he wanted to take her up and get used to her new temperament. At least that would be one less 'unknown.'

He lowered himself into the prototype seat which had two steel tubes protruding from either side at its back. The smell of a BF 109 cockpit, a combination of leather, acrid cordite, rubber, high-octane fuel and oil at first, repelled one. But once you were inside, the warm aromas closed around you like the smell of your favourite old lounge chair.

Checking his mirror, Michael stared at his own head, dark, wavy hair above penetrating green eyes that suddenly seemed too serious and world-weary for the boyish face that contained them. He shook his head and went through the start-up procedure carefully. Because of the new forward position of the seat, he struggled to reach the engine primer control and could only operate the elevator trim wheel with the tips of his fingers.

'Not good!' he said to himself.

Putting on his leather helmet, goggles and gloves, he tapped Donald once for luck, as he always did and gunned the Daimler-Benz engine into noisy, rude life. The twenty-four hungry cylinders ripped apart the silent air over the airfield, and Michael laughed at the sheer joy of it. He forgot his fear as he taxied across the wet grass carefully and turned onto the long, flat strip of short grass of Vendeville's runway. As he taxied gently towards its end, slowly weaving, so that he could see over the long nose, he passed three of the newer Focke Wulf 190A's. He admired their smooth, aggressive lines, but he felt glad he had been allowed to hold on to Daisy for this last mission. It would be a fitting end for his companion, who had been with him since 1939.

Taking a deep breath after turning around at the end of the airstrip, he pushed forward the throttle with his left hand and waited for the tail to come up. It took much longer than usual. His airspeed hadn't increased enough when he reached half way down the grassy causeway to the sky. He swallowed.

'Eight hundred kilos of dynamite behind my ass! Oh well, at least I only have half a fuel tank under me!' he said to himself.

Michael eased back on the stick as late as he dared, and the aircraft lifted lightly into the air.

'Just needed a little speed, eh baby?'

***

Now Michael led the formation, diving on London. They emerged from under Tower Bridge, almost line abreast. Michael saw how little the City had changed. Apart from the preponderance of men in khaki uniforms, barrage balloons and slit covers on car headlights, it really hadn't changed at all. For just an instant, he wished he could walk down Charing Cross Road with a pocket full of shillings and half-crowns. And then all hell broke loose. Two destroyers were moored on the right bank of the Thames, and somebody had told them what was coming.

"Damned Tommy luck again! Just in the wrong place at the wrong time. Planners didn't tell us about this!" he said out loud.

40 mm and 20 mm cannon fire as well as 0.50 inch machine gun bullets sliced the air all around the little Messerschmitts, and ahead little black clouds started to pock-mark the sky above the bridges from the ineffective Ack-ack.

"We're too low! You'll hit your *own* buildings!" Michael shouted inside his cockpit. But the British gunners were reckless in their determination to down the Nazi attackers.

Tracer from the cannons ripped through the air in a line just ahead of his aircraft's nose, and Michael instantly banked to the right. He didn't have to worry about his two wing-men; Joachim had been with him since France during 1940 and had the rank of Oberleutnant Staffelkapitän. Gustav, much younger, still flew a 109 better than any other pilot Michael knew. Joachim had been a natural choice as yellow-2, but it had been a surprise when Gustav volunteered for such a dangerous mission. They jinked left and right, almost in unison, as the destroyers spat orange flame and black smoke.

'Wonder if Gunther left any ammo in this thing?' Michael wondered.

As the bow of the furthermost destroyer glanced the bead of the sight, Michael pressed the firing button on his joy-stick. The nose of the 109 juddered as the MG FF cannon opened fire, sending tracer arching into the water just short of the ship. As he turned left again, Michael lifted the nose slightly and had the pleasure of seeing a few hits on the hull of the ship and a panic of activity on her fore-deck.

"Thanks Gunther!"

London Bridge came up fast, and Michael began to think they would make it when he felt a mighty explosion behind him. He had no time to look.

"God help us!" he muttered, just as Daisy's wing-tips passed under the modern bridge. As the sky went dark for a moment, he glanced to his right and breathed a sigh of relief. Joachim's aircraft still shadowed him, although black smoke poured from his engine and Michael could see a lot of damage to the top of the nose.

'You won't last long, Joachim. Better ditch!' he thought.

But he knew his friend wouldn't give up while there seemed a way to keep his bird in the air.

The gunfire stopped at last, and they passed under Southwark Bridge, then Blackfriars.

"Now!" he shouted.

Michael pulled up on the stick, and yellow-1 pulled lazily up, away from the muddy Thames. Steering to the right, Michael lined up on Somerset House, which looked just like the models they had studied. He peered down over the cockpit edge, looking for The Strand. Its long curving gully stretched out below him while he slowed to 380 Kmh, as they had practiced. The slower speed would be necessary to allow more accurate aiming when they reached the Palace. Behind him the others would be slowing even more to create a big enough gap that if any of them crashed or blew up in mid-air, the explosion wouldn't take the others out.

The Adelphi Theatre flashed by to his right. Michael smiled at the pleasant memory of an evening there. Recalling the practice runs over streets marked out in chalk on fields near Audembert, he peered through the windscreen, watching for Trafalgar Square.

"There it is!"

In a blink of an eye he passed it by and flicked the nose of his aircraft up, slightly more than he normally would, to clear Admiralty Arch. Only then could he drop below roof level since reconnaissance and spy-photos had shown there were no telegraph wires crossing The Mall. As he pushed the nose down, the engine coughed twice and then continued its snarling scream.

"Out of fuel."

He felt a massive explosion rock the tail of the aircraft and knew that Joachim had met his maker. A moment later red and yellow light flickered across the edifices and shadows of the pale building along The Mall, making them blush in the early afternoon. Michael closed his eyes involuntarily for a moment. Then he forced himself to focus. Somewhere behind him, he hoped Gustav still followed, so he had to get this right. He eased back further on the throttle and saw the airspeed indicator touching 330 Kmh, the correct speed for the attack.

Somebody fired at him. A machine gun round pinged harmlessly off from the nose armour in front of the cockpit. He aimed the nose of the aircraft in the general direction of the fire and pressed the trigger, emptying the last few cannon shells into the unseen target. The entrance to Churchill's bunker, the secondary target, flicked past on the left, but his stare fixed on Buckingham Palace, half a mile in front of him. In that moment, all suddenly seemed quiet and calm. Michael could barely hear the engine, and an image, unbidden, came into his head of Anna's soft red lips. He tried to push it away, but then he heard her crystal-clear laugh, just as he had last heard it in Oxford.

"Not now!"

He tried to focus and went through the procedure in his head, all within a fraction of a second.

'Arm. Press cockpit release. Aim. Eject. This is it. No!'

The exclamation seemed spoken by an unfamiliar voice, a part of him he didn't recognise.

Suddenly he saw himself, back in Oxford, on the day he and Anna had borrowed two bicycles and ridden out to the country for a picnic. England looks at its blooming best in June, and they had found a field, laced with white daisies and poppies, to eat in. After, they had laid on their backs looking at the scudding clouds. He began trying to teach her how to make a Jewish-harp from a blade of grass, stretched between her flattened palms, and they gave up, laughing.

"What do you want to do when you leave Oxford?" she asked.

He rolled over to look at her beautiful face with her hazel eyes, floating mysteriously under a bewitching wave of ebony hair. Until then, they had only been friends, but that wasn't as the way he had wanted it.

He put the tip of the blade of grass in his mouth. "Oh, I don't know … . Go back to Germany perhaps …  There seems to be a lot of opportunities for physicists over there … ."

"No, I mean what do you want to do with *physics*?"

"Oh … . I want to know how the universe works, and what makes stars and all about light and … ." He looked at her, but she seemed lost. He continued, "But what I really want to know, is what makes women the way they are. What makes *them work*?"

She smiled, and he felt a curious tightening in his stomach. "I think you will need more than physics for that!"

"I suppose you mean meta-physics, or … or something." He nearly said 'biology,' but that would have been too awkward.

"I will show you if you like." She looked down at the grass but then seemed suddenly emboldened. "I will show you everything!" She looked at him, and their eyes met. "Then you will know," she added.

How could you not fall in love with a girl that offered to show you all her secrets?

Suddenly, Michael felt released. He has been focused for months so totally on the mission, his real mission that he had forgotten for a moment the motivation that had driven him; his desire to see Anna again. Now he just had to focus on getting down.

'Strange that only now I stop pretending! Did I really think the others could tell from the way I flew?' he wondered.

He knew the untried ejector seat might go off during a rough landing, either crushing his head against the canopy frame or cutting his neck with shards of Perspex. He pulled the nose of the Messerschmitt up to soar above the Memorial to a German Queen, in front of the Palace gates, up and over the Palace itself and pulled back the canopy eject lever to his left. An instant later, the canopy jettisoned. The sudden, violent flow of air whipped around the cockpit's remaining armoured windscreen and slapped at his face. Through squinting eyes, he throttled back as far as he dared and lowered the flaps.

'I hope this explosive really is as stable as they say!' he said to himself.

In the distance, just where he aimed for, he could see the flashes from the AA guns in Hyde Park. When he had studied the maps, the only possible place for a landing proved to be a narrow strip alongside The Serpentine. Even then, it seemed much too short for a wheels-down landing. On such uneven ground and with possible obstacles, the delicate undercarriage of the 109 would collapse and send the aircraft cart-wheeling or tumbling end over end. It had to be a belly-landing.

As the tree tops of first Green Park and then Hyde Park floated by, Michael searched hard for the head of The Serpentine. Somewhere behind him, he knew Gustav would be about to eject, and he expected a loud explosion any second.

'I just pray the ejector-seat works for him.' he said to himself

The engine coughed a few more times, shaking the whole aircraft, and then the engine note shifted down a few octaves before one last cough and then it grew silent. The blades continued to turn. Michael turned the pitch control to the coarsest setting, to get a little less resistance from the wind-milling blades. He floated, only about thirty feet above the ground now.

To his left, where he hadn't expected it, he suddenly saw the reflections from water, the lake. He banked gently to follow its northern shore and squeezed the wing-tips between an old building and the bank of the lake, where it turned to the north. He banked gently to the right and eased the aircraft down into the soft, English grass. The impact nearly wrenched his teeth out of his mouth, and his head hit the soft padding on the gun-sight, designed to cushion just such a blow. He felt completely disorientated for a moment as clods of grass clattered against the rear fuselage and tail-plane. With one last judder the aircraft came to a halt, rocking slightly from side to side. He shakily released the harness and stood up in the cockpit. He jumped to the grass just as a blinding flash assailed his sight from behind Daisy. A moment later, he saw a burst of light from a gigantic fireball rising in the sky behind The Palace. The sound of a thundering explosion, ripping the air apart, followed, a moment later.

Michael looked back at the ugly brown furrows in the grass that marked the trail the Messerschmitt had left behind. Some way back they appeared to twist right round. It seemed that the aircraft had spun through a full circle on the hard, July soil when the wing-tip hit a park bench and then continued on. Either side of the crashed aircraft, not far apart, were two AA guns, pointing to the sky. They had stopped firing, and the gun-crews looked with gaping mouths at the German pilot and his aircraft.

'Passed right through them!' he mused.

"Sorry old girl," he said, patting the side of Daisy. He started to walk towards the gunners, taking a Regie 4 Brand cigarette from his silver case in his shaking hand and putting it in his mouth.

"Have you a light, please?" he said in precise English, as he approached the nearest man. But at that moment, two men in khaki uniforms brandishing Enfield rifles stepped up to him from behind and shouted "Handy hock!"

It was 4.29pm.

***

At 7.20pm, Archibald Gates stopped outside the large oak door to his superior's offices in the Security Services. He had been told not to go home but wait until summoned by telephone. The telephone call had come, and now he stalked down the corridor. Archie, as his friends knew him, had achieved the status of a middle-ranking civil servant. Flat-footed and from a wealthy family, he had read too many Biggles stories before the War. He had no known talents other than patience, a certain smooth and easy obsequiousness and a keen aptitude for chess. He mused downwards, looking at his scuffed black, patent leather shoes. His feet were two inches too long for his five feet eight frame.

The door opened and a hand waved him into the room. From behind the dazzling light of a desk-lamp, pointed vaguely in his direction his director spoke.

"The Palace affair earlier … ."

Archie nodded.

"Winston sees it as a counter-threat after Operation Upkeep, that Dams affair. He wants a response. I have seen everybody else in your department … ." A smiling face replaced a mop of spare blonde hair, for a moment, when the director looked up from the memo in front of him. "Sorry for keeping you late Archie. I don't have much hope you will come up with anything, you're not a creative individual, but I need every brain we have on this."

Archie nodded.

*Wonder why he always has to have that damned lamp shining in our faces. Swine!*

"Well that's it. Go away and think about it. Come back tomorrow with an idea. Oh, one other thing, the pilot who survived, a … Oberleutnant Michael Dorfmann, keeps asking for an Anna Styles. The usual thing … . Won't give more than name, rank and number but then asks for her."

Archie nodded again, furrowing his brow.

"Could be significant. We located her. Pick up the dossier from my secretary. That's all we have. Good night, Archie."

***

"Anna! Anna! There's somebody to see you, from the Ministry!"

Anna looked up from her final scribbled decode attempts of the day and laid her pencil squarely next to the pad. She stood up and walked to the door.

"Which Ministry?" she asked.

"I don't know."

The tall man with slickly greased black hair look very tired, but he smiled at her and extended his hand. He twisted hers slightly as they shook, in an old-fashioned gesture of gentlemanly solicitude, as if he were about to kiss it.

"I drove straight here from London, but what with the constant air-raid warnings and checkpoints, it took a lot longer than I would have liked. Sorry."

Anna shook her head in confusion. "But what are you here to see me about?"

"You need to come with me. Orders, I'm afraid."

"But … ."

"Sorry, but you are needed in London. Anything you need will be sent later."

"Oh well! If I must. Wait just one moment."

She returned to her desk and took her pastel-blue jacket, a gift from her Uncle in Venice, from the back of the chair and returned to the hut entrance. The man held the door open and guided her to a large, black car. She climbed in the back and sank into the leather seats, luxuriating in their scent, but crossed her arms to indicate her disapproval.

On the drive to London, the man attempted to engage her with platitudes and light discourse, but when she asked for clues about their destination, he remained silent.

By the time he woke her, they had reached London, cloaked in blackout, night without stars. She stepped, sleepily, out of the car, through a black door and followed him up a narrow staircase to a rude little room, painted only in green and brown. The driver smiled once and left her with another man, grey-haired, whose white shirt and purple tie looked as crisp as if newly pressed.

"Please sit," the man said with the authority of a new doctor. "Miss Styles?"

"Yes."

"I want to ask you a few questions." The door opened behind her and an elderly lady brought a cup of tea and placed it in front of her. The blue and white porcelain cup rocked delicately on its saucer and two digestive biscuits sat beside the cup. "Sorry. There's no sugar," he continued. "But I know you have milk with your tea." She nodded. "Anna Nicoletta Styles; mother, Italian, father, English. One younger brother. Hm." The man, older than the driver and with hair going silver, cleared his throat as a punctuation. "You graduated at Oxford with a first in Mathematics … . Brilliant student with great potential … . Hm. Praise indeed." The man lifted up his face from the single double-spaced, type-written sheet of paper and smiled. His cold, blue eyes sent a shiver down her spine.

'He thinks I'm an uppity female!' she mused.

"And now you are work at Station X?" The sentence had only the faintest hint of a question in its inflected ending.

"Yes?"

"Well … what do you think of it there?"

"I don't know what you mean." She still felt half asleep. She lifted the porcelain cup to her lipstick coated lips and sipped. The tea was only lukewarm, so she drained it. It tasted stewed and she repressed a little shudder.

"Do you *like* it?" He seemed to be getting impatient.

"Oh. Yes. Most of the time it's really rather fun. I like the work too. Useful, I mean, I feel that I'm doing some good."

"Good," he echoed. He drew the sheet towards him and turned it over. It had type on the back, too. He leaned back in his chair and made a church with his fingers.

"If I was to ask you whether you would like to make a more … useful … contribution to the War Effort, what would your first thought be?"

Stunned, she lifted a digestive from the saucer and nibbled it. "Well, I would have to know what it was, of course. If it wasn't … too dangerous and was really useful, then I don't see … . I mean, I would like to help."

"Um. Your parents were *both* interred at the beginning of the War and were released in March. Regrettable mix-up with your father, but of course he *had* taken Italian Citizenship. Have you ever wondered why you were recommended, and accepted, for X?"

"Yes, actually. Many times."

"Quite. You have talent … and we wanted to keep an eye on you. Part of the reason your parents were released early was, *because* of your performance." She nodded nervously. "But of course," he added slowly, "they could *soon* be sent back."

"But … ."

"Does the name Michael Dorfmann mean anything to you?" He knew it did. Her heart skipped a beat.

"Yes. We dated at Oxford. He was a physicist. I … we, were in love."

"Today, at about 4pm, an attack was launched on Buckingham Palace, you will no doubt have heard of it on the Home Services. Oberleutnant Michael Dorfmann crash-landed his aircraft in Hyde Park and has been taken prisoner." He paused to watch her reaction. She stared at him, as if at a ghost. "He has, of course, only given his name, rank and serial number … but he keeps asking for you."

"I … I see."

"We would *like* you to meet him, but we want his co-operation. I don't know if you know this, Miss … Styles, but we have quickly learned, during this War … in this department, that even good German officers can often be persuaded to give us at least some information and help us. Do you see where I am going with this?"

"I … I'm not sure … ."

"Well, let me be specific. We want *your* Michael Dorfmann to tell us all about the attack; the explosives they used, how they planned it, who authorised th- … in fact, anything he can tell us. He is, after all, a high-ranking officer. All we are asking is that you pick up where you left off. We will do the rest."

"Then, what you said about my parents … ." Her brow creased, and she looked darkly at the man opposite her.

"War can be unpleasant Miss Styles. I just wanted to make it quite clear where we stood. Are we clear?"

"Bastard," she said quietly, once, under her breath. The man did not react. "Yes. Yes, I would like to meet him. How soon can it be arranged?" she asked, quite composed.

***

Archibald Styles couldn't sleep that night. He had finally come up with one good idea, the first in his life, and he knew it would propel him to the top of his career ladder.

Waiting to catch a late train home from Euston, he had been pacing up and down at the end of the platform, going over what he knew of the raid that day on the Palace, Oberleutnant Michael Dorfmann and Anna Styles. As it often did, his mind played out various classic set pieces from the best international chess championships, in the background, a mental twitch he couldn't control. Another pacer interrupted his thoughts when they both met head on. Both shifted in the same direction so blocking each other's path again. It irritated Archibald, but as he finally passed the man, muttering, a double-bluff move he had once seen sprang into his mind.

He heard himself say, "That's it!" quietly. Then the whistle of a train eased it from his mind. His own train then arrived, and he had traveled half way to Aylesbury before he managed to retrieve the idea.

"Do exactly the same to the Germans! Attack the Bunker! Leak intelligence out, so they think it's a bluff, whereas in fact, we will actually do it!"

His idea, in the form of a single line memo, lay on the desk of his superior at 8.45am the following morning. By lunchtime he had started to think it wasn't such a good idea at all, and by 4pm he accepted that his idea would not be the one chosen. He was, therefore, very surprised when his phone rang, and that familiar, supercilious voice asked him to, "Come at once."

The familiar desk lamp shone in his face as his superior delivered the verdict. "Archie. I never thought I would say this, but your idea is exactly what we need. Winnie likes it. The project is yours. What do you need?"

Archibald felt too taken aback to say anything, except, "Give me half an hour."

In the following thirty minutes, repeated images of his favourite hero, Biggles, screaming down from the sky in furious attacks on Jerry, invaded Archibald's mind while he tried to come up with the bare bones of a project that might work. He didn't even know how to fly, let alone the techniques needed to bomb the Bunker. One thing he had learned in the Civil Service; if you didn't know something technical, there would always be somebody to ask. So in the end, he knew he needed one thing and he wrote it down on the memo he took back to his superior: a pilot expert in low-level flying. By noon the following day Archibald had his list of eligible pilots. He could only see one name on the list.

***

*2am 14<sup>th</sup> July. Telephone call from Adolf Hitler's office in the Reichtag to the office of Reichsmarschall Herman Göring:*

> *"First you lose the Battle to dominate the British skies, and then you insult them with a secret mission to attack their Royal Head! And you don't even tell me! Imbecile! I should have you shot for insolence! You had better do better defending Italy, or you will regret not having been shot!"*

The Hurricane's propeller stopped spinning and Richard Earlgood could only hear one thing; the 'tick, tick,' of hot metal cooling down. He closed his eyes and leaned back against the headrest, revelling in the ecstasy of survival. He didn't move until his ground-crew clambered on the wings and tapped on the canopy.

"You alright, sir?" said Beattie, as Richard pulled back the canopy.

Richard's jut-jawed, but down-beaten, face creased in a big smile that always cheered those around him like rays of sun. Pale marks around his blue eyes contrasted with his oil-covered cheeks as he ripped off his leather flying helmet and goggles, releasing his black wavy hair. "Yeah. I think so. Sorry about the ol' gal, though!"

His crew Chief's joined the face of Beattie, peering down at him. "She's a bit of a mess sir, but we'll have her right as rain by tomorrow. The old Hurri may be slower than a Spit, but at least the cannon-rounds go straight through! Tea's up in the mess, and there's somebody to see you."

"Really? Who?"

"Don't know, rightly. Funny looking chap. Ministry type."

"Oh."

"You been up to your tricks again, sir?"

"No. Not lately. I want to make Squadron Leader, before Jerry gets me."

With a pained glance at the large holes in the fabric on the rear fuselage, Richard headed for the green-painted, wooden hut where tea awaited.

*If it had been a Spit, I would be dead now!*

"They told me your plane's been damaged! Are you alright?" An awkward, gangly young man with clean white skin, tightly cropped brown, curly hair and very large feet, welcomed Richard with a mug of tea.

"One of those Focke Wulf 190 jobs. Fearsome. We were jumped! Only three of us made it back! These damned raids over France do more damage to *us* than the enemy!"

"Ah yes. The Butcher Bird! Isn't that what you *chaps* call it?"

"Well, yes, some of us *chaps* do!"

Richard perched on the edge of a large oak table and reached over to pick up one of the three white cups of muddy tea which had just been poured.

"D'ya get one, Mister Earlgood?" shouted the station cook.

"Nope." After a few sips of tea, he put the cup down and drew off his gloves. "So what's cookin' then?" The young man's forced use of 'chaps' inclined him to be suspicious, but

Richard, being 'different' himself, had learned not to make fast judgements.

Archibald blurted out, "Low level pilot! I need one. And I hear you're the best!"

"Ha! Who told you that?"

"Eiffel Tower, 14th May 1940? Wellington Bomber. Leeming airfield, August 1940? Short Stirling, I believe?"

"Ah, well the lowest span of the Tower is *hundreds* of feet high, plenty of headroom *there*! The Stirling was fun though." Richard sucked in his breath at the memory of his punishment after flying underneath one of the new Stirlings coming in to land on a windswept Yorkshire airfield during the height of the Battle of Britain. He had emerged under the nose, his cockpit between those great wheels only seconds before they squealed on the concrete.

"Well, you clearly have talent. Hr-hm. If I may say so," Archibald whispered, leaning closer, conspiratorially. "It may have been a thorn in the side of the RAF, your … er … practice before, but right now it's exactly what we *need*."

Richard looked at him suspiciously.

"It would mean promotion … ?"

"Oh well, that's it then. No problem! Are you telling me, with my history, that they're willing to promote *me*! I'm probably the only pilot in the RAF, from the Battle of France who still *isn't* a Squadron Leader! It must be *suicidal*! Not that I care much, but I do want to survive … . Sorry, I am really very tired. I haven't had leave for what seems like years". He stroked a greasy smudge on his forehead.

"All I need, initially is somebody to help me plan it. I have very little technical knowledge of planes … . Apart from a few stints in a Tiger Moth, paid for my father I might add, I know very little. I need somebody who knows technicalities and tactics … . And low-flying of course."

"Aircraft. A pilot never calls it plane. It's an *aircraft*."

"Right."

"All you need is a planner?"

"Yes. For now. And your name is the only one on my list."

"Where do I sign up?"

"Good. Glad to have you aboard." Archibald thrust out his hand. Richard shrugged and then took it.

"I understand you will need to get the release from your C/O. Then grab your things, and I will drive you to London."

"One thing before you go," said Richard's C/O as he picked up the signed release form in the cramped office. "God knows why, and given your antics under my command, this isn't my decision, mind … but I have been instructed to promote you to temporary rank of Squadron Leader. As of now! Good luck. Maybe at last your low-level flying skills will have some use!"

***

Anna' heart fluttered uncontrollably as she fumbled for the last cigarette she knew nestled in her handbag.

"You can go in now. Five minutes. No more. I will knock on the door when your time is up."

To her surprise, she had been told Michael waited in the very same building in which her interrogation had taken place. In fact, he waited only a few doors away, but she couldn't meet him until he had been fully debriefed. She had been given a room at a cheap hotel nearby and brought back the following afternoon. There, a guard led her to an adjoining room with a few hard chairs and asked to wait.

She stood up, straightened her skirt, snapped shut her handbag and smiled at the man, who led her down a short length of corridor to a door which he opened. Stepping through it she immediately stopped, seeing a tired looking man in flying uniform, sitting on a chair. He jumped up, and the door closed behind her.

"Anna!"

"Michael?"

"Anna, dear." He rushed over and clasped both her hands between his. "I can't believe they have … I mean … ."

"No. I know what you mean … ."

"Well, let me look at you!" He spun her round him. "You haven't changed one bit, apart from your hair being shortened and … yes … you are even more beautiful … ."

She blushed. "Thank you, Michael. I … I don't have long. Just five minutes, they said. I know you can't tell me much. But what have you been doing? How are the family? Heidi and your mother?"

"Fine! Fine. I have been doing well, Oberleutnant now! Or was! I have no idea what will happen to me now. I flew on a raid against your Palace, but I couldn't do it! I … ."

"Yes. They told me … ."

"Anna! I missed you," he said after a long silence. "I wanted to see you so *many* times!"

"Did you?"

"Yes. I know … I was a young fool, believing the Third Reich needed me and, more stupidly, believing the *Third Reich* stood for something fine and grand!"

He drew her down to a chair next to his, not letting go of her hands. He gently massaged them between his, and she felt some pain, some bitter resentment, ever-so-slightly melt inside her. She resisted the feeling. They sat for some time, looking into each other's eyes, reading thoughts and half-lost memories.

"I thought about you a lot Michael, but you left me in a lot of misery. You can't expect me to … " She gathered all her resolve for one moment. "Why did you ask for me?"

He looked confused for a moment. "Why did you come?"

She felt at a loss.

'He suspects me. What do I do?' she wondered.

"I … I'm not sure. I suppose … maybe I was curious … . I don't even know why I'm here. Why they brought me, I mean."

"I know. Don't worry, soon we will spend more time together."

"You think so?"

He stared at her for a long moment, drinking in her beauty and flinched once at the look of lost innocence in her eyes.

She heard a sharp rap on the door. She turned and walked out of the room.

***

Richard drove from London up to his old digs in Yorkshire for the last time. There were only two suitcases to pick up in the annex to the farm where he had been staying. He knew it would be a long drive, and he had been on the road for seven hours already. Dusk approached when he drove into a storm.

With the tiny Austin Ruby's single wiper blade struggling against the torrential rain, he regretted not taking his things with him before. As usual, he found his mind pondering the strange conundrum Archibald had landed on him.

He didn't know the target, he didn't know the weapon, and he didn't know the terrain. So far, all he did know was that he had to find a way to get a fighter to a location, five hundred miles away, have time to make a circuitous approach to a difficult target at ground level and then fly four hundred miles back to a safe landing somewhere.

Once at the target, the aircraft had to be able to negotiate narrow flight paths between obstacles as little as thirty yards apart and drop a weapon-load of at least one thousand pounds.

Automatically, he had thought of the Hawker Hurricane. Not only did he have considerable experience with it, but in theory it could carry two five-hundred-pound bombs. The snag? A big one. It only had a maximum range of six hundred miles, barely enough for the outward leg of the mission. After he, Archibald and a pair of civvie-street ordinance experts had gone over the rough idea in a Whitehall office, he had spent the next three days racking his brain to think of a solution. So far, he had none.

Two points of yellow light suddenly flashed in the slit-beam of the car headlights, too close to avoid by braking. He swerved and nearly turned the car over on the slippery road before skidding to a shuddering halt.

"Damn! What the *hell* was that?"

He climbed out of the car and, pulling his jacket collar up against the driving rain, walked back along the road. There, forlorn on the rough tarmac, sat a bundle of brown fur. Clearly it had been wounded, and his first instinct made him want to walk away.

"*Damn!*"

He walked around the shape and saw that it was a rabbit. Its nose twitched in the rain, and it looked down at the road, avoiding his gaze. Its ears were back against its head, and it shook violently, terrified.

Again, he had the urge to walk away, but before he could think any more about it, he had bent down and scooped the frightened ball of fur up in his arms. He saw blood on its right, front leg. It squealed when he touched the leg.

"Seems to be broken. There now, it's alright."

It seemed too exhausted to struggle much. After a few feeble wriggles, it lay still. Richard walked back to the car and put the creature on the rear seat. He went to the boot, took out a picnic blanket and wrapped it around the poor animal.

As the car rumbled on in the rain, he was reminded of one Christmas day, ten years before, when he and his older brother, Martin, discovered a starling, frozen into the snow. They had brought it inside and warmed it up in a bed of straw lined with woolen sheets, placed near an old boiler. To their surprise the starling recovered quickly but showed no sign of wishing to leave. It had stayed, fed and kept warm, in their house until Boxing Day when it finally showed its readiness to leave by pecking on the window pane. The memory made him laugh.

"You'll be alright, little one," he said to his new passenger. "Richie will take care of you." This suddenly reminded of his brother, Martin. Only Martin called him Richie.

A tear wetted the corner of his eye. Martin's first card had arrived in January:

> Reached Southampton. Can't wait to see you and
> the family. Want to fly again. Martin.

The week before that, a telegram from the Foreign Office had been the first indication that he was still alive, after his Stirling had been shot down over Holland. Richard couldn't wait to see him and hear all about his adventures. He never tired of Martin's stories of hairy 'wizard wheezes' in Stirlings.

"Just like a builder with vertigo! Only good for lifting and dropping heavy weights from a low altitude, that's what the powers-that-be now say about the Stirling!"

"That's it!" Richard suddenly shouted out loud in his car. "The Stirling! There has to be some use for the old crates!"

He drove on, singing to himself all the way to the farmhouse where he picked up his things. He left the rabbit with the Shentons, who owned the farm and promised to pay the vet's fees to have its broken leg fixed. They pleaded with him to stay the night and shelter from the storm. Saying good bye to the protesting farm-owners, he left with the two suitcases on the long drive back to London.

He wouldn't arrive back in London until 3am. This didn't leave much time for sleep before the next briefing. It had been foolish to drive, but he so rarely had the chance to drive the Austin these days and loved the Yorkshire Moors. On the way he wondered about Short Stirlings, the rabbit and a pair of black, nylon panties he had found under the bed. He had packed them too, so as to save Mrs Shenton the embarrassment.

*Must have been a girl who was dating one of those Yanks on the nearby B-17 base. Funny I don't remember. Must have been too drunk!*

***

Richard could barely contain his excitement as he took his place around the enormous oak table in the planning room at Whitehall. At the end of the room, a large-scale map of Europe completely covered the wall. A ladder, on rails, rested to one side beneath it. Archibald introduced Richard to his own superior; a tall, spare man in his fifties with blonde hair and a melodious, but dark, baritone voice.

Two planners, both from MAP, the Ministry of Air Production were there. Richard also saw a man with grey hair and a purple tie, rather astonishing in such austere times and such austere company.

Richard listened patiently to Archibald's briefing on progress so far and a summing up of the difficulties. He could contain himself no longer and, not knowing Whitehall etiquette, stuck his hand in the air for permission to speak. All faces swung towards him.

"Yes, Richard?" said Archibald.

"I think I have the solution, how to get a fighter there, wherever 'there' *is*."

"Well," said the man with blonde hair. "We're listening."

Suddenly Richard wasn't so confident. The idea seemed ludicrous. "Well sir, I was thinking about it last night and a fighter, such as a Hawker Hurricane, could be carried to the target by a bomber, maybe the Stirling, and then fly back. What's the maximum load a Stirling can lift?"

The sentence sounded way too short, and the silence following it alarmed Richard. He had the urge to apologise but bit his lip just long enough. The blonde-haired man began to nod, slowly. "Archie?"

"It's brilliantly simple. Yes! I think, perhaps it could be done." He turned to the two MAP men. "What do you chaps think?"

"No way! It's never been tried. And in the time we have … ," said the younger man, who had a slight American twang.

"Hang on Andy" said the other. "Don't forget that Liberator affair. And also, Short have experience with this, the Empire flying boat and Mayo. A Stirling *can* lift roughly the weight of a Hurricane. I would need to *check* … ." The other raised his eyebrows but acquiesced.

"What's the Liberator affair? And what's Mayo?" asked Richard.

"Dan?" said the acquiescent Ministry-man.

"Oh … . The American's have been messing about with a Liberator carrying a fighter. They tried a Hurricane, the only fighter we have tough enough and light enough, but the Hurricane pilot was killed. Pylons detached, along with the Hurri in a slight dive after a long flight. They used a *modified* Hurricane, I think … ."

"One of those Hurricanes modified for catapult launch by the Navy?" asked Archie.

"Yes. Something like that. All hush-hush. Even I don't know much. The Yanks aren't talking about it."

"And the Mayo?" prompted Dan.

"Yes. You may remember, before the War, 1937 newsreels, Short had an Empire flying boat modified to carry a four-engined mail aeroplane called the Mercury. Worked quite well, actually. Ha! Anyway, if anybody could do it, Short could. The Sunderland is a development of the Empire class, and the Stirling has basically the same wing."

"There you go!" said Richard. He picked up a pencil in front of him and slammed it down for effect.

"So what we are actually talking about here is a *Super Weapon*!" said the man with blonde hair. "Winnie will love *that*! Our answer to Big Ben! But wait a moment … . As you may have heard Andy imply, we have a deadline for this mission. The date is *critica*l! It must be executed on or before 2nd September. That's forty-eight days from now until D-Day."

"Why then?" asked Richard. "And what's Big Ben?"

"I can't answer the second question. The first, because Intelligence tells us that the work on the Bunker is due to be finished by then. After that date it will no longer be possible to penetrate inside the bunker with a bomb. But there is another … more *pressing* reason. Winnie thinks, that even if the operation fails in its primary objective, this mission will create maximum embarrassment for Göring, who authorised the attack on the Palace. If this happens, and he may even be removed from command by Hitler, it might just disrupt the Luftwaffe enough to hinder or even stop them resisting an invasion we are planning." Everybody in the room suddenly sat bolt-upright. The hairs on the back of Richard's neck stood on end at the word 'Invasion.' "We believe that anything which might cause division within the German High Command is worth the risk." Silence fell in the room. He continued, "Are you *sure* this can be done? Can we actually find a way to transport a fighter on top of a bomber, test it and fly the mission in that time?"

Archibald swallowed once. "We have to."

"Good," answered the blonde man. "Now, I have something to add. In the room next door, we have a young woman, Anna Styles, who was, before the war, the girlfriend of the pilot who survived the attack on Buckingham Palace … ."

"But … . I thought all three died!"

"That's a rumour we've been deliberately spreading. In fact, contrary to the rumours, this was *not* a suicide mission. Each aircraft had been fitted with something called an ejector-seat; a seat fitted with rockets to throw the pilot clear of the aircraft. Despite this, our pilot, their leader, seems to have decided not to attack the Palace and instead crash-landed in Hyde Park. He's quite well and in our keeping." He paused for this to sink in. "He has been asking for Anna by name, and we believe he may be persuaded to help us plan this mission." Richard's eyes widened as the penny dropped. "Yes, Squadron Leader, I think you might now guess what the mission is … and the target. If you do, it would be most wise to keep that guess to yourself. In time, of course, you will be told clearly the target, but since this mission depends on surprise and the utmost secrecy, you are bound, by law, on punishment of death, to keep everything you learn of it to yourself. Is that quite understood?"

"Of course, but … ."

"Let me continue. In a moment, you will meet Anna, and we would like you to liaise with her and Archie, so that she can gain as much useful information from Oberleutnant Michael Dorfmann as possible. Archibald?" Archibald placed a brief case on the table and took out a single white sheet. He slid it across the table to Richard. "On this sheet is all we know about the attack on the Palace and Michael Dorfmann," the blonde-haired man continued. "There is also all *you* need to know about Anna Styles. Memorise it and destroy it before you leave here." He concluded the meeting. "Gentlemen, we will meet again in one week's time, precisely. By then, we must have a detailed plan and an itemised list of everything you need; men, aircraft, equipment. Is that clear?" Everyone nodded. "Good. Good day to you, Gentlemen."

While Archibald spoke with his superior outside the office, Richard studied the single sheet of paper.

Two details interested him most besides the 'ejector-seats;' the explosive used and the Wing of the pilot. The report detailed the explosive as '850 kg of RDX.'

*What on earth is RDX? And how do you get that much into a Bf 109?*

The Wing of the German pilot; JG26, had been one of the two most infamous German Wings of the Battle of Britain.

*At last I get to meet one of them, face to face!*

Archibald led Richard out into the corridor and to the door of the next room. He fought off the pilot's questions. "But Archie, how can I plan this if I don't know … ."

At that moment he saw Anna for the first time and was silenced. She smelled of Pears soap.

"Richard, this is Anna Styles. Anna, this is Richard Earlgood."

"Hello," she said, smiling. She held out a well-manicured hand. The man facing her clearly appreciated her looks. Unimpressed by this, she looked beyond his stare. He had the lived-in good looks of a square-jawed film star, but there seemed something coy about his gaze. 'He slouches!' she also noted to herself, scoffing. However, his smile, which broke out as soon as she spoke to him, made her want to smile back.

"Hello," Richard finally replied. "Er … pleased to meet you."

Anna's mood of confusion momentarily lifted, and she smiled appreciatively. All three sat at a small table, and Archibald outlined the situation.

"This must be difficult for you. Are you still in love with him?"

"Richard … ?" Archibald protested.

"Sorry … . I am always too direct. Born in the country, you know," he said to her.

"Oh, it's quite alright. As a matter of fact, I prefer a little directness. Just lately things have got so complicated. No … . I don't think I am."

"So what do you want me to do?" he asked.

"Well, actually this may be simpler than we all imagine. I think Michael wants to help. I don't think he any more considers himself a Nazi. If it were possible to secure his release … ."

"Yes?" asked Archibald.

"I think he would tell you everything he knows about how the mission was planned and who was involved. In return for guaranteed safety of course, for him and me. That's what he said in my second meeting with him this morning. You see, there are German spies here, who might have him killed … ."

Richard looked at Archibald, who replied, "Let's start with some simple things. Richard, if you were working with this Oberleutnant Dorfmann, what would be the first thing you would want to know?"

"Well, what did they practice on? How long did they practice, and how do these ejector-seats work?"

"That's three. Let's just start with one. The first one: what did they practice on? Miss Styles, if Michael is willing to give us that answer, we would consider that the first step to his rehabilitation and possible release. How does that sound?"

"I will try," she replied.

***

"My brother's on Stirlings. Why don't we go and see him?" Richard's casual comment in the back of a black Riley, travelling down the Mall, had been met with a frosty stare from Archibald. "What?"

The meeting in Whitehall a week after Richard met Anna, had gone equally well. Richard had his list prepared of what he needed; five Hurricanes which included one in reserve and one for experimentation; four Stirlings, again including one in reserve; three good fighter pilots experienced in low level flying; three good Stirling pilots and crew; an airfield with a secluded hanger, mess, accommodation and an area of countryside to practice low-level flying over.

"You must surely guess that we can't involve your brother. He was the first British airmen to travel all the way out of Holland, across France to Spain using the French evasion line. He can't fly over France again, at least not for now. He knows too much." Archibald's face softened to a smile for a moment. "I did think of him. Knowing your family's history, it was one of the first thing I thought of. But it wasn't long before I found out about his gung-ho adventures!"

"Archie. Has anybody ever told you, you talk like Biggles sometimes?"

"Ha. Funny you should say that. I've read all the books. I'm an *enormous* fan!"

"It doesn't surprise me. But listen. Martin may not be able to actually fly on the mission, whatever it is, but we need somebody to advise us on Stirlings, and there's not much he doesn't know. He's one of the best we have. He's training pilots at a Heavy Conversion Unit in Suffolk now, No. 1657 at Stradishall. Let's drive up tomorrow and see him?"

"Well … we do have to start somewhere. And now we know pretty much what we want … I will have a word with the boss."

As a result of his conversation, they both found themselves on a train to Bury St. Edmunds the very next day. An RAF staff car met them at a station, whose signs had all been removed, and took them to the vast airfield at Stradishall. Soft rain had just started to patter on the tarmac from a grainy sky when they reached the gates and showed their passes to a guard.

As the car sped along the perimeter, Richard remembered the girl in Whitehall. "Has Anna come up with anything yet?"

"I'll tell you later. Is that Martin?"

A taller version of Richard, with the same angular face but blonde, curly hair and a livid patch devoid of hair at his right temple, jumped up and down, waving both arms at the approaching Riley.

Richard wound down the window and Martin's woolly head poked inside the car before it had stopped. The two brothers grabbed each other and bellowed with delight.

"Richie! You little devil. So you are on special ops at last, eh? So bloody good to see you. It's been so long, and so much has happened. Couldn't get down to London, I'm afraid!"

"Ha! Bloody Hell! Marty. How the hell did you get back? After pranging a Stirling, you hardly deserve it. Don't know why they're letting you fly another! How's mum and dad?"

"Fine! Fine!" By this time the car had stopped and Archibald had stepped out of the opposite side of the car. The driver waited patiently until Richard had climbed out and then sped off.

"Come on, chaps! You're just in time! Just taking this old bird *up*!" He strode towards a Short Stirling, parked facing them on the tarmac, one hundred yards away. Even at that distance Richard thought it looked big. "Just had her two-hundred-hour inspection check, so I need to take her up. Thought you might like to come along!"

"Martin, this is Archibald. He's the chap from Whitehall who masterminded this operation. My boss!" Richard grinned at Achibald, who was obviously even younger than Richard.

"Pleased to meet you!" shouted Martin over the sound of the port outer Bristol Hercules engine, which had just been started up.

"She's a monster!" shouted Richard. "Bigger than a Lanc."

"You haven't seen one before?"

"In the air, but not close up on the ground. Of course, you know the rumours. Not sure I'm keen to try … ."

"Nonsense. Queen of the Skies, she is. Once you get to know, her she is a real *Lady*. Tough as old boots, too."

Richard swallowed and glanced at Archibald, who looked very pale.

The aircraft stood like some oblique monumental piece of architecture on its formidable undercarriage. It seemed to be poised, leaning forward, and had a bullish, brutish look about it.

As they avoided puddles and passed between the undercarriage, stooping for no good reason apart from reverence and fear, Richard noted that the tops of the great wheels were above his head. The second engine had started and now a third. The air throbbed and hummed cyclically as the engines reached the same pitch. The noise grew intense, but the vibration didn't feel unpleasant. The fourth engine started just as the three men reached the rear entrance hatch in the fuselage, near the tail.

They climbed a short ladder and stepped into the dry interior of twenty tons of aluminium and steel.

The sheer space inside impressed Richard immediately. He had been inside a Wellington once, but this seemed like a whole different concept.

*Even a ladder up to the top turret! It's vast!*

"Wrong name for it then!" shouted Archibald in Martin's ear.

"What?"

"Short!"

"Ha!"

"That old scarf! You still have it," said Richard, pointing to a tatty blue strip of knitted wool around his brother's neck.

"Ha! Not the original. I lost that in France."

"You haven't changed … !"

Passing the rest bunk, they edged past the Flight Engineer's seat, the Navigator's seat and climbed up a short ladder on the left side to the two pilot's seats under the greenhouse-sized canopy.

A man in oily blue overalls climbed out of the pilot's seat and squeezed past Martin, shouting, "All yours! Number One engine has two new cylinder heads, and Number Three has a new oil cooler! We ran her up earlier! Keep the revs down a bit for the first hour or so!"

Martin took the pilot's seat on the left and pulled on a flying helmet from the dashboard. He passed one to Richard, who sat in the second seat. "You're second pilot. Do what I say as we take off."

Archibald leaned on the seat backs and peered out over the airfield. "We must be thirty feet up!"

"Parachutes are underneath us! Archie, there is another one and a helmet stowed by the Bomb Aimer's position, down there!" He pointed through a narrow entrance under the main control panel, through which they could see the Perspex Bomb

Aimer's window and the nose gun-turret. "But you won't need them! Pretty reliable, these old crates!"

A head suddenly appeared by Archie's ankles, from beneath the raised flight deck. A bleary-eyed man with brown, curly hair, clutching a tattered crime thriller paperback, grinned up at him. "Just having a nap! Tell Martin I'm taking up position!" Archibald passed on the message.

"That's 'Cloudy' Callum! My Navigator! Never go up without one!"

"I already did ground-checks … and pilot's checks!" shouted Martin in Richard's ear. "Engineer's checks are done!" After checking the oil pressure and temperature for each engine and going through the remaining pre-flight checks, Martin set the flaps one third out, set the trim tabs to 'neutral' and kicked the rudder left and right. "Is it moving?"

Richard peered down the considerable length of the fuselage and nodded, confirming the correct movement of the rudder. They repeated the procedure for the elevators and then ailerons, although Martin did his own visual check for these. He leaned out of an open panel in the canopy and waved to the ground-crew, who pulled the chocks from the main undercarriage wheels. Taking all four main throttle controls on the centre column in his fist, he slowly moved them forward in the gate, the right pair slightly ahead of the left to counter the Stirling's tendency to swing to the right. The rev indicator showed 2000 rpm. The engine roar rose, and slowly the aircraft began to bump along the rough concrete pan. He manoeuvred the aircraft onto the taxi-way towards the end of the runway and spoke into his mike, calling the control-tower. "J-for Jessica. Requesting clearance for take-off." He grinned at Richard. Only Martin heard the response. He boosted the engines slightly and the aircraft turned until it lined up on the main runway. There, it stopped. Martin closed the canopy panel and wriggled in the seat, making himself comfortable. Archibald noticed a fresh tattoo of a love heart and the name Francine on Martin's bare forearm. His heart pounded with excitement, tinged with apprehension, at the prospect of take-off in the RAF's first heavy bomber.

"This is the best bit!" shouted Martin in Richard's ear "Put your hands on the throttles below my hand! Whatever happens, keep them evenly spread, and if anything happens to me during take-off, push them all the way forward smoothly. Wait until the airspeed is at least 100 mph! Then pull back on the control column! Don't forget your flaps and the undercarriage, considerable air resistance from them! Not like the early Hurricane! You don't have to wind them up yourself! Just push this lever forward here!" He indicated a lever on the left side of the main throttle console, retained in the down position by a catch. "Safety catch here! Then select 'Up.'" He pointed to a switch on the main control panel. "Ready?" Both Richard, and Archibald nodded vigorously. "Right then! Off we go chaps!"

Martin pushed the four throttle levers gently forward in their gate. The engines roared, and the Stirling rumbled down the long runway. It took quite a distance to reach any great speed, and then Martin eased the control-column forward to lift the tail. The sound from the engines, as Martin pushed the throttles all the way forward, was deafening. The end of the runway approached fast, and Archibald felt the urge to close his eyes. At the last moment, Martin eased back the control column, and the great aircraft lifted gracefully into the air. The trees of Suffolk whizzed under the wings as they slowly climbed into the blue July sky. Martin retracted the undercarriage, then the flaps and trimmed for flight. They gently banked to fly north and at 12,000 feet he levelled out. "On the ground she's a duck, but now she's a swan!" He throttled back, and the engine note became just a pleasant rumble in the background. "Here, Richard. You take her." With dual control, the two pilots didn't even have to swap seats, and with a barely noticeable dip of the wings, Richard took control.

"She's lovely!"

"Well, not all would agree with that. She *has* her moments."

In a clearing sky, a flight of Spitfires passed them, flying south, the leader waggling his wings in greeting. After a while, Martin suggested Archibald have a try.

"Oh, no, not me."

"Go on!" Archibald, pale faced, but grinning like a school-boy, climbed into the co-pilot's seat and gripped the control-column as if his life depended on it. "Just hold her steady. Okay. You have control. We train pilots who have flown twin-engined jobs; Blenheims, Wellingtons, some Whitley crews not many of those left now. It's bloody more dangerous than Ops, I can tell you! Two crashed in the last month, both crews lost.

All of them." Archibald's hands shook slightly. "Okay, now turn gently to port. That's it, pull back slightly or she will dip a wing too much, and you might slide." Martin gave the Stirling a little more throttle to keep the nose up, too. "That's great." After they completed the turn, he took back control. "I have it. What's that? Oh, okay. Navigator says there's heavy weather over the wash. Better strap yourselves in."

Archibald twisted round and glanced at Cloudy. Leaning back in his chair, arms crossed, he looked for all the world as if he were fast asleep.

"But … ," said Archibald.

"Archie, old boy. Go to the Bomb Aimer's position and lie flat. There are brown paper bags if you need them, to your right." When Archibald had got into position, Martin grinned at Richard. He put the Stirling into a gentle dive and let her build up speed to her maximum of 255 mph. "You know, with these short wings, she's no good at heights and not so good at many things … . But she is good at this … . Ha! Ha!" With that, he pushed the throttles suddenly forward and turned the steering wheel on top of the column to the right. The Stirling executed a complete, elegant roll and came back to level flight. "You can't do *that* in a Lancaster!"

Richard's eyes were popping out of his head. "But! You mad bugger! You're not supposed to do that! It's not supposed to be possible!"

"I know. There's some chap actually loops a Lancaster though. We need to keep up! And she's quite good at this *too*!" With that he executed a barrel-roll and again came back to level flight before executing another one, in the opposite direction. This time he held her upside down for a few seconds and loose items in the cockpit fell from the floor to the canopy, floating past their faces and random directions as he put her into a slight, inverted dive.

"Stop it Martin! You'll kill us!"

"Ha! A-ha! That's it for now. Some boys actually *looped* a Sunderland, so that *should* be possible too, but I never tried it yet."

"You're mad! No more. I need to check on Archie. Keep her steady, okay?"

"Fine."

Richard clambered down through the opening in the control panel, to where he could see Archibald prone on the floor. He had pressed his face against a brown paper bag and was retching. Richard shook his shoulders. "You alright, Archie"

Archibald turned around, face was white with terror and shaking violently. "Just been a little bit … sick. Should we have done that?"

"No. To be honest, I didn't even think it possible. You mustn't tell anyone."

"No." With that, a pale grin passed over Archibald's wan face.

They landed safely back at Stradishall, the Stirling flouncing along the runway before settling unceremoniously on the concrete and rolling almost to the end. As soon as they were out of earshot of Martin, Archibald turned to Richard.

"We must have him." A strange look of recognition came in Archibald's eyes, and suddenly he said, "Yes, we must have him!"

***

Archibald called Richard to tell him to meet Anna for tea in Claridges, the next day.

"How's it going with her? Has she come up with anything?" he replied

"Oh yes. That Dorfmann chap is most co-operative. He has come up with everything we wanted to know and much more. Seems he can't keep quiet. Almost too good to be true, really. I would like your opinion on Anna, whether you think we can trust her … ."

"Alright. I'll use my best detective skills to probe her inner motives!"

"Be serious, Richard. Just be subtle."

He found her waiting patiently, sipping tea with white gloves on and wearing a grey three-piece with a matching hat. She looked gorgeous. He thought her Italian ancestry showed in the way she looked, dressed and carried herself.

*Class!*

"You look smashing!"

"Thank you. I took the liberty of ordering a pot for two and two buttered scones! Well of course, it's not butter … since the Ministry is paying … . Real sugar too!"

"Oh, right!"

"I used to come here with my parents when they did their main shopping trip before Christmas! A childhood memory … ," he added, lamely with a faint blush.

"How wonderful! My parents never brought me to London when I was little. I had quite a sheltered childhood." She, too, blushed.

"Hm. So how has it all been going … ?"

"You mean my work? I … I can't spea- … "

"No. I meant with Michael."

"Oh. Sorry. Yes, you're right. Down to business."

"No! I … sorry. It's just that … ."

"Don't apologise." She gave him a direct look, and he became lost for a moment in the variegated hazel colouring of her irises. "I think it's been going well. I mean, I'm not an expert at these things, but Michael quickly answered your main question. They practiced on his airfield with the roads marked out by rope, buildings too, although some were fabricated out of cardboard and plywood. He's happy to talk about the modifications to his aircraft, a Messerschmitt 109 E." She pronounced the aircraft name accurately and easily, as if familiar with the name.

*Maybe she's in intelligence, Air Intelligence. Or maybe an Ops. Room plotter.*

"I see." Richard leaned back in his chair. "Doesn't it worry you a bit? He seems awfully forthcoming."

"No, Mr Earlgood – I mean Squadron Leader Earlgood – I know Michael. I think he genuinely has become disillusioned with Hitler's war-machine and wants to help. However, he won't give any information about personnel, or the location of his Wing. Firstly, we know this anyway, and he knows this, but I think he wants to protect his friends. He seems happy to talk about the actual technicalities of the mission, called Blue Flower, and the command structure above him."

The sting Richard had felt at her use of formal titles in her response, made him take a risk, to win back her trust. "He must really be in love with you …"

"I beg your pardon?" she asked, smoothly but politely.

*I'm too common for her. Oh well.*

"Sorry. My mistake again. I assume too much, sometimes. What did he say about modifications to his aircraft? Of course, I know the details … ."

She laughed. He wasn't sure why. "He said, and I quote, 'She handled like a pig, or like a sow … . Isn't that the word? Like you when you had eaten too much at Oxford!'"

Richard raised his brow, shocked at her challenge. "Okay I didn't expect such detail." He smiled. "Any more details?"

"Yes. He said the 'C of G' was too far back but that the MF FF cannon in the engine and some ammunition left in it, helped counter this. He wished he'd had a radio, so that he could have talked to his friends before they died. Let's see, oh yes, and he said the ammunition came in handy, because he could shoot back at the two destroyers. He wanted to know if he hit anything. And why they were prepared to fire across river when they might have hit a building or civilians. Oh, and he asked, 'Did they save Donald?'"

"Donald?"

She smiled again. "I may tell you, one day. It's a private joke."

"Oh." He thought for a moment. "So why did he do it, volunteer for a mission that he didn't even intend to carry out. Surely, he could have just flown over and landed on any RAF airfield, they would have loved to have him!"

"Yes, that's something I'm working on. I'm not sure yet. At least I'm not sure of the truth. It will take more time … ."

"Oh. I see … ."

"But I'm glad you asked. At least you're direct." She suddenly flexed her shoulders, and he could see a great tension released within her.

"It must be tough. I cannot imagine what they're putting you through."

"Yes. It's not much fun, to be honest. I … I could do with a bit of light relief."

Wary of her formidable intellect, and a trap, Richard hesitated before speaking. "What are you doing tonight? We could do a show, or just … dinner?" He held his breath.

"No … I don't … I don't really feel like doing any of that. What were you going to do?"

He laughed. "Well, to be honest, I had planned, sometime this evening, to drive up to Yorkshire. I have a patient who I need to bring with me to our new digs tomorrow. Archie and I are going to our new base in Stradishall."

"Patient? What patient" She looked intrigued.

"Well, a rabbit actually. I found him, or her, wounded on the road. Some friends, my old landlords, are looking after him, but I promised to pick him up. I'm not sure what I'm going … ."

"Oh, how sweet! May I come?"

***

# Chapter Two

Transmitted by radio ham near Dover, night of 17th July 1943:

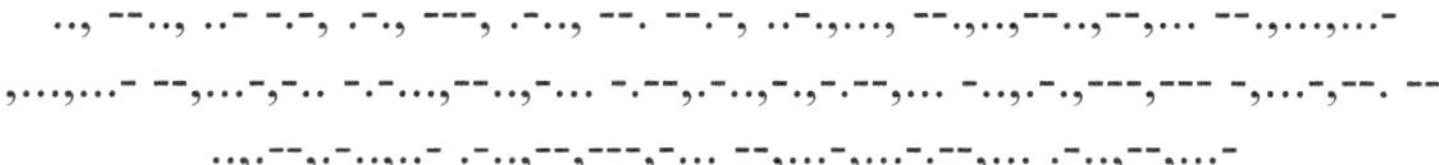

Adolf Hitler threw the progress report for the Führerbunker on to his desk and studied Eugen Vögler, CEO of Hochtief, the company building the bunker.

Until now, using forced labour, the work had progressed on time, and the Führer did not appear to want to have one of his tantrums just yet. Eugen nevertheless felt on the verge of shaking violently, and the strength seemed to leave his legs.

"It's good of you to come all the way from Essen, just to keep me informed, Herr Vögler. I appreciate that. Tell me what you need to get this done on time, and I will make it happen. We have a shipment of very healthy Jews, all male and of prime building age, arriving from Poland this week. I was thinking about … ah well, that's a secret for now." He wagged his finger comically, and Eugen Vögler thought for a moment that Hitler could be both charming and endearing, which surprised him. But the black undercurrent of projected menace could still be felt in the air. Failure would not be an option.

"Yes, mein Führer. Many of our workers are not of the highest grade … and not … erm … worthy of the work."

"That's settled then. Tell my secretary how many you need, what age and height, and it will be arranged." With that, Adolf Hitler's face turned back to paperwork on his desk. Confused, not knowing if he should go or not, Eugen Vögler stood stiffly, almost to attention. The Führer looked up at him, and those pale, grey eyes, seemed to regard the CEO with innocent curiosity for a moment. "That is all."

***

Richard went straight from Claridges to his little rented flat and packed his things before going to the Ministry. They had their first Operational Briefing, and he wouldn't have time to pack before picking up Anna. His heart fluttered at the sound of her name in his head. He wasn't sure if Archie would approve of his date that night. He arrived late for the briefing and without his notes which he'd accidentally packed, along with his books.

"Sit down Squadron Leader. Glad you honoured us with your presence, finally," said the blonde-haired Ministry man. The two MAP men were sitting near him. The other man with silver hair wasn't present. Richard hardly noticed this as he entered the same room of the previous meetings. His mouth had dropped open at the sight of his brother, Martin, sitting next to Archibald. He mouthed the word, "How?" silently. Martin shrugged his shoulders. Another man sat next to the blonde-haired man. The hat placed on the table in front of him had plenty of gold braid on its brim, a Group Captain's cap.

"Now then gentlemen, continued the Ministry man, acting as chairman, this is the first official briefing of project False Promise. In a minute you will learn how appropriate that code-name is, but I hardly need reiterate, everything that goes on, and is said, within these briefings is Top Secret. Now over to Archie, whose project this really is. He dreamed it up! Archie?"

"Thank you … sir. I would like to start by welcoming Squadron Leader … *Richard* Earlgood, and I'm pleased to inform you, Richard that you've finally be cleared for all top-secret information on this mission. Your brother has also been cleared, and I might say, we only cleared him so quickly, because he *is* your brother … . We only had to check the parents *once!*" The joke seemed a modest one but drew enthusiastic laughter. Richard nodded, magnanimously.

The blonde-haired man waited for the jollity to subside before clearing his throat. "I am still not at liberty to tell you where we are invading immediately after this operation, but if you read the newspapers, you will have a pretty good idea. It's very close to a small island we *are* currently invading."

*We're invading Sicily. It must be Italy!*

"Now, on the wall at the end, you will see the mission marked out at large scale. As you can see, the target is Berlin. My idea, in brief, given that the Prime Minister wanted a response to the attack on Buckingham Palace, is a simple one. Attack Hitler's Bunker!" He paused.

"But it's impregnable!" protested Martin.

"Yes, for normal bombs, it is. But we don't intend to destroy it. Projectionist, if you please." The lights were switched off by a man in a suit, who had been hovering near a projector, silently. He flicked a switch and the wall, to the right of the door, displayed a large grainy photograph of what looked like a garden within a city. "I know it's a bit grainy. Sorry about that. This photo was taken at enormous risk, by a member of the German underground." Richard heard a murmur of astonishment in the room. "Oh yes, there is such a thing. It's a photo of the back garden of the Reich Chancellery two weeks ago. It's an incredible stroke of good fortune for us that Hitler is having an extension to his Bunker built. I have outlined here, the extent of the new Bunker. As you see, it will extend right out into the Reich Chancellery garden. But what interests us are these two excavations here, close to the Chancellery wall. They go right through to the Bunker. They are building temporary air-ventilation towers here. Eventually these towers will be well out in the garden and presumably automated, so that they can be quickly shut. They are usually open but can be closed during an attack. According to information gained by the underground, a gas canister of cyanide or some such poisonous gas, dropped right here against the wall, would poison anybody sheltering in the bunker. What we plan to do is bomb the Reichtag on a day when we know Hitler is there. This will send him down to the Bunker, and there we will kill him with poisonous gas."

Richard stared at him, the irises of his blue eyes focused to a pin-point. "Poisoned gas? Isn't that against the Geneva Protocol?"

Archibald looked nervously at his superior and sat down.

The blonde-haired man toyed with a pencil. "Nobody is forcing you to take on this mission. Indeed, at this point, you are simply a planner, Squadron Leader Earlgood. You are free to drop out at any time. But the badge will be staying here. If you want my *opinion* … any pin-point mission that can shorten the war, with the death of only a few top Nazi brass, is worth bending the rules of war a little. And whether we succeed or fail, I am quite certain that Germany will not make a fuss about it. Indeed, I am quite sure they will keep the outcome of this raid as quiet as possible." The two men stared at each other for almost a full minute. The blonde-haired man looked away first. Richard cleared his throat.

"But won't they be expecting just such an attack?" he asked.

"Just a minute Squadron Leader. Since your brother is here too, hadn't we better ask if he wishes to continue … under the circumstances?" the blonde-haired man interjected. He nodded to Martin.

"It's fine with me, I have seen the Nazis at close-quarters. They fight dirty, so why shouldn't we?"

Richard shifted in his seat. Something about the way the chairman of the meeting had put the last question made him uncomfortable.

"Now, to return to your question of the Germans expecting such an attack," the blonde-haired man continued, turning back to Richard. "That's the second part of my plan. We have already launched a campaign of disinformation. We have passed a rumour among RAF, Army and Navy types that we're planning to bomb the chancellery with a special type of X-ray bomb." There were sniggers from the pilots present. "It's a double-bluff of course. For those of you unfamiliar with chess or such terms, we expect the Krauts to guess quite quickly that this attack is a myth. Then, if they *do* discover anything, they will instantly dismiss it."

"But how do we get the bombs placed that accurately?" asked Martin.

"Yes, I thought you'd ask that. Richard and I have figured it out. At first, I thought a Mosquito could do it, but the problem is that you have to get in real close, negotiate trees, buildings and telegraph wires, and you just can't do it with even something as nimble as a Mossie. You might just do it with a fighter though, say a Hurricane. Richard will lead three Hurricanes, that ought to do it, each, carrying two 1000-pound gas canisters, in an attack right into Hitler's back garden."

"Incredible!" said Martin.

"This is where you come in, Martin. To get them there, they will have to piggy-back on three Short Stirlings. These Stirlings will be escorted to Berlin by the rest of a normal bombing squadron, who will create the diversion by bombing the Reichtag. Of course, it will need to be incredibly accurate to force Hitler out, so it will have to be carried out at low level too. The three Stirlings will then break away, dive down low over the outskirts of Berlin, release the Hurris and fly home. Now if you will just step over here." He led them to a large table underneath the map at the end of the room. A blue cloth had been draped over it. He pulled the cloth off, revealing a large-scale map of the area of Berlin around the Reichtag. Using a long wooden pointer, he traced the path of the Hurricanes. "They will fly up the River Spree as low as possible, avoiding flak just as the Germans did in London, turn left into Unter den Linden, fly all the way down it to the Brandenburg Gate, take a left, turning through almost 180 degrees and come across Hermann-Göring-Straße, thought you'd like the irony of that, then these trees and gardens until they are over the Chancellery gardens here, where they will drop the canisters. Goodnight Hitler!"

"Then what?" asked Richard.

"What do you mean?"

"I mean what about us?"

"Ah, that bit of the puzzle has only just fallen into place. Of course, you knew I was looking for a way to get Hurricanes in and out of Berlin, that's when you came up with the idea of the piggy-back, Richard. Well, the Hurris will then have enough fuel to make it all the way back to Holland where they can land in one of the many big, flat fields. Martin helped us here. Martin?"

"Richard, remember Bernard, the Dutch student who stayed with us in '32? And you stayed with him the following year?"

"Aha."

Richard remembered a day in 1933 when he and Bernard had crawled to the edge of a reed bed, to watch some kind of wading bird.

"That's rare," Bernard told him. "Let's see if we can get the eggs."

"No." Richard felt appalled. "That's not right. Let's just watch." At that moment, a shot rang out and the wader took to the air. It rose above a line of trees, its wings beating frantically, and then he heard a second shot. The little bird veered to one side and disappeared over the horizon.

*Wow! That was close!*

A single one of its wing feathers floated to the ground. Later, Richard found the feather and kept it. He still had it in a little wooden box of childhood memorabilia.

"Well I know I was a bit of a cad to him then," Martin continued. "In fact, until I got shot down, I never felt very interested in Europeans, but then I thought of him. We ditched here in Veluwemeer, near Elburg, and that's when I remembered him. Only three of us got out, and we asked for him in the town. He's in the Dutch resistance and passed us down the line, eventually. Anyway, make it to here, and he'll help you."

"Yeah! If we can make it to there! That's a long way for a Hurricane. What happens if we can't release the canisters, or have to go around for several attempts, or get damaged?" He looked at the man with blonde hair, who didn't answer. The room fell silent. "Okay."

"What about the vents?" asked Andy.

Archibald smiled weakly, glad of the distraction. "Ah, that's the other crucial part of this mission. The vents need to be open. The excavations around the foundations are sealed up every morning. There is a chance some gas would get inside but probably not enough to do the job. We have a plan for opening the vents, but it's sketchy right now. Martin helped us with the first part. Martin … ?"

"I remembered Bernard has contacts in the German resistance, so he is trying to make contact with them now. There are two possibilities. The Germans are forming a small Brigade of Dutch Waffen SS. The Dutch Resistance have two of their own men inside. One of them could possibly get inside the Guard detail in the yard. The second possibility is getting inside the Bunker itself and getting out to open the vents from there. But that is highly unlikely … ."

"*Unlikely*! Damned impossible! Even the Waffen SS idea sounds mighty thin! How about the work detail itself?"

"No, replied Martin. It's the obvious route, but they are Jewish prisoners. Their every move is watched, and they spend each night in a high-security camp."

"So!" shouted Richard, turning to Archibald. "You are asking me to fly in there, with a heavily loaded Hurricane which probably can't reach anywhere safe afterwards, and attack the Bunker, Hitler's very own Bunker, mind, and hope that the gas, or poison, will be able to reach the bastard, because some poor sod has managed to open the vents from *inside* the Bunker! It's the maddest plan I ever heard. Archie, I thought you were a *genius*. Now I just think you have a few screws loose! Even if I *was* prepared to do this, I couldn't possibly ask anybody else to go!"

"Somebody has to do it, and somebody *will* do it," said Archibald, quietly.

"There's just one other point," said the blonde man. "Dan?"

The MAP planner cleared his throat. "We have done all the calculations and … the Stirling's will struggle to take off carrying Hurricanes and the bombs; there's only one or two runways in the east of England long enough. Stradishall is one of them. Even then, the weight factor is going to be critical and a struggle. I'm not sure, with the right sized bombs, it's possible."

"So is that it, then?" asked Richard.

"We did think about keeping the bomb size the same but taking fuel out of the Hurricanes!" added the blonde-haired man, indignantly.

Richard counted to ten, silently. "Thanks," he said, finally. "Wait a minute, Anna told me that Dorfmann's 109 had all the guns removed apart from one. That's the answer. I don't like it, but what if we remove all the guns apart from two?"

"Yes. I don't know off the top of my head," said Dan, "but I think that would save about six hundred pounds or so. We will try that. The rest of it is something that needs to be worked out as we go along," concluded Dan.

"To get down to practicalities," cut in the blonde-haired man. "Your contact at MAP is a Group Captain Devonshire. He's plenty of combat experience but has been seconded to the office of the Chief of Air Production. He also knows Bomber Harris. He'll be invaluable in getting the men and materials we need to complete this mission. He's been put in overall charge of this operation, which is to be called False Promise, but his role is purely an organisational one. Operationally, he has strict instructions not to interfere and will take his lead from the two Squadron Leaders Earlgood. Short say they will have a prototype Stirling carrying a Hurricane mock-up in ten days for a test flight at Rochester airfield. I expect you both to be there, Richard and Archibald. By that time, I want this mission planned out in every meticulous detail. That means you, Martin and Richard, have until then to select your crews and pilots and begin practicing. Archie has had an area on Dartmoor set aside where we can lay out the main streets and the river in three dimensions. I think that's all." He closed the meeting. "You all know your tasks. I want success, and Winnie expects to get it! The attack needs to be on 2nd September, no later, but the best weather would be a day with low cloud cover all the way to the target, so it could be earlier. Therefore, we have less than seven weeks to build and test this combined-aircraft contraption, train the pilots and crews, plan the mission, practice until perfect and execute it. We will meet again eleven days from today. Good day gentlemen."

"Fancy a pint?" asked Martin, slapping his younger brother on the back as they left the room.

"Can't. Not now … . Meeting a bird … lovely girl. You know how it is … ."

"Boy, you sound a bit frosty. Is it something I said?"
"Yes. You didn't seem that bothered about the gas. Doesn't it bother you?"

"Not really. War is dirty. We will only be killing Herr Adolf and a few of his cronies. I daresay this sort of thing happens a lot in wars, behind the scenes. Oh, the Gentlemen's agreements are all very well, but with Hitler, the gloves are off! *Well* off!"

"Well … I guess you're right. I'm sorry. I haven't seen the Nazis first hand like you have. What was it *like*?"

"I'll tell you later, over a drink. We must do it soon, though. We haven't really talked for what? More than a year now."

"Sure. Of course, if we're working together, there will be loads of time together. Maybe tomorrow, Marty. Okay?"

"Fine."

***

Richard's thoughts spun like a whirlwind as he hurriedly said good bye to Archibald and Martin and drove to Anna's flat. He didn't remember actually volunteering for the mission, and yet he felt committed.

*But it's all so sketchy!*

He repeated that to himself at the end of many chains of thought and nearly ran over a cat, before knocking on the blue door with the number fifty-nine.

"You look startled!" she said as he guided her into the passenger seat of the little Austin. "Is it good news?"

"Ha! I don't know. I … er. I can't tell you."

They drove north, stopping at a pub for dinner, and arrived at the farm not much before midnight.

"He's been quiet. Won't let anybody near him though. Squeals if you so much as look at him. Vet says he will be right as rain in another week. We would keep him if we could, but … ." said Mr Shenton, guiding them through to the cellar where the patient sat quietly. As soon as he saw Richard, his ears pricked up, and he hopped once towards the visitors.

"Well I never! He remembers you!" said Mrs Shenton.

Richard scooped up the little bundle of fur, whose little nose twitched furiously. Richard stroked him. The rabbit put up no struggle. "There now, little chap. Did you think I had forgotten you?"

Anna leaned in and stroked his head. She pulled the two silky ears together, and the little rabbit's nose stopped twitching, but he eyed her gratefully. "We have to think of a name. Is it a he?"

"Oh yer. The vet said so." offered Mr Shenton.

"Jackie" suggested Richard. "For jack-rabbit."

***

Over a cup of Horlicks, Richard tentatively explored their next move.

"Do you have to get back tomorrow?" he asked Anna. "I mean; I should have asked. I don't know what work you do … ?"

"No. I don't have to be back. At the moment I'm the property of the Ministry, but there's nothing planned for tomorrow. How about you?"

"Nothing. The day after, Archie and I are going down to Rochester. But nothing until then. I just have to move in to my new digs."

"Where are you going to, then Richard?" asked Mr Shenton.

"We have a hut at RAF Stradishall."

"Where's that then?" the farmer asked.

"Near Bury St. Edmunds."

"Quite a drive then. Why don't you both stay the night? Both guest rooms are empty at the moment."

Richard studied his cup carefully.

"That would be nice," replied Anna, "If that's okay with you, Richard?"

They were both awoken by the crowing of the farm's old cock. An hour after dawn, they were well fed on eggs, ham and fried bread and on their way to Suffolk.

"Where's the ash-tray?" asked Anna, lighting a Dunhill cigarette, while bending forward to keep the lighter out of the roaring wind.

"There isn't one!" shouted Richard, slowing the car, helpfully. "Sorry. I guess you're used to Bentleys and Rollers?"

"Not likely. It's a gorgeous day. Let's have a picnic!"

"With what? Dandelions and Dunhills?"

"Ha! No. We can stop at a pub and get something, a sandwich or maybe a bakery … ?"

"Alright."

They stopped in the next town and bought some bread, cheese and herrings, ginger-beer, a knife and two paper plates before continuing on. Richard turned up a narrow farm-track above a railway cutting at lunch time, and they laid out their feast on the old blanket he had wrapped Jackie in on the day he found him. The rabbit sat quietly in a little carrying cage which the Shentons had provided.

"Let's let him out," Anna suddenly said, touching Richard's wrist.

"What and let him escape? He wouldn't last long with that leg."

"But let's just see if he *wants* to escape?"

"Are you mad?"

"Please … ?" she asked, with a moue.

Richard complied reluctantly, releasing the catch on the cage.

The rabbit hopped awkwardly until it emerged from the cage and then just stopped, its nose twitching.

"Go on, boy?" Richard said, encouragingly.

"Oh look Richard. He doesn't want to *go*! He wants to stay with you. I knew he *would*! Now you can keep him!"

"Is that what you wanted? You wanted me to have his permission?"

"Yes. Sort of … ." He reached out and took her hand, gently. It felt warm. Her skin seemed so soft and smooth. He leaned in to kiss her. "Don't … ."

"Oh. Sorry … ."

"No. It's not what you think. Contrary to your belief, I did not grow up rich. My parents were just very strict. It's Michael … . I'm not sure if I'm still, well, I don't think I'm still in love with him, but I *do* love him, and I want to give him *something* … I don't know how to explain … ."

"Go on. I have time." He leaned back and pulled up a blade of grass to chew.

"Well, I don't know … . It's just that they, we, want information from him, and I … I don't know how to do that, without giving something back! It's the sort of person I am, I suppose. Silly, I know … ."

"No. Not silly … . Awfully honourable though."

"Yes. I'm glad you understand. It's only for now. It's not permanent."

"I wish you wouldn't do that!"

"Do what?"

"Be so open, so direct. It makes me fall for you even more!"

"Oh. Sorry. I'll try not to do it."

"So what kind of work do you normally do … I mean, before this Blue Flower thing?"

"Oh that! I can't tell you! I know it's awful, but it has the same security rating as your project."

"Oh? And how do you know about that? I was going to say that *I* can't tell you about my project."

"But I know about it. It's called False Promise, and today you are moving in with the Secret Ops. chaps already based at Stradishall."

"Sh! Don't say all this too loud."

"Why? Are you afraid Jackie is working for the Germans?"

"No, but he might have friends … ."

Richard crawled through some clumps of grass, looking theatrically behind bushes for spies. She laughed, delighted at his little joke. He came back and sat beside her.

"And here's me trying to keep all this a secret from you."

"It's very dangerous, isn't it? What they want you to do …?"

"I'll say. But no more than some of the fights in 1940. I survived those, so I will survive this."

"But how can you be sure."

"I'm sure. I may be mad, but I'm lucky and mad."

"I know a little about you. I've seen your file … ."

"I have a file? I didn't know that."

"Yes. You are known as a 'wild pilot.' Your father was a barnstormer. I guess that explains why both you and your brother are pilots and good ones too. But you … you keep getting into trouble."

"Yes. It's a constant problem … ."

"But surely … . You've been a pilot since the War in France, so they should have promoted you … ."

"Not with *my* record. I just can't help it. Sometimes I just have the urge to push the limits, prove that I'm alive!"

"Tell me about your father."

"He's still alive. He lost a leg in an air-accident in '35. Since then, we had been living on the bread-line. Before that, it was a good life. We travelled around when I was very young. We even went to Egypt once. Later, we settled at Croydon. There were always good crowds there, so we could make good money."

"You worked with him?"

"Well, me and Martin just used to help with the aircraft, preparing it and collecting the fare or the money from the audience when he was stunting."

"And your mother?"

"Dead. Killed in the Blitz, along with my sister, Joanne. I miss her. After my father was injured, she had to become the bread-winner for a while. But she's really a very quiet woman, I mean was. Sorry. You know … homely."

"I'm sorry, Richard. So sorry."

"It's alright. I am used to it now. Only … ."

"What?"

"Well, Archie said something funny to me. Odd, I mean. At the time I didn't think much about it, I was too flattered, but since a briefing … it has been on my mind. He said mine was the only name on a list he had of good low-level pilots. Now I *know* that *isn't* true! There are a few, not a *lot*, but a few. So why me?"

"Perhaps because you haven't been promoted? A big carrot for you?"

"Maybe."

She let him think for a moment

"Is that what you like in a woman; quietness?"

"No. I don't think so."

"Hm." She seemed far away for a moment.

"So what is your next task in this great mission of ours?"

She sighed. "Oh. I have to tell Michael about his friends, in the raid. They both died. He knows about the first, he crashed in The Strand. The second pilot used the … ejection-seat, but the parachute didn't fully open, and he hit the wall behind Buckingham Palace."

"He'll be very upset."

"Yes."

***

Richard took Anna with him to Stradishall; he needed to drop his things in his new quarters. They had no plans after this.

"How high is your security clearance?" Richard asked. "Only I'm not sure they will let you thought at the perimeter … ."

"Well, we will find out then, won't we?" He glanced at her and saw a delightfully mischievous twinkle in her eye. "How about you, Jackie?" she asked, swinging around on her seat. "What's your clearance?"

They were allowed through the gates after Anna showed her pass. Richard's eyebrows went skywards, though he said nothing.

Four black-painted Lysanders, parasol-winged light-aircraft used by the Secret Ops squadron, were just being towed out of a large hanger.

"Must be flying tonight. France, probably," Richard commented. Glancing over to the main apron in front of the larger hangers, he added, "Looks like all the Stirlings are up too." His was the next hanger along the apron, and he pulled up the car outside a green-painted blockhouse, fifty feet from the last hangar. He opened the passenger door for her and led her into his place-of-work. The few staff that had already been assigned to the project all looked as if somebody had died. "So what's the air of gloom for?" Richard asked the lowly orderly, recently transferred to Stradishall. The red-haired youth, Mackay, seemed to be the only one smiling.

"I have to call Mr Archibald … ." Richard said.

Anna giggled and whispered, "Mr Archibald … ?"

"Nobody uses his second name here. It's Top Secret," he whispered back. "Let's go into my office." He led her down a short corridor and opened a flimsy door into a musty room at the back of the block-house. "My Chateau, Mademoiselle!" he announced, with a flourishing sweep of his arm. "Please be seated while I contact my butler." He lifted the receiver of the black telephone and called the three-digit Whitehall number. "Archie? Yes, this is Rich … ard. What's the low-down? Oh before you start, I have Miss Styles with me. Oh, fine … . Well, yes, as a matter of fact, I had noticed that her pass seems to get her just about anywhere … . Right … . Oh, I see … . Yes, I'll be there. Yes, it's fine here. There's not much to eat though. I will have to take Miss Styles somewhere *out* to dine, if you understand what I mean … ." He grinned boyishly at Anna, before replacing the receiver. "I have to meet him at Rochester tomorrow as planned. Just confirmed. I wonder what everyone around here is looking so sad about." He opened the door and called for the orderly.

"What's going on? Why'd everyone looking so glum?"

"Ah, hello sir. It's Mr Martin, beg your pardon, Squadron leader Earlgood, sir … ."

"Nevermind. What about him?" Richard felt the cold grip of fear tighten around his heart.

"Well, sir. He had just moved in his stuff, as it were, when a call came in for volunteer pilots for the raid tonight on Hamburg. Some dumb fool had left the Station Tannoy on. It had only been intended for the crews in 1657 Squadron who were filling in for missing crews at Downham Market … ." Richard's face had dropped, and the poor orderly couldn't stop talking. "You know how it is sir … these big raids. They're often looking for replacements for 214 Squadron Stirlings … . Anyway, the Squadron leader heard it and went rushing off. We later heard he had taken off in B for Beer."

Richard mastered his emotions. "What time are they due back?"

"Oh five-hundred, sir."

"I thought Martin had been transferred away?"

"Not until tomorrow, sir."

***

Richard drove Anna to the nearest pub, which served them a passable meal, but he didn't feel in the mood for conversation. As soon as he could, he drove her back to the station and left her alone in the car, while he visited the Control Room.

"No news, yet," he said, driving her back to the blockhouse. "I was going to drive you back to London, but I can't leave now. I'll try and arrange a car to the station for you … ."

"Please don't bother. I couldn't leave now. I can sleep in a chair if necessary. I want to stay up with you. I have never seen bombers returning. My work's always behind closed door, so removed from the real … ." Her words petered out.

"You were going to say 'action … .'"

"Yes. Sorry. I didn't mean … ."

"It's alright. I *do* know what you mean. It must be difficult for you … ." Suddenly she took his hand, and he squeezed hers.

They brought Jackie inside, and the orderly found a cardboard box and some old rags to line it with. Soon the convalescent sat munching contentedly on canteen vegetable scrapings in his new accommodation.

"Let's go outside. They'll start coming back soon," Richard said as 4am approached. They had been served numerous cups of weak tea from an old canteen during the night, but these were just to sooth their nerves. Neither felt tired. "Damn," he said when they were out of earshot of the blockhouse. "Why did Martin *have* to go and *volunteer*!"

"I thought he just *trained* pilots?"

"Yes, but Operational Conversion Units still contribute to the main force on some raids. They are dual purpose units … . Welcome to the the grimness of war."

Anna lit a cigarette. "It's my last."

"Sometimes I wish I smoked … ."

"Here," she said, holding out the cigarette for him.

"No thanks."

She glanced up into the black dome above. "It's such a beautiful night. It looks like the night has been sprinkled with fairy dust. Shame some men might die up there."

"*Might* ... . Will."

They walked slowly up and down the apron in front of the Secret Ops hanger. At 4.30am, the runway lights came on, and a lone Lysander gracefully floated down on to the concrete strip. It slowed within a few hundred feet to taxiing speed. The pilot gunned the engine from time to time as it moved towards the hanger. There the pilot cut the engine, and the Lysander rolled to a stop only fifty feet from Richard and Anna. Three shadowy figures rushed out to push the little aircraft into the waiting hanger.

"One home," he said, quietly.

"Probably more in the back," she added.

He looked at her, curiously. "You know much more about operations than you let on."

"I'm not stupid, you know." This time he took her hand. "Such a black night now. The clouds have come over. There's a moon up there, but I can't see it. Can you?"

"Not for a while. The clouds keep covering it. Gloomy. But then it always is these days. Have you seen a radar screen?"

"Yes."

"I sometimes think it's as if England is an image on a radar screen. Even on the sunniest day there is an insidious gloom penetrating everything. I wonder if Hitler can even see us mere mortals!"

She squeezed his hand.

At 5.10am, just as dawn started to raise its curtain of light, the first engine could be heard in the distance.

"Here they come!" said Richard.

The first Stirling to land had only three engines running and flak damage pocked its long fuselage. The pilot landed the struggling aircraft delicately, and then, after a gap of almost fifteen minutes, another three aircraft landed.

"Sir! Sir! Where are you?" The young orderly came running out of the blockhouse and Richard broke into a run towards him. Anna stood still, waiting for the news. Richard walked slowly back to her and seeing his grim face, she feared the worst.

"He's coming in on three engines!" Richard said, shaking slightly. "Have you still got that cigarette?"

"No. I finished it. Will he be alright?"

"God knows! The bloody fool! He didn't have to go." Richard began to pace up and down. Anna tried to keep up, consoling him and encouraging him.

"Sir! More news. It's not good, I'm afraid," shouted the orderly from the blockhouse door.

"Oh God. What *now*?" Anna followed him as they walked up to the red-haired orderly, little more than a boy.

"Their electrics are shot up!"

"Oh Christ!"

"What does that mean?"

"Means the undercarriage might not come down, and they may not have flaps. They will come in too fast! On any other aircraft it might not be too bad, but on a Stirling … . You see, the undercarriage is very long and a bit delicate. I've been reading up on it. Christ, bloody Air Ministry!"

"Why?"

"I'll explain later. There he is!"

Just above the horizon, Richard spotted B-Beer, approaching much lower than the previous aircraft. Its remaining three engines were screaming at maximum revs to maintain what little height it had. The cowlings were glowing red hot in the early morning haze.

"Port outer is out. Come on Martin! They're lowering the main undercarriage. That's good. They've left it bloody late. Come on! Do it!" Richard said to himself.

"Why so slow?" Anna said, holding on to his sleeve.

"They're winding them down manually. Have to! No electrics. It would be better to belly-land, but he hasn't got flaps, so he will come in too fast. But if he lowers the undercarriage, it probably won't lock, and then the aircraft might cartwheel! Its a sticky bloody business. But if anybody can do it, Martin can."

The Short Stirling lined up on the main runway and began to lower slowly towards the airfield. The port outer propeller blade wind-milled gently, with no sense of purpose. All over the airfield, eyes were glued to the incoming wounded aircraft. Nobody moved. No bird sang.

The rumble and crackle of the three Hercules engines grew louder, and then Richard shouted.

"There! They're coming down! Yes!"

Below the wings and tail of the Stirling wheels could be seen descending, not quite fully extended yet. Rather than a sleek bird, it began to look like a stalky chicken looking for a place to land. Anna gripped Richard's sleeve tightly.

"Oh. I don't want to look."

The aircraft had descended to only one hundred feet above the grass, and only a few fences lay between it and the end of the friendly runway.

"You can do it, Martin. Come on," whispered Richard. "It looks like they're down! The wheels are down!"

Then the Stirling's shadow sprang ahead of it along the concrete strip as its pilot lowered it gently down and down.

"It's going way too fast. He must be doing one two five!" Richard held his breath as the main wheels approached the runway. Then, the port inner engine coughed twice, and the port wing began to drop towards the concrete runway. "Oh Christ, no!"

Richard heard the sound of scraping metal. Sparks flew off the wing-tip. But whoever piloted the aircraft just managed to haul the port wing tip up long enough for the port main wheel to touch down. The huge rubber tyres squealed once, twice, and then the aircraft whistled across the airfield with the remaining two engines cut.

"He'll never … ," began Richard. But he stopped speaking when the left undercarriage of the huge bomber collapsed, and the wing crashed to the ground. Anna buried her head in Richard's sleeve, but he wrenched himself away and sped towards his car. "Stay here!" He jumped over the door, into the car and thrust his keys into the ignition. All the while he kept one eye on the Stirling which, sparks flying from the wing-tip, had begun to slew around to the left, onto the grass. Then the second undercarriage leg collapsed under the strain, and the aircraft began an elegant three hundred and sixty-degree spin. Richard gunned the engine of the Austin and raced across the grass towards his brother's stricken aircraft. From all over the airfield, fire-tenders, ambulances, cars and trucks of all descriptions raced towards the scene of the accident, hoping to find survivors. Nobody thought about the probability of an explosion and their own safety.

Richard was the second to arrive, and the Stirling had just come to a halt, its wings rocking gently from side to side. Clouds of grass floated across the crash site, some blades settling on Richard's hair, but he didn't notice. He had scrambled out of the car and started running towards the cockpit, where he could see at least one figure emerging from the emergency hatch in the top of the Perspex 'greenhouse.' As he reached the fuselage, the figure jumped down onto the wing and then down to the grass. It was 'Cloudy Callum,' the Navigator.

"Where's Richard? Is he alright?" Richard said, grabbing the man by the shoulders and steering him away from the wreck.

"Oh he's fine, old man. A few scratches, but nothing a pint and a WAAF won't put right. Probably checking everybody else by now. Tricky landing, what?"

"Is everybody else alright?"

"I think so. Let's stop. They'll be out in a moment."

Both men stopped at a safe distance from the wrecked bomber and turned to watch for the others.

The first man to arrive at the crash had stopped his car at the rear of the aircraft and had opened the rear hatch, near its tail. In single file, slowly, brushing themselves off and straightening their hair, came the rest of the crew. Last of all came Martin. He straightened up once his feet were on the grass and took off his flying helmet. He replaced it with his cap and walked up to Richard. Richard could contain himself no longer and ran up to embrace him.

"You bloody idiot! What were you *thinking*? You're damned lucky to be alive!"

All around them trucks, fire-tenders and ambulances were arriving, bells were ringing, and men were rushing up to the stationary aircraft.

"Aah! Nothing to it really. We *were* lucky though. You're right. Could have been a right mess! Pretty poor landing though! I don't think my students will be very impressed. My last operation flight with the squadron too. On well. Fancy a pint? That is, if the bar's open."

"Yes. This time, I won't refuse. And I'm buying! We'll have to pick up Anna."

"Who's Anna?"

"The girl I told you about."

***

Richard drove Martin over to the blockhouse where Anna waited, looking pale and nervous. When he saw her, Richard had the urge to run up, envelop her in his arms and kiss her. It was a spontaneous thought that surprised him. Instead, he smiled and she smiled back.

"Anna Styles, this is Martin, my brother. He made it!"

"Thank God! Hello Martin. We thought you were a gonna!"

"Ha! Not so easy to kill. We were a tad lucky though! How do I look" he said, turning to Richard.

"Like you've been in a plane crash!"

"Hmm. This is the new quarters, isn't it? Can I go inside and tidy myself up?"

They followed him inside.

"Who's this then," he said stooping to get a close up look at the little rabbit in his box on Richard's floor.

"His name's Jackie. Richard found him on the road."

"Cute little mite, isn't he? Looks like me."

"Ha!"

"Martin thinks all women find him cute," emphasised Richard. Then Martin did something that surprised his brother. He took off his blue scarf and wrapped it gently around Jackie's furry neck.

"There you go, little chap. That will keep you warm." The rabbit sniffed Martin's fingers, its wet nose touching his fingertip for a moment.

"Bloody hell. He likes you too!" exclaimed Richard. "You can't give him the scarf though. It's your lucky scarf. He's already had enough luck, and he has me."

"He can be my mascot. If I last as long as him, I'll be happy."

"I'll knit him a little version of your scarf," said Anna.

***

Anna, Martin and Cloudy loaded themselves into Richard's car. A black Riley followed them to the Officer's Mess where two bottles of scotch were released from their hiding places.

"This will have to do, until the pub opens!" shouted Martin's rear gunner, Eamonn 'Tiddler' Frost.

"Don't forget we have to be at Rochester for 2pm," Richard shouted in Martin's ear. As Martin lifted the first glass of scotch was to his lips, Richard noticed that his brother's hand shook uncontrollably. He hooked his arm around his brother's with his own, glass in hand, to toast each other in the traditional way. He braced his wrist against Martin's, and the drink reached its destination without a drop being spilled.

"Quicker by train … . That way we can get blind drunk, too," Martin replied, after downing the scotch in one, eyes closed.

They did get merrily drunk, singing plenty of good, old-fashioned English pub songs and dirty renditions of them created by bored RAF officers. Both men treated Anna as 'one of the boys,' and she took up position between them for each rousing chorus and raucous dance.

***

"Here we are," said Archibald. The black, unmarked car whisked them through the checkpoint after barely slowing for the driver's face to be checked, before they were speeding down the apron towards the main factory buildings of Short Brothers. "This is where they assemble the aircraft, apparently." he added. The airfield seemed pock-marked with bomb craters.

"Göring's Luftwaffe has been having a good try at stopping production," offered Martin wryly, glancing at the craters.

Richard's head throbbed viciously. Too much scotch, too early in the morning, followed by a long train journey on a hot, sunny day, had been too much for it. They had travelled down to London on the train and left Anna at Liverpool Street.

"We're going to be busy for a few days," he told her, taking her hand gently in his. "The pilots I picked from a list Archie gave me, will be arriving along with some aircraft, at Stradishall. Would you mind if I call you when I next have some time?" He felt not the least trace of guilt at making the offer.

She showed not the least trace of discomfort when she smiled and said, "Alright." She looked at him as if expecting something.

Richard wanted to kiss her but felt awkward. He hesitated. "When are you next seeing the German pilot?"

"Michael? Today, probably. I have to tell him … ."

"Yes, you said …"

"Maybe you would like to meet him?"

"Me. Well … that would be interesting. Is it possible?"

"I could arrange it. I have to go. Call me?"

"I will."

The black car stopped outside an office next to a giant hanger on Rochester airfield. Richard and martin were led into the office and showed their passes to a guard. He waved them through onto the main factory floor.

"Wow!" Richard's mouth fell open. Before him were row upon row of partially completed Stirlings, stretching as far as he could see. The sound of machinery, hammering, whistling and singing echoed around the vast interior of the assembly plant. The jolly atmosphere offered a stark contrast with the world outside the factory.

"This is where we mate the wings to the fuselages," said a man in a grey suit, wiping sweat from his forehead with a white handkerchief. "Richard Rose. I heard you were coming. I have been sent to show you our special little project!" He was an energetic, short, almost bald, man, his few tufts of white hair combed neatly against the side of his head. As he turned this way and that, endlessly restless, he reminded Richard of a white vole seeking food in a reed-bed. At times a strand of hair would obscure one lens of his round, black framed glasses. "Follow me."

"You are Sir Richard Rose?" queried Martin.

"Yes. I suppose I am, but I don't allow anybody to call me that. Senior Management wouldn't have it anyway. We're strictly informal around here … . Ha! Ha!"

He led them across the floor of the vast space and through a white door into a smaller and much quieter, space of the same height. Before them, they saw a single, half-completed Short

Stirling, with a strange framework attached to its spine, just behind the cockpit.

"We're using an Mk III for the prototype, but it really has been quite easy. You see, during the development of the Stirling we actually designed a version to carry a fighter. We had the drawings for the carrying cradle already completed. Took me a while to find them … . Silly thing is, I designed it, so I should have known where to find them!"

"What fighter … or fighters, will it carry?"

"Well, the obvious choice is the Hurricane. It's stronger than the Spit and about the same weight. That's what we originally had in mind, and I understand you do too."

"Yes. When will you put a Hurricane on it and try it out?"

"Well, we were thinking of using a mock-up, but the Ministry of Air Planning has sent three Hurricanes our way, they were never used by the Navy and were in storage. Quite lucky really; they're ideal. If they can stand launching from a catapult, they can certainly take a joyride on the back of our Stirling."

"When can we see one?"

"Well, this one should be ready in five days. With the Hurricane of course. We'll contact you, and you can come down for the trial."

"When will the other three Stirlings be off the production line?" asked Martin.

"You mean when we put them together?"

"Err, yes. They're going to be Mk IIIs?"

"Oh no. MAP wouldn't have that, far too valuable. I imagine Harris would have a fit if we did that. No, these will be rebuilt Mk Is. They will be quite adequate for the purpose. Better, in a way as they don't even have a top turret!"

"No, and they have Exactor carburetors and pitch control! I'm not happy about that! Richard, we have to say something!"

"Oh, you don't like the Exactor system?" asked Sir Richard.

"*No*. And I don't know any pilot who does. They are a menace. No doubt they're fine on paper, but in service … ."

"Yes. I have heard there have been some difficulties. Well, that's all that can be spared, I'm afraid."

"Could they be updated, have the Exactors taken out?"

"It *could* be done. Out of my hands though."

There followed an awkward silence.

"Martin crash-landed an Mk I this morning. Lucky to get out!"

"Really? My dear fellow. Sit down. Can I get you anything? Something to drink? Are you alright? I had no idea!"

Martin smiled. "I'm fine. The old queen got a bit pranged up though. I felt a bit shaky until I had had a scotch or two."

"What actually happened?"

"Electrics shot out. Luckily the undercarriage came down but not the flaps. What nearly finished us was the engines. First one overheated, and we couldn't feather it properly. Then just before we touched down, the other failed. Basically, we couldn't cool them, because the engine gills are electrically operated too. Now, if you had the undercarriage and the feathering electrical, and the flaps and gills hydraulic, it would give the pilot more options. Its unlikely both would be out."

"Yes. Yes, I see what you mean. I will have a chat with the chaps. Was anybody else hurt?"

"No, we were all okay."

"But the aircraft's a right-off, I suppose?"

"'Fraid so."

"Ah well. Shame about the 'crate!' Ha! Ha! That's what you chaps call 'em isn't it. Mind you, I am jealous. I would love to be flying one myself!"

Richard started on a circuit around the Stirling. The others followed. "So how will the Hurricane be attached and detached? Electrical locks of some kind?"

"I was thinking more of explosive bolts … " said Sir Richard, uncertainly. To the blank expressions of the two airmen he added, "That … seems the most secure method. After all, the Stirlings may, I presume have to take evasive action?" His prompt for more information met stoically blank faces. "If you could tell me more about the mission? Where you are going? What altitude?"

"I'm afraid we're not authorised," replied Richard. "Somebody no doubt will tell you in time. You're probably right though. Evasive action is likely. You're test flying in about five days?"

"Yes."

"Who will be in the Hurricane?"

"No one. A plastic dummy, probably."

Both airmen nodded.

"We'll be here."

With that, Sir Richard Rose showed them out of the factory. In the car, on the way back to London, Martin voiced his misgivings.

"I don't like this 'cheapest solution is fine' approach. It's all being done on the cheap! I know we're expendable, but not *that* cheap!"

"I know what you mean. I've had that feeling from the beginning."

"Maybe Harris doesn't believe in it after all."

"It's almost as if it doesn't matter that much whether we succeed or not."

"No."

***

Michael paced up and down in his small room, his windowless cell, in Piccadilly. The heat felt oppressive, and he had stripped to the vest and the trousers, which he had been given to replace his own. He didn't like looking untidy, but he hadn't been allowed to bath properly since the raid and only allowed a bar of soap, one towel, a hairbrush and a Gillette razor blade. The last he had only been allowed under supervision of a guard with a gun. All of this, and he only had a forty-watt light bulb, which glowed dimly, naked, from the centre of a dappled, duck-egg green ceiling. At least the colour represented something familiar; a utilitarian austerity. He heard footsteps outside, and the door opened. Anna stood there and a guard left her.

"Anna!" He rushed over and took both her wrists in his hands. He leaned forward and kissed her lips lightly. She blushed.

"Michael." She looked around, pulling away slightly from him. "What a horrible room. How long have you been here?"

"Since yesterday. The guard told me this is where I will be for some time. I think they are trying to break me down!"

"Listen Michael. There's something I need to speak to you about." Anna clasped her handbag between her two nervous hands, as if wringing it, and paced up and down. "Sit down." Without thinking, Michael sat down. Anna then placed her handbag on the single table. "There's a chance you might be able to get out of this room, at least for a while." She glanced at Michael, who nodded slowly. As she turned, she reflexively glanced up at the ceiling rose above the light-bulb. She could see the crack, behind which she knew the microphone had been placed. She looked down before turning to face Michael again. "If you can give me some indication that you can be trusted, that you no longer consider yourself a member of the Nazi Party, then you could come out for a day with me." She hastily added, "Would you like to meet an RAF pilot I know? His name is Richard. He's a Hurricane pilot. He would like to meet you."

Michael shook his head slowly. "So this is blackmail. I thought it was too good, too fortunate for me to see you … ."

Anna pulled out the other chair and sat facing him. "Michael, let's be honest … . Think about it. Of course, they *want* something. That's the only reason they let me *see* you!"

"So you are one of them! You are working for British Intelligence? I should have known." Anger clouded his normally smiling face.

For a moment she felt at a loss. "It's not that bad. All they want is a sign from you. Something!" She shook her head in exasperation. "How do you feel about Hitler?"

A half-formed smile creased the corner of Michael's mouth. "I *could* think that this is a trap and that you will betray me. But I know you better than that." He paused and then stood up. He walked away from her, while thinking. He recalled the speech he had prepared and spoke. It wasn't difficult to sound genuine as it reflected what he had begun to feel about Hitler. "As it happens, I … despise the man. Ha! For a moment, I was afraid to say that! But now, of course I am free. Your government will protect me, and believe me, the safest place from Herr Hitler right now is London. Anna, I haven't told you this before, but many of us in Germany hate what Adolf Hitler has done." He spat the Nazi Leader's name. "I even contemplated joining one of the many conspiracies to remove him!" Anna's eyes widened in hope. "Yes! At the Russian front I saw there the inhumanity, the … what is the English word, a *good* word, the 'barbarity' of it. My faith in the National Socialist Party faded there. But ambition brought me back to France. I still thought I believed in Hitler. I actually came up with the scheme to attack Buckingham Palace myself. But part of me always knew I couldn't do it." He sat down again. "It's all such a mess. I finally realized, when I was flying up The Mall, that what I wanted was you, and if I carried out the attack, I would never see you again."

He looked crestfallen, and Anna wanted to hug him. But she held to the plan given to her by her superiors. "What if you knew there was a plan to assassinate Hitler, a plan in London?" He looked up, hopefully. "A plan to be carried out from the air?"

Michael stirred. "Well, yes. I would, I *might* … want to help. But what could I *do*?"

"Might or would?" Her stern, hard expression surprised him.

"*Anna*? You ask a lot. I have only just escaped from the Third Reich! I have lived there for … . No, you are right. It's my decision to make." He looked up at the ceiling for guidance. He hardened his thoughts and then his face. "If I *could*, I would kill Hitler myself. But I won't kill Germans indiscriminately." He looked at Anna.

She smiled. "I'll see what I can do."

"And the pilot. May I meet him?"

Anna touched the back of his hand, resting on the table, with her fingertips. She picked up her handbag, stood up and left without saying a word. Michael stared silently into space for a long time before he moved.

***

# Chapter Three

Adolf wiped his mouth with the white napkin and pushed away the plate of fresh alpine vegetable and mung bean salad. His chef's new creamy sauce gave it just the richness needed to 'hit the spot.' He felt almost sated. Only one thing could complete the feast. He slid open the drawer to his left, picked up a cream puff from pile on a blue plate there and felt the cream ooze between his teeth as he bit into the succulent delicacy. When he finished it, he again wiped his mouth clean, stood up to let Blondi into the Reich Chancellery garden. He bent down stiffly, and Blondi put her wet nose against his. He grabbed her by the ruff and clutched her to him. Both hearts beat together as fur met skin in mutual love and affection. Then Blondi yelped and pulled away from him.

"So you want to play, do *you*? You never grow *up*!"

He picked up a rough piece of broken branch from the muddy construction site and walked on. He had made sure the workmen left one area of grass undisturbed, near the back and to the right of the garden. When Blondi reached it, he threw the stick and sat down on a bench that had been placed there for him. It was nearly 5pm, only lunchtime for him. He had only been up a few hours, but for once he felt happy and wanted to enjoy the sun before it sunk beneath the trees.

He smiled again at the news he had received only minutes before eating. The British! Such determination! A Gestapo report had reached him about a motor-torpedo crew picked up off the Dutch coast when its fuel tank had been ruptured during an attack. Normally such a report wouldn't interest him, but one member of the crew had squealed about some secret plan to bomb the bunker with X-ray bombs. X-ray bombs! As if such a thing could exist. Still, he had always been a cautious man. Such rumours often hid a grain of truth; just as well he had started to enlarge and strengthen the Führerbunker. But what could it mean? The young sailor thought the attack might be timed for September. It had to be a bluff. He had planned to be in the Berghof in the early part of September before the air grew too cool. Perhaps they meant to attack him there instead? That would be easier. He would remember to cancel at the last moment but would tell no one in advance. Let them bomb an empty palace!

***

When Richard and Martin arrived back at Stradishall, they saw five Hurricane IIa's parked at the dispersal area beside their hanger.

"Bloody hell! They look almost new!" he said to his brother. "Things are looking up!"

The small canteen that served as a mess in the blockhouse, had filled with orderlies and the three pilots Richard had chosen from the short list drawn from pilots he had flown with. They crowded around Richard and slapped him on the shoulders.

"So you've got yourself promoted at last! What's it all about?" said a baby-faced Australian with blonde hair and a wispy moustache. Martin thought he still looked about sixteen.

"Todd! Good to see you! I can't tell you much yet, but you'll know the basics tomorrow. Martin, this is Todd McKenzie, older than he looks. I have flown with him since France in '40. This is Bob Crawford, 'Slick' to all and sundry for obvious reasons," Richard said pointing Martin's outstretched hand toward that of a shortish, but handsome, man with dark, Bryl-Creemed hair and a friendly grin, "And this is Eric 'Razor' Sutton," he said turning to a man with brown, tightly curled hair, sporting a black patch over his left eye.

"Got it in a tussle with a FW 190 late last year. I got him in the end, an eye for a life, like, as I always say!" Razor replied with a Geordie accent.

Martin smiled wryly and shook his hand warmly.

"Chaps," said Richard. "This is my brother, Martin. He's a bomber pilot, on Stirlings, and one of the best. I can tell you we will be working very closely with him. So get to know him. He's not a bad sort, although I wouldn't trust him with your girl, especially if she's French."

The little dig by his brother amused Martin, and he laughed wholeheartedly. "You noticed. Tell you later."

"Two Squadron Leaders and three Flight Lieutenants, what's this then, some kind of excuse for a nightly foray into London for booze-ups?" commented Slick, slightly older than the other pilots.

"That's not why I chose you … ," replied Richard.

"Sir," said the orderly, MacKay, from a half-opened door. "There's a call for you from Mr Archibald. Urgent, he says."

"Ah, okay. If you'll excuse me a moment. Mackay, I want you to break out the best booze we have for these chaps. And then find the best food we have on the station for them, alright?"

"Yes, sir!"

"Hello … . Richard, its Archie. Listen, I don't have much time. Things are starting to move quickly. We just had a visit from the Royal Engineers. We have requested their services to build the mock-up of the Berlin Streets for you, and they're up for it. When I asked them how long the whole thing would take, they said *two weeks*! *Minimum*! Anyway, the powers that be think it will be alright, but we need to get them started on it tomorrow. I'm at Liverpool Street now. I can be there in just under two hours. Can you arrange an Ops. Room for us on the Station?"

"Yes. I don't see why not. Do you want all of us?"

"No, just you and Martin. My train's just about to leave. See you later."

At 8.30pm, they convened in one of Stradishall's three Operations rooms. The wall displayed a very large-scale photograph of the small section of Berlin around the Reich Chancellery, stretching east and north as far as the river. Some of the buildings were outlined in red.

"Accurate maps of this part of Berlin are impossible to come by these days," said Archibald. "A high-flying Spit took this yesterday; it's completely up to date. This is your target!" He pointed to a red cross over the Reich Chancellery rear garden. "Now, what you have to decide, tonight if possible, is the route you are going to take to get there."

"But I thought you had it planned?" exclaimed Richard.

"We did. But there's a problem. Since the beginning of the War, there has been a massive expansion of telephone lines in central Berlin and, unfortunately for us, the Germans have chosen to string them between the tops of buildings. Consequently, Unter den Linden is festooned with cables at just the height you were to be flying!"

Richard walked up to the grainy photograph. Close up, he could see little detail but could make out individual people on the streets, unaware they were being photographed. "Why can't we come in from the west, across the park? Then there would be no obstacles?"

"You could, but that park is filled with the best ack-ack crews in Germany. They have everything there, light stuff and 88s, as well as the really big stuff."

"I see. Okay how about coming from the north, say down this street here, what is it?"

Archibald referred to a map on a table. "LuisenStraße. Yes, you could, possibly, although the turn off the river would be very tight, and the street is narrow. Only about seventy feet. But how would you then get around into Unter den Linden. The turn here would be too tight."

"Yes, I suppose you're right. The south is no good, because no river. I am guessing that's why the Germans were so nearly successful on Buck Palace. A river is easy to fly up, and it's below building height, so nobody can shoot at you!" Archibald smiled ironically to himself, thinking of the two civilian casualties from their own guns that day in London. "I can't see any other way than straight down Unter den Linden. If we can't go down there, it's over the park, but that's suicide, unless there is total surprise."

"Which there won't be," added Martin. "A squadron of Stirlings, three of them carrying Hurricanes! The first thing the Germans will think is 'suicide attack.' They will have everything in the air including all the lead in Berlin."

"Yes," said Archibald, quietly. "You can see our problem. I hardly like to ask you to do it, now. At first it seemed a good idea, but now I'm not so sure."

"Cheer up. We'll think of something. Hm … . What if we fly a Stirling up Unter den Linden, just above rooftop level, but with it trailing a grappling hook. That would take down all the cables … ."

"Yes! That could *work*! I hadn't thought of *tha-* … !"

"Wait a *minute*!" cut in Martin, exasperated. "Are you *crazy*? There's no way that Stirling would stay in the air. It might reach the end of the street, but then what? It would be so weighed down, it would crash. It couldn't possibly gain height!"

"But what if it could drop the grappling hook?" suggested Richard.

"'Still … . I don't think … ."

"Let's keep it as plan B for now," suggested Archibald. "We need something better."

Fired up, Martin stood up and paced in front of the photograph. "What if we bomb the street with the Stirlings at the same time as the Chancellery. We would have to use some special kind of filler for the bombs; something that cuts through telephone cable. How wide is the street?"

"It's over one hundred and fifty feet. The central reservation is about twenty feet, so that's about sixty-five feet either side," answered Archibald

"That's plenty for Hurricanes, isn't it Richard?"

"Yes … ."

"Well then, we only have to take down a few poles or cables, and the whole lot should come down. Should be possible … ."

"That's it then, said Archibald. I'll get the boffins started on it right away."

"Of course, there is one potential problem here," added Richard quietly.

"What's that?" asked his brother.

"The Krauts only have to have a couple of guns at the end of the street, by the Brandenburg Gate, and they will have an easy shot. We will be right in the middle of their bulls-eye for what, twenty seconds?"

***

Richard gathered the pilots together in the same Operations Room the next morning. The large photograph and map had gone. All except Richard had gone drinking in Martin's favourite pub, called The Black Dog, the previous evening, and the faces staring at Richard were weary and uncertain.

"Today we're going on the first practice mission. I've just heard from the boys in Whitehall; Sappers have been up all night and have already laid enough markers on Dartmoor overnight for us to try a little practice. Now, Obviously I can't tell you much about this mission. When we get there … ." He walked over to a blackboard and drew two curving, parallel curves on its right side. "You will see white paint marking out this shape on a flat area. This is a river. This is where we will begin our attack run. I can also tell you that the Hurricanes will be carrying 1000-pound bombs." Three right hands shot up in the air. "Wait until I finish, and then I'll take questions. Now, here you will see another pair of straight lines on the grass, approximately 150 feet apart. We turn from the river, between these lines and fly straight down them for about 4000 feet, before making a sharp left hand turn of about ninety degrees, another one here and then climb away to finish. We must do all this at about fifty feet or less. Martin will be coming with us in his Stirling C-Charlie to observe, and we'll formate with him on the way back." He drew a crude outline to represent the Stirling in plan view on the blackboard and placed three smaller shapes to represent the Hurricanes beside it; one next to each wing-tip and one behind. "Three of us will be in these positions and the fourth, with us each taking turns, will fly twenty feet above the Stirling's back. This Stirling has been modified slightly. Its radio aerial from the mast behind the cockpit to the tail, has been moved to the tail-plane, here. Just remember that. Don't even think about getting into this area here, between the left wing and the tail. You'll be safe enough just above the fuselage though. Any questions?"

Again, three hands shot up. Richard pointed to one.

"Razor?"

"1000-pound bombs, Rich. The Hurricane can't carry bombs *that* 'evy!"

"They can. That size of bombs had already been used, it's just not widely known yet. However, these Hurricanes are going to be modified. I think I can tell you that they will be *very* modified Hurricanes. The ones we have now are just for practice. They will have all armaments removed apart from two Brownings." His audience shook their heads, disapprovingly. He nodded to Todd, the blonde Australian

"Why Stirlings, skip. Surely, they are old crates now. Why not Lancasters?"

"Martin might be better able to answer that later, but the one thing the Stirling … has in its favour, is manoeuvrability at low altitude. And this we will need. It has one other … structural advantage which I can't tell you about, but let me tell you it's the ideal aircraft for this mission. Slick?"

"What's all this business about flying so close to the bomber" replied Slick in nasal Queen's English. "Damned dangerous if you ask me. Twenty feet? Can't you tell us why?"

"Actually, we will start at twenty feet, but later we will get it down to ten. And no, I can't tell you why. I *do* want you to get to know the Stirling intimately thought. I want you to get it to the point where you could fly all around it at less than ten feet in your sleep. Any more questions?"

Three heads were shaking. Razor muttered, "Too many questions … ." Richard eyed him. "But let's do it!" he continued, grinning, his grin appearing even more lopsided by his eye-patch and slight gap between his top incisors.

"Right. Now a few last points before we leave. First of all, you can trust Martin with your wife, I mean life." This met with chuckles. "And you will have to. He's the best pilot in Stirlings there is; what he doesn't know about them, isn't worth knowing. Secondly, in all likelihood, some of us won't be coming back." He looked at the stern, but determined, faces. He felt suddenly emotional. "This is going to be a very tough mission, carried out at low altitude, and you will need to do your very utmost to pull this off. Make no mistake." He grinned at the blonde Todd and the cocky Slick. "And now my last point. I know I have a reputation as a bit of a clown, as a trick flyer and a bad dresser." This met with guffaws. "It has been said I'm not able to handle responsibility. I hope to prove that wrong, and I would be grateful for this one chance to prove it. But I know that you may already feel differently. I have been chosen for this mission, precisely because of my low-flying skills … . Anyway, what I wanted to say was that if you feel uncomfortable with me leading this mission, now is the time to speak up."

"We'll give you a chance!" shouted the boyish Todd, laughing. Slick cuffed him around the shoulder.

"Right, let's go."

***

This would be Richard's first operational flight as acting Squadron Leader. They arrived over Dartmoor safely, having flown most of the way there at less than one hundred feet. Using the new VHF radio, Richard had instructed them on avoiding obstacles. "Watch out for any type of vertical structure. It might not look it, but it could be the anchor point for some kind of cable. If in doubt, fly over it!"

Twice they had nearly hit telephone cables. Once, they narrowly avoided a windmill. Only the nimble manoeuvrability of the Hurricane, the only fighter which could out-turn a Spitfire, Me109 and FW 190, saved them. By the time they reached Dartmoor they were all sweating, party from engine heat at low altitude in late summer and partly from fear.

The Stirling had taken off ten minutes before them and, having quite a respectable top speed and not having to avoid obstructions, had arrived ahead of them.

"There's Martin, circling ahead. I'll go in first," Richard announced. "You chaps circle here until I call you. Then do exactly the same as I do. If there are any trees on the route, hop them." As he dropped towards the lines marking out the imaginary river, Richard could see huddles of Royal Engineers, next to their trucks, waving at him. He waggled his wings, before lining up between the two painted white lines. He throttled back to 150 mph and dropped right down to 50 feet dodging between the odd tree on the gentle slope of the moor. Then, he saw that the Army had cleverly placed the whole area of the mock-up in a valley, so that it could not be seen by curious eyes. He saw the white lines of the road that led into Unter den Linden, come up and turned into it without difficulty. He remembered that this first section of this road, whose name he couldn't remember, ran into Unter den Linden. Narrower here, perhaps only 100 feet, Unter den Linden then opened out. He followed the slight curve to the right.

*This will help protect us if they do put guns at the far end.*

Suddenly the white lines stopped. Richard felt at a loss for a moment, as he flew on, but then they started again, just where he would have expected them to be.

"Sappers didn't get as much done as I would have liked last night!"

Then he saw the imaginary Brandenburg Gate marked out ahead. On cue, he wrenched the joystick hard to the left, lifting the nose slightly to hop over the imaginary three-storey buildings that ran out from either side of the gate. Turning onto Hermann-Göring-Straße had been no problem, and then another tight right-hand turn took him onto a heading straight for the back garden of the chancellery. At the last moment, Richard pressed his gun trigger which had been set to 'safe.' It gave him a feeling of satisfaction to think that if this had been for real, he would just have dropped his bombs right on the target.

*Seems all too easy!*

He pulled up and returned to the circling fighters. "Okay Todd. You give it a go. The lines run out half way along the straight street but then start up again." He heard only a studied silence from the other pilots at the word 'street.' The young Australian flew accurately along the river and turned onto the long street, bounding over the few trees along the way. Richard felt pleased to see that he had no problems until he reached the Gate at the far end. The Hurricane pulled up but was going too fast, and its left turn brought it out too far away from the Gate to make the second turn into the garden. Missing his second turn Todd came over the VHF.

"Sorry skip. Messed that bloody up!"

"Too fast. Try it at nearer 150. It's a bit sluggish at that speed, but you *should* make the turns. Okay, next up. Slick."

The second Hurricane fared much better, as did the third, piloted by Razor, both making their last turn successfully.

"Right, we'll try that a few more times and then it's home for lunch. I want this to become automatic for you. Tonight, the Sappers will start building facades of the buildings at the turns, so it will steadily become more realistic and more difficult over the following weeks." Richard told them.

"Wish we knew what it's all aboot, like" Razor in his Geordie accent.

"Sorry."

On his last run, Razor pulled up to clear the imaginary obstacle he didn't yet know mimicked the Brandenburg Gate and started to make his turn when the engine spluttered twice. At such low altitude he had no choice but to straighten out instantly and look for a flat area to crash land. The others saw him disappear over a slight rise and drop into a valley beyond. They watched the skies for the expected plume of black smoke, but it didn't come. Suddenly, they saw the Hurricane climbing above the horizon, and Razor's voice crackled over the radio. "I'm awkay. Must have been dirty fuel lines. She nearly gave out but cut back in just before ah touched down."

*Bloody hell! That was close!*

"Okay. Back to base," Richard ordered. "Razor, you go straight home, alright? Don't take any risks until that Hurricane's been checked. You other two follow me."

They formed up with the circling Stirling, also fitted with VHF radio, unusual for a bomber, and Martin came over the radio. "Nice work chaps. Got some nice photos. You were all at about 50 feet I reckon. Bit dodgy with Razor. What do you want me to do, Richie?"

"Far too close for my liking, Marty. I nearly lost one. 'Could have done better,' would be my report on myself. Just fly a straight course home. Stay at 200 mph. Keep her straight and level. We'll do the rest."

"You're too hard on yourself, Richie. Right oh. All follow me!"

On the return flight they each took turns flying at each wing-tip, just behind the tail and above the fuselage at 20 feet. The last would be the most tricky and dangerous. Richard tried first and quickly decided five minutes would be too long to keep it up for. He broke away after two.

"Ha! Ha! Chicken, are we?" quipped Todd.

"Knock it off, kid," cut in Slick, in uncharacteristically direct language.

"Ha! I heard a story about you … ." Only silence came from Slick's radio. "What floats to the surface in the cream of RAF wives?" Again silence. "A mouse called Slick."

"You Aussi, cocky little ba-ahstard. One of these days you will get *too* cocky." Richard grinned.

When they approached Stradishall, they could see Razor's Hurricane already at dispersal.

"Special Ops Squadron Leader to Blueberry Control, A-Apple, B-Beer and C-Charlie request permission to land."

"Blueberry Control to Special Ops Leader. Permission granted. D-Dixy already on ground safely."

The other three Hurricanes landed and taxied to line up with Razor's D-Dixy. The Stirling, F-Freddie, landed shortly after, and Martin taxied it to the main Stirling dispersal area. As yet the custom radio aerial had attracted little interest from other crews on the squadron, who thought it must be just another electronic warfare measure or counter-measure.

***

Richard had a message to call Archibald when he reached their small Mess.

"Hello, Archie? Yes, it's Richard."

"How did the first day's practice go?"

"Oh fine. Nearly had a hiccup with one of the Hurris. Engine nearly conked out at low altitude, very low! It all went kay though. The Sappers are doing a fine job."

"Good. Tomorrow they will start bringing in materials for the facades. They have permission to cut down trees too if they're in the middle of any of the 'streets.' Should give you a better run."

"Um. I wonder. No, you know Archie, let them leave the trees. They were only small anyway, not much grows on the moors. Even if the Stirlings do bomb the telegraph wires away, there will still be some obstructions."

"Oh. Alright. We'll be bringing up the model diorama tomorrow too. Only for you to look at, but it's as good as we can make it. Next best thing to being there. The chaps have been working on it around the clock. Unfortunately, they still have quite a lot to do, but they will work on it at nights. Anyway what I wanted to ask you … ."

"Yes … ."

"Anna has managed to persuade this Michael chap to meet you. In fact, he's really rather keen. And we're convinced he's ready to switch sides. Well, with Anna around you can hardly blame him, can you?"

"No." Richard said, uncertainly.

"Anyway, *tonight*, if you are willing. Can you get the 7 o'clock train?"

"Yes. Of course."

"Good. Come straight here. We've set aside a nice room for you. There will be food, wine and music."

"Listen, Archie. I suppose you know I have been seeing Anna?"

"Ah yes. We know all about it. None of my business, old boy. As long as you don't expect too much, you know … . She's probably still in love with him, after all. My superior thinks so. Just don't let Michael know."

"Yes. I think so." He tried to sound certain.

***

Michael went over that conversation a hundred times before he arrived at Whitehall.

*Does Archie know something I don't? Do they approve or not? Or are they using me in some way I can't see?*

He still mused over it when he opened the door to a well-lit room, populated by only two individuals; Anna and a smart, dark haired man in a cheap suit. They were both seated at a large table set for dinner, but the man immediately sprang to his feet, pushing the chair back on the oak floor with a loud scraping noise. Anna rose slowly.

"Richard, Squadron Leader Richard Earlgood, this is … Oberleutnant Michael Dorfmann."

Richard took off his cap and stepped forward to shake hands with the smiling man.

"Squadron Leader Earlgood. It is a very great pleasure to meet you. Forgive my regrettable state of dress. I have only the clothes they have given me. They took away my own, no doubt to check for secret maps and such." He laughed, awkwardly. "But then again, what is suitable for flying an Me109 is hardly suitable for dinner!"

The ironic pilot's joke broke the ice.

A waiter briskly entered the room as they seated themselves, on the three sides of a table-end. Anna sat between the two men. The waiter poured three glasses of white wine and left the bottle before departing.

"We have food, wine, even music … ," Michael said, indicating a gramophone set with his hand. "It's much better than what I have been used to recently."

"Oh? I'm sorry about that. Anna didn't tell me. I hope it's not too grim."

"It's not The Ritz."

"If I might say so, your English is almost perfect. But of course. You met Anna at Oxford. I had forgotten. You probably stayed in The Ritz."

"Yes. As a matter of fact, I *did*, once or twice. Usually too sozzled to appreciate it though. Ha!"

Behind the bon-hommie, both men were sizing each other up. Richard could read nothing in the steady gaze of the Luftwaffe pilot's green eyes.

"So why 109s?" asked Richard, suddenly. "Surely 190s are faster."

"Ah! Have you flown a 190?"

"No. But we have one. We know all about it. It's a very fine aircraft."

"Yes … . Yes it *is* a fine aircraft. But it doesn't turn as tightly as a 109, and it's not so good at high altitude. Perhaps it's just the way I have been trained to fly, but I prefer the 109. We are old friends. Perhaps you and the Spitfire are the same?"

"I fly Hurricanes."

"Ah. Then indeed we do have something in common. We both prefer outright manoeuvrability to speed."

Richard edged his wine glass away from him on the white tablecloth. "Yes. I was an aerobatic pilot before the war."

"Really? How fascinating! Clearly, we have never met in combat or you would have shot me down!" They both roared with laughter, but Anna felt confused. It seemed like a bad subject for a joke to her. Michael reached over and placed his hand on the back of Anna's, delicately. "Darling. We pilots have a strange sense of humour." Richard involuntarily jolted at the sight of the touch.

*Damn. I'm giving too much away. Fool, Richard. Fool.*

"How about the ejecting seat?"

"Ah! It's very cramped and fits badly. There are scratches all over the cockpit of my lovely Daisy where they clumsily fitted it."

"Daisy?"

"Yes. My 109 Emile. It's one of the rare ones, with the cannon between the engine cylinders. It's a lovely aircraft. You should take a look."

"I nearly forgot, Michael," said Anna, reaching into her handbag on the table. "They gave me this." She pulled out the rubber Donald Duck character which had been retrieved from the crashed Messerschmitt. She gave it a quick squeeze, and it made a bronchial honk sound. Both she and Michael laughed before she handed it to him.

"Donald! My Donald. I missed you!" He put the rubber duck on the table next to him. "Thank you very much Anna, and please thank your … erm  … associates for me. I don't suppose I will ever see Daisy again. But I'm sure she can be easily repaired. I would like it if you flew her, Squadron Leader."

"Richard. Call me Richard."

"Thank you. I'm honoured. And you should call me Michael." Despite himself, Richard had begun to like the polite German.

"But Michael, can't you tell me a bit more about the seat?"

"Ah. Of course. Well, it works on compressed air in two tubes. These act like barrels of a gun and fire it up and backwards, away from the aircraft. Of course, you have to eject the canopy first, and there are explosive bolts to do this. I did that before crash-landing. The seats were put in at my request, actually. In fact, the whole attack had been dreamed up and planned by me! Ha!"

Richard sat up, astonished at the candour of the man opposite. "Really? Does anybody know this?"

"In Germany yes. Here, not yet. Nobody asked me! But just to finish answering your question; the seats were designed and built by Heinkel. They originally built them for the He 280, you are familiar with the design?" Here, Michael broke dangerously away from his brief; mentioning secrets he wasn't authorised to reveal.

"No, actually."

"Ah, it's an experiment jet-fighter."

"I'm sorry? What?"

"Ah. I can see they haven't told you. It's the next generation of fighter. Ask your superiors to let you in on their secret. I don't mean to scare you with what *we* are up to. I believe you chaps are up to something similar."

"I see. Yes, I will have to find out more."

"As I was saying, the seats were designed by Heinkel, and I had them modified to fit the 109. It was a tight fit, I can tell you, and I couldn't reach all of the controls properly, the elevator trim wheel."

"Ah, yes that *would* be awkward." Richard smiled, grateful to be back on familiar territory. He still wanted to move onto something which interested him more. "Can I ask again; why did you actually want to attack Buckingham Palace? If you studied at Oxford, I just don't understand … ."

"You didn't ask me, actually, but I knew you would. You want to know why I'm not grateful, why I would hate the King and his family enough to try and kill them. Well, it's not that simple, but basically, I was an angry man and ambitious. And, I think … caught up with the National Socialist ideals. Let me explain. When I left Anna, foolishly, as it turns out, I was inspired by the ideas of the Leadership in Germany. I wanted to become part of it. During the Spanish Campaign I decided to join the Luftwaffe. I had been inspired by watching the Oxford Cadet Squadron just before the war, but I never believed I would be a pilot. I thought I would become a scientist. I was a talented pilot, and after becoming an ace during what you chaps call the Battle of Britain, I was sent to Russia to form a new Squadron. They wanted me to fly a Focke Wulf 190, and I was given one, but I gave it to somebody else. I kept Daisy. Then … I don't know what happened … . Perhaps I missed Anna, perhaps I just decided a senior position in the Luftwaffe was the course for me. I had this idea that if I could carry out a very bold and successful attack against a British target, I would be promoted and get to Berlin. Perhaps it was a combination of both, or just desperation to get away from the Russian Front; it really is terrible there." He shook his head. "Anyway, as you British like to say, to 'cut a long story short' I didn't hate the King at all. In fact, I *am* grateful for my Oxford Degree. I just became caught up in ambition, foolish ambition, and a confused wish to be with this woman again. At the last moment, I knew I could not do it and so … . Oh yes, and I knew the ejector seat would probably not work either! Ha! Yes, it worked in the Heinkel, but the cockpit of a 109 is *so cramped*!" He laughed raucously at his own joke and both Richard and Anna joined in. Richard found that he really liked Michael. He seemed a very honest man.

They were served the meal; a very presentable roast lamb, complete with real potatoes and real carrots, all soaked in gravy. They were almost silenced by this, but half way through, Richard asked his final question.

"So how do you feel about Hitler? Do you admire him, respect him?"

"Adolf Hitler must be killed. That's all there is to it. There are many conspiring to do it. I myself nearly joined such a group. I was ambitious, yes, but once I had seen what Nazism was doing to ordinary Russians and Germans, the poor Jews, I knew there was more than one Germany I could rise to the top of."

"You hate him?"

Michael rolled the base of his wineglass between his fingers while he thought over his answer, studying the table top seriously. "I hate what he has done to Germany, to ordinary people, and what he plans to do, yes."

Richard nodded. That would have to be enough.

After they ate apple pie for pudding and drank coffee, complete with brown biscuits, Richard stood to leave.

"I must be getting back. My new squadron will be wondering what has happened to me!" He bit his lip at his slip of the tongue.

"Richard is forming a Special Operations squadron," added Anna. Richard's open mouth was silenced by a confident and determined glare from her.

"Really? I see. Well, I do hope I find out more. I hope we meet again, Richard. I will be most interested in what you're planning. Could it be anything to do with attacking a certain Herr H?"

Richard nearly fell over with shock. At that moment, the door opened, and two guards in khaki uniforms, holding Browning rifles and wearing holsters with pistols, marched into the room. They led Michael away. "Good bye Richard and Anna!" he said, as the guards swept him down the corridor.

Richard sat down again. "The poor fellow! What an extraordinary chap! And what on earth just happened?"

"Don't worry. He'll be alright. Don't worry about False Promise either."

"Archibald Gates told me I had clearance to tell him a little, the aim of the mission. You see they think we can use him. And security is so tight, as you see, that he can't possibly get away or pass on any information."

"Oh. I see."

The door opened again and the mysterious man with blonde hair stepped in. "Thank you Anna. That was very well done. We recorded a lot of very useful information. I hope you enjoyed the meal." His eyes seemed to indicate that they were no longer welcome.

Richard felt incensed. He felt used. "*Anna*! What's this all about! You never told me we were being recorded!"

"But I didn't *know*!" she said, distraught. She stood up and threw down her napkin. Richard stood up, picked up his cap and left. He didn't look back.

Richard took the train back to Stradishall and arrived, tired and confused. He put himself straight to bed. The long hours and complexity of the operation were beginning to get to him. And now he no longer felt sure of Anna.

*****

For the next three days, they continued with Martin, practicing on the way and on the way back from, Dartmoor. The sappers worked tirelessly and building facades began to grow at the intersections of the marked-out streets and river. By the third day, the second storeys were complete. The model had also arrived at Stradishall. Richard noted with irony that the facades were only approximations of the actual Berlin buildings. A spy would still not guess the real location. He felt uneasy each time he walked around the model, kept in a locked room of the main office complex. With each day, its miniature detail increased at a much faster rate than the full-sized model. He began to notice a very large building, as it grew, in the corner between the River Spree and Schloßplatz.

*If it gets much higher, we won't get around that corner. We'll have to find an alternative route!*

*****

The red-hot anger that Richard felt towards Anna had not abated when the call came for the trip to Rochester. This time, Martin and he were met at the gates of the aerodrome by Sir Richard Rose. Richard, in particular, felt nervous about seeing his ideas put into action.

"Thank you driver. We'll take it from here." Sir Richard said.

He ushered the two brothers into his own black car and waved aside a Corporal, who demanded their identity papers. The black car sped across the aerodrome at a dangerous speed, the tires squealing as it navigated the concrete taxi-ways, just as heavy rain started to come down in sheets. The car screeched to a halt beside the smart officer who materialised as a Group Captain from the rain. He climbed in and the car sped on.

"I'm Group Captain Devonshire," said the man, tall and gaunt, with silver hair. "Over there! Although you can't see it. You *will* do, in a moment," he said. "While we have time, is there anything I can help you chaps with?"

Both pilots started talking together and then stopped. Richard nodded for Martin to continue.

"When we will get the Stirlings? And will they be Mk Is or Mk IIIs?"

"Well this is the first one. It's an Mk I. If this all works, you can fly it away sometime this week. Of course, we need to try a fully loaded Hurricane, but that I will leave to you and the chief test pilot. The other two will be Mk IIIs. There's not much differ … ."

"Thanks. Thank you very much!" Martin' face beamed.

"When do we get the Hurricanes?" asked Richard.

"Ah. That's a bit more of a problem. We'll prove the rig using a normal Hurricane I, but of course it won't have the range, and the Stirling would struggle to keep at any kind of altitude for long with all that weight. I would suggest you use a similar arrangement with the other Stirlings when you get them."

"When will that be?"

"Oh, if this test goes well, within the next two weeks."

He finished speaking just as he stepped out of the car, which had pulled up behind a rope barrier. On the other side, he saw an amazing sight. A Stirling, with a yellow belly, sat there. On its back, over thirty feet in the air, squatted a Hurricane, painted in light sea blue. For just a moment, Richard felt like a mad scientist.

*It was me who dreamed this up!*

Martin's mouth dropped wide open. A pilot in white overalls, balding, but with a hooked nose, waved to them as he disappeared around the rear of the fuselage, doing his final inspection. That done, he wiped his hands on his overalls and walked over to the two brothers. He grinned and held out his hand.

"Robert Benjemin Binnie at your service! Everyone calls me Benjy." His sharp, wise eyes darted curiously from brother to brother.

"Richard Earlgood," Richard replied, taking his hand warmly, "And this is my brother, Martin."

"Pleased to meet you. So this is all your bloody daft idea, is it?"

Richard grinned, sheepishly.

"Well today, we'll see if it works. I must admit I always wanted to fly the Empire Mayo composite, but I never got cleared for flying-boats. Now is my chance! See you later!"

With that, he walked back to the tail section of the Stirling and climbed in.

A plastic dummy's face stared alertly ahead inside the Hurricane cockpit. The cradle that supported the fighter consisted of four vertical struts with cross braces between them laterally and a single one each side, running down at an angle from each of the front pair of struts to the rear. The rain eased and pale, yellow sunlight reflected in a large puddle between the observers and the bomber-fighter composite aircraft.

All four Hercules engines slowly kicked into life. The pilot waved from the cockpit before taxiing away to the far end of the aerodrome to their left. To Richard it seemed like an eternity before they finally saw the Stirling come rumbling down the runway towards them, throttles fully open. The Hurricane's own propeller blades were in the feathered position and static, so as to create no resistance to the air which flowed around it. As it passed, the tail of the Stirling lifted, but still the bomber remained firmly on the ground.

"Come on!" whispered Richard. Martin shielded his eyes against the sun lancing through the clouds. He said nothing. It looked as if the Stirling would never leave the ground, as it slowly sank almost out of sight over the horizon towards the far end of the aerodrome, but then at the last moment, it lifted slightly and then slowly, so slowly, rose into the sky.

"Phew! I thought he wasn't going to make it!"

"Just being cautious, I expect," said Sir Richard Rose behind them.

"Well, it's in the air, Sir Richard."

"Don't call me that, please! Yes. Quite a sight, isn't she!"

They watched as the pilot executed a very slow turn to the left, away from them and then straightened out, to bring the colossal composite aircraft back over the aerodrome. All heads tilted backwards as the black shape cast its shadow over them.

"Funny how yellow appears black in shadow," Richard said. Martin opened his mouth to say something, but a loud crack cut him short. The Stirling suddenly lurched to the right slightly as it turned. As it revealed its back, they saw that the Hurricane hung at a bizarre angle, off the side of the bomber.

"Oh my God!" said Sir Richard. "I have to go to the Control Tower. He may need me." He ran and climbed back into the car, which sped off at top speed.

When Richard again looked into the sky he could see that the Stirling's crew were lowering the undercarriage. It looked like the pilot would attempt to land immediately, whether lined up on the runway or not. No one spoke as the bomber seemed to lurch from side to side. Each time, the Hurricane seemed to rotate a little more, until it faced at ninety degrees to the bomber. The pilot managed to turn again to the left and line up with the runway. Just as the bomber touched down the fighter slid off the bomber's back and cart-wheeled into an ignominious heap on the grass. The uneven weight distribution caused the right undercarriage of the Stirling to collapse. As it swung around, the right wing-tip caught the grass. The wing-tip dug deeply into the soft soil, and the aircraft went into a spin on the ground, the other undercarriage collapsing too.

"Oh no," Richard heard himself saying, under his breath.

Violently spinning now, the left wing tore loose, and then a gout of flame shot from a crack in the wrecked wing. An instant later all the onlookers ducked as a huge explosion rocked the aerodrome ground under their feet. Fire tenders, rushing towards the accident, stopped where they were as bits of aircraft and sods of soil came fluttering down out of the sky. The largest pieces of the aircraft, engines and bits of the tailplane, were spread over a half mile radius.

"There can be no hope for *them*," Martin said.

"God, what an awful mess," Group Captain Devonshire added. "Listen, there's no point you chaps hanging around. You'll just get in the way. Why don't you head off, and I'll call you later at Stradishall with any news. You can borrow my car and driver."

Reluctantly, the two brothers complied and climbed into the back of his car.

***

The sombre mood the two brothers brought back with them soon infected the whole blockhouse. No call came from Devonshire, through to Stradishall. It didn't need to. They both knew what the outcome would be. Richard felt as if his guts had been ripped out. The hopelessness of the mission that upset him. The loss of a man, older than him and probably more valuable, a man who had risked his life for Richard's idea, upset him deeply. Nothing seemed to be going right. During a meagre meal, nobody talked.

"I feel so bad," said Richard, so quietly that Martin barely heard him. "Men died today, because of my idea!"

"Not your *idea*. The idea is *good*! It was the execution that was bad."

"Do you think this will be the end?" Richard had asked Martin, pushing his plate of unfinished food aside.

"I don't think so. These things happen, Richard. Set-backs and deaths … are inevitable. After all, this is war."

"Those poor men, though."

"They knew what they were doing. It's a way of life, being a test pilot, or crew. They were just doing their bit. In a way it just shows how much people are prepared to do, how far they are prepared to go. We're all in this together, you know."

"I suppose … ."

"How's it going with that girl of yours? Anna?"

"It's not. We're not talking."

"Oh."

"I think … she betrayed me. Oh, I'm not sure. I met that German pilot, though. The one in that attack on Buck Palace? Nice chap, actually."

"Really. Did he tell you much?"

"Quite a lot. Actually, a hell of a lot. He actually wants to *kill* Hitler. Well, he says he does, and I believe him."

"Then why the hell … ."

"I know, it doesn't make sense."

"How about showing me this model you keep talking about?"

"Nah. I don't think I'm in the mood."

"Well, it's too early for bed. Would you rather go for a pint?"

"No."

"Well then … . Come on."

Richard unlocked the door to the room that housed the model of Berlin. Martin stood beside him, the only other person authorised to view it.

As Richard had feared, the building between the River Spree and Schloßplatz had grown too high, to five storeys.

"We'll never get around that!" he pointed out.

"Hmm. I see what you mean."

"But there is this space on the other side of the river. Mainly low housing, two storey. We could turn right further south, here, and that would give us a much wider turn. Yes, I think it could be done. We'll have to get the Sappers to model it, so that we can try."

"And then you have another problem … . Remember, there is a hill on Dartmoor where that open space is."

"Err. Yes. Good point. It's shallow though. Maybe they'll have to do some digging."

"Do 'em good."

Both brothers laughed for the first time since that morning.

"Look, the Chancellery is taking shape at the back. You can even see the earthworks. So that's where you have to get the bombs or canisters. Right down next to those little towers. Bloody hell! I don't know how you're going to do that, Richard!"

"Neither do I … yet. Look see those white cocktail sticks stuck in, all along the side of Unter den Linden. Some bright spark has written a note here. The white poles are thirty feet high. Very useful that. It's given me an idea. We could get some real thirty-foot poles planted on Dartmoor. It would help a lot. Got a pen or pencil, Martin?"

"No, but there must be something here." They hunted around and found a pencil one of the modellers had left behind. Richard left a note on the sheet of paper:

What is the building on the corner of the river and Schloßplatz? Please can you label the main buildings?

Richard called Archibald's night secretary, requesting the measured poles and the modification to the right bank of the river, before he went to bed.

***

The practice flight to Dartmoor the following day started in a brighter mood. Devonshire had visited them early that morning with the report on the crash at Rochester.

"Not much left of the crate. Crew all killed of course. Lucky it was only three. Now look at this." He took out a 10" x 8" photograph. It was very grainy but showed the base of one of struts which supported the Hurricane. "We had three cameras filming either side of the runway, this is where we expected any structural failure to occur. Luckily, they carried on filming when it was in the air, and one of them took this shot just after the Hurricane slipped. You can see the strut has failed at the root. I talked with Sir Richard. He assured me they would have it strengthened and would use the new structure on three new Stirlings. There won't be time for another trial, I'm afraid. This will have to work! Or be modified in the field!"

"How long before we get them?" Richard asked.

"The modification is simple, apparently. You should still get the Stirlings within two weeks."

"Should?"

"Yes. You have a point. I will make sure of it."

***

When the unusual flight of four Hurricanes and a Stirling arrived over Dartmoor, Richard saw that four white poles had been erected on one side of 'Unter den Linden.' Work hadn't yet started to the right side of the 'river.' He also saw that somebody had let a herd of sheep stray onto the mock-up of Berlin.

"Bloody hell. Sheep! That's all we bloody *need*! Now chaps, you see those white poles. They're thirty feet high. So today we will try for thirty feet along that street. Keep your cockpit below the top of the poles. Alright?"

"Roger skip. I'll give it a go," Todd called.

"Okay. But I'll go first."

Richard flew down the river and turned left into Unter den Linden, his mind full of the model building which he now knew they would have to avoid. Seeing the first white pole approaching, he let the Hurricane sink lower, but the top of the pole flashed by, below his wing-tip. He felt sick as he pushed the control column forward just the tiniest touch. He nearly yelled, as the Hurricane headed towards a slight rise ahead. He pulled up just in time and tried to settle down until he reached the sharp turn to the right. The last pole flashed by, just above the cockpit.

*Thank bloody God!*

"It's *bloody low*!" he said over the radio. "Todd, be careful of a slight rise between the first and second pole. Take your time. Remember, no faster than 200."

"Al-right! Going in."

They watched as B-Beer sank lower, until it looked as if it was actually sliding along the grass. The near midday shadow completely disappeared under the brown and green fighter. Richard saw the Hurricane jump as Todd cleared the rise, but then Todd messed up the left turn.

"Sorry about that! I see what you mean about that rise. Nearly scared the pants off of me. I need a toilet break."

Ribald comments from the other two pilots preceded silence, as Slick took his turn. The flock of sheep scattered in all directions each time a fighter passed overhead and then gathered itself together again. As Slick reached the rise, the flock broke apart again, but one unfortunate ewe ran under the Hurricane. Sure enough, the Hurricane jumped in the air, but this time, they heard a lot of swearing from the cockpit. Something white and red seemed to fly away from the hurricane in fragments.

"Bloody hit one! Bloody sheep! I was *that* bloody low! I think if it hadn't bloody been there, my prop would have hit the ground! Just warned me to pull up in time! Soddin' 'ell that was close!" Behind the Hurricane, on the grass, lay bits of one sheep spread over a wide area, white wool smeared with red blood. "Some of it's in my radiator I think." The engine coughed as Slick slowly gained some height.

"Can you make it back Slick?"

"Not sure. Wait. Give me a minute of two." As the others watched, the fighter gained altitude until it circled above them. "It's okay, I think. As long as I don't try anything too clever. I'll just circle around here for a while and watch you chaps."

"Alright. Razor, in you go." Razor achieved the distinction of being the first pilot to negotiate the rise without difficulty. "That sheep is definitely dead," he commented dryly.

"Bloody waste!" said Slick over the radio.

Each of the remaining three pilots tried two more runs each. Then they formed up with the Stirling for the flight home. Not long after they had left the area, Slick came over the radio. "I'm losing oil pressure fast. I think I'm going to have to land. There's an airfield near here, isn't there Richard?"

"About five miles. We'll stay with you until you land." Slick landed safely. "See you later, Slick."

However, early that evening they saw C-Charlie come in for a faultless landing on the main runway. When the Hurricane came to a stop outside their hanger, all the other pilots of the special flight were waiting to hear how he had managed to get the Hurricane repaired so quickly. Slick climbed down from his aircraft carrying a mysteriously large sack.

As he passed them, he said simply, "Mutton for supper, boys!"

"Oil pressure, eh?" Richard commented.

***

Hugo Knopfl and Klaas Zapruder stepped onto the pavement. They had to move briskly to let the convoy of Wehrmacht vehicles pass. Half-tracks carrying troops and pulling 88mm guns rumbled, creaking, over the cobbled stones. One of the camouflaged SS troops waved at them. Above, a cloud passed in front of the sun, casting the town square into dusk instantly. Sonneberg was one of those pretty German towns, nestled in the fold of verdant hills, populated by slate-roofed houses with walls painted many colours. Ironically it was the home both of toy-making and the Dutch Waffen SS.

Klaas waved back at the soldier leaving.

Hugo threw the butt of his cigarette on the ground. "Don't do that," he said in quiet Dutch. "Why pretend when we don't have to anymore?"

"You're right. We won't be coming back."

"That's not what I meant. Come on."

They started walking up the hill in the cloud-formed dusk, towards the road that led out of the square. The barrel of a parked Tiger tank pointed directly at them, but they ignored the implied threat.

Hugo tried to look relaxed as he passed other SS soldiers and officers, particularly the officers, but his nerves were stretched as tight as a bow string. He peered around every corner looking for somebody or something suspicious. Both he and Klass were veterans of the bitter siege of Leningrad, and only in the spring of 1943 had they returned to Sonneburg, Germany. There, the SS Volunteer Panzer Grenadier Regiment de Ruyter would recuperate and reform. As they walked, not speaking, Hugo saw the grueling expanse of time he had served under cover in the SS contract to almost nothing. At last they had a mission he could believe in. He didn't mind killing Russians, but killing Germans had been his motivation for joining the volunteer Dutch SS unit. Within days he would probably be dead. However, it would be a good death, something his dead parents would be proud of. He stifled a laugh at the naïvety of a political power that thought it could murder innocent civilians and yet recruit their children to fight.

"Almost there," said Klaas, quietly. Hugo could hear the man who had become his friend breath out slowly, softly. When they entered the bar, they would have to be good SS officers again. "What time do we have to leave?"

"Ten. Maybe a bit before. Don't drink more than three pints, but make it look like five. Spill as much as you can."

Hugo often longed to walk up the hill, on through the village of Neufang to the Observatory he had seen once on manoeuvres. His student days studying physics had been left far behind in this war.

Looking up at the darkening sky, he mused that it wasn't just a quirk of the moody weather that diminished the glory of the mighty Reich. Only one red flag, with a black swastika, now fluttered indolently in the town square. No longer did every week feature a parade of soldiers and armour, cheered on by excited Germans. If they paraded now, a few hungry children would be their only audience.

***

They both left the bar just before 10pm, holding on to each other for support, apparently blind drunk.

"Klaash! You are a dumpkopf! I despise you!" shouted Hugo.

"'Ugo! You stink."

"Whidch way?"

"Left."

"Are you shure?"

"Shure? Who's shure of anything, these days! Lead on!"

They stumbled up the hill, slipping on the cobbles, towards the trees that marked the first field on edge of the little town.

"We are toy soldiers, Klaas."

"Are we?"

They reached the trees, just as a tank search light snapped on, and swung towards them.

"Quick!" cried Hugo, pushing Klaas out of the way of the probing light-beam.

"Halt!" cried a voice from the top of the tank.

"Where is it?" said Klaas, in frustration, rummaging through the hedge at the base of the trees.

"Got it!" whispered Hugo. He stood up clutching a dark suitcase, tied closed with course twine.

Hurriedly, they both pushed out through the trees into the beam of light, smiling artlessly. Klaas leaned against Hugo and pretended to zip his fly.

"Just peeing! Mr Gestapo! Even Hitler lets us piss!"

They stumbled towards the tank. The beam of light and the end of a machine-gun barrel followed them back to the square.

"Get back to camp or I'll report you for being *drunk*! *Bastards*! Who says you should have leave while we have to do guard duty?"

"Herr Wagner!" They both laughed at the joke.

"Ah! Yes. Your new Commander." The man on the top of the tank laughed.

Just outside the barrack grounds, Klaas and Hugo stopped and untied the twine knots by match-light. Inside were two black SS uniforms of the old LSSAH type, now worn only by special units in Holland and Denmark and one other place, the Reich Chancellery. Underneath the jackets were two of the peaked caps with the totenkopf, two thick strands of gold rope and one thin one, de-marking the elite units of the German Army.

"At least we won't have to press them!" muttered Klaas.

"Bernard has done well."

"Yeah. But it was a woman who packed these." Both men fell silent. They could imagine a woman's delicate hands folding the cloth.

Hugo rummaged in the pockets of the jackets for papers. He found an identity card, pulled it out and held it close to the lit match Klaas held up.

"SS-Hauptsturmführer Casper Drall," he read out. "Good. Quick. Let's bury it and get back to camp."

***

As soon as they had cleaned up after the Dartmoor practice, four of the pilots piled into a staff car Martin had borrowed and headed for The Black Dog. They had already alerted the chef to the illicit contents of the car's boot. Just before they left, Martin caught Richard staring into the far distance through the window of his quarters.

"What's up? Pining for that girl? I thought you were angry with her."

"I was … am. Oh I don't know. I was thinking about her last night. Actually, since the crash at Rochester, I've had this niggling feeling that I'm being unfair to her. Something inside me is telling me to trust her. But I just don't know. I mean … she *did* say she hadn't known the room was bugged, just before I left. But I didn't believe her then … ."

"Ah … so that's what it's all about. So, do you believe her now?"

"I don't know. I only know I'm *not* certain she was lying to me."

"Well, give her a chance then. She's a great lookin' gal. It would be a shame … ."

"Yes. Okay. Okay, I will. Go and wait in the car. Tell the boys I'll be out in a minute. Keep them off my back for a couple of minutes, alright?"

"Will do."

Richard paced up and down in the hallway for a few minutes before rushing into the mess and grasping the telephone receiver to his ear. He almost put it down before he finished dialing Anna's number, which he knew by heart.

"Hello?"

"Hello. Anna? This is Richard. You said I could call … ?"

"Yes. How are you?"

"Oh well, you know. There was a big crash at Rochester the other day, which got me down, but then I was thinking … and I thought about you … ."

"Really? What did you think?"

"Err. Well, that's rather complicated. Can it wait until we eat?"

"Eat?"

"Yes. This is a bit complicated too, but one of my pilots, a chap called Slick Crawford, accidentally killed a sheep today, and we're having what's left of it cooked at Martin's favourite pub. It's right near the station, or so I'm told. It's called The Black Dog. Would you … I mean, I would like … it if you could come. Sorry, that sounds … ."

"Okay. When?"

"Well, now. If you can start out now, you'll get here before we finish it, at least."

"What's the number of the pub? Do you have it? I'd like to book a room. Then I don't have to worry about coming back tonight."

"Um. I don't know it. I've never been there, actually. Wait a moment … ." Richard rushed outside to get the number from Martin.

"Go on without me. I'll follow in the Austin," he shouted before returning to the block house.

He gave the number to Anna.

"See you later then. I think there's a train every half hour, so I shouldn't be too late. Don't eat it all without me!"

"I … we won't. See you then. Bye."

"Bye."

When they arrived at the pub, Martin and the other pilots all had to visit the toilet, which seemed very odd to Richard.

"Get a round in and order a table for six, but don't mention the you-know-what!" called Martin over his shoulder, as they disappeared through the door in the rear of the lounge.

"Four beers and a scotch, please," Richard told the taciturn bartender, who had a white cloth slung over his left shoulder.

"Right. Out from Stradishall, are you, sir?"

"Well, actually … yes!"

"Stirlings, is it … or the other type?" he said, tapping the side of his nose.

"Ah. The other type, I suppose."

"Good. I mean, I understand sir. Always good to have an officer *and* a gentleman to serve. You're welcome any time."

"Thanks awfully. Can I also have a table for six?"

"Fine. Silvie! Table for six. Wife'll be out in jiff, sir. Party is it? What's the occasion, if I might be so bold? We do a fine line in birthday cakes, if you want them." He leaned over the bar, closer to Richard. "We even have some of those little candles. Hard to get now, what with the War … ."

"Ah no. No birthday. Actually, we were doing a spot of target practice yesterday and had a bit of a prang. We're all okay, though."

"Prang? Target practice? Sounds a bit irregular. What did you say you were flying, sir?"

"I'm not sure if I should say … . Fighters actually. I s'pose I can tell you that much, if you really must … ."

"Fighter! You cheeky blighter! Get out of here! We don't serve your mob here. You should know that! Strictly bombers we *are*!"

Richard's mouth hung open, but he glimpsed Martin's grinning face next to a pillar at the other end of the bar. Then all the other three pilots broke into tears of laughter.

"It's okay, barman. He's with … me!" gasped Martin, leaning on the bar for support. "Poor ol' Richie probably doesn't even know about the feud!"

"What feud?" asked Richard, indignant and confused.

"There was a feud between Bomber Command and Fighter Command in these parts; it involved kidnaps, raids and all sorts. I guess you chaps down south didn't hear about it. Which is good." Richard shook his head.

"Ah. Sorry sir. Don't mind them," said the bartender, placing the last of the drinks in front of Richard. "Squadron Leader Earlgood has played this particular prank before! Martin. I think you'd better introduce me to your friend."

"Certainly. Mr Maytree, this is Richard Earlgood, my younger brother!"

"Well, I don't know … I didn't even know you had one, and here he *is*! Mr, well I'm not sure what to call you … Mr Richard Earlgood, welcome to our little inn. Silvie! Where are you? I believe you have a little something for me, Martin."

"Uh-huh."

"Ah there you are Silvie. When you finish laying the table open the back door for Mr Earlgood, the elder. Ha!"

When Anna arrived, the remains of the sheep had already been roasted and were served soon after with roasted potatoes, carrots, peas and gravy. It seemed like a meal fit for a king to Richard. The drink flowed and so did the conversation. At last there came a pause, when the last slice of plum-pudding had been consumed and they waited for real tea to be served.

"I brought this," said Anna, taking a tightly wound wad of blue wool from her handbag. She unraveled it and Richard saw a miniature of Martin's scarf, which he still wore. Both brothers laughed out loud, and Martin wrapped it around Richard's neck.

"Suits you, Richie!"

"But it's for Jackie, not me. I must say Anna, it's really jolly good! Did you knit it yourself?"

"Um Hm."

Martin looked nonplussed, but Anna peered archly at Richard, remembering the rubber Donald Duck. Richard found himself lost in her hazel eyes and wanted very much to reach out and touch her. She smiled, and then the moment had gone. But both kept casting little glances at each other for the rest of the evening, as if checking the other remembered the little moment.

Richard had introduced the three new pilots as soon as Anna had arrived. Only now did she engage each, in turn, with her precise and curious mind.

"So, Todd … ? I hope you don't mind me calling you that."

"No. Sure … . All the chaps do. And the ladies."

"Ah. And I bet there are … have been, a few of those."

"A few." He rotated his beer glass by its rim.

"Your boyish good looks and those blonde curls are the main attraction, I bet."

"Hey!" chipped in Razor. "It's his brain they're after. Everyone knows that!"

Todd grinned artlessly at Razor but became serious again when he looked at Anna.

"Where, in Australia, are you from?"

"Ah, you've been?"

"No, but I would like to look it up and know about it. The more you can tell me now, the less I have to look up!"

"Ah, well I'm from near Dah'win. It's a lot hotter than here! My parents have a ranch. A sheep ranch, as it 'appens!" There were roars of laughter at this. "There's not much there, in my little town. A windmill generator, a few broken down cars and a creek, which all us kids used to swim in when we should'a been at school."

"Sounds idyllic. As you know, it rains far too much here!"

"Yes, but your women are prettier."

"Oh, I'm sure that's not true."

Somebody must have started pulling Todd's leg, because he slowly slid under the table, protesting. Razor and Slick suddenly straightened up.

"He's doing what boys in his neck of the woods do all day long. Ha! Ha!"

Todd's blushing face reappeared next to Anna.

"Don't listen to them!" she said, helping him up into his seat.

"Oh, I don't! I was engaged once!"

Suddenly the faces around the table grew serious. Anna felt caught

"So what happened to her?" she asked cautiously.

"Killed by a stray bomb. While she was staying on a farm too, in deepest Devon. Tch!"

"Oh. I am sorry." She flicked a glance at Richard, who still stared into space. "And you, Bob. Why do they call you Slick?"

"Mystery to me. I guess it's 'cause I'm so serious. Kind of English sarcasm. I'm not really that serious, young lady, once you get to know me."

"Where are you from? Your accent … it's  … hard to place!"

"She's on to yer, mate!" quipped Todd, nudging Slick.

"Like Richard … . We're both home county boys, him Kent and me, Oxford."

"Oxford Street, more like, like!" added Razor. "And I suppose you want to know about this," he said, looking comically at his patch with his good eye. Anna laughed. "As I told young Martin here, I got it in a scrap with a Focke Wulf 190."

"Actually, I was more interested in your nickname. Why do they call you Razor?"

"That's a good one. Tell us, mate?" asked Todd, laughing. Todd nudged him out of an obstinate silence.

"Oh. Well it's real daft, like." Anna leaned forward, cradling her glass of wine. "Well, me da sent me this cut-thrort razor, like as a keep sake. It belonged to me grampapa … . It's real precious to me now, like, since my pap's gawn.  Anyway, we all use Gillettes now, you know, those little safety razors. But one day we ran out, just before a dance, like … ."

"So ee says, 'I got a fix for that, lads,' and whips out this dirty great razor like a scimitar." said Todd, laughing until he almost choked. The other men laughed raucously. "It must be pre-WWI at least!" added Todd on the end of a long breath out. He snorted, short of breath, and his head hit the table.

"Oh. You alright, man?" asked Razor, lifting up Todd's face by his curly hair.

There were hoots of laughter at this. "Who's for a round of tag-drinking?" asked Slick when they had all stopped laughing.

"How do you play?" asked Anna.

"No respect for me da, who's gone, like," Razor said into Anna's ear, gesturing towards Todd. Anna shook her head at the confusion around her.

"I'm so sorry," she said into his ear. He looked into her eyes, and she could see tremendous sadness and an emptiness there. He leaned towards her.

"Sometimes I don't know if I can go on. Sometimes I want to be with them …" He suddenly grinned. "Do you want to play or not? It's simple. Get 'em in, Todd, while I get things started."

Razor went to the bar and returned with a sheet of thin note-paper and a pen. He tore the sheet into six narrow strips and handed them out. "You write on here, in not more than ten words, what you did, with who and where in your first sexual experience. Now it has to be with the opposite sex, in this particular case.  Queen's Rules! Write it clearly, and then roll up your strip into a little ball. Nobody is going to know whose it is, because we'll place it in an empty glass and draw it. We're too drunk already to guess handwriting."

By this time, Todd had returned with three Pints each for the four pilots, except Richard, who had shorts of scotch. For Anna he lined up three glasses of white wine. Into an empty glass, Razor put his roll of paper and handed the pen on to Richard. Each, in turn, wrote something down and put their ball of paper in the glass. Anna blushed as she wrote hers down, with her back turned.

"The rules are simple," said Richard. "Starting with Razor, he can drink a large gulp of beer or say one word of the statement on his piece of paper. Go on, Razor." Razor shook the glass and took out a ball of paper. He unrolled it and read out the word 'Barn.' "Now, each of us will do the same, going clockwise. You can choose to drink one gulp and say a word or drink two gulps. You can't make the same choice more than twice in a row. Off we go!" The game moved quickly. Of course, within a very short space of time they were all blind-drunk and hadn't clue who had done what, with whom and where. They all roared with laughter at the hilarious suggestions made about each other's sexual prowess. Anna laughed as loudly as any. The game ended in much confusion and with no conclusions being drawn. But the glasses were empty.

"So what do you think about Hitler, Richard?" asked Todd after they had calmed down and shared a few tales and thoughts on the War.

"Pretty much the same as everyone else." He looked at Anna, wondering at the reason behind Todd's choice of subject. He quickly looked away.

"I think he's mad. But I don't think he's all bad. I heard he loved animals. I don't hate him." He drained his glass of whisky, as if to end the conversation by punctuation.

"But would you kill him?" persisted Todd.

"He needs to be killed … if he cannot be taken alive, and I doubt he can. If he could be put on trial, that would be the best, but I don't think that can happen. No, he must be killed. There's no other *way*."

"Hm." Todd studied his glass seriously.

"Of course it could be done from the air … ." added Richard.

Todd and the others stared at him intently.

*Shit! Now I've gone too far.*

"By three Hurricanes!" he added, trying to sound ironic. He backed it up with a nervous laugh. None of the others joined him. Anna's foot touched his leg under the table.

*Now I've definitely gone too far!*

"Look at the time!" said Todd. "We have to go back soon or there'll be trouble getting in. We have to be up early to … ."

"Ah, ah aah!" cut in Richard. "Naughty! *Naughty*! I think you've had enough to drink, my Lad!"

"I think we all have," added Razor. "Time to be off. We don't want to spoil a good evening. Settle the bill, Martin. Ha!"

While the others gathered themselves together and stumbled out to the staff car, Richard said good bye to Anna.

"I don't know what to make of them!" as Richard held her coat open for her arms by the door.

"Oh, they're alright."

"Yes. I didn't mean that. I mean that there was a lot of laughter and yet a lot of … well, pain. Why were they all laughing so much when they have been through so much?"

"I know what you mean. I was going to mention something myself. Tonight was the first time I heard of Todd's engagement; must have happened after I was transferred from his squadron. I knew about Slick's daughter and Razor's parents but not that."

"Razor lost both parents?"

"Um hm."

"Oh. That's sad."

"Yes, but it means all three, and I have lost family. Do you think …?"

"*What*? Hasn't *everyone* lost loved ones?"

"Yes. Maybe … I just wondered … Did you book a room alright?"

"Yes. But listen. I think we need to have a little talk. Can you find a way to double back, without the others knowing?"

"I think so, yes. What's it all about then?"

"Just do as I ask. My room's at the back, second from the far right as you look from the back garden. I think you can climb up, because there's a shed under it. Don't be too long, or I'll be asleep."

Richard dutifully followed the staff car for a few miles, before slowly dropping behind. The other pilots were too drunk to notice. He parked in a lay by for a few minutes and then drove back, to park a few hundred yards from the pub.

*Should I be doing this in my state? I could kill myself!*

He dropped onto soft grass from the fence near the shed and then clambered onto the low building. A light came on just above him, and the window opened.

"Shh!" he heard.

"Anna!" he whispered.

"Hurry up."

Finding a foot hold, he then grabbed a thick velvet curtain Anna had draped out of the window. He hauled himself into the room and collapsed headfirst onto the floor.

"You idiot! I think the whole village heard you!" Anna closed the window and pulled the drapes, which reached the floor, across the window. They sat giggling for a few minutes, waiting to see if anybody else would stir. Apart from their own giggles, they could hear nothing.

"Now what was it you wanted to speak to me about, Miss Styles?"

"You nearly blew it in the pub! What were you *thinking*?"

"Oh, that! It was a bit silly of me, but I *am* their leader!" He stood up stiffly to attention and saluted a water-colour of flowers on the wall.

"Oh, you fool, Richie!"

"*Richie*! Only my brother calls me that!" he said, acting offended.

"Yes. I'm sorry. I guess I haven't done anything to deserve that kind of intimacy."

"No. No, you haven't. But you could do … ."

"I could?" She lay back on the bed covers and let her hands lie, palm up next to her face, her fingers naturally folded slightly showing the bright red polish on her nails. Richard strode to the bed and fell on top of her.

"You gallant fool," she whispered.

"I know. But you know, it's all in the line of duty for an RAF officer. Now about that intimacy … ."

"Yes … ?" Her hazel eyes opened wide, and even through the blurred vision of drunkenness, Richard thought her the most beautiful thing he had ever seen. Without thinking, he kissed her and pulled away to see what effect it had had.

"Ah, that's what you had in mind. Now can I call you Richie?"

"No. No, indeed not. You have earned just the 'R' bit so far."

"Really. That's quite a lot for just a kiss."

"Actually, you're right. Damnably simple of me to bargain so poorly, *what*! It's been a while since I visited the bazaar in Timbuktu. You must forgive my manners and my style."

"Oh, I do. For your style anyway."

"Good. I think this is more what I had in mind, for the, what is the next letter after … after … ."

"Do you mean the 'i' in Richie?" she said innocently.

"Yes, that's it." He struggled with the buttons of her blouse until he had three undone. There he paused for a breather. "Damnably hot in here, Miss … Miss  … what was your name again?"

"Miss Styles. With a 'Y.'"

"Yes. It would be. I often ask myself why when I get to the third button and find it's not the last … ."

"And how many buttons *would* be the equivalent worth of the 'i.'"

"Well, let's see." He pulled her blouse out of her skirt and counted all the buttons. "I count eight, so that's eight!" He continued unbuttoning until he had her blouse completely open, and he stared at her brazier. "Now I think you need to turn over."

"I do?"

"If you want your debts to be paid. You have already called me Richie twice!"

"I have? I must stop doing that or I will be completely naked."

"Ah, I think you might have finally mentioned what I had in mind." He crawled up the length of her body and kissed her mouth long, hard and passionately. He moved to her ears, and delicately tracing around the contours of her earrings on her lobes with his tongue, kissed her neck below her ears.

She writhed on the bed in pleasure and told him, "I'm prepared to do it, oh Master." He sat back and watched as she unfastened her bra. "The lights," she said. "There!" She pointed to the light switch. He stumbled to the wall and turned out the lights. For a moment, a pitch black fell, but then he remembered the curtains and felt for the velvet drapes. He pulled them back slightly, and a warm glowing light flooded the bed chamber.

"Does this earn your intimacy?" she said, completely naked. Richard couldn't wait. He stripped and snuggled up to the vision of beauty, warm and soft, which had suddenly become his world.

***

# Chapter Four

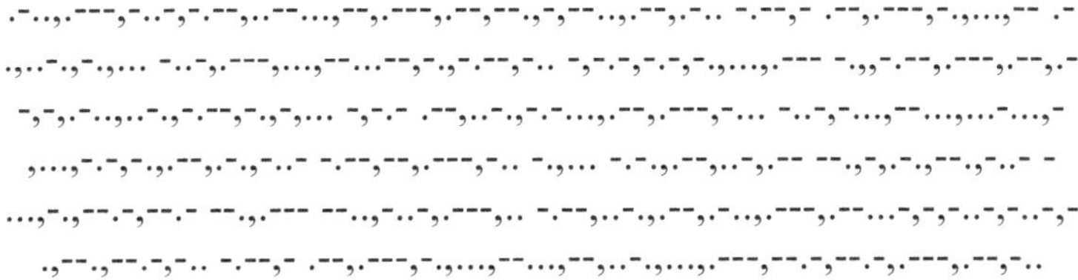

"It's today, Richard," said the voice on the telephone. "It's the 31ˢᵗ. We need to keep things moving along … Richard?"

"Listen Archie. I have a something I want to say to *you* … !" Richard's anger rose so fast that he had to take his cap off and put his hand on his forehead to cool it. "I am *not* your baby-sitter, and I am *not* a Secret Service agent. I am a pilot. And that is *all* I am!"

"That is not what I recruited you for. I … ."

"No! I *know* what you recruited me *for*! I have been doing some thinking. All the pilots have something in common; we have all lost loved ones to the Nazis. Admit it! That's why you recruited me; to do your dirty business. You *knew* it was against the Geneva Protocol, so you want people who are filled with hatred. It's not enough to *ask* us to do the job. You have to *manipulate* people into doing it, forcing us to do it!"

Richard heard only silence on the receiver for a moment. Archibald finally answered with a hushed voice. "Look here, Richard. Careful what you say on the telephone, please! Also, I didn't like it myself at first … Originally, I had hoped ordinary … Look I can't talk about this easily on the telephone. I just didn't realise it would be so sensitive at first. I know, I was naïve. But when I asked for a list of pilots, and the only name was yours, I asked why. That was when D … my boss told me what we had to do. I hated it. But there it is." Archibald sounded deflated. Richard felt slightly guilty but still angry. "And we're not forcing you."

"Oh yes! Like we have a choice! We're all …" Richard couldn't find the right word until he spluttered out, "… crippled. Emotional cripples!"

"Two guards, at all times. Plain clothes, so they won't be obtrusive. Just take him somewhere nice. Make it a nice afternoon. Understand"

"I still haven't forgiven you for last time, Archie. Don't think I have. That bugging was despicable!"

"*Richard*! Alright. Anyway, be at the station at 12.36. Alright?"

Richard slammed the receiver down. He reached the station near Stradishall just in time to see Anna, Michael and two burly men in suits descend from a carriage onto the platform.

They made a comical sight, driving along with the Austin's hood down. The two guards, perched high on the rear seat, looked studiously at the landscape each time Richard glanced at them directly or in his rear-view mirror. The escapee Michael grinned from his squashed position between his two guards.

Three days had passed since the overnight stay in The Black Dog. Richard had risen early with a hangover. Anna woke just before he left.

"I won't tell Archie or his boss about last night," she murmured before falling asleep again. He kissed her neck once, pulled the covers over her and padded out of the pub. The front door had been left on a latch, so he deftly lifted it and crept out of the pub.

Now the clouds rolled over Norfolk as they drove east, looking for a new beauty spot.

"It's going to rain," said Richard.

It did, and he had to pull over to put the hood up. But the rain quickly cleared, and the air filled with that fresh scent that follows a summer shower. Richard had been morose, but the fine weather and the limited time he had with Anna forced him to put aside his quarrel with Archibald. He stopped near a river. They climbed over a stile and followed a rough path to the river bank. There, they laid down a thick picnic blanket. The men in Whitehall had thoughtfully packed a large hamper with sandwiches: ham and egg, cheese and chicken. In addition, they found ginger beer, lemonade, tea in a flask, cutlery and napkins.

"Not bad," Richard had to admit.

Anna divided up the food according to preference, and the two guards took up positions flanking the party.

"At last. Some freedom! And privacy!" said Michael. "Anna and I often used to ride into the country at Oxford. The English countryside is very beautiful. As beautiful as Germany. Different … but just as beautiful. Perhaps more so when you are with somebody who is herself a picture of beauty. Isn't that so, Richard?"

"Ha! Well, I don't think the two are the same."

"No. Not the same. Did Anna tell you about the time I tried to teach her to play the Jewish harp." He took a thick, long, blade of grass and stretched it between his flattened palms to make a reed. He didn't notice Richard flinch slightly at the word Jewish. He blew over the reed, making a sound like the caw of a crow. "Ha! Almost like peacetime. I had forgotten … ." He seemed lost in a reverie for a while. Richard and Anna exchanged glances.

Richard finished the last chicken sandwich, and Anna poured him a cup of tea.

"Ah, this is the life," he said, laying back on the blanket.

Michael remembered his coded mission instruction number one; compromise Italian Beauty.' With a painful twist of emotion in his own heart, Michael determined to try harder winning back Anna's heart. "Have you ever played skipping stones?" he said suddenly to Anna. She shook her head. "I'm not sure. I don't think so."

"Come on then. I'll show you." He surged off to the riverbank, and the two guards sat bolt upright. Richard thought he saw the glint of a gun barrel. He watched impatiently as Michael skipped flat stones across the gently swirling river water. Anna tried a few times, with Michael holding her wrist in the correct position, but her stones just sank without skipping once. She smiled over her shoulder at Richard, and he smiled weakly back. Michael grinned at Richard like a little boy. When Richard felt he could stand it no longer, Anna broke away and came back to sit beside him. Michael continued skipping stones, as delighted as a child with a complex new toy.

"He's such a kid!" Anna said.

"Yes. Charming though. I can see why you loved him."

Anna smiled weakly. "Richard. There's something I need to tell you. Something strange has happened. I didn't mean for it to happen … ."

Richard felt a pain in his chest. "Go on. Tell me!"

"I think I still love Michael. That is, I have fallen back in love with him."

"But … . The other night?"

"I know. Don't be angry." She took his hand and quickly kissed his wrist while Michael wasn't looking. "I … I'm very … fond of you … ." Richard smarted at the word 'fond.' He pulled away from her and stared into space. "No Richard. Don't do that."

"Do what?"

"Withdraw from me … . Abandon me."

"But you don't *want* me."

"I didn't *say* that."

"But how, then … ?"

"Look he's coming back. We can't talk about this. I feel very strongly about you too. That's all I can say. Just be patient."

Michael returned and sat beside them, oblivious to the conversation that had just taken place without him. Richard's emotions were a maelstrom during the remainder of the trip, but he thought he had managed to hide his feelings from the dashing German pilot who threatened to take his girl.

***

Rudolph Eineger strolled past the cigar seller in front of the Hotel Adlon, Unter den Linden 1 and released two buttons on the front of his black, leather trench-coat, almost a uniform for Gestapo officers. Berlin still baked in the late summer heat, and he let the cool air of a capricious breeze enter between the lapels to cool him. It felt pleasant to leave the office for a few hours.

'I should do it more often.' he thought. 'After all, now I am senior enough to do as I like.'

A passing blonde frau smiled conspiratorially at his handsome face, framed by dark hair trimmed to not more than half an inch in length. He had a livid white scar on his left cheek which she thought only made him more handsome. He twisted to watch the lithe swing of her hips as she receded into the distance. Then he continued on to the Eden tea rooms near the Tiergarten, where he took a seat and unfastened the rest of his coat buttons.

"Two coffees please, oh and biscuits, if you have them."

"Of course, sir," said the waiter who fussed around him. "Heil Hitler."

Coffee was another luxury only senior Nazi officials could afford. Eineger rarely indulged himself. Work, a little sport, reading, a woman from time to time, those were his needs. He had no time for love, or marriage. He was in thrall only to the Führer.

"Rudolph!"

"Ah … . Herr Schtickel!" he replied to the thin, blonde official, leaning over him, the title of 'Herr' being an old joke from their days at the Academy.

After some small talk, Eineger broached the subject of his interest.

"Bruno. I need some … that is, I would like to know how you think the Chancellery feels about a certain subject … ." By 'Chancellery,' both knew that Eineger meant the Chancellery gossip network and not the official channels. He often used Schtickel in this way and in return gave information of his own. The problem with German Intelligence, as Eineger often reflected, was that all departments were so busy trying to gain favour with Hitler, to save their own skin or to gain power, that often those departments hoarded information. In effect, it had become a medium for barter among the adepts.

"Ah! And I thought you just wanted to spoil your old friend! Well, go on … . What can I help you with?"

"This morning I received a dossier from a Luftwaffe … debriefing centre near Dunkirk. An RAF crew, shot down a few days ago, has finally revealed, after some subterfuge on our part, information about a new secret weapon and where it is to be used." He looked up at his friend, hopefully.

"Go on … ."

Eineger laughed, awkwardly. "Well, it sounds foolish, but they believe the RAF has a new x-ray bomb!"

Schtickel's smile looked indulgent and slightly condescending.

Eineger continued uncertainly. "They were overheard saying that it will be used on the Reich Chancellery soon, perhaps in the next month. Who knows?" To Schtickel's down-turned eyes, he could only respond by continuing, "Now, I wouldn't *make* anything of this, but I have another dossier, built up over the few weeks, which has similar intelligence. We have another RAF crew picked up in the Channel, who said a very similar thing. We also have amateur radio traffic saying the same thing. And we have reports, I don't have anything official, of British seamen saying something similar. In fact, we have much information from all over the Western perimeter of the Reich, so much so that I'm forced to conclude there is something to it."

"I see."

"Well?"

Schtickel leaned very close to his friend. "X-Ray bombs! Raids on the Chancellery! Rudy, I would forget these things. They are foolish rumours!"

Eineger knew this standard response. It would be for the benefit of anybody overhearing their conversation. Schtickel would drop some subtle hints and start a rumour within the Chancellery. Eventually, by whatever arcane route it took, the rumour would reach the ears of Hitler himself. Then, after a delay of perhaps a week, he would hear from his friend what the Führer thought of the intelligence. This made for an efficient system: Hitler would hear every breath of a rumour within the Reich, and officers like Eineger would learn if his information might take him further up the ladder.

"In any case," continued Schtickel, "H is on holiday in Bavaria for the first two weeks in September."

'H,' of course, signified Hitler, and this little speech was Schtickel's way of telling Eineger what he personally thought of the rumour; that the main target might be the Berghof. Eineger almost interrupted. But this time he played a dangerous game. In fact, he intended to play his old friend Schtickel. It hadn't escaped the young Gestapo officer that his SS friend, senior in rank and senior by association with the Reich Chancellery, always benefited most from their little game. Schtickel could use the flow of intelligence traffic to oil the cogs of the Chancellery machinery while adding grease to Eineger's own particular pole. But this time it would be different. Rudolph Eineger knew the intelligence to be pure gold. The pieces of the puzzle fitted badly, but he saw a picture there. The RAF had to be up to something! But he detected that his friend had missed the subtle nuances of the information. Hitler wouldn't.

Normally, Eineger would hold back enough information keep his own stock high but give enough detail for Schtickel to verify some of the intelligence. This time, in a few days-time, Schtickel would find out that the RAF crew had not been interrogated in Dunkirk. Hitler, given his unearthly instinct, would realise the value of the information and would ask for more detail. Schtickel would come unstuck, and, impatient, Hitler would demand to see the officer responsible for the intelligence. At last, the Führer would come looking for Rudolph Eineger. He *would* have his day in the sun! He would lose an ally of course, but Schtickel had never really been a friend. He had used Eineger.

They parted with a handshake, after finishing the coffee and sweet, sugar-covered biscuits.

At 3am that night, Rudolph Eineger sat bolt upright in his bed. He must have been tossing and turning and had woken up sweating profusely. A thought nagged at the edge of his consciousness, but he couldn't identify it. He climbed out of bed to get a glass of water. Padding over to the washbasin in his kitchen, he turned the faucet and cupped his hands under the running, cold water. Splashing it on his face, he stopped, rigid.

"It's not the Berghof. It's a double bluff!" he said out loud. A cold thrill ran down his spine. This would either make his career or be the end of the Führer.

***

At last, he had been left alone. Michael Dorfmann sat nervously down on the leather sofa in the small, but well-furnished, studio flat. He expected it all to evaporate in front of his eyes at any moment. He had finally been given his own flat after being released from the holding cell somewhere near Whitehall. There were two guards outside and probably microphones inside, but at least they had left him alone.

Outside, a cat meowed somewhere close by the window, and a bell tinkled as a cyclist rode by. On a table, draped in a shiny green chenille with tassels around its hem, were the two things he had requested; a violin, in its case, and a metronome.

'No radio,' he noted.

Michael Dorfmann wasn't an accomplished violinist, but after two hours 'sawing away', as his Oxford teacher used to call it, he felt he could make a fair sound on the instrument. Satisfied, he put it back in its case and placed the metronome on the mantle-piece, just in front of a large mirror. He set the small weight to sixty beats per minute and set the pendulum swinging. It had grown dark outside. He drew the drapes closed. Then he dragged the heavy chair into the centre of the room and sat on it, facing the metronome. Just as the Gestapo doctor had taught him, he began to breathe deeply and focused completely on the swing of the pendulum.

"I am feeling deeply tired, and I want to sleep," he said, over and over to himself in a hypnotic fashion, until he felt him to be in a limbo between consciousness and unconsciousness.

Then, suddenly, he woke, and the address; 14 Hansard Mews, filled his mind. He memorised the address and then a phrase that seemed to go with it: 'Behind the door is a brown envelope.'

He suddenly felt incredibly tired. He stood up, stopped the metronome and threw himself on the small single bed in the annex. There, he fell asleep.

***

The Stirling made a distinctive whistling sound as it came screaming in low over Stradishall, so low, in fact, that the newly cut harvest chaff in the field just beyond the runway rose into the air in whorls, created by the draft of the bomber's wing-tips.

"Wow!" shouted Richard, holding his cap onto the crown of his head with one hand while waving at Y-Yankee.

"Phew! That is what I call real flying!" added Todd, waving both arms like a semaphore signaler.

It was 5th August. The three Hurricane pilots had just returned from another training flight on Dartmoor. The sappers had completed all the building facades right up to the Chancellery garden, and they had even completed the cut into the hillside. This mimicked the space to the right of the five-storey building which Richard now knew to be the Berliner Castle.

In his briefing before the training flight, Richard had explained his change of tactics.

"We've built you a detailed model of the area we're going to attack. There's an obstacle here … five storeys high, which prevents turning directly on to this heading. But if we bank sharply to the right, there is space here, and then we can make the turn … I think!" There were discontented murmurs from his audience. "I know. It looks tricky. The sappers have cut into the hill and placed, for now, some thin poles with flags on top to represent the high obstacle. We'll approach at about 160 mph and then speed up after making this turn. Oh, one other thing. We were, until today, officially D-flight of 1657 Conversion Unit. As from today, we are 700 Squadron, but that name is to be Top Secret. None of you are to talk about this mission, or the Squadron, to anyone, including your mother, girlfriend and sister, from now on. Any questions?" There had been none. In the event, after half hour of trying, none of the three pilots had been able to negotiate the Berliner Castle.

The call Richard and Martin had been waiting for, had come through from Group Captain Devonshire that morning.

"The second test flight of the Stirling and Hurricane composite proved successful, and the first aircraft will be ready today. If Martin could come down, their test pilot would like to check him out on the thing!"

"Take good care of her, won't you? Two more will be ready within three days." was the last thing Sir Richard Rose said to Martin before he took off for Stradishall, with only Cloudy and himself on board.

The Stirling made one more pass and then floated down onto Stradishall's main runway, with Martin at the controls. The heavy aircraft slowly taxied the odd-looking aircraft towards the apron in front of 700 Squadron's hanger. All week-long, men had been constructing a vertical extension to their vast hanger, adding another twenty feet of height to the centre portion, leading to speculation at the base that an airship would be housed there. Looking at the four strange pylons on top of the Stirling's fuselage, it would now be apparent something would be carried on the bomber. But what? Only the crews of 700 Squadron knew. Their quiet, knowing looks were met with incessant questions and ribald comments from the rest of the air crews on the base.

Two tractors towed the Stirling through the hangar's vast doors, and they were sealed shut. Passing through a small door into the dim space inside the hangar, 700 Squadron's pilots walked around the monster aircraft.

"When do we get one with a Hurricane on top, like?" asked Razor.

"We can only fly, with the Hurricanes mounted, at night," Richard told the men. "See those crane rigs up there? They are to mount the Hurricanes. The first one should arrive in a few hours and be mounted overnight. We'll try it tomorrow night. We have a lot to do Gentlemen and very little time, in which to do it. We have to step things up! From now on, we will fly two training missions each day. And a third, at night if necessary, to train on the combination."

***

The arrival of the first Hurricane had been delayed at the last minute. It arrived with the other two on the night of the 6th August. This, however, allowed the hanger assembly rigs to be completed, so that all four Short Stirlings were only equipped with their piggy-back fighters that night.

To Richard's complete and gleeful surprise, the Hurricanes delivered were Mk II's and not the rickety Mk I's he had been expecting. A little heavier than Mk I's, the Hurricane Mk II was more robust and could carry bombs as standard. These already had bomb release mechanisms fitted. The Mk II also had some enhanced safety features which made the pilots happy.

By 4.30am they were ready for take-off. The briefing, two hours before, had been the first time the fighter pilots met the two bomber crews Martin had selected for the mission. Martin asked the pilots to stand up. He introduced Geoffrey Hutchinson, blonde, who walked with the aid of a walking stick and had a black and white collie dog called Kettle sitting quietly beside him. Fitchell, Hutchinson's front gunner impressed Richard with his quick wit, which had all the crews laughing raucously.

Richard closed his briefing. "You all know the flight plan. I expect all navigators to get their aircraft to Dartmoor within minutes of sunrise. We can't be seen by the public flying these top-secret contraptions, but we will have privacy over the model … city, as you all know it is by now, and we need the light for the Hurricanes to do their stuff. Todd, Slick and Razor, the Mk IIs' as you know, are heavier, so getting around that first corner is going to be even trickier. So far, none of us have made it. The only thing that might help slightly is that the Mk II have metal-covered ailerons. They distort less so should be more efficient. You will also have noticed that your aircraft now has practice-bombs fitted. There is also now a target marked on the wall at the end of your run. These bombs contain flour, so let's see if any of us can hit the target. Everybody give it your best shot today. Let's go!"

"Richard … sir?" called Slick, raising his hand. "When are we gonna learn the target?"

"You'll know … soon enough. Perhaps too soon!"

Each fighter pilot climbed gingerly up the makeshift ladder and strapped himself in his Hurricane. The Stirling crews took their positions and the hanger doors were opened.

All four Stirlings were hauled as far as the end of the runway by tractors, and then sixteen Bristol Hercules engines fired up. A few sleepy station staff and civilians turned over in their beds, disturbed by the roar of the engines, but they were quickly returned to the land of dreams.

Richard remembered the new instructions from Sir Richard Rose. Short had solved two problems quickly; how to stop the Hurricanes from shearing the pylons during flight and how to shorten the take-off run. The first they had achieved by lengthening the front two pylons, thus angling up the nose of the Hurricane. This gave it more lift in flight and put less stress on the pylon structure. Coincidentally this had led to the second solution. When Sir Richard Rose had first seen the Hurricane mounted at the new angle, he had immediately wondered if running the fighter's engine at some moderate revs would help provide more lift for the dual-rig. After some experimentation, they had found that running the Merlin engine at 2500 rpm did indeed provide some extra lift but not enough to stress the pylons.

Richard started up the Merlin and let it idle, while Martin went through his last checks before take-off. As soon as he heard the Hercules engine revs rise, he throttled up to 2500rpm. The Hurricane shook from side to side, and Richard felt a rhythmic rocking motion.

*God. I hope I'm not going to die now, before we've even started!*

He turned on his VHF radio and switched it to transmit.

"Don't mess this up, Marty. Keep listening, everyone. If the take-off goes wrong, I may as well transmit something useful."

He settled into his seat and checked his harness one last time, as the huge Bomber, carrying the fighter like a mother bird carrying her fledgling, rumbled down the concrete strip. It gradually gained speed. Richard was surprised how early the Stirling tail lifted.

"Sir Richard really has improved take off a lot!" he said into his microphone.

A moment later, the violent shaking and rocking ceased as the bombers wheels left the concrete. After a minute, he cut the Merlin and revelled in the feeling of peace in his cockpit.

*Flying in my Hurricane while not even operating the controls is the best thing ever!*

"Chaps, you are gonna love this!" he said into the microphone.

"I hope so, like!" answered a single, nervous voice.

***

A few minutes after sunrise, the flight of strange looking aircraft dropped out of the clouds over Dartmoor. Richard fired up his engine once more and prepared to separate from the Stirling.

The red light started flashing on his dashboard, to indicate he could release the fighter. He pressed the green button underneath the canopy on the right and heard the four bolts detonate in the top of the pylons. He had been holding the joy-stick firmly in his right hand, and now the Hurricane suddenly felt lighter on the controls. He eased back on the stick and the fighter gently separated from the bomber. He took care to keep his airspeed up to avoid the Stirling's tail and then throttled up to take position in a holding pattern over the model on the moor below.

"Easy as *anything*!" he shouted into his helmet, jubilant.

All of the other three Hurricanes separated from the bombers successfully, and after checking each other's aircraft over, they dropped down to start their approach to the model of Under den Linden.

Richard would be the first to try the now-complete route. He marveled at the building skills of the sappers. He had memorised the model of Berlin and, apart from false windows and decorations, the plywood facades resembled quite closely the real thing. In some ways they were too accurate. It worried him that one of the pilots or a civilian might recognise them.

"Going in!" he said, breathing hard. "If I screw this up, don't do what I do … . I'm going to take the corner at 140 with prop pitch set fully to 'fine … .'"

The other pilots, including those in Stirlings, listened to his heavy breathing as the Hurricane dipped and flattened out just twenty feet above the moor. Richard weaved the little fighter over the hillocks and between brakes of bracken and wind-torn trees, with violent movements of the control column and rudder.

"Coming up to the turn … too fast … ." He veered violently to the right. "Can't … ." He flicked left, narrowly missing the lip of the dell the sappers had cut into the hill. A few moments later the Hurricane had climbed level with the other fighters, and Richard's calm voice came over the radio. "Botched it, I'm afraid. Nearly, though. I reckon 130 might do it. Razor. You go first. Turn about a second before you think you want to. The controls are slow to react that near the ground, maybe too much turbulence or updraft off the hill."

"Roger. Going in, skip." Razor made a similar approach, but at 130 mph the fighter felt sluggish, and his wing tip clipped a gnarled oak tree. "Shit!" he said over the radio. Just before he reached the five-storey building, he flung the fighter violently to the right, but its airspeed was too slow. The wing tip sank towards the gorse, and only a quick correction the other way brought the wing tip back up in time. Even so, the Hurricane's propeller threshed another gorse bush as it scraped over the rise and dropped into the valley beyond. "Bloody fuckin' 'ell!" came over Razor's radio. "That was too loew, like!"

"Okay, take a break, Razor. You next, Slick!"

Slick didn't fare any better, but after approaching at 140 mph and missing the turn he flew over the buildings and dropped down into the long, straight corridor between the building fronts, Unter den Linden. "It's like Hollywood!" he shouted, excited. "At least I'm going to drop my bombs!" He made the turning at the end, next to a structure that looked to Richard too much like the Brandenburg Gate and dropped his bombs against the target wall. He missed by only ten feet. "Quite easy really … if only we could get around the turn … . Let's see you do it, Toddy! Go on, lad!"

"Going in! Watch this!" Todd approached and reduced his speed to 135 mph. He swung violently into the right turn and then swung again immediately to make the left turn. At the very last moment he had to pull up to avoid the building facades on the far side of the long street. "Bugger it! I damn nearly made it! That was at 135 mph, skipper!"

Richard remained silent for a long moment.

*Bloody fool. Still, maybe that's the right speed.*

"Okay Toddy. Bloody stupid, but you may have just cracked it. I'll give it a go."

Richard tried the approach at 135 mph but miss-timed the turn and couldn't equal Todd's effort. He flew on down the valley, past the eastern end of 'Unter den Linden.'

"Right. Off you all go. Todd. Show us how it's done!"

Todd did no better than his previous attempt, and the other two were closer, but still failed to make the turn. They each tried one last time, this time dropping their flour 'bombs' close to the target.

Richard felt tired and dispirited. His voice showed it as he said, "Okay. Let's go home."

***

Michael needed an excuse to get out of his flat. He needed the English to really trust him. His chance came the next day from an unexpected direction.

"Lieutenant Dorfmann, sir! I am to accompany you to a meeting with a Miss Styles and a Squadron Leader Earlgood.

We only have thirty minutes … that leaves you fifteen minutes to get ready." The surly guard avoided the German officer's unblinking gaze. "I will wait outside," he added just before the door closed.

One minute before 2.30pm, a door opened in front of him, and the guard ushered Michael Dorfmann through to a small room in Whitehall, barely furnished, except for a large oak dining table, surrounded by ten chairs. Sitting on two of them, facing him, had been Richard Earlgood and Anna Styles, but both stood up.

"Michael!" said Anna, smiling. Richard reached across the table and extended his hand. Michael took it and sat down. "How have they been treating you?" she continued.

"Fine," he said uncertainly, then more confidently, "Yes. They have given me my own flat, with two guards outside the door of course!"

"Yes. I heard. Progress," she said quietly. She placed her hands flat on the table and slid them a few inches towards him, as if she wanted their hands to touch. He glanced at Richard and smiled weakly. Richard clasped his hands together firmly on the table.

Richard began, "Michael. I can't tell you the details, but I'm leading a squadron that is doing … research into low-flying. We are trying … at the moment, to work out how to negotiate tight turns, very tight turns, in Hurricanes and we're failing. I noticed that the turn you had to make across Trafalgar Square was pretty tight. I wondered how you did it. Can you tell us?"

A silence settled between the two men. Richard thought that Michael was calculating something. He answered with a single word.

"Flaps."

"Really? I had thought of that … never tried it. Not recommended on a Hurricane."

"The Hurricane is a good aircraft. Not good in a spin, in fact … terrible, but you can make very tight turns. If we could do it in an Emile, you could do it in a Hurricane. I can show you if you like."

Richard looked at Anna. "Well, that's very good of you … . I'm not sure the … ."

Anna coughed, quietly and Richard stopped speaking.

Michael looked from one to the other, then down at the table and smiled, slyly. Their familiarity had not escaped him. When he spoke again, Anna noted a coolness each time he glanced at her.

The German turned to Richard again. "Please … . I want to prove myself."

"Well … . I … I'll see what I can do. Could you give me a little more *help*? I mean, how much flap; how early, before the turn; during … ?"

"Well, that depends on the aircraft. Obviously, I know it best in an Emile, which is a very good aircraft. The Hurricane … . I have flown *one* … ."

Richard sat up, astonished. "You have?"

"Only once. I'm sure it will be fine, but I never had the chance to try."

"Well, I certainly don't mind you trying. We'll have to see what the Ministry men say." Richard stood up and shook the German's hand. He went to the door and held it open. A guard beckoned, and the guest left Anna and Richard alone.

"He's hurt," she said, quietly.

"Hurt? Why?"

"Us."

***

Richard felt astonished at Archie's response thirty minutes later.

"Yes, he can fly a Hurricane. Didn't Anna tell you? We want him on our side. If we can *get* him!"

"I didn't know! She never said anything! But do you think it would be safe?" Richard paced around the Whitehall table.

"Well, of course, we have to set it up in the right way. We don't know for sure where his allegiance lays, yet. No good if he gets back to Germany in one of our fighters. My bosses would have a fit!" He looked at his big feet and snapped them together as if standing to attention. Then he grinned artlessly at Richard. Richard wasn't sure why, but he felt that something must be going very well, at last.

***

# Chapter Five

Coded message from CS-6 to British Intelligence:

hsl 7z7h vlxn nz6d nzc vllc cd.k6dfdc, zx ;fl9kxdc.

Richard had succeeded in persuading Archie's boss to recruit his former ground crew, and now he watched them preparing the two standard Mk II Hurricanes on a blustery RAF Atcham airfield.

"Okay. Ready for you Lieutenant Dorfmann!" shouted Beattie to the German standing next to Richard. Michael Dorfmann threw his Lucky Strike butt on the grass and winked at Richard. "Now, you will see what a German pilot can do with your English fighter." His two guards looked on, sourly.

"Fine. Remember to keep your radio on at all times, like I showed you."

"Will do. See you upstairs," the German said. He waddled to his Hurricane, his motion impeded by the parachute hanging down the back of his legs.

Richard's crew chief, Fleiming, wiped his oily hands on his thighs and strode up to the British pilot.

"All ready for you, sir! She's not top-flight, but she'll do. A little heavy on oil … but we gave you the better of the two. Funny business though, sir. Why do you want to get mixed up in all this? Keep him in front of you all the time."

"Thanks, Chief." Richard waddled over to his aircraft and climbed in. He went through his last pre-flight checks and then fired up the Merlin engine. With the noise cutting out all other sound, he grinned as he saw Beattie pointing to various controls to help the German start up his aircraft.

*Forgotten already!*

As arranged, Richard followed the other aircraft out on to the take off strip, marked on grass. He pointed his nose into the wind and gunned the throttle. The lightly fuelled Hurricane bounced eagerly over the small hillocks, as it gained speed, and then leaped into the air. Richard looked ahead and saw the second Michael's Hurricane climbing away. Richard turned his

VHF radio to 'transmit.' "Course south east. Don't forget where you are, Michael. This is Shropshire. You have enough fuel for one hour, so you can't even reach the coast. If you try and escape, you will end up captured by a British farmer or his wife. If you're lucky, they will be English. If you're unlucky, they'll be Welsh!"

"Ha! Thank you, Richard. I will remember that. I think I want to fly this lovely aircraft for a little while first. But you know, I bet I could make the coast if I leaned the mixture right out!"

"Don't be tempted. There are two squadrons of Spits ready to scramble South East of here, and another Mosquito squadron which will chase you anywhere. They have orders to shoot you down on sight. You haven't a hope!"

"Ah! That's what you think!"

"Testing guns," said Richard over the radio. A short burst of .303 ammunition burst from the eight-gun ports of the Hurricane.

"Testing guns," said Michael. He pressed the firing button. His Hurricane flew serenely, quietly on. "Ha! Ha!" Richard grinned at the German's humour.

"We're approaching the Shropshire border," said Richard. "Let's drop down to 50 feet and see what you can do." The two fighters dropped down into a wide valley, dotted with a couple of farms and a few herds of lazy Fresian cows. "There! See those three oak trees. Can you fly tightly around them?"

"We'll see!"

Richard flew a lazy circuit, a few hundred feet above the valley, while Michael dipped down to a height of only twenty feet. He slowed the Hurricane to 160 mph. "How slow will it go before stalling?" he asked over the radio.

"That close to the ground, we have tried 135, she's good for that."

Michael aimed just fifteen feet to the right of the clump of trees and extended the flaps to 15 degrees just before he reached them. The Hurricane started to side-slip toward the ground, but Michael gunned the engine to its maximum power, and the fighter seemed to drag itself around the trees in a painfully sharp turn. Richard could hear the engine straining even over the engine noise of his own aircraft.

"Whooo!" shouted Michael.

"Not *bad* … ." Quietly, Richard felt very impressed. "Okay, so tell me what to do; I'd better try it." After Michael had run through the techniques, Richard dropped down to thirty feet, so that the Hurricane seemed to be scudding across the grassy slopes of the valley. Behind him green wakes rippled and swirled from the propeller wash. He dropped his airspeed to 135 mph. At the last moment before reaching the trees, he selected 15 degrees of flap and gunned the engine, just as Michael had instructed him. He pushed the rudder pedal hard right and banked the Hurricane to the left using the joy-stick. The airframe seemed to complain at the abuse, but the sturdy aircraft responded to his command, and he clawed his way around the clump of trees at a tighter angle than he had ever experienced before. The blood rushed towards his feet with the G-force, so he had to swallow hard and compress his stomach muscles hard to avoid blacking out.

"Suck in your breath!" shouted Michael over the radio.

"Thanks. A bit late, mate."

"He thinks he can fly, now!"

"One more time and then let's go home!"

On their return journey, Richard spotted a low bridge over a river. Its central, long span had to be not much more than twenty feet above the little choppy wave-lets.

Lower than anything I have tried before … but I'm not going to be out-flown by a Jerry!

Richard's blood was up. He put the Hurricane into a dive without a word, aiming under the broad arch of the bridge. The Hurricane rocketed through the span, light becoming dark, and then light again as Richard diced with death and emerged into life on the other side. "Do that!" he said, jubilantly.

"Yes. I think I can." Michael put down the Hurricane's nose and nervously approached the span. He adjusted the controls in fleeting little twitches, the Hurricane not being as sensitive as a Messerschmitt Bf 109. He closed his eyes, held his breath as he went under the bridge and then heard the boom of the great Merlin engine, bouncing off the brick and concrete.

He bit his lip to stop himself saying, "Phew!"

Richard felt angry with himself. He never could control his emotion when faced with somebody as daring as himself. He *would* prove himself better. Before he had thought of the risks, he banked the Hurricane to approach the bridge from the other side, but this time he aimed for one of the side spans. Richard guessed that the span could not be much more than a propeller diameter above the green-brown water.

"This is going to be great or kill me. Now which … is … ." He burst into the bright light again, alive, before finishing his sentence, "… it!"

"Not bad, Englishman! I'm not going to try that! I don't know this aircraft well enough!"

"A likely story!"

From the radio Donald Duck seemed to say "I'm not a stupid duck!"

"Ha! Ha!"

*Damn! I like the man.*

***

Richard Earlgood didn't waste any time taking 700 Squadron back to Dartmoor. He shook Michael's hand and patted him on the shoulder, as the guards took the German away. Then he climbed back in the Hurricane and took off for Stradishall in a borrowed Hurricane.

"We take off in one hour!" he told his men when he arrived. On the way to Dartmoor he explained the reason for the impromptu practice. "I think I know how to get round that turn … . It's the flying equivalent of a hand-brake turn. In case I don't make this, drop your speed to 135, just before you turn, put on 15 degrees of flap and right rudder, left aileron and push the engine to maximum boost."

He approached the turn at 135, at the last moment going through the move Michael had showed him. The Hurricane strained as it turned towards 'Unter den Linden.' For a moment, Richard thought he wasn't going to make it. He wondered how strong the plywood facades were in front of him, but he heard no sound of impact. The propeller kept turning and suddenly he found himself flying serenely down the long street at twenty-five feet.

"Whoopee!"

"Yes! Well done, Skip! You made it." The other three pilots rapturously congratulated him.

***

The night after they buried the suitcase, Klaas Zapruder and Hugo Knopfl were on a train to Berlin. They had left the barracks early in the evening, on the pretence of another drinking binge and then changed into their SS uniforms. Catching the last train from Sonneberg, they travelled north through the night. Their commanding officers would assume they had collapsed, drunk, somewhere, and a search party would be sent out for them in the morning. But they wouldn't be posted missing until at least the following night. By then, they would be in Berlin and much harder to trace. They sat, two carriages apart, on each train and only met once at a prearranged time in the corridor of a carriage. Without speaking, they both lit a cigarette, official SS fare but in reality, only cheap Turkish tobacco flavoured with mint. Both smoked them down to the butts; their code for 'all clear.' They knew it might be the last time they saw each other alive, but the train's corridor had become too packed to speak. When they arrived in Berlin, they both exited the station separately. Hugo caught a tram towards Templehof Airport, while Klaas booked himself into a cheap hotel as SS-Hauptsturmführer Kristoph Junper.

Hugo, posing as SS-Hauptsturmführer Casper Drall, walked to a building called Columbia House, near the airport, and crisply saluted the guard at the main entrance. His heart raced. Bernard, his contact in the Dutch Resistance group CS-6, had given them information passed on from their contacts in the German Resistance group, the White Rose, that Columbia House was a secret prison used by the SS and Gestapo. It held some Jewish Prisoners used as slave labour in Berlin. Hugo had false papers, ordering his transfer to temporary duty at this prison, from a German SS officer now dead and believed to be the only one who knew Drall well. If background checks were made, as they probably would be, it would take time, a very long time, to deduce that this Drall wasn't the original one. Beyond this, Hugo would be on his own.

"SS-Hauptsturmführer Casper Drall, reporting for temporary duty as Guard in the Reich Chancellery." He did his best to look bored and stared down his nose at the guard, checking his papers. He continued, "I'm tired, hungry and need of a good whore, so if you don't mind … ." He spoke perfect German, inherited from his German father.

"Sir! Report to the Commanding Officer, up the stairs to the right, turn right on the first landing and third door on the right."

Hugo had to bite the inside of his lip to stop himself saying, "Thank you."

His luck was in that night. When he reached the third door on the right and knocked, an adjutant answered and told him the Commandant had gone out to supper. Hugo explained the purpose of his transfer and flourished his papers. The orderly, clearly not surprised by anything, showed him to a vacant room.

"I will tell the Commandant about you in the morning. He will issue your orders. The canteen is on the third floor. They will fix you a sandwich if you ask nicely. And of course, you're free to go out and see the whole of our wonderful city. Good night, sir!"

Hugo felt immensely relieved. He had to sit on the bed just to steady his nerves. Hungry and determined to gain as much information as possible, he made for the canteen and struck up a conversation with the chef on duty.

"So what's it like working here?"

"Oh, same as any other place. The Commandant is okay though. He's an old bastard, just seeing out his time. I think he got kicked out of the Russian front, this is not a desirable posting! Unless you like the food!"

"Umm," said Hugo, mouth full. "Not bad! Where do you get the ham?"

"Ah, that would be telling! You here long?"

"No. Only for a few months."

"You here to replace that Bertmandt?"

"I think so. What happened to him?"

"Who knows? Stabbed in the neck, while drinking one night. Working here, you make a lot of enemies. Mind you, he was a particular type of bastard. I hear he liked to pull out prisoner's nails."

Hugo nodded slowly, feeling bile rising in his throat.

"Bert … what was his name again?"

"Bertmandt."

"Did he have any close friends here?"

"One I think. Frankus. But he was more like his sidekick. Watch him! He would sell his own mother for a quick step up the ladder … ."

"So he won't miss his mate, then."

"Nah. No worries there."

"And the Commandant. What sort of man is he?"

"Strict, you know … discipline and all that. Likes a sharp salute and nice uniform. Likes talking about the old days … I don't know how he got into the SS; he is always complaining about Hitler, sorry, the Führer … ."

"It's okay. You're among friends." Hugo finished the first of two sandwiches and offered the chef an SS cigarette.

"Thanks."

"How is he on red tape?"

"Hates it. If you dress smart, salute beautifully and like a few glasses of schnapps at night, he will love you like a son."

"Thanks. By the way, how can I get this uniform pressed tonight, so I have it by 6am?"

"Easy. We have our own laundry press. Hans, one of my mates, operates it. Only during the day mind, but if you have five Reichmarks handy, he doesn't mind a bit of extra work."

"Good." Hugo handed over ten Reichmarks. "Keep five for yourself. Where do I leave the suit … and the boots?"

"Outside your door. What's your number?"

"Twenty-two."

"Ah Bertmandt's old room! You *must* be here to replace him! Hans will pick them up in thirty minutes. Have them all back on time … and the boots polished."

"Good night."

"Heil Hitler!"

"Yeah."

Hugo found himself practicing saluting and snapping his heels for a solid hour before laying down and falling into a nervous sleep.

***

"Ha! The efficiency of the SS never fails to surprise me, but even so, I find this a little incredible!"

Hugo had been summoned to the Commandant's officer at 7am and had just executed as near perfect a salute as he had ever managed. His heels stung from their sharp contact. He looked down at his papers, which were being scrutinised by the old SS officer.

"I barely remember your Commanding Officer from the academy, and yet he somehow knows I need a replacement only three days later! How can you explain this?"

Hugo stared straight ahead for a moment and then decided to take a risk. "I don't know, sir. Perhaps it's not just efficiency. You know what they say; there are eyes everywhere."

"Yes … . Yes, I know what you mean … . Do you care for a schnapps?"

Hugo smiled broadly. "I would like that very much." For a moment he thought he had pushed the informality too far by not qualifying his answer with 'sir.' But a returned smile gave him all the reassurance he needed.

"Your service record is excellent. I don't see why you cannot go to work immediately. I hate red tape. We'll have to check your details … . But we'll do that later. Prost!"

***

In the week since his late-night revelation about the RAF's double-bluff Rudolph Eineger had not been idle. He had made himself a pest with every Reich Chancellery contact he had; looking for every possible weakness in the machinations of the great building's operations that the British could exploit. Of course, there were many ways the RAF could kill the Führer, for instance just bombing it at the right time, but this did not have a high probability of success. Any raid by heavy bombers always gave plenty of warning, plenty of time to get down to the Führerbunker. And that thought had led Eineger to an inescapable conclusion. The only sure way to kill the Führer would be to destroy the bunker itself with Hitler actually in it. Even were he not actually killed by the attack, he would be so tightly sealed in, that subsequent raids could finish the job before he could be rescued. Yes, it seemed viable.

Eineger's first line of enquiry had been to investigate the SS staff in the bunker. But so far this had come up blank. No civilians, other than Hitler's personal friends, were allowed to enter. So his friends had been the next line of enquiry. This had also drawn a blank and proved somewhat dangerous to continue.

Then, by a lucky chance, he had discovered something few knew about; that Hitler had begun a project to extend the

Bunker into the back garden of the Chancellery. Eugen Vögler, CEO of Hochtief, which had been contracted to handle the work with the SS, had next come under Eineger's piercing gaze, but frustratingly, he had come up clean as a whistle. Not a card-carrying Nazi, Vögler nevertheless proved above suspicion. For a brief moment, Eineger thought he saw a connection. Vögler seemed up to his neck in debt, but a quick check revealed that he would be paid such an enormous personal bonus for the work that this would more than write off his debt. He had nothing to gain and everything to lose by not completing the job.

In desperation, Eineger began to go through the staff of Hochtief and even those of the companies that made the equipment being used.

Finally, at 11.32am, and in need of a cup of proper coffee, Rudolph Eineger slammed shut the final blue paper folder and stared at his ink blotter.

"Nothing!"

Could it be the Jewish slaves working in the garden? Eineger had thought of this and dismissed it several times. Or even the SS guards watching them? This seemed so outlandish that he smiled at himself before dismissing it. He had to find out where the slaves were kept and snoop around there. It didn't take him long to find the location; Columbia House, near Templehof Airport.

"I want to see the Commandant," he said when he reached the front gate thirty minutes later.

"He's not here, sir!"

"I am SS Oberleutnant Rudolph Eineger. I need to see a full list of prisoners and any information on each."

"Yes Herr Oberleutnant!" The guard directed him to the Commandant's office. "The adjutant will help you!"

The adjutant helped willingly, with terror in his eyes. "Here is the full list of current prisoners. Which in particular would you be interested in? A name?"

"This is fine, thank you. Something to drink, if you please, and then I want to be left alone."

"Cognac? Schnapps?"

"No alcohol. Coffee or fruit juice."

"Right. Certainly." The Gestapo frightened all men, but this one with the livid scar scared the orderly more than most. He returned a few minutes later with a china cup of real hot coffee on a silver plate, laden with sugar and a pot of cream too. The Gestapo officer barely glanced up, as the adjutant placed the tray in front of the Eineger on the vast oak table. "Will that be all?"

"Yes." But then, as the adjutant left, Eineger continued, "Where can I find you if I need you?"

"I have to go and help the new SS Guard get settled into his duties. After that, I will come straight back. It will take about an hour."

"Fine."

Eineger started turning the pages of the prisoner list. They were in sections, each secured with a paper clip at top left, and each typed in single-spaced lines. Some of the sheets had little more than the 'name' and the 'religion' column completed, but some had the 'region of birth' column completed, others the 'region of previous' work and a few more, the 'trade' column complete. A very few had all columns completed. Eineger had just decided to focus on the complete ones first when he became distracted by the single word 'new' in his mind.

He slapped the sheets down on the folder in frustration and then acquiescent, he stared into space. "New? New? What is *new*?" He cast his sharp memory back and then came up with the answer. "Ah yes, the new *Guard*. Hm. I want to find out more about him."

Eineger trusted his instinct totally. But at that moment he became distracted again. The telephone rang in the adjutant's office, next to the Commandant's. It rang nearly thirty times before stopping at last. But five minutes later, it rang again. And then the black phone right in front of Eineger rang, also thirty times. He looked at it as if it were one of those large black beetles he had seen in Egypt; something he despised and wanted dead. There followed another short pause, and then another telephone rang somewhere far away in the building. This continued, moving from one telephone to another for over ten minutes. Finally, the beetle-telephone rang again, and Eineger counted patiently to thirtieth ring. To his extreme annoyance, it rang an uneven thirty-first time, and this prove too much for him.

"Why doesn't somebody answer the God-damned telephones around *here*?" The last word echoed off the row of filing cabinets against the wall in front of him once in the silence that followed the last telephone ring. And then he heard the sound of distant jack-booted feet running up steps. They came ever closer, and then the door was flung open. The adjutant stood facing him, breathless, his face deathly pale.

"Herr Oberleutnant! The Führer's wishes to see you at the Reich Chancellery immediately. A car has been waiting outside for nearly ten minutes!"

"The Führer? Himself?"

"Yes Herr Oberleutnant! I'm sorry nobody could get hold of y- … ."

Eineger leaped out of his chair and ran through the door before he heard the end of the sentence. He buttoned his leather trench-coat furiously as he ran down the stairs, fearing the Führer himself might even be in the car.

"Damn! Why now!"

When he reached the street, a black Mercedes flashed its headlights at him, and he walked briskly to it. A huge, polished door swung open, and he climbed in.

The car took him swiftly up Mehringdamm into Wilhelmstraße, the driver expertly overtaking cars at every opportunity. Within five minutes, they pulled up outside the Reich Chancellery and a secretary ushered Eineger inside. As he strode to Hitler's office anti-room, he went over in his mind what he planned to say.

"Wait here, please, Herr Oberleutnant. The Führer will see you in approximately five minutes," said a secretary

Five minutes became ten minutes. Then the huge doors to the Führer's office opened, and a red-faced General swept past Eineger.

"You may go in, now," added the secretary.

Rudolph Eineger unbuttoned his coat, considered taking it off and then decided against it. He walked through the doors and then sought the figure of the Führer himself. There he was, at the far end of the room, a tiny figure in a tall, leather chair. He appeared to be looking at something to his side, on the floor. Eineger strode purposefully to the place at a long table, just to Hitler's right.

"Herr Eineger. Please sit down," said Hitler, in a melodious, yet empty voice. "I won't waste your time; I know you are a busy man. So am I, these days. Rumours have reached my ears, as indeed rumours always eventually must, that the British have some new … X-ray bomb … . And that they are going to use it to try to assassinate me."

Peering over the table edge, Eineger could see the famous Blondi, eating a brown biscuit like the ones on a plate in front of the Führer. Hitler suddenly swung to face the young Gestapo officer and fixed his coldly grey eyes on Eineger's. The gaze sent a shiver down the young man's spine. He had been in Hitler's presence several times, but he had never been stared at directly. He didn't think the Führer recognised him.

"I believe that to be true, meine Führer."

"Indeed. I heard from Herr Schtickel that you are the source of the … information?"

"Yes."

"And yet the provenance could not be verified … ."

The statement hung in the air like a great, grey axe.

"That is probably correct. I have often passed on information which I knew would come to your ears, meine Führer, but this time I needed to be sure it would reach you … accurately." Eineger let his practiced words hang in the air.

Hitler stood up and walked towards a set of double doors at the end of the room. Blondi immediately stood up and padded after him, her claws making little echoing taps on the marble floor.

"Come with me, Herr Eineger."

Rudolph Eineger wondered if the day of his death had come. Hitler turned right, walked down a short corridor, with Blondi brushing against his thigh, and then opened another set of doors to his right. The cool draft of air wafted some drapes and the Nazi flag from the garden beyond. He heard the sound of a pick axe biting into heavy mud and gravel accompanied by birdsong.

"Do you like animals?" Hitler asked over his shoulder.

"Oh yes. Very much."

Hitler sat on a wicker chair and ruffled Blondi's ears. "Go and say hello to the nice man," Hitler suggested. Blondi's tongue lolled as she paced towards Eineger. He immediately dropped to one knee and ruffled the Alsatian's ears. Blondi looked into his eyes and both blinked at each other.

"Ha! She likes you! That's good enough for me. Throw her a branch. My bones ache today."

"Here Blondi. Fetch!"

"No need to tell *her*. She *knows* what she's doing … ."

"Now, Herr Eineger, I can quite see why you wanted to get a message through to me without needing to trust the messenger. It's quite bright of you. I don't trust most of them, myself. *Now*, perhaps, you may feel you can tell me, freely and in confidence, what you know."

Rudolph Eineger remained silent. Hitler's eyes widened slightly in surprise.

"Herr Schtickel, I will probably need to keep my eye on. I have seen your face a few times, but since you don't yet serve in the Chancellery, I presume you might find such a position attractive."

This was the green light Eineger had been waiting for. He revealed his true sources and then continued, "I can have the files delivered to you today, Meine Führer."

"I don't think that will be necessary," Hitler said quietly, taking the stick from Blondi's mouth. "Personally, I think the target is the Berghof, but I am curious why you were at that prison when we found you today. What is it called?"

"Columbia House. I have been wondering what weaknesses there might be in the Chancellery. What might offer hope for a would-be assassin, with or without an X-ray bomb."

Not more than one hundred feet away, scaffolding draped with tarpaulins covered the excavations around the base of the Chancellery wall. A prisoner in striped uniform emerged pushing a wheelbarrow of soil and gravel. He crossed the muddy ground on lined-up planks and then deposited the soil onto a high pile near the back of the garden. An SS guard followed him all the way there and all the way back.

"And you suspect the Jewish prisoners?"

Eineger felt skewered. A drop of sweat formed on his brow as he furiously tried to recall if he had told anybody that he suspected, not the prisoners, but one of the guards. After almost collapsing with the effort, he realised he hadn't. He had no wish to stick his neck out on a long-shot hunch; that was not how he operated. It would do for now to let Hitler think prisoners were the main suspects.

Withholding information constituted a crime, punishable by death. Eineger suddenly felt suspended between life and death. He had always been good with numbers and had been training to be an actuary before joining the Gestapo. His particular speciality had been risk. It hadn't escaped his attention that while before the two possible outcomes of his investigation had been his own promotion or Hitler's death, now they were his own promotion or his own death.

"Yes. I don't know how it might be achieved, but a Jewish prisoner can be impersonated just as easily as, or more easily than, anyone else."

Hitler nodded slowly. "I still think it's the Berghoff. I want you to find out more about this … 'bomb,' Herr Eineger. I am putting you in charge of the investigation. Any funds you need will be made available. Speak to my secretary before you leave. I don't think it's the Jewish prisoners, though. The SS guard them day and night, and the SS have enough problems. Leave all that to them. I would like to know how you found about our little bit of building work in the garden. But I suppose it's your business to find out these things. I'm busy, so that conversation will have to wait for another day. For your information, I'm going to the Berghof anyway, at the end of August, probably for ten days. I'm not going to let the RAF or the American Eighth Air Force spoil my lovely walks in the last of the sunny days. However, if you hear anything more, you must let me know immediately. Even if you feel you need to come personally. Is that alright with you?"

"Yes. Certainly, meine Führer. I understand completely."

"And in the mean-time, not a word of this conversation with anybody. Understood?"

"Yes, meine Führer."

"Good. Help yourself to biscuits on the way out. Say good-bye to the nice gentleman, Blondi."

The Alsatian barked once and Eineger patted the top of her head, before walking back inside the Chancellery.

'What a great man. So cultured, so intelligent, so subtle in his thinking. I don't see how anybody can see him as the demon the English portray him as,' Eineger thought. He had instantly forgotten the terror he had felt earlier.

***

The next practice run to Dartmoor would be the first using proper bombs. The 500lb bombs had to be loaded under the wings of the Hurricanes after the fighters had been mounted on the Short Stirlings for safety reasons. The intricate rig that had been devised by Short to do this took the ground crews time to get used to and proved clumsy to use. For this reason, the preparations took a whole day and night, and the practice didn't take place until the 10th August.

The flight down to Dartmoor, just before dawn, went smoothly, but then the trouble began.

Richard, as usual, wanted to be first to try the course with the bombs, and he missed the turn into 'Unter den Linden,' clipping the top of the first building on its far side with his left wing.

"Blast and damn! No good, I'm afraid. The bombs make a huge difference. It felt so sluggish and I daren't give it the full 15 degrees of flap."

The other two pilots fared no better. When Richard tried again, he used the full 15 degrees of flap, but quickly straightened out and had missed the street altogether when he felt his aircraft begin to shake violently.

On his third attempt, he still could not make the turn and flew over the plywood 'roof tops' before straightening up and dropping down into 'Unter den Linden.'

"At least I may as well drop the damned things!" he shouted.

As he turned near the 'Brandenburg Gate,' he noticed two small figures, a man and a woman, waving at him from a ridge to the right. Richard tried to focus on his bomb run and hit the release mechanism deliberately a few moments too early. The two heavy bombs ploughed into the soft Dartmoor soil a few feet in front of the plywood walls that marked the edifice of the Reich Chancellery.

Who the hell are they?

He swung the fighter to the right for a pass above the two new spectators, fearing they might be civilians. Flying low just in front of them he saw that the woman had dark hair and looked pretty. He recognised her; Anna. The man in the ill-fitting suit next to her could only be one man, Michael Dorfmann. Richard felt furious.

"Going in skip," said Todd over the radio.

Richard circled around for another view of the couple on the ground but heard a yell over the radio.

"Jesus … !"

*Damn. I should have been paying attention!*

"What's happening, Razor," Richard shouted.

"It's not good, like, skip."

Richard glanced over to the tricky turn point and saw a plume of smoke rising from the ground. "Oh no!" He aimed the fighter directly for the cloud, preparing to crash-land if necessary to save one of his pilots in trouble.

A weak voice came over the VHF. "I'm okay I think skipper. That bomb nearly did me in!"

Richard arrived at the source of the plume; the wreckage of Todd's crashed Hurricane. One wing had been completely ripped off and the other folded above the cockpit as if the aircraft felt bashful about its disheveled state.

"What happened, Todd, Are you alright?" Richard radioed.

"Yes. Okay. Arm's a bit sore. Tried the full 15 degrees. Bomb ripped off in the turn, took some of my wing with it. Had to belly land."

Richard's elation almost made him whoop with joy.

*He's alright!*

Richard could see an army truck churning up mud in its effort to reach the stricken aircraft. An ambulance could be seen, approaching the practice area.

"Okay. Everyone else home for tea. The Army will take care of Todd now. Nothing we can do."

The flight back seemed interminable to Richard. He felt very angry about a lot of things; most of all about Anna and Michael, only slightly less so about the bombs and least of all about Todd's recklessness.

As soon as he landed, he called Archibald.

"Archie?"

"Hello? Richard?"

"Yes. It's me. What is this ridiculous idea of letting Anna near the practice area? And even crazier, who the hell authorised a dodgy German to be there?"

"Now calm down, Richard. I can honestly tell you, neither was my idea, but this is just the way it's going to *be*. There is *nothing* I can do about it!"

Archibald's own indignation showed through in his voice, and Richard's anger lost its vehemence. "I suppose it's that blonde-haired boffin?"

"I can't say. I think it goes further. I can't speak now. There will be another Whitehall briefing on the 13th August. You'll find out all you need to know then."

"Fine. Just don't let that German near me until then."

The receiver on the other end went dead, and Richard found himself listening to a continuous tone. After some moments, he replaced his receiver.

***

Richard would not have his wish fulfilled with regards to Michael Dorfmann.

That very evening a call came through from the gatehouse on Stradishall, while Richard and Martin were relaxing over a game of chess.

"Anna and that German are here," Richard said to his brother, putting down the receiver.

A few minutes later, Anna and Michael walked in to the blockhouse. Richard and Martin looked up from their game of chess, while Jackie sat silently watching from the comfort of a beaten-up wicker chair which had been furnished with a cushion.

"Jackie!" shouted Anna, running over to the little rabbit, whose nose twitched furiously. "Oh look! He's still bandaged. And where is his scarf?"

"He doesn't wear it all the *time*!" Richard protested.

"Where is it? I want to show Michael!" Richard retrieved the blue scarf dutifully, and Anna wrapped it around the young rabbit's neck.

"A little flyer! All he needs is goggles!" quipped Michael. "How is that pilot of yours?"

Richard stared at him icily before smiling. "Todd has just returned on the train. His arm's strained and in a sling. He has a few cuts and bruises but nothing too seriously damaged, other than his Australian pride."

"But one lost fighter … ."

"Yes … . But we can replace it easily enough." Richard looked at Anna questioningly.

"Michael has become part of this operation now, he is helping us. He has already helped you and, in fact, Archibald is talking about the possibility of Michael coming with you. He needs to know anything any of the other pilots know." She let the proposition hang in the air. Martin and Richard looked at each other, incredulous.

"Now hang on!" shouted Richard. "I'm trying to put together a highly sensitive mission here. We're all risking our necks, and not one civilian can know about this. And then you two turn up on Dartmoor, watching as if it's some fairground display … !"

"Now Richard … ," Anna replied, quietly. "I know you think … ."

"I don't know what to think … !"

Anna looked to Martin for help. Michael looked at the floor. The air crackled with tension. Michael, at a loss what to say or do, walked over to Jackie and knelt down in front of the rabbit. He stroked those long, furry ears and laughed at the silky smoothness of the fur. "He's such a cute little chap!"

"He's our squadron mascot. We're thinking about painting roundels on him and a serial number!" quipped Martin.

"Oh Martin, that's cruel," replied Anna.

Richard let a long blast of air out through his lips, and then his anger had gone. Martin lit a pipe and started reading a newspaper. "Anybody for tea?" he said from behind the security of the middle pages.

"I need to go for a walk," said Richard.

"Oh yes. Good idea. Can we come?" asked Anna.

"Oh, I suppose so. I can't seem to shake you two, anyway."

Outside the blockhouse Anna spotted four bicycles. "Oh Richard. Can we go for a ride around the airfield?"

"I suppose so. As long as Michael doesn't take one and make a run for the Channel."

"Oh Richard," Anna said, ribbing him with her elbow. "Michael doesn't even have guards now. See!" She gestured to the apron around them, devoid of other people. "Tomorrow I have permission to take him to Harrods, to buy him a proper suit." Michael grinned and went to choose a bicycle.

"Hm. I had an argument with Archie," Richard said Anna quietly. "I told him that I thought the pilots had been selected, because they were emotionally … damaged by the Nazis." He let out his breath. Anna stared at him. "I know. I know, it was foolish, but you know what? I was right. He had *no* answer!"

"Well, what did you expect? That's the way they operate."

"How about you. Did they try something like that with you?"

"*Something* like that."

He reached out to her. Their fingers touched, and they clasped hands for a moment.

"I hate this whole damned war. It's turning us *all* into Nazis! We're no better than *them*!"

"You and I are! Perhaps not those like …"

"Archie? Oh, I know it's not his fault. He is just as naïve as I was; taken in by it. When I get back, if I get back, I hope things will be different." He looked into her eyes, but she couldn't quite catch the intent there. "The trouble is I don't think they want us to come back!"

"Come back," she whispered.

"But you want Michael to come back, too." The moment of intimacy had gone as quickly as it had come, replaced by an old anger that grew again in Richard.

The sun had just set, but the evening still felt warm with only a slight breeze from the south west. The clear, moonlit dusk gave a dreamlike quality to their excursion. Richard remained sullen as they rode while Michael and Anna joked about everything they saw. At the very southern-most extreme of the airfield. Richard stopped. He thought he had seen something large, moving furtively in the undergrowth.

*Perhaps they don't trust him so much, after all!*

The thought cheered him. "Let's rest awhile." He sat on tree stump while Anna stood nearby and Michael wandered about.

"So good to be free, Richard," the German said. "I can't tell you … . For a while I … . But anyway, how is your mission going? I saw the bombs are giving you trouble?"

"Yes. Everything is giving us trouble. We cannot negotiate the course. The bombs are too heavy … . We need more fuel … ."

"I recognised the street … . Unter den Linden. You need to be careful. Any civilian who has been there might recognise it."

"Yes. I said the same to Arch … . But apparently the Army are doing a pretty good job of keeping anybody away from it."

"But the Luftwaffe reconnaissance? There is a flight which goes down to Exeter every day. A friend of mine flies the Focke Wulf 190. He only needs to detour one hundred kilometres or so. Then you will be caught. His aircraft has everything stripped out, I tell you it will do 450 mph. You would never catch him!"

"Yes. Well it's just another risk." Richard smiled at Michael, remembering why he had liked the man. He seemed genuine. Richard felt grateful for any opinion that resembled his own.

A movement high up in one of the elm trees, swaying in the slight breeze, caught their eye. A large, shadowy bird took clumsily to the air.

"Heron, most likely," offered Richard. "No water near here. He must be some way from home."

"Like me," added Michael.

***

Michael Dorfmann marvelled once again at the splendour of Harrods. He had last visited it years before noticed no change. He waited until they had bought the suit and Anna became consumed with curiosity with some trinket before executing his plan. He let himself be carried on by the vociferous crowd and then darted into a stair well. He exited Harrods and walked quickly to Knightsbridge tube station. Within twenty minutes, he exited Kensington Olympia Station. Then he walked the short distance to 14 Hansard Mews. It was 5pm and already dusk. He watched the silent house from across the street. He saw a window, to the left of the blue front door, and then a garage with a blue-painted door. He could see almost no sign of life in the salubrious street at all, only a cat, sitting and quietly licking its paws near the other end of the street where it turned to the right to join the main street. A train rumbled by only fifty feet or so from Michael. He put a cigarette in his mouth but then didn't light it. He knew somebody might see the smoke. A black cloud crossed the moon and another freight train rumbled slowly by.

'Now,' he thought, but his legs wouldn't move. He took one last look at the door and shook his head. Within half an hour, he had returned to Harrods and made a point of getting the store staff to make a public announcement:

"Would Miss Anna Styles please come to the reception desk on the first floor? Your friend is waiting for you." He waited half an hour and then went back to his flat. He found Anna walking nervously up and down in front of it, smoking a cigarette furiously.

"Where have you been, *Michael*? I looked everywhere!"

"I don't know! I looked around, and you had gone!" He pretended to be slightly angry himself. "I waited for over half an hour, and then I went to the reception desk. I made them make a public announcement and then waited another half an hour. When there was no sign of you, I came back here!"

"Oh. I didn't dare make an announcement! For one thing I can hardly say, 'Michael Dorfmann, please come to reception,' *can* I? And anyway, I wasn't sure what you were doing." She looked down at her neat suede shoes.

"Oh Anna! I'm sorry! Thank you for not getting me into more trouble!" He lifted her chin and kissed her lightly on the lips. Her lipstick tasted sweet. He licked his lips, and she smiled.

***

Hugo Knopfl heard the telephones ringing all over Columbia House. He wasn't surprised when the Commandant's Adjutant finally gave in and ran off to answer one of them. He smiled ironically to himself

"Luck is always an important ingredient of success!" he whispered to himself. By incredible good fortune, he had already found himself assigned to the guard detail for the Reich Chancellery garden. The luck wasn't so much in the choice but the speed. In fact, the Jewish prisoners were only currently used for two projects; building work on Templehof Airport and the work in on the Führerbunker. He had orders to start the next day. For now, he familiarised himself with the prisoners' details and the rules of the prison.

The adjutant returned in a very agitated state. "No less that the Führer himself trying to get hold of a Gestapo officer! What he was doing here, I have no idea! But to have the Führer's secretary calling every telephone in the building and nobody answering … I will probably be shot for this! Or at the very least sent to the Eastern Front!" He paused to catch his breath. "The Commandant will be back soon, so I have to go. I'm sure you will find all you need here. The main meal is at 6.30pm in the ward room. You will be expected to wear a dinner-suit if you have one. If not, that will do. The evening is generally yours to do with as you wish. I suggest you try Berlin's night entertainment. One of the other officers will most likely be pleased to show you the sights!" He winked once, unconvincingly and left.

Hugo wasn't late for dinner. It proved more extravagant than he had expected, and when it finished, two hours later, he felt bloated and slightly drunk. He decided to walk for a while towards the Tiergarten and then perhaps take a tram from there.

At around 10.30pm, he found himself in Marienstraße, a narrow street of late regency buildings, just north of Unter den Linden and just over the river. He hadn't intended coming so soon, but the address found for the two agents by CS-6 drew him. Outside number twenty-two, he saw a grey metal letterbox, just out of the reach of the light cone from a street lamp. The letterbox lid was unlocked. He lifted it and dropped in a rolled-up ball of paper; the pre-arranged signal that all was well. He couldn't see a second ball of paper inside.

From there, he caught a tram across town and had a few pints of watered-down beer in a quiet bar. Nobody talked to him except the taciturn bartender.

Hugo's first guard duty began the following morning. He expected a tap on the shoulder at any moment. A grey bus arrived at 7.30am and drove them up Mehringdamm into Wilhelmstraße. Unlike his journey in the black Mercedes, this one took almost an hour. Neither the guards nor the driver seemed to care. The haggard prisoners, in their shreds of uniform, tried to avoid Hugo's gaze. He knew they cared for very little any more.

At the Chancellery, one of the other SS guards showed him where to form up behind the prisoners and demonstrated how to hit them in the middle of the back with his rifle butt whenever he felt the need for a little more speed. Hugo resisted the urge to punch him. Using servant's corridors, the carpets temporarily covered with dirty tarpaulins, they were soon in the Chancellery back garden. It began to rain just as the prisoners began working. When the other guard offered him a cigarette, he smiled and smoked it obligingly. The prisoners had a ten-minute break at 11am and lunch at 12.45pm; this latter consisting only of a chunk of black bread and some watery broth. The SS guards ate thick wedges of delicious, fresh white bread accompanied by cheese and sausage. They washed this down with hot coffee. The prisoners were given nothing to drink.

The rain cleared after lunch. The prisoners continued shifting piles of gravelly soil from the Chancellery wall to the far end of the garden in wheelbarrows.

Several times when he felt nobody could see him, Hugo took a long look at both of the curious little towers near the Chancellery wall. He knew these were the towers that housed the ventilators for the bunker below. He and Klaas had been briefed to find a way to open these during the day. Which particular day they needed to be open on he didn't know yet. He could see the wooden slats were closed now. By the end of the day, he had looked at the vents from all sides and could see no visible levers or controls of any sort which would open the slats.

Once only, Hugo thought he saw a small figure with an Alsatian dog emerge from a door in the Chancellery. The figure threw the dog a stick in an area roped off from the building site. 'Could this little man be Adolf Hitler?' Hugo thought.

The work detail would finish at 4.30pm. At 4.15pm the prisoners downed tools and tidied up. A few minutes later, Hugo noticed a large tipper-truck back towards the garden from the other side of the trees at its far end. The driver gunned the diesel engine several times to overcome undulations on the rough ground. Hugo guessed this truck would be the means to remove the large piles of soil.

That evening, at dinner, the ageing Commandant regaled Hugo with war stories. Hugo found the man pleasant and amusing. Forced to drain more than a whole bottle of schnapps, Hugo only found one moment unpleasant during the whole evening.

"I have sent for authentication of your papers from your command, Casper," the Commandant said, while Hugo sipped some soup. The unfamiliar name hung in the air for a moment before he realised *he* was being addressed.

"Fine, meine Commandant. I trust all will be in order."

"One thing though. They have requested I send a photograph of you … just to be sure. Would you mind? Tomorrow morning one of my men can take the photograph."

"No. That's fine."

***

# Chapter Six

zgahinkt toinz Yzgxzykozk galmkxalkt

The people sitting around the briefing table in Whitehall on the 13th August now included Anna, much to Richard's discomfort. The gaunt Group Captain Devonshire sat patiently watching, his cap placed squarely in front of him on the table.

"Update us please, Squadron Leader Earlgood," the blonde-haired man, asked.

"Thank you. Well on one front, we made progress. We found a way, with the help or

f our esteemed German friend, to negotiate this bend here." Richard pointed to a plan view of the Unter den Linden area in Berlin on a wall of the room with a stick. "In short, we can use the flaps and over-boost the engine for a short space of time, to get around this obstacle, the Berliner Castle, on the corner of the River Spree and Schloßplatz."

There were smiles of appreciation from around the table.

"On the other hand, we tried the day before yesterday with the new 500-pound bombs, and we lost an aircraft when the bomb tore free of its harness. We also found, with these bombs, we can no longer get around the corner." He coughed and paused. "We find we can easily enough bomb the Chancellery wall here. This corner by the Brandenburg Gate is not a problem. The main problem remains for us the turn off the River Spree and, of course, any telegraph poles along the main street." With that he could think of nothing more to add.

"Thank you. Archie?"

"Thank you. I have only a few points to make. We now have some members of the Dutch resistance CS-6, posing as German SS, actually inside Berlin, and its believed one of them has managed to attach himself to the working party in the Chancellery garden." There were exclamations of astonishment from around the large table. "The other point is that one of the things they have been tasked with, on their nights off … ." This brought laughs of derision from the audience. " … will be to scout out Unter den Linden and map out any obstacles we need to destroy. That's it from me."

"Thank you Archibald. Group Captain Devonshire?"

The gaunt man stood up without acknowledging the invitation and started talking in a very cultured, home-counties accent. "We believe … the problem with the weight of the bombs can be overcome by removing the machine guns. Together with their ammunition, these weigh about 850 pounds. A further weight reduction can be made by only half-filling the wing tanks. This would also help manoeuvrability in turns … ."

Richard stood up, and the Group Captain paused, looking at him. "No, not *all* the machine guns! It may be just a psychological thing, but I don't think that's a good idea! As I know from talking to Michael Dorfmann, having some kind of defence acts as a deterrent to would-be attackers. We should retain two guns at least." The Group Captain acquiesced with a slight nod. "And as for losing *more* fuel! No. We already barely have enough fuel to reach Veluwemeer. We may have barely any chance of surviving the attack, but for any that do, I will *not* take away their last hope of rescue. Anything less would be asking them to commit suicide. I'm not going to command a suicide mission!" Martin nodded in support. The Group Captain pursed his lips. The blonde-haired man looked steely-eyed at Richard but said nothing.

Archibald, at a nod from the blonde-haired man, stood up. "So we are agreed that we will try with six machine guns removed from each aircraft?"

Richard nodded. He glanced at his brother.

"Yes," Martin added. "We have to do something. It worries me that the Stirlings can barely get off with the 500-pound bombs. The other day, Amalfi Douglas barely got off at all. I think he had reached the grass before the thing lifted off. I agree with Richard, we can't expect the fighter pilots to lose more fuel, though. Can't anything be done about the performance of the Stirlings?"

One of the two men from MAP spoke up. "We can try and lighten the Stirlings. They don't need any of the bomb release mechanisms or cradles. There is quite a bit that could be removed. I bet we could save at least 1000 pounds."

"Then please do it," added the Group Captain.

"Yes. What are we waiting for?" added Richard.

"Now … the route," said Archibald, brightly. "We have been talking to the boys in the Eighth Air Force, and they have agreed to co-operate. We will need to plan D-day, the day of the attack, to coincide with one of their big raids." With that, he pulled on a piece of string, and a large map of Europe rolled down to cover the earlier plan of the Unter den Linden environs. A long piece of red sticky-tape stretched out from Stradishall, across the Netherlands, towards Hanover, and then angled south slightly towards Berlin. A blue piece of tape started from Suffolk and joined the red line to run alongside it as far as Hanover, where it looped around and returned to Suffolk. The red line split into two other lines at Berlin. One returned to Stradishall, the other to Veluwemeer in the Netherlands. "The idea is that you chaps will take off just ahead of the main force, on its way here … to Hanover. But you will be flying slower and will fall behind by the time they reach their target. This will look as if you are stragglers on German radar, but you will drop down to a few thousand feet and complete the run in to Berlin at this height. This should completely throw Heinz, we think. They won't be expecting you at all when you arrive."

Martin's eyebrows rose. He stood up. "You do realise we can barely reach 10,000ft with the fighters on our backs. Are the Yanks prepared to fly that low?"

"Hmm. Good point. I will have to check with them. We thought you would be able to reach 15,000ft at least."

"And if we're floating around way below the Yanks, we are going to be wide open to attack!" added Richard. "How about some escort. Mosquitos, maybe?"

"Yes. We did think of that," Archie replied. "Trouble is, if we give you escort, it makes for a bigger sort of blip on the radar, and then there is more chance of you being noticed."

"Well, let's see what Archie comes up with after he has talked with the Americans," said the blonde man.

"One thing we are missing," added Archibald. "We don't know at what height you want to cover the ground to Berlin and how you want to approach it?"

Richard turned to his brother. "Martin's best to answer the first."

"Well, I think 1000 feet," replied Martin. "At that height it's too low for anyone to get under you or stay on your tail for long. We are too high to hit any masts or anything; believe me, these contraptions don't handle too well, so we don't want to be dicing with anything on the ground. We can use the terrain to avoid radar and also to make it difficult for enemy fighters. As for direction, Richard, and I haven't thought about it. Looking at the map, since we have to approach the River Spree from south east, it might make sense to steer a course as if we are going to Frankfurt, further east, and then turn north. This would probably confuse them."

"And how about the flight of six standard Stirlings you are to command, those that will bomb the Chancellery?" asked Archibald.

"Yes. Good question. It might be an idea if they stayed with the main force and then flew on to Berlin at 15,000 feet. They don't need a heavy bomb load, so it should be possible. That would *really* confuse the enemy. I would have to co-ordinate it over VHF though. Is that possible?"

Archibald spoke up. "Provided we use some kind of code, then yes. It's possible."

"Okay. It's going to have to be timed exactly right," added Martin. "They have to bomb the Chancellery minutes before we bomb the bunker. Too early, and Hitler could be gone by the time we get there, too late, and he might not be there yet."

"Alright," said the blonde-haired man. "Archie, get the planners working on this. Anything else anybody?" Heads slowly shook from side to side. "We meet again in one week."

Richard caught up with Archibald in the corridor and grabbed his sleeve. "Look here, Archie," he said, swinging him around. "I have decided to continue with this … operation, but I have just one thing to say to you." Archibald stood there, waiting. "When this war is over, people like you will not be able to find a hole to hide in. Your type will end up either behind bars or creating crossword puzzles for the Evening Standard! At least then you can do less damage!" Archibald looked down at the floor, turned and walked away. Richard suddenly found that all his anger had left him.

***

Richard and Martin hugged each other briefly on the concrete runway at Stradishall and then took their positions inside their aircraft. For Richard this meant climbing up the ladder to the escape hatch on the Stirling and then using another ladder hooked over the leading edge of the Hurricane to climb up to his aircraft. Once there he signaled, and Cloudy pulled down the ladder into the gloom of the Stirling interior. Richard climbed into his cockpit and closed the hood. It was the 15th August, two days after the last meeting in Whitehall. Short had sent out a group of engineers to remove the bomb mechanisms from the Stirlings. Engineers from Hawker had also arrived and assisted with the first fitting of the 1000lb canisters they would be using for the attack. These were particularly difficult to load on the special rig set up in the hangar. The Hawker engineers had also removed six of the eight browning machine guns and their accompanying ammunition handling equipment. It was just before dawn. All three pieces of work were complete, and the first trial of the new configuration would commence in a few minutes.

"You okay up there, Richie?"

"Fine. Nice view. Just make it a smooth take off. Alright?"

"Of course. Aren't mine always?"

"And absolutely no aerobatics. I don't want to fall off."

"I wouldn't let you."

Martin left one of his three VHF radios, dedicated for communication with his brother, turned to transmit, while he went through the last pre-flight checks. Richard's pulse raced and his heart thumping as he waited for the intense noise that would signal time to fire up the Merlin. He swallowed and tried to breathe evenly.

Today, the load on the four Hercules engines will be the greatest yet. Will they stand up to it? Can this great lumbering monster take off?

"Time to add your noise to the Stirling's, Richie," Martin shouted into the radio. Richard barely heard him as the Hercules engines powered up. The gills were fully open, allowing the greatest flow of air around the red-hot cylinders of the radials.

"Starting up." Richard quickly went through his own start up procedure; throttle half open, propeller control fully forward, supercharger set to moderate, radiator shutter open, ignition set to 'off.' Then he pressed the engine starter on the left side of the front panel and the booster button. The Merlin kicked into life, and he released the starter button. He held the booster button, next to the engine starter, down for a few seconds while operating the hand pump, until the engine ran steadily. He increased the revs slowly to 1000 rpm and kept it there. The Merlin made a curiously contrasting sound with the Hercules. The Merlin almost shrieked compared with the discordant rumble of the Hercules.

Richard felt a jerk as the Stirling eased forward and then trundled on to the main runway. Martin lined it carefully up and then paused.

"Ready?" he asked his brother.

"As ever!"

"Let's go."

Slowly, painfully slowly, the dual-aircraft combination gained speed. All the Stradishall hangars were behind them before the tail of the Stirling finally lifted. Until this moment, Richard had thought Martin might abort. Now he knew his brother intended to take off, no matter what.

"We're not going to make it, Martin!"

"Not on this day perhaps … Just a few … more … moments … ."

Suddenly the concrete runway ran out and the Stirling's great rubber tyres bounced on the grass. They lurched into a dip, and then with one violent wrench, the great bomber and its little passenger fighter, were airborne. "We're … up!"

"Yeah. Barely!" Richard held his breath as the bomber struggled to gain height. The top of a row of elm trees lay across their path. Richard closed his eyes as the Stirling's undercarriage, not yet fully retracted shredded the tops of the trees.

"Whew! The old farmer won't like that!" There came no answer from inside the Stirling. Richard tried to peer over the side of the nose of the Hurricane, but he couldn't quite see the bomber's cockpit. The two-aircraft composite continued to shake violently as it clawed its way slowly into the sky. Then Richard heard a different sound. At first, he couldn't quite place it, but then he knew it. He knew it as if he had been waiting for it all his life. One of the Hercules engines faltered. He could see thick white smoke pouring from the cowling of the starboard outer engine. He knew this engine would always be pushed hardest on the Stirling, because it had a tendency to veer to the right, and the pilot could only compensate by boosting the outer engine on that side.

*Not good.*

That thought would be all he had time for before things became very chaotic.

The Short Stirling's right wing started to dip.

"We can't make it together, but … maybe apart. I'm releasing you … ," shouted Martin over the radio. A moment later, Richard saw the red light flashing on his dashboard and pressed the green release button. He heard the four bolts fire on the pylons below his fighter. Without time to think, his instinct made him push the engine boost to maximum, 16 psi and push the revs to 3000 rpm. He felt the fighter drifting away from its cradle but in a sickening side slip toward the ground.

*This is going to be tricky!*

At no more than 100 feet of altitude, there would be no time for niceties. Richard hunted for a flat area to land in the fields below him. The dawn's dim rays gave just enough light to see a row of elms directly in front of him, so he allowed the fighter to continue its swing to the right. With the Merlin at full combat-boost and little more than 130 mph airspeed showing the controls were almost unresponsive. He had to jerk the job-stick fully to the right and left to get a reaction from the ailerons.

*Only one way down now.*

He decided to try and land parallel to the elm trees, but then he heard a loud metallic scraping sound and then a bang. The joy-stick was almost wrenched from his grip before he managed to correct, and the fighter continued on its flattened course to the ground. From the corner of his eye, he saw the damaged wing tip of the Short Stirling appear under his left tail surface. Something hung from the end of the bomber's wing. He had no time to consider this as the ploughed field rushed up towards him. He cut the engine and pulled up the nose of the fighter at the last moment.

*Oh no!*

He saw he would hit a ploughed field, across the ruts. A little laugh escaped inside him as he remembered the note in the pilot's handbook for ditching; 'before touching down, execute a shallow turn to stop the radiator digging in.'

There came a sickening crunch, and then his neck almost broke as he snapped forward in the harness. Something broke loose from the control panel and hit him on the head. The nose of the Hurricane had dug into the soil of the field, sending mud and stones slamming into the cockpit hood. It shattered, sending pieces of Perspex flying around Richard's face. He felt himself passing out. He instinctively closed his eyes and pulled his arms up in front of his face. Another sudden jolt smashed his left arm against something on the left side of the cockpit. And then he knew no more.

Richard regained consciousness but could not see properly. At first, he couldn't remember where he was. Then he remembered the crash. He felt very uncomfortable and in pain.

*My arm! At least I'm alive!*

Somewhere in the distance he heard a faint crump. He knew it to be the sound of the Stirling crashing somewhere, but he felt too dazed and in pain to move. He tried to sit upright but again lurched forwards and hung in the harness straps. Then he heard a welcome sound; the sound of a bell.

*Fire-engine? Ambulance? Don't care as long as it arrives soon.* Those were his last thoughts before he passed out again.

Arms were pulling at him, and voices were asking him lots of strange questions. He could make little sense of anything when he came to. The cold blast of dawn air made him suck in his breath when the men pulled him out of the smashed cockpit and laid him on a stretcher.

"Have you in a nice clean hospital bed in no time … with a pretty nurse to take your temperature, sir!" said a comforting voice.

"Whash tha shmell?" he heard somebody say. It was him.

"Glycol and fuel, most likely. Lucky it didn't go off, I'd say! And bloody lucky those dirty great bombs weren't armed!"

His flying suit, soaked with fuel and glycol, let the cold air seep into his aching bones while they loaded him into the ambulance.

He managed one last question before he passed out again. "Is the Stirling okay?"

"Don't know, sir."

***

Richard awoke and opened his eyes. A bright light dazzled him. Daylight streamed through a window somewhere behind him. He could feel the heat on the back of his neck. He had been propped up on two pillows and his left arm heavily bandaged in a sling. His face stung painfully. It had a thin layer of bandage wrapped around it. There were other plasters on various parts of his body, and he ached all over.

"Ah. Awake at last!" A sweet female voice had Richard scanning the room for its source. A pretty nurse began changing the sheets on the bed to his right. He could just see her, by stretching his painfully stiff neck as far as it would go in that direction.

"Hello," he mumbled. It sounded like, "Heflo."

"Hello, Squadron Leader Earlgood. Your mouth is probably a bit sore, I think you swallowed a few teeth. But you still have your tongue … ! Ha! Ha!"

"What elf is damajed?"

"Well. Not too bad, actually apart from the severe concussion; you have a very large bump on you head. You have a fractured arm, quite a few nasty cuts to your face, some whiplash; strain to your neck and back and various other cuts and bruises. Should have you up and about in a week or so. You won't be flying again for a little while though."

"Mm. How is my … ?"

"You have somebody next to you who you might know."

"What?"

 She nodded to Richard's left, and he craned his neck to look at the patient lying sprawled on the bed, both legs in bandages and his face covered. Suddenly the right hand came up, and the right hand signalled a Victory-V. "Hey Richie!" said a muffled voice beneath the bandages.

"Martin! You're alife! Ha!"

"Barely. How about you? How do you feel?"

"Oh. A little stiff. Whaf's happened?"

"I was going to ask you the same. You first."

Richard recalled what he could remember of the crash and his rescue. "And you?"

"Well … Sorry to say only Cloudy, Fitchell and I made it. After your graceful exit, which left half your tail attached to our poor Stirling's wing, we were buggered. One engine down is not too bad but smashed up wing as well! Hmph! Anyway, I tried to gain a bit more height, and we executed a very slow turn to the right, we can't have been far from you at that point, and then I tried to make for the runway. We didn't quite make it! The number one engine gave out under the strain of full boost for so long, and we went in, quite steeply I have to say, but … under control, nevertheless. Unfortunately, some silly bugger has been digging a trench for an ammunition dump over that side of the airfield and they didn't tell me! We ploughed straight into it, and the poor old girl jack-knifed. We lost the left wing straight away, but, fortunately, the fuselage broke in two. That's what saved us. The radio operator and Tiddler copped it in the rear, it caught fire along with the left wing. We were lucky! It was a sad end for them and the old girl. Now I have nothing to fly!"

"Don't worry. We'll foon find another F-Freddie. But what did you fay about Fitchell? I fought he was Hutchinson's gunner?"

"He was, but we had him along with us. Jonesy was ill. Anyway, the replacement won't be F-Freddie. It will be X-X-Ray. There's been a change of plan. If we're going to do this, we had better do it properly. The Stirling's will have call-letters near the end of the alphabet. That way, you idiots in your toy-planes won't get confused!"

"I thee. Well we know one fing for fertain."

"What's that?"

"Thoth bombth are too big. We aren'f going to gef off wiv those."

"Yes. That's true. I have been thinking about … ."

"We came up as quickly as we could!" Anna announced, bustling in with Michael behind her. She stooped and kissed Richard's bandage on his forehead. She took Martin's hand lightly, but he yelped playfully.

"Aw! Careful!"

"I'm so glad you're both alright. I would have been worried sick if they hadn't already told me you are alright. We brought you some chocolate and apples. We couldn't get oranges."

"Fanks," said Richard. "How are the boyth?"

"I don't know, Richard. I haven't seen them … . Michael may be able to tell you something?"

Richard looked suspiciously at Michael.

"I just wanted to say that that was a fine piece of flying," Michael said, grinning. "From what I have heard there are very few pilots alive who would come out of that alive! As for your friends, I've just met them, Richard. Archie brought us up and introduced me."

"Two minutes!" the pretty nurse called to Anna and Michael.

"And?" asked Richard, tersely.

"Fine men. I liked them although I don't know what they made of me. I have been asked to fly your replacement Hurricane … until you are fit again. They say it will take you at least two weeks before you can fly again … ."

"Like hell it will!"

"Time's up!" the nurse called.

"Good bye, Richard." Michael reached down to shake the injured man's hand, but Richard played up his injury by keeping his hand flat on the bed.

"Don't be mean!" said Anna. "I will see you tomorrow. We are staying at The Black Dog. Bye!"

"Don't look so grumpy!" said Martin. "It might be quite innocent!"

***

Three days passed before Rudolph Eineger felt he could visit Columbia House again. The previous afternoon, the file he had requested, on the military service history of the new SS guard Hauptsturmführer Casper Drall, had arrived. Unlike the prison Commandant, he could not wait for any photographic confirmation of the SS officer's identity. He could see very little personal detail in the records; born on 3$^{rd}$ September 1923; father a boot maker; mother a housewife; and brought up in Bremen with a sister, Heidi. However, his military record looked quite impressive, showing medals won for bravery in the Belgian campaign and in Russia. Casper Drall had been awarded the Iron Cross, First Class, in the battle for Tobruk and most significantly, had sustained a serious injury to his temple, from shrapnel.

Telling his adjutant his destination, Eineger left at 7am for Columbia House, but when he arrived he found that Casper

Drall had already left with the prison detail of Jews for the Chancellery. His suspicions were raised further when the questioning of another guard revealed that *this* Casper Drall did not appear to have a facial scar on his forehead. However, Eineger could not snoop around too much. His curiosity about Drall exactly balanced his terror of Hitler finding out he had disobeyed the Führer's wishes by visiting the prison. Reluctantly conceding he could not make any more progress there, he had begun to put on his coat when an officer asked him to take a telephone call. It had come from his own office.

"Sir, we have arrested the SS officer!" his adjutant told him. For a moment Eineger felt confused.

"Which officer? Who?"

"He was posing as one of the SS guards on duty at the front entrance to the Führerbunker!"

Eineger's heart leapt against the inside of his rib cage. "I will be there in fifteen minutes! Put him in the cell and leave him. I don't want anybody to speak to him. Understand?"

"Understood, sir! There is one other thing, sir. He's been shot, twice. He opened fire on the officer arresting him, so they had no choice!"

"Damn! I want the officer's name. Stupid idiot! How bad is he? Will he last?"

"I don't know sir. Should I get a doctor?"

"Yes! Yes! Of course! Get one right away." Eineger slammed down the telephone receiver and ordered a car and driver from the prison adjutant.

With the heavy rush-hour traffic and a driver who talked too much, it took Eineger nearly half an hour to reach the Gestapo building.

By the time he reached the prisoner's cell, the doctor on call had just finishing putting temporary bandages on the man in bloodied SS uniform. Even at a glance, Eineger could see that the uniform was out of date. He could not see how such a uniform could have gone unnoticed for any length of time.

"How badly hurt?" he asked the doctor, impatiently.

"One bullet is too close to the heart. He won't last more than a few hours, I don't think. There is no point trying to remove the bullets."

Eineger nodded. "Everyone out! Out!"

He took the wounded man's head in his hands and raised it up.

The man grinned at him and spoke in German. "Hour? I would say minutes, Herr Eineger. I have heard all about you since my arrest. You might inspire terror in your subordinates, but for me you hold no fear!"

Eineger's made his voice sound kind and patient. "Yes. I only want to know two things. What is your name and who do you work for? I know what you are here to do." As Eineger expected, he saw a tiny glint of something like astonishment in the dying man's eyes at the last sentence.

"I will tell you neither."

"Then I shall have to use force. I don't want to. Your time is nearly up. Make your death as painless as possible."

"And allow the Führer to live? Never. What is a little pain for me if I save the people of … Europe." The dying man gasped for air. Eineger could see the second gun-shot wound had penetrated his lungs. Pink foamy blood bubbled out through the black jacket. Eineger knew this to be one of the most painful wounds a man could sustain. He feared using more pain on this man, who already looked so close to death. Consequently, he tried persuasion for twenty minutes. Finally, he knew he had no choice. Leaning over the man, and grinning in his face, he found the bullet hole with his fingers and forced his index finger deep into the hot, sticky wound. For a moment the dying man passed out. And then he groaned and opened his eyes. They looked far, far away, to a place his interrogator could not imagine. Eineger twisted his finger slowly.

"You will tell me what you know. There are worse things than death."

"I, I cannot … . Oh, dear God … ! No, please." But suddenly a smile came over the dying man's face. "I don't think you can follow me here, Eineg- … ." Klaas Zapruder slowly relaxed, letting the white light come towards him. God was with him and had shown him the way to escape. He allowed the feeling of warmth to flow over him and willingly let life leave his body.

Eineger was left with his finger inside a dead body. Repulsed, he withdrew it and wiped it on the black SS tunic. He left the cell in a silent rage and found the nearest wash basin. He scrubbed his finger raw before ordering the body of the unknown man to be removed.

Eineger brooded over the prisoner's death for several hours. Still the record of the new guard at the prison tugged at the edge of his mind; he wasn't convinced the dead man had been his main prey. Like a cat landing on its feet after a long fall, Eineger knew where he had to go. He knew the Jewish work detail would arrive at about 5pm. At 4.30pm he left in a black Mercedes for Columbia House.

The traffic had been much worse than he expected, because of a military convoy. And then, when he reached Mehringdamm, the traffic halted completely. A bus had been blown up by terrorists. Eineger's black Mercedes finally reached the bus. Like an insect crushed by a giant boot, the front of the bus remained intact while the rear had been spread all over the wide road. Unlike a squashed insect, red blood of the many dead German passengers had splashed all over the bus wreckage and road. Eineger often felt glee at the death of non-Germans, but the sight of his dead countrymen left a sour taste in his mouth.

His car sped away, darting in and out of traffic before again becoming trapped. He thumped the seat in frustration. An air-raid warning siren had just started, and the traffic ahead had come to a complete stop. Men and women were running for shelter everywhere.

"But it's not even dark!" he shouted to nobody in particular.

"They are coming early tonight!" his driver said.

Eineger didn't hear him. He had already leaped out of the car and started to run south, down Mehringdamm. He finally reached the prison, out of breath, at 5.15pm. He immediately asked the guard if the work detail from the Chancellery had returned.

"Yes, sir!" Reassured, Eineger walked calmly up to the Commandant's office and entered after knocking once.

"I need to see Hauptsturmführer Casper Drall, immediately!"

"Very well," said the gaunt man behind his desk. He called for his adjutant, who led Eineger to Drall's room. Eineger pushed past him and opened the door. The room was empty. On the bed lay a black SS uniform, of the same type as that worn by the man they had captured earlier.

"Where is he?" Eineger demanded.

"I don't know, sir. Normally he would be expected at dinner."

***

Hugo Knopfl had returned from the work detail knowing he would not attend dinner in the prison that night. For three nights now, he had returned to Marienstraße and checked the letterbox for a sign from Klaas. He himself had dropped a match box with three matches in it the previous evening to indicate that all was still well after a further three days. He felt inside the box but only came up with his own box of matches. He saw nothing from Klass. Now he felt very worried. This could mean that Klaas had been killed, captured or come under surveillance.

After quickly changing, he left the prison and walked up Mehringdamm to the nearest tram stop. Before reaching it, he noticed a man in a long leather jacket running south along Mehringdamm.

"How peculiar," he mused. "He looks like Gestapo, but they never run. Unless … ."

He climbed aboard a tram and returned to Marienstraße. As on previous nights, he saw no sign from Klaas. A cold shiver ran down Hugo's spine. He had to face the fact Klaas had probably been compromised. This made his own position very precarious. For a moment he considered running. Then he calmed himself. He had to think. Firstly, he dropped a folded piece of paper into the letterbox from his pocket. It contained a fairly detailed sketch of telegraph poles, wires and other obstructions he had observed and memorised while walking down Unter den Linden. Then he took another tram to his favourite bar and drank slowly, alternating between ersatz coffee and schnapps until 10.30pm. Finally, he caught a tram back to Columbia House. He left the tram two stops early and walked down Mehringdamm.

Rudolph Eineger could barely control his fury when he learned that Drall had left while he had been in the Commandant's office. He returned to Drall's room and started searching the room. He went through all the suit pockets and the contents of a small bedside cabinet. He found nothing incriminating. A few receipts, a torn menu, some lines on a piece of paper, which Eineger could not decipher, seemed to be all Drall possessed. Eineger went to the Commandant's officer and requested instructions be given to two SS guards to wait inside a storage room near Drall's. He ordered that nobody else should know what he intended to do. The two guards were to come to the room when Eineger called for them. Then Eineger returned to Drall's room, sat on the bed and prepared himself for a long wait.

Rudolph Eineger prided himself on understanding the criminal mind. One of his great uncles had been convicted for murder, seemingly just for money. As a consequence of the family stigma, two of his uncles had become policemen, and therefore Eineger felt himself almost uniquely qualified in the field of criminology. He knew if he waited patiently enough, his prey would come to him.

Hugo reached the pavement opposite the prison and hid in the shadows. The air raid earlier had passed, and the street had become almost empty. Few needed to walk near Templehof station at this time of night. He looked intently at the doors to the prison. It looked normal. He waited. After fifteen minutes, he felt it seemed too quiet. Nobody had entered or left. He decided to wait a little longer. He saw lights go on and off. And then one of the other officers approached the gates on foot wearing an evening suit. He smoked a cigarette quietly before knocking on the gates and gaining entry. Still Hugo waited. A few lights, high up in the building were turned on or off. Finally, a familiar face emerged from the front gates, lit a cigarette and set off down a side street. It was Hans, who operated the laundry press. Hugo relaxed. He thought it must be safe. He strolled over to the gates and knocked. The guard admitted him, so he went straight to his room. When he opened the door, he found a man wearing an unbuttoned trench coat sitting on the bed. Like a bullet to the head, he knew he would die. A moment later he recognised the man as the one he had seen running down the street earlier that evening.

"I am Rudolph Eineger. I'm a Gestapo officer. And you are … ?"

Hugo didn't know how long he had been tortured. The single, naked light bulb's insistent glare gave the only light, but it indicated neither day nor night. He lay on his back, his two wrists strapped to the head frame of a small bed somewhere in the bowels of the Gestapo building. He had had neither food nor water since his capture. He guessed that he had been in the cell for two days. During that time, five of his fingernails had been removed and most of his intestines. A blood-soaked bandage had been clumsily wrapped around his midriff, but it did little more than provide purchase for the cockroaches that were feasting on his entrails. Now he only wanted to die. He knew if he couldn't find a way to do this himself, his arm would be removed that night using a blunt knife; more than he could bare to contemplate. He had worked out how to leave the world. Now, he just required the strength to do it. But he became distracted for a moment. Suddenly feeling quite warm and calm for the first time in days, his mind drifted to a sunny place, far away. He thought he imagined the voice of a young woman talking to him; soft and sweet. Then an image rushed into his mind of a yellow flower. When he had unfolded the SS uniform in the suitcase, there had been a single yellow flower pressed between the shirt and the jacket. Klaas had guessed that a woman had packed the clothes. He had been right. Since then, Hugo had often imagined a woman's pretty hands folding the clothes. He wondered who she was and what she looked like. Since serving in the SS, he had only once experienced the kindness of a woman, whom he wasn't paying; while starving in Leningrad an old woman had given him half of her own half a loaf of bread. She grinned toothlessly at him and then shuffled away. Memories of women before the war were now less than dreams, too far away to be recalled. Now, he only had the thought of the woman in the resistance who had packed his uniform. A tremendous peace came over him, and then he found himself crying. He was only twenty years old, but now he had to do something he believed he never would. Hearing a guard opening doors in one of the corridors he knew the time had come. Using the noise outside as cover, he twisted his body painfully, so that he balanced on the edge of the bed. He put his right upper arm against his throat and then forced his weight over the side of the small bed. It rocked once. He wriggled again, and then it toppled over, forcing his whole weight onto his neck, which had itself become trapped over his outstretched arm. He already felt incredibly thirsty, but now the pain in his throat as it rasped for air overcame him. He had one last chance to think of the fields of his home in the Netherlands before he blacked out. Moments later, he died.

Adolf Hitler became incandescent when he learned that an intruder had actually been working in the Chancellery garden for three days. He immediately called for Eineger, and together they discussed what to do. On Eineger's advice, Hitler ordered the work on the Führerbunker to be continued day and night and to be completed within two weeks. He also ordered a concrete wall, fifteen feet high and five, thick, to be constructed twenty feet away from the Chancellery wall to protect the two ventilation towers and the excavations. He also sent a message to Göring demanding a crack squadron of fighters be brought immediately to Templehof airport specifically to protect the Reich Chancellery. Finally, he announced that he would leave for the Berghoff the next day and would not return until a Berlin rally, in two weeks' time.

***

Richard still felt too stiff to move the day after his accident, but on the following day he forced himself to walk to the door and call for the nurse. She felt shocked to find him teetering there, but he pushed her away and ordered her to fetch his clothes. As a military nurse she had no choice but to obey and helped him dress. She fashioned a new sling for his arm, called for a staff car and smiled as he saluted her at the door. As soon as he left the building she called for his superior to order his recall. She tried every number she could find at Stradishall but quickly found that he had no superior there.

Richard soon reached the blockhouse and found himself being fussed over by the rest of his elite squadron. They showed him a photograph of his crashed Hurricane. He couldn't believe he had escaped alive from such pile of smashed metal. What remained of its tail, intact, reared high above the ravaged soil. "Wow!" he said.

"We were goin' to visit you today, but this damned Nazi bastard insisted we fly doon to Dartmoor, like," said Razor, wryly.

"How did it go?" Richard asked dryly. His speech had lost its slur over the last twenty-four hours. The effect of the concussion and the soreness in his mouth were wearing off.

"Oh. You know. We're getting better at the turn, but nobody dares use bombs, not even the 500 pounders. He's a good pilot, like. But he's … well … ."

"He's a bloody Kraut!" cut in Todd. "We don't want to fly with him, but a Group Captain Devonshire turned up and said we 'ad to!"

"Well. I'm back, so you will be flying with me now. Where's Beattie and Fleiming?" The two ground crew were called, and Richard ordered them to make his replacement Hurricane ready for a flight.

"Who will be flying her, sir?" asked Fleiming.

"*Me!*"

Fleiming grinned. "Right you are, sir!"

"Where's Dorfmann now?" he asked his men.

"At The Black Dog, most likely." Todd looked at his feet.

"With Anna, I guess?" Nobody answered.

Within fifteen minutes, Richard had eased his arm out of his sling into a borrowed flying jacket and parachute. He had to be lifted into the cockpit of his aircraft, but he immediately felt as at home, as if he had been on his parent's old sofa before the war. The fighter responded to his thoughts as if he were in a dream. He fired up the Merlin and taxied to the end of the runway. The bumps jarred his fractured arm painfully. As soon as he became airborne, he breathed a sigh of relief.

*I can fly! They can't stop me, now!*

He did a few circuits and then set off for the coast to fire the guns. Just about to turn for home, he saw something glinting in the sun below him and to his right; a German intruder heading for home. Richard turned quickly and opened up the throttle to add 5lbs of boost, enough to keep him ahead of what he now knew to be a Junkers 88. Since it was late morning, the sun lay east of them, and he kept up-sun of the twin-engined bomber. His fuel gauge showed him to be dangerously near the limit of his range when he turned and dived on his quarry. Having no idea how much ammunition he had on board he waited until the last moment, until he could see the horrified face of the pilot, before he opened fire. Bullets ripped apart the bomber's canopy as he dived under the German aircraft. He pulled up and executed a half-Immelmann to come up behind and above the bomber for another burst. It proved unnecessary. The bomber had already begun an uncontrolled dive towards the

North Sea. He watched until he saw the mighty eruption of water as the bomber hit.

*Nobody is getting out of that alive!*

Then he turned for home.

A trawler later confirmed his kill. 700 Squadron was ecstatic. Martin hurriedly arranged a trip to The Black Dog, much to Richard's chagrin. He found out that Anna and Michael were in, but when he knocked on their doors, he heard no reply. For a moment, he thought about bursting in, even knocking down the doors, but his civil upbringing prevailed.

***

In fact, Anna had brought a Polish Jew to meet Michael. Having learned from Michael that he believed his best friend from childhood, another Jew, had been killed by the SS, Archibald had recommended the meeting at the behest of his superior. A Pole, Witold Pilecki, had been flown over from Warsaw a few days earlier, to give evidence in Whitehall of the holocaust, something not widely known at this stage of the War.

"Michael … ." Anna began in her room at The Black Dog. "Please say hello to Witold Pilecki. He has a story to tell you."

Michael reached out his hand to Witold, but the Pole refused it.

"My best friend was a Jew, and I believe he was killed … hot in Berlin, by a rogue SS officer." Michael said in his clipped, but accurate, English.

Pilecki nodded, slowly. He answered in faltering English. "He was not rogue, Herr Dorfmann. This is SS policy. They … erm do a policy of complete destruction of Jews … in camps. Death camps. I escaped from one, Auchwitz, in April. I tell you it is horrifying place."

Michael looked at him, somewhat sceptically, with one eyebrow raised. "I have heard of these camps. But nobody has seen one. I hear they are quite comfortable. People work there and are fed and looked after!"

"No. No, not true. You are naïve if you believe this."

Michael glanced at Anna. He already felt angry with Hitler. But he wasn't sure if he felt ready to hate him. She nodded, encouragingly. "Go on. Tell me what you know."

"What I *saw*. With my own *eyes*! Women and children, get off train, go into camp and divided, men and boys, healthy women to right, old people and children to left. They go to shower. But it is not shower! It is gas chamber! All are killed! All! It is terrible. Then they bodies burned. In ovens … until just bones."

"No! I don't believe it. It's not possible. Nobody … even SS are not that … barbaric!" Again, he glanced at Anna, but her she returned his gaze steadily and gave nothing away.

"Yes! Yes, they are. Animals! And they think *we* are animals!"

"And what happened to you? Did you work? How did you survive? What is the food like?"

"Food! Food. If you are lucky, you have small piece of bread and soup. Like water! Sometimes kill people for one piece of bread. Nazis don't care. They laugh! All people … how you say in English … skeletons in there. I was worker, yes. I worked in 'Canada.' Big warehouse. Choosing clothes and shoes and other things to keep. Oh my God! Watches, jewellery, even gold … what you say?" He looked at Anna for help and pointed to his mouth.

"Teeth," she ventured.

"Yes. Teeth. Even teeth!"

Michael shook his head. "No. You must be wrong."

"You think I lie? Look into my eyes, Herr Dorfmann."

Michael, slowly, reluctantly, brought his gaze to bear on the Pole's eyes. Cool and blue, they stared calmly back at him without a flicker of guilt or doubt. Michael had met many liars in the last few years. He had also met many brave men and learned how to identify the truth. He held the Pole's gaze for only a few moments and then looked down with pursed lips.

"Anna, he said quietly. I must go back to Berlin."

Suddenly the impact of the meeting dawned on Anna. They had heard an intelligence report that day, revealing that the Waffen SS agents had been caught. She had assumed replacements would be found and that Michael would still fly with Richard during the attack. Now she saw what the blonde-haired man and Archie must have seen only too clearly and now Michael too. There could be only one way left to get somebody in the bunker. Michael could do it. How naïve she had been!

"No!" she whispered. Michael reached out and clasped her hand. Then, unexpectedly, Pilecki offered Michael his hand. The German took it. As they clasped hands, Michael could feel that the Pole shook uncontrollably.

***

"Hi Archie. What's happening?" Richard picked up the receiver handed to him by Slick.

"I hear you not only survived but shot down a Junkers 88!"

"Ah well. Just wanted to prove I wasn't too badly hurt. How are things?"

"Crisis! The operation is in crisis, Richard. The briefing has been brought forward to today. 3pm. And bring Anna with you. See you there."

Martin, Anna and Richard were the last to arrive at the Whitehall meeting. During the train journey down to London, Richard had hardly spoke to Anna. At first, she smiled and tried to make conversation, but in the end, she gave up and only talked to Martin. Richard sulked.

An ominous silence met their entrance to the room with the long table. Archibald stood up.

"Gentlemen. The mission may have to be aborted. Firstly, the two Waffen SS agents have been arrested. They will be tortured. We don't know yet if they have revealed anything. We will know if the two ventilation towers move or are modified. We *do* know Hitler has changed his plans. According to intelligence reports, he left for the Berghof today. He has ordered a wall, fifteen to twenty feet high, to be built just outside the two temporary vents, and we have reason to believe work will now continue on the bunker around the clock until it is complete. There are also further intelligence reports of a fighter squadron, possibly Dorfmann's old squadron, JG26, being transferred to Templehof Airport. In short, Hitler knows pretty much what we are up to. He may not know when, and he may not yet know how."

The blonde-haired man nodded in grim approval of Archibald's speech. "Gentlemen, there are the further difficulties faced by Squadron Leader's Earlgood with the bombs which resulted in a fatal accident the other day at Stradishall. In short, the mission may not now be either achievable technically or operationally. Your views gentlemen? Glad to see you are up and about Squadron Leader Earlgood. Both of you, in fact. What is your view?" He nodded towards Richard.

Richard let out a long sigh. "Well, most of this is news to me. It's bad. I must admit, it's difficult to see how we can continue. But on the technical front, I do have one idea … . Well actually, it was Martin's. At first, I was sceptical. Martin … ?"

"Well, yes. I had the idea lying flat on my back in the ward. I only managed to run it past Richard on the way here. Basically, I wondered why we couldn't remove the undercarriage from these Hurricanes completely. They will be no use on the mission since they will be launched from the Stirlings and could probably ditch in Veluwemeer, near Elburg in the Netherlands."

"At first, I thought it was a crazy idea," added Richard. "But the more I think about it, the more sense it makes. Without the undercarriage and six guns and possibly a bit less fuel, I think we could possibly carry 750-pound bombs and make the turns. I think 1000-pounders are definitely out though." He turned to the boys from MAP. "You chaps will have to come up with smaller bombs, I'm afraid."

"Very good. Let's try it, said the blonde-haired man. How long will it take?"

"It would be better if you can remove everything to do with the undercarriage," cut in Richard. "Hydraulic lines, electrics … the lot."

"Phew," said one of the MAP men. "That could take weeks … ."

"Oh. Better just make it the main gear, then," Richard replied.

"In that case, a day! We'll get somebody at Hawker down to do it. But you know you will only be able to try it once or twice at most on a Hurri we modify. Each time it goes in the drink, which I might add is a risky do, it will have to be rebuilt. Not all of you will get to try it."

"Just let me fly it; see how it handles. My boys will be okay with that," replied Richard.

The blonde-haired man nodded to Group Captain Devonshire, who stood up and went to the screen. He pulled down a white sheet with a plan view and elevation of the Chancellery garden. He cleared his throat.

"We have been studying the implications of this wall. As you can see, it effectively blocks us from feeding gas directly into the vents. We don't think this is intentional on the enemy's part, but now if we drop the canisters outside the wall, it would be unlikely that enough of the gas would get sucked in to cause the effect we want."

"So we knock the wall down!" said Richard, impatiently.

"Well yes, precisely," replied Devonshire. "The only problem is, the only aircraft that can do it is your Hurricane. So that means we need more."

"And that means more Stirlings … ," added Martin, quietly.

"Precisely. We believe three more Hurris could do it with 500-pound bombs. The wall is unlikely to be thicker than five feet."

"But you're not sure … ," interjected Richard.

"No. No. A lot of this is guesswork. It has to be. The enemy is on to us, and now it's a game of chess. We have to out-think him if we're to succeed."

"Well. That will mean more crews and more training!" added Richard. "And how about this move of JG26. That's Focke Wulf 190s isn't it? We don't have a hope against them, encumbered as we will be by these bombs!"

Archie spoke. "We thought of that. These three new Hurricanes can carry the full complement of machine guns. Once they drop the bombs they can provide 'top cover.'"

The logic of the suggestion momentarily silenced Richard. Then he remembered another problem.

"What about the telegraph wires in Unter den Linden?"

"Ah yes. The Waffen SS agent did manage to scribble down a rough sketch of the street. We have prepared a drawing from it."

Archie handed a large sheet round the table. It showed Unter den Linden, with a number of 'x's marked on it, many joined by a thin, hatched line.

Richard looked closely at the diagram. "The 'x's are poles, the hatched lines wires, I presume? How do we deal with those?"

One of the MAP men stood up. "We've been working on a new type of bomb. It carries small, razor-sharp blades made out of tungsten steel. They will go through those wires like a knife through butter. One of the Stirlings bombing the Chancellery can fly up the street, drop a specially timed stick of these bombs, and Bob's your Uncle!"

"But the poles?"

"They will probably remain. We will mix in some blast-bombs which will take some of them down but not all."

"Hmm. Martin, you will have to select a pilot to do this."

"Of course. I will think about it."

Richard nodded. "Well that only leaves the date. When would we have to go?" asked Martin.

The blonde man stood up and walked to the diagrams on the wall, the first time he had addressed them thus. "Gentlemen. The only option we have left is to move D-day forward to 20th August when we know Hitler has to attend a rally glorifying the Reich in Berlin. He has been planning it for a year, and he simply would not cancel this. We believe … ."

A stunned silence fell in the room for a moment before the man began to speak. Then both Richard and Martin shouted together:

"20th August!"

"Yes. That is the only way. Any later, and the bunker will be finished, the vents replaced. Earlier and Hitler won't be there." He let -the information sink in.

It took Richard a moment to gather his thoughts sufficiently to say anything. "Well, for one thing, there is no way we can train all the new crews, modify the Hurris, get enough practice with these canisters and be ready to fly on the 20th August! That's just 15 days! And even if we could, who is going to open the vents?"

"Squadron Leader Earlgood. Are you telling us, that we cannot achieve what we are asking for on this mission?" asked the blonde-haired man. Suddenly Richard sensed the whole political will of Whitehall in the voice of the man addressing him.

"No sir. I am not saying that." He stood up and addressed the whole room. "We will do it. We will find a way to do it. Give me the men and equipment, and we will get the gas near the vents."

"Very well," the blonde man replied, curtly. "I have another question for you. Until today, we had thought it possible that we could select one of your pilots to lead this operation, that is, if you were not willing. Now, I am not sure we have that option."

"Are you ordering me to lead it?"

"No. I have no military rank, and therefore I don't have that authority." He nodded to Group Captain Devonshire.

"We would prefer you to volunteer," the Group Captain said.

"I don't see anybody else that can do it," replied Richard.

"Then, as you say … ," continued the blonde-haired man. "There is still the question of the vents. Anna?"

Richard looked down at the table as Anna spoke in her quiet, but controlled, manner.

"Last night I arranged a meeting in The Black Dog pub between Michael and a Polish Jew who had escaped from a concentration camp. Michael was very touched by it. I have never seen him so emotional. After the man left, he was very angry and then almost cried. He wants to go to Berlin. He wants to try and get into the bunker, posing as an escaped war hero!" She lifted her eyes, and Richard could see they were brimming with tears. Now he felt so guilty for his early mood that he could not take his eyes from her. She glanced at him, and a moment of electric emotion rippled through them both. It made Richard want to cry out.

"So gentlemen … . There you have it. We now have a volunteer to get into the bunker. And what is *more*, he's much more likely to succeed than his predecessors."

"But can we trust him?" said Richard. He immediately regretted his question.

"Anna trusts him," said the blonde man. "And in any case, we have no choice. The mission has got to go *ahead*. There is a slim chance that, even if he cannot open the vents, the gas might still find a way in through the excavations."

"Of course, we need to give him something to return with as a prize, to make damned certain he will be awarded a medal by Hitler himself. If we time it right, that will be the day we launch the attack. Dorfmann will be able to give us twenty-four hours warning ahead of this date. The prize … . We think we should allow him to escape in a Spitfire, a new Model … . Or at least that's what we want the Germans to think. The MAP boys are working on this now."

Both the MAP boys grinned mischievously and nodded.

"So there you have it. We go … on the 20th August. Gentlemen. This will be the last briefing but one before the mission. You all have jobs to do. Now are there any final questions?"

"I have one," asked Martin. Can we look at that map again, the one of Europe?

Archibald pulled down the large map. Martin strode to it, beckoning Richard to join him. "If we now have twelve Stirlings and Hitler is expecting us we are going to have the whole *damned* Luftwaffe after us all the way from the Netherlands to Berlin! Especially when they see these strange looking aircraft! We have to come up with a better plan for the route. What are these mountains here?" He pointed to a small range of mountains running roughly in a line to the south east, only a few hundred miles from Berlin.

"The Harz Mountains," said Archibald. "Geography was my strong subject at school," he added, grinning.

"Right. How high are they?"

"I don't know, but I do remember they have some pretty tricky gorges, deep, with lots of bends."

"Hm. What do you say Richard?"

"I see what you are getting at. If necessary, we could slip into those and get lost. Even Focke Wulf 190s would have a hard time getting the bead of a site on us in there. Trouble is, we will probably all end up flying into a mountain ourselves. Archie, can you find out more about these gorges; how many and how deep; how wide?"

"We will get Air Intelligence on to it right away. A Mossie can fly over and get some detailed pictures."

"While you're at it, we need regular updated photographs of the Chancellery back garden."

"Of course. There are regular flights by high-flying Mossies over Berlin, every week I believe. We can't do it more regularly than that or it will raise suspicions."

"One last question," said Martin, sitting down.

"Go on," said the blonde-haired man.

"What does this gas actually do?"

"I can't tell you that. It's Top Secret. Not even Archie here knows. But you will be told when you return. If that is the last question, I have one last point to make. Not a word of any of this to Dorfmann. He has agreed to fly back to Germany posing as an escaped prisoner. He will attempt to get into the bunker and tell us when he's there. He will leave in the next few days, and the less he knows the better, both for him and for us. Gentlemen, the attack will go ahead. This meeting is ended."

***

# Chapter Seven

zgahinkt faxaiqmkmkhkt untk kotkt Vrgt lax jkt
Bkxyzuyymkmkt LK

The little, blue aircraft dropped out of the sun and floated down on to the long airstrip at Audembert. It touched down lightly and bouncing once. A few mouldering transport aircraft sat forlornly in one corner of the airfield; Dorfmann's old airstrip had become almost disused now. Mainly used by high-ranking Nazi commanders who needed to fly to Berlin occasionally, a few Fiesler Storchs and Bf 108s were lined up on its apron for this purpose. One single FW 190 sat rusting to their right. Michael Dorfmann taxied over to a spot near the control tower and cut the engine of the Spitfire.

A single refuelling bowser rumbled out to meet him.

"Wow! A Spitfire! Have you captured it?" said the young German driver.

"You might say that, yes. It's the very latest prototype. Can I use the telephone?"

Within minutes, not only JG26, now based in Berlin, but the whole Luftwaffe and the staff of the German high command in Berlin knew of Dorfmann's achievement. He requested his own ground crew be sent to Audembert. After they had arrived by air, and he had been debriefed by the Luftwaffe, he had been feted by the local dignitaries. Gunther had been particularly enamoured of his new charge.

"With the new bubble canopy! First I have seen! What is she then?" he asked.

Michael ran his hands affectionately over the sleek Spitfire's nose. "An Mk XV. She's a prototype."

"How the hell did you manage it?"

"It's a long story. I'll tell you later."

In fact, the Spitfire was a plain MkXVI but modified to take the new bubble canopy. Supermarine had experimented with this canopy on various models for the past two years. Several prototype MkXVIs had been built with one over a year before, but the production run had started using the standard canopy.

The Spitfire in front of Gunther had been in service for almost a year. Michael had an inkling of this but had not asked questions when he had been shown the aircraft.

That evening he had been ordered to catch the train for Berlin. He would be accompanied by a Gestapo officer and two SS soldiers. In Berlin he would be given a more thorough debriefing, before arrangements for his inevitable awarding of an Iron Cross, First Class would be made. Insofar as his original secret mission seemed to have been needlessly abandoned, some of the German Intelligence found his story hard to believe.

On the train, Michael had time to think about the previous few days. Events had moved like a whirlwind after the meeting with the Polish Jew in The Black Dog.

The very next day he had met with Richard for the last time. He and Anna had visited Stradishall and, as the sun went down, they took a stroll out to the airfield perimeter.

"Remember last time … that heron?" said Michael, laughing. "It's a sign of luck, I think."

"No, I think that's a stork," replied Richard.

"Ah … storch. No … I'm sure it's a heron. In my country anyway."

"No. It can't be. Oh well, anyway, it doesn't matter."

Richard noticed Michael's hand brushing against Anna. It made him hot with jealousy, but then he remembered how wrongly he had judged Anna only a few days before and what danger Michael would soon face. His jealousy became aroused again when Michael put his arm around Anna's shoulders, and she did not pull away.

Richard stepped close to her and smelled the aroma of Pears soap again. He felt like punching Michael. "So which of us is most likely to come back alive?" he blurted.

"Ha! I would say you are. There is no hope for me. If I can succeed in the mission, I will most likely be shot, or something worse. But many men have tried to do it. Perhaps I will succeed. I will try and stay alive, and then I will win the heart of my Anna." He kissed her lightly on the cheek. She blushed, looking down.

"Well, if we both survive, she's going to have to choose, isn't she?"

"Now listen boys. It's no good bickering. You may think a woman can't handle relationships with more than one man at the same time, but I can assure you I *can*. So if that's the way it's going to be, that *is* the way it's going to be."

Both Michael and Richard were stunned into a silence. As Anna walked ahead, grumpily, they held back.

"You know it's highly unlikely we're both going to get back," Michael continued. "She's one hell of a woman."

"Yes. Whoever does come back will have won her." Richard kicked a stone and watched it skip along the concrete surface of the taxi-way.

"And you know what … she will be loyal to him for the rest of her life."

Both men avoided each other's eyes. Later they went for a last drink at The Black Dog. Richard didn't invite the rest of the squadron. The only moment of note came when Richard asked Michael if he missed his fellow pilots in JG26.

"Some, yes. Most, no. The ones I miss are the ones who I've known the longest with one exception."

"Oh? Who's that?"

"Voss. Gunther Voss."

"Why? What's he like?"

Michael sucked in his breath through pursed lips. "You don't want to meet *him*! Good pilot and natural killer. Ruthless! He has thirty-eight kills. More than *me*!"

"Tell me about him."

"We first flew together on the Russian Front. But I never liked him. He was an accountant before the War, or at least training to be one. I never was sure; he didn't encourage conversation. There is a coldness about him. He talks about his kills as if they are entries in a ledger, no emotion at all. I can't be like that. Even though I'm glad I have shot down so many British aircraft, I always think about the pilots who didn't get out. I'm always glad when I see a parachute. Gunther is not like that. If you see him, watch out. He always has a black cat holding a bomb, you know, one of those theatrical bombs; round with a big fuse, on the nose of his aircraft. Usually he's number seven. All Jagdgeschwader 26 aircraft have a gothic 'S' painted on a white shield."

"So why did you keep him?"

"When I came back to JG26? Simply because he was good."

After the drinks, a staff car arrived to take Michael and Anna to the station. After Anna and kissed him and squeezed his hand before climbing into the back seat of the car, Richard couldn't think what to say to Michael. Instead he just offered his hand, at last looking the German in the eye. Michael smiled, and Richard relaxed.

"Good luck, Michael."

"Good luck to you too, Tommy. You won't need quite as much as me!"

"No. I dare say. We're all depending on you. The whole squadron."

With that, Michael turned and climbed into the back seat of the car.

***

Fleiming's last words, before closing the Hurricane's canopy, rang in Richard's ears.

"Are you sure you're ready for this, sir?"

"The arm's a bit stiff, but I shot down a Ju 88, didn't I?"

"I didn't mean the arm sir, I meant your eyes. They're bloodshot, sir. When did you last get a proper night's sleep?"

Now he found himself approaching Rochester on top of the Short Stirling. The dawn sun's reflection on the port wing dazzled him and hurt his eyes. He had never felt so tired in his life.

*Am I safe flying this thing? Probably not. Has to be done, though.*

"Ready for release, Richie." Martin's voice came over the VHF radio. Martin piloted a Stirling for the first time since the crash, but he flew the bomber smoothly. Michael saw the Thames Estuary sparkling like a ribbon of glittering silk on the horizon ahead.

"Ready." Richard went through his last checks and then fired up the Merlin. He raised the revs to 1800 and set the boost to 6 lbs. He waited.

"In thirty seconds," said Martin. "Four, three, two, one … ."

There were four metallic bangs as the bolts in the pylons released. The Hurricane drifted slightly above the Stirling, and then Richard pushed the engine to full revs. The fighter climbed away from the bomber and flicked to the left to do a circuit around the Rochester factory. Richard wanted to reconnoiter the ditching site as thoroughly as possible. He dropped down to just above the waves of the estuary. It was a glorious morning, and a white Short Sunderland parked on the bank to his right shone in the sun. The little waves on the river were like ripples of silvered blue metal, constantly shimmering and shifting in the dawn light.

*Looks calm enough.*

The Hawker engineers had stripped out the undercarriage from an old Hurricane Mark I and shipped it down to Stradishall. There they also fitted it with buoyancy tanks instead of fuel tanks in the wings and an inflatable raft. This would pop out of a compartment under the nose of the fighter automatically when the aircraft ditched. At the last moment, they decided to remove the guns too, nervous that the raft and buoyancy tanks would not keep the fighter afloat long enough to be recovered. This aircraft would be the only one available for a test ditching of the fighter before the mission, and Richard would use it. His first impression was that the aircraft felt much lighter on the controls. The fighters for the mission would only have two guns each, so this aircraft would be a good match for that final configuration. Only the bombs were missing. Richard avoided the temptation to try some aerobatics with such an old aircraft, but he felt heartened by its light and nimble responsiveness.

"A-Apple to Tiger control. Are all your recovery vehicles in place?"

"Tiger control to A-Apple. Affirmative. We're all ready for you. What's the wind like out there?"

"Steady and from the East, I think. I will set the trim slightly to compensate, but I don't think it will be a problem. I'm more worried about her digging in!" Richard looked to his right as he beat up the river one last time, ten feet above the waves. Four launches, two with RAF roundels on the hulls, were slowly moving towards the lane, marked out with buoys where he had to ditch. He lifted the nose of the Hurricane and went around one last time. This time he flew a lot further east before turning and lining up with the river. As he slowly dropped lower he saw the first marker buoy coming up under the nose.

"A-Apple to Tiger control. This will be it. Please don't leave me in the water. I can't hold my breath *that long*!"

"Tiger control. Understood. Don't forget to open your hood."

*Damn! Forgot that. That's a bad sign!*

Richard opened the canopy and slid it back as far as it would go. He checked his harness had been tightened enough and then throttled back. The aircraft floated slowly down to just above the wave-lets. At the last moment he banked slightly to the left and lifted the nose as the pilot's manual recommended.

*I wonder if anyone's ever done this and survived!*

Because of its belly-mounted radiator, the Hurricane was singularly ill-equipped for ditching; one of its few weaknesses. Richard's heart leaped into his mouth as he felt the left wing touch the water. A sharp jolt slammed him forward in the harness. This time nothing hit his head, but the little fighter slewed round to the left before settling into the water. The sudden deceleration almost jolted Richard's fillings out of his teeth. He had expected the fighter to spin on the surface of the waves, but, in fact, it had come to almost dead stop straight away. Now he could hear the sound of the raft inflating and water rushing into the fuselage beneath the foot wells.

He punched the harness release on his chest. He had to hit it twice before it released. He stood on his seat and looked around him.

"Over here, mate! We can't get any closer. Catch!" A man threw a length of rope while perched on the front of a launch, only thirty feet away.

Richard grabbed it. He climbed out onto the wing of the fighter, where his feet were washed by the cold water. Shortly after, a dinghy chugged up and barged against the wing. Richard stepped into the dingy.

*Safe!*

The nose of the fighter began to slip beneath the waves. Two other dinghies secured ropes around the tail and attached buoyancy floats to the wings with more rope. Richard sat on the deck of the launch, watching as the launch crew secured the Hurricane and then towed it to the dock.

"Three cheers for Richard!" went up a cry as the launch pulled alongside the dock. All of 700 Squadron lined up, bomber crews and all, to welcome Richard ashore.

"All hail the conquering hero!" shouted Martin, striding up to clasp his brother. "That was impressive. You may be one of the first ever to ditch a Hurricane successfully. Your boys thought you were going to die!"

"Yeah. Well I wasn't so sure I wouldn't. I need a pint. I'm shaking like a leaf."

In the nearest pub, Richard talked them through the ditching.

"She's not so bad in flight. I mean she's pretty close to what we will end up with, almost identical once we've dropped the canisters, or bombs … whatever you want to call them. Turns on a penny and light as a feather. A bit touchy perhaps, but you'll get used to that. Probably more like a 109. Michael would have loved her … ."

"But what about the ditching, like?" asked Razor.

"Well. Not as bad as I thought. Like the manual says, you just dip a wing just before touch down … she turns once … . But I was expecting a cartwheel. I guess I just did it right. If you overdo the turn, she will cut right in, and then it will be painful."

Two crew from the one of the launches came in accompanied by some engineers from Short. The two crewmen doffed their caps at Richard.

"Brave man," said one of them.

"We heard about your escapade. We also heard that n most fighters it would be nothing, to do it intentionally in a Hurricane … that's something else. I want to shake your hand." He came over and put a large, oily ham of a hand in Richard's.

"Well, we better get back soon," Richard said, ruefully. "We have the new crews arriving this afternoon. I'm not looking forward to briefing them. It's going to be a steep learning curve. Too steep, I fear."

"They'll be fine," said Martin, patting his brother on the back.

They caught a transport aircraft back from Rochester airport to Stradishall.

***

The briefing room at Stradishall thrummed, crowded with twelve Stirling crews and seven fighter pilots. Sitting quietly in the corner of the stage, from where Richard now spoke, the Station Medical Officer surveyed the faces below him disdainfully. Most of his audience pulled furiously on cigarettes producing a blue haze which floated above them.

"Now, for a lot of you this is your first briefing with 700 Squadron, so a deeply heartfelt welcome!" There were boos and hisses from the core members of the squadron.

"Sh … Let me just introduce you all first. Please stand up when your names are called. First, the new Hurri p- … Hurricane pilots"

"Hurris will do!" shouted out Todd.

"Thank you Todd. Good to know you're awake! For the new Hurri pilots we have Johann W Grutsberger, Known as Grutsy to all and sundry and a Canadian." A dark-haired man with a big black beard and moustache stood up and stared solemnly at those in the room. "Eugene Blalock … . An American … Baseball player, isn't that right Eugene?" A very tall, well-built man with black hair stood up.

"That's right, sir!" He grinned pleasantly and turned through a full circle.

"And last, but not least, Frank Lenoit!"

"Bonjoir Monsieurs! Et Madames!" announced a shortish man, wearing an oily red silk tie around his neck, which he swore to all brought him good luck.

Everyone in the room looked around eagerly for the mentioned females. None were to be seen. Guffaws of laughter broke out.

Of the new Hurricane pilots, Richard only knew Lenoit personally, although all the pilots had come recommended as experienced and able pilots. Richard winked quickly at Lenoit, who smiled back warmly.

"Thank you gentlemen. And now the Stirling pilots. You can meet their crews later. But for now … the pilots. First there are the three aircraft that will carry the support Hurricanes – Hurris. Joseph Mitten … ." A small, shy man stood up and nodded. "When we have finished painting Joe's aircraft you will see six kills on its nose. Isn't that right Joe?"

"Six and a half, actually," Mitten said, quietly. The room immediately hushed in reverence to hear anything more he might say.

"Almost as many as my seven!" added Richard, seeing the awkwardness of the new pilot. "Then there is David Evergreen."

A lanky man stood up and announced in a Scottish brogue, "Aye! That's me!"

"And finally, Roger Oakly." To a large round of applause, a blonde, tousle-haired man stood up, waved a pipe at everybody and swivelled through a full circle, grinning mischievously.

Richard went on to introduce the six support Stirling pilots who were to drop bombs on the Chancellery. Finally, he introduced the existing pilots in 700 Squadron.

"Now, 700 Squadron has been training intensively for a mission to bomb a very small and specific target a long way away. To do this, we are going to use Hurricanes and Short Stirlings. At this point, I can't tell you the route, target or any other details. What I can tell you is that we will be practicing at a location on Dartmoor which has been modelled to closely resemble the real target. Some of you may even recognise it. If you do, keep mum. This is a top-secret mission, and we cannot reveal anything to anyone outside this room except a few individuals known to me. Security has been tight at Stradishall so far, but now we have more of you it's going to be tightened even more!" Jeers and laughter met this. "The lead group of three composites, with Martin and myself as leader, will be Red Section. The other composites will be led by JW Grutsberger and will be Blue Section. The six Stirlings bombing the Reich Chancellery will be Green Section. You will all have VHF radios and can keep in touch on pre-set frequencies which will change using a timer. You will be in contact with Martin who will have three sets. He will be coordinating things, like HQ if you like, but relaying things to me. Most of the decisions will be made by me, and when necessary Martin can patch me through to all of you. By the way, you won't even know the radio frequencies. This is to keep the enemy foxed and keep security tight. Neat little idea, that!"

There were nods of approval from the audience.

"One other thing. If any of you bomber crews get hit and you know you cannot maintain your height, drop your Hurricane. That way at least both of you will have a chance. And Hurri pilots, if things get really thick on the way there, I may ask you to start your engines. Let them tick over at 1500 revs, in case you have to make that hasty departure. Now, you're all volunteers … ."

"No, we're bloody not!" shouted one, lone American voice.

Richard looked for the source. "Blalock … . You *were* asked if you wanted to volunteer?"

"Like hell we were. We have just come to the end of our tour, and we were told we had to do this mission. They said you were short of crews … ."

"Oh no! That's not right. Well, we shall have to replace you. And I will have a word with your squadron C/O. I specifically asked for volunteers. This is going to be a tough mission … ."

Blalock's crew went into a huddle. For some minutes an intense discussion went on while Richard looked on. Suddenly, Blalock's head emerged, grinning.

"It's alright skip. Now we're here we may as well do the damned thing! We were told anyway; if we completed it, if we survived, we could do the next tour at a training school!"

There were cheers from the audience.

"Oh well … . That's fine!" added Richard. "Now, where was I?"

"You can't tell us *anything*!" said some joker from the bomber crews.

"Right! But what I can tell you is that you will be flying night and day for the next week, so that you can get this right. Take a look at this!" He pulled down a large diagram, identical to the one in Whitehall, of the mock city street layout on Dartmoor. "This is what you'll be practicing on. You fly down here, turn into this … corridor here, fly along it, bank around to here and drop your bombs here. We have marked out a 15 feet high wall, the most likely height, here. You three new Hurri boys will have to blow that apart before the rest of us can lay some special bombs just inside. This all has to be done at between ten and twenty feet. I'm told you all have some experience of low flying. Now the tricky part is this turn here; we've tried lots of techniques for getting around it, but only one works." Richard went on to explain the technique Michael had taught him for negotiating the turn.

"You already have been instructed in take-off and launching from the Stirlings. Later I will brief you on ditching the Hurris. Because as you may not know yet, they won't have any undercarriage."

There was a sharp intake of breath from the audience. It created an eerie hum like a wind.

"It's a very steep learning curve. Now I must confess … ." Richard paused for a moment, and the audience hushed, sensing things were becoming very serious. "When I was told I had to train an extra three bomber crews and three fighter pilots, I thought it would be impossible in the time left. This is a very dicey operation. In my opinion, even the most experienced, skilful and well-practiced among us has less than a 50/50 chance of coming back." He paused again to let that sink in. "But if you new boys do exactly as I say and follow the lead of the existing members of 700 Squadron, ask them as many questions as you like and listen to their answers, you have a slim chance of coming back. I wish I can say more than that but I won't lie to you."

"Gibson's lot did an incredible job on the Dams Raid. They didn't turn the tide of war, but they did deal a mighty blow to Jerry. If *we* succeed, we *will* turn the tide of war. Now if any of you wish to drop out, now is the time to do so. Just hand your names in to the secretary on the desk outside or post a note, and no questions will be asked. There will be no shame in turning down this mission." He looked at the serious faces watching him. All looked rapt. None turned away.

"Gentlemen, we have about nine days to get this down pat. The first practice mission is for Hurri pilots only, take off in thirty minutes. In three days-time, if you're ready, you'll take off on the back of a Stirling."

With that, his audience stood up one by one, and a murmur broke out. Richard stepped over to this brother.

"How did I do?"

"Fine. You're becoming a real leader."

"Yeah! I was scared like hell! I had to lean on the table to keep on my feet! Do you think they swallowed it?"

"Swallowed what? You gave them the truth. We *can* succeed, and some of them *may* survive. *May* … ."

***

The practice on Dartmoor quickly became chaotic. The new Hurricane pilots could not make the turn after being shown the way by Todd, Slick and Razor. Even after six attempts each they still could not do it although on the last attempt, Lenoit came close.

"We will do it next time, Monsieur Earlgood!" he said with typical French bon-vive. The new pilots were flying with dummy 250lb bombs. Combined with the weight of the undercarriage, this roughly approximated the weight they would fly with on the mission. The other pilots now flew not with dummy bombs, but the original sacks of flour. This gave them the all-up weight they would have on the mission. Richard, Todd and Razor turned the walls of the mock-up Chancellery white, while they derided Slick for missing the target and hitting the replica of the new wall.

"That won't be there, like, on the day, man!" Razor quipped.

"You hope!" Grutsberger replied.

That night, the area on Stradishall, around the 700 Squadron hanger, thrummed with activity. Without enough space for the new bombers in the hangar, the space behind it had been requisitioned for the purpose. The RAF Battalion furiously engaged in building thirty-foot perimeter walls around the space to enclose the first new modified Stirling, due to arrive that night. Hawker had sent ten of their best engineers down to assist, and these were joined by a similar number from Short. Richard and Martin looked on bemused.

"It's like a bloody ant's nest!" the older brother mused.

"Yes. It's getting to be a very big operation. It scares me, being responsible for this lot."

"Not *dying*, then? Ha! Ha!"

"I haven't had time to think about that. There is a lot riding on it now. I wonder how Michael's getting on."

***

"It's a very pretty aircraft, Hauptmann Oberleutnant Michael Dorfmann. Perhaps not as unique as you seem to believe it is, but we'll come back to that later. Would you mind telling me how you *acquired* it?"

"It's all in the report I submitted yesterday."

"But I would like to hear it from *you* … . And in as much detail as you can manage."

Michael didn't like the supercilious tone in the Gestapo officer's voice when he said the word 'manage.'

"Do you mind if I smoke?"

"No, please. Go ahead." The Gestapo officer leaned forward, into the cone of light given out by the desk lamp, and offered up a silver, cigarette lighter to the cigarette between Michael's lips. The young German pilot took a long drag on the cigarette, letting the nicotine wash over him, soothing him, before beginning. He had heard that insofar as the Gestapo were very cynical men, flattery could not work and would probably get an adverse reaction. Therefore, best way to lie to them was to seem more cynical than them.

"The hypnotism worked, as planned. I went to the safe house, but they were watching it. Naturally, I had to be cautious. It wasn't easy getting away, even once. I had to leave a woman, Anna, in Harrods to get there. Another chance … ."

"Ah yes. Anna. I have read your file. I know all about her. A very intelligent woman, who now works for the British Intelligence, does she not?"

"Yes. All part of the plan."

"Yes, I have spoken to the Intelligence officer who planned this with you. The Führer doesn't trust him … ."

"As I said, another chance didn't come up immediately. And then I became aware that Anna was trying … wanted to recruit me as a double-agent. This was what we wanted, so I went along with it." Michael paused, not knowing what reaction he would get.

"And what was the inducement?"

Michael smiled ironically to himself. "Ah. Well, you're a man of the *world* … Have you ever loved a woman, given her up and then wanted her back?"

"No. No, I don't think I have. But you were pretending? In reality you're loyal to the Führer?"

"Yes, but Anna was the inducement." Here was Michael's lie. "Not love. I simply wanted her. But of course, I told them that I hated Adolf Hitler and wanted him dead."

"You're lying! Why would they believe you?"

"They organised a meeting … with an escaped prisoner."

"Prisoner?"

A cold chill ran down Michael's back. But he also felt a thrill. "From a Juden concentration camp. He said that men, women and children were being gassed, put to death, as soon as they arrive."

Michael caught the glint of fear in the Gestapo officer's eyes through a weak smile. "But that is complete *nonsense*! You must know *that*! They are treated with respect!"

"No. I believe him. I know a lie when I see it." The fear suddenly became openly visible in the eyes of the man sitting opposite Michael. The man arched forward.

"You must not speak of this. Are you insane! It's treason to talk of this! To believe it will bring your own death!"

"So it's true, then." Michael nodded slowly to himself.

"I … I cannot say. It may be true. No … no, it's not true. But even to speak of *it*!" The Gestapo man stood up and paced around the room. He clearly had become flustered. He called for coffee and then changed his mind. He called for two cups of coffee.

"Please … drink. It's the real thing. Let's forget about that whole thing we just spoke about. So … they believed your little story, and you agreed to work for them. But where does the Spitfire come in?"

"That's easy. They simply wanted to test me. They took me to Biggin Hill and showed me that brand new prototype. They asked me if I wanted to fly it, I said yes, and so I took it up. Of course, I guessed that the tanks were almost empty of fuel. It was only ten minutes, and they sent another pilot to watch me."

"Yes, yes. But why not an ordinary Spitfire? Why did they risk you crashing the, as you call it, latest model?"

"I don't know. Perhaps they thought I would not risk my life to escape with an ordinary Spitfire. But I think they wanted me to compare it with the FW 190 … to tell them where it was better and where, worse." This was the weakest part of Michael's story, and he had to steal himself to silence when he finished speaking. The last phrase hung in the air like a chimera. He was sure his interrogator would pick holes in his statement. But after a long while, the Gestapo man nodded slowly and closed the file in front of him.

"Of course, you know the aircraft is, in fact, probably a modified Mk IX?"

"No. I don't think so. It's much later than that. I expect the experts will soon confirm that it *is* a prototype."

"Well. We will see. In the mean-time, you will stay in the Esplanade Hotel; all expenses paid. We have a few more checks to do, but I don't suppose there will be any problems. In a few days I will write to the secretary to the Führer's under-secretary and recommend the awarding of a medal for you. I expect it will be the Iron Cross with Oak Leaves this time. Stay out of trouble. If you are going to enjoy a woman, be discrete. Personally, I enjoy blondes. Good day, Hauptmann Oberleutnant."

"Thank you."

***

It was the 14<sup>th</sup> August. Michael Dorfmann had been in Berlin six days. The White Rose had passed on the location of the drop box in Marienstraße to British Intelligence. The young German pilot had to leave a coded message indicating the date and time of his medal award ceremony, but he couldn't get there. He knew there were spies in the Esplanade Hotel, and as soon as he stepped outside, there would be an anonymous looking black sedan waiting on a street corner. Frequently a man would follow him for several blocks before another took over; a pattern he had been taught to recognise. He had tried every technique he knew to shake them, but none had worked.

'The British will think I'm dead!' he mused as he put on a raincoat to leave the hotel once more.

This time he waited until the very last moment before hopping on a passing tram. The tram sped on, and at first, he thought he had lost his tail. Then he noticed the familiar black sedan following him. He hopped off opposite a large department store and ran in. He used the stairs to get to the top floor, the men's outdoor wear section, and pointed to a deerstalker hat, tweed coat, jodhpurs and shiny boots.

"I will be back in five minutes. I'm a thirty-eight-inch chest, shoes size forty-two," he told the attendant, showing his Luftwaffe Officer papers. The attendant nodded sceptically but

Michael knew the man would have little choice but to obey such a high-ranking officer.

Michael went to the toilet and came back five minutes later. The attendant handed over a large paper bag full of cardboard boxes, and Michael handed him two hundred Reichmarks. At any moment he expected a hand on the shoulder. He guessed the tail would be working his way up the floors and would have left a driver to watch the front entrance. Michael went back to the toilet and changed quickly. Then he took the stairs back to the ground floor and walked out through the revolving door with the deerstalker pulled low over his face. He turned right and walked casually along the pavement, swinging the bag which now contained his old suit. He turned right at the first opportunity and then left at the next turning. He continued in this zigzag fashion for thirty minutes. At last he felt sure he had lost his tail. He then caught a tram in the general direction of Marienstraße and walked the rest of the way. He quickly dropped two boxes of matches in the grey metal letterbox. One contained twenty broken matches, indicating the twentieth day of the month. The other contained five matches, indicating 5pm, the time he had been told he would be meeting Adolf Hitler in the Chancellery. As British Intelligence well knew, Hitler never rose in the morning. Michael quickly left and worked his way back to the Esplanade Hotel in Bellevuestraße, just south of the Tiergarten. A call on the room telephone half an hour later, from the Gestapo officer who had interrogated him, had been designed to do two things; make sure he still remained in the hotel and remind him they were observing him. The cold voice also said, "Do you expect to go hunting, Herr Dorfmann?"

"I was thinking about it during my leave; yes."

There followed a long silence on the other end of the line. "Very well. Good luck if you do. There is not much left to hunt in Germany these days. Only men."

With that cold riposte, the line went dead. Michael found himself sweating when he replaced his receiver.

***

"Let's talk." Richard waited, holding the telephone receiver firmly to his ear, to hear what Archibald Gates would suggest.

"I'll drive up this evening. We can talk over a meal. Fix something up at that pub of yours. I'll pay."

"Fine." Richard thought Archibald sounded tired and strained. British Intelligence had heard from the White Rose that Michael would be meeting Adolf Hitler on the 20th August at 5pm, as expected.

Archibald had just told this to Richard, who then replied, "Two days! It's too close. We'll never make it! The new crews are only half trained. They will be cannon-fodder if we go then!"

Unexpectedly, Archibald arrived with Anna. Richard led their car to The Black Dog from the station in his little Austin.

"Remember this?" Richard asked Anna, opening the door for her and pointing to the Austin.

"Ha! Yes. We had some good fun in it. How's Jackie?"

"He's all better now. I'm toying with the idea of releasing him. If I come back alive, I think that will be the time to do it."

They each remained silent for the rest of the drive.

"How is Michael doing?" Richard asked Anna, who had sat beside him.

"I don't know. He must have still been alive two days ago. That's a good sign."

Richard shook his head. "It's an almost impossible task. I mean what the hell is he supposed to do once he even gets inside the bunker, *if* he can get inside it?"

"That's up to him, Richard," replied Archibald, leaning over Richard's shoulder from the back seat. "He seems like a resourceful fellow. We just have to hope … . Apparently, he's a big hero. The German newspapers are full of stories about his exploits with that Spitfire, apparently!"

"You look tired, Archie. Things getting a bit rough in Whitehall?"

"You could say that. Winnie went bonkers when he heard of the new plan. It won't be good for any of us if we mess this up."

"Great! Well, frankly, there's not much chance of us getting it *right*!"

"Don't say that, Richard," Anna pleaded, clutching his sleeve in her gloved hand.

"How are things going at Stradishall?" asked Archibald later in the pub, as his plate of lamb arrived.

"Great! You should see it. It's like some unearthly dockland. Cranes everywhere! Everywhere I look, I see bits of Hurricanes and one hanging from a crane. If there are any German spies around, they must know something is up by now. The rest of Stradishall can hardly miss it either! Late at night, if you are high up enough, you can see everything lit up like an open-air factory!"

"Yes, security has been a problem. The closer we get to the day, the more I think this is a mad idea. And I'm to blame!"

"No, it's not that. The idea itself is sound, it's just the timing. We don't have enough time. I gave the whole squadron the day off today, because we have been flying day and night for a week. They are all exhausted. It's a minor bloody miracle we haven't had any deaths already, in the air anyway. A mechanic died the other day when a bomb broke loose from its cradle and fell on him; another death I feel personally responsible for."

"What does Martin think?"

"He agrees with me. Can't we have just one more week?"

"Can't be done. Hitler is skittish. Intelligence reports are that he will stay in Berlin for a few days and then will go on some kind of tour. Nobody knows where. If we don't do it now, the opportunity will be lost." Until this moment, Archibald had avoided Richard's eyes. Now he put his knife and fork neatly beside his plate and looked directly at the Squadron Leader. "Richard. We both knew the enormity of the task when we took it on. Only you had the skills to do it. There have been enormous problems, and you've found a way through them all. Only you could have done that, I believe. There is so much at stake now. We just have to get it done!"

Richard saw a look, almost like pleading, in Archibald's eyes. At that moment, the two men became friends. Richard smiled. "Okay Archie. If there is no other way, we will do *it*. Even if there *is* such a small chance of any of us coming back."

The conversation turned to small talk after that and Richard only noticed later that Anna had been holding his arm for some time. He put his around her, and she leaned into him.

"Turn the music up!" shouted a voice in the lounge. Big band music had been playing softly for some time. Now the sound of Glenn Miller's 'In the Mood' blasted out of the speakers.

"Fancy a dance?" Richard asked Anna.

"Yes! Let's!"

They danced until pub closing time while Archibald smoked, watching them and grinning when he caught their eye. Anna even persuaded him to dance with her once, but he wasn't a good dancer, and his over-large feet stepped on hers too often. The last orders bell rang. Richard and Anna were holding each other close in a slow dance.

Archibald touched Richard on the shoulder. "I have go to back to London. Listen, can we step outside for a moment where it's quiet?"

"Of course."

Outside, the evening air had begun to bite.

"Cold for August! I just wanted to say, Richard … that I wish I were going with you. I would give anything to be a fighter pilot. But I just don't have it in me, you know."

A red-mist came over Richard's eyes. But he no longer felt angry with Archibald. "It's terrible, Archie. Shooting down a German fighter; it's like a drug. You can't get enough of seeing the bits flying off it. But then you see the pilot … ." Archibald touched him lightly on the shoulder and climbed into the staff car.

Anna and Richard danced on and only broke apart when the 'last orders' bell rang.

"I didn't book a room!" whispered Anna in Richard's ear.

"Let me ask. Excuse me. Do you have any rooms available?"

"Ah Squadron Leader Earlgood! Or one of them to be precise! How are you? Yes, we have two room actually. If my memory serves me, we have the same room the lady had last time!"

"We'll take that one then."

"Right! Let me just get the keys."

"Do you think they know?" Anna whispered, like a little mischievous girl, as they climbed the stairs.

"Know what?"

"That you were in my room last time?"

"Oh. I don't know. Who cares?"

Anna took his hand and led him into the room, which felt cold. They lay together on the bed while the log fire slowly heated the room.

"You are so serious," she said, poking his nose. "Is it that bad?"

"Yes. It's tomorrow and we're not ready!" he said. They were both solemn but began to kiss solicitously. In a sombre mood he slowly undressed her, and they made love. She didn't expect the exuberance of the last time. Richard didn't say a word while they made love. When they were finished, she reached up and kissed his lips once, like a little child kissing a white rose. He fell across her, and they fell asleep.

He awoke in the middle of the night to see Anna watching him.

"I guess you and Michael made love in this room too? I just remembered that the last time wasn't with me but with him." He could hear no anger or jealousy in his voice, and after a long while Anna answered:

"We didn't make love." She kissed him, and he knew it to be the truth. He closed his eyes. She wanted to hold him forever. She wanted to stop him leaving in the morning.

***

# Chapter Eight

317q487j 59 t9oer8wy ro68ht r8wy q43 8h 5y3 q84

Richard sat in the cockpit of his Hurricane atop Martin's Short Stirling X-X-Ray near the end of Stradishall's main runway, just after 1pm on the 20<sup>th</sup> August. It was D-Day, the day of Operation False Promise. Above Stradishall the six Stirlings of Green section circled, waiting to escort the six strange bomber-fighter composites to Berlin. They waited for the 'Go' signal from the Control Tower.

Richard had slept little the previous night. Every detail had been gone over in his mind until the tracks of his thoughts seem to have completely worn though to the bedrock of his soul. It had been very dark there.

An English mist that morning had made the bombers look like the ghosts of lost aircraft; their noses poking out of the silken veil. Guards paced tensely around each aircraft and nodded to Richard when he passed.

He had given Jackie one last pat before walking to the mess hall.

"When I get back, little chap, I'm going to set you free. See you in a few days." The little rabbit's nose bobbed up and down in response. Richard circled around the back of their hanger before continuing to the mess hall. With their Hurricane cargoes, the Stirlings had sat silently waiting for action, their noses pointed to the sky in that familiar majestic pose that only Stirlings have. All the aircrew all been offered a full fried breakfast that morning and roast beef for dinner. Richard had forced himself to eat as much as he could, fighting against the fear that made the air feel like lead and made time slow to a standstill.

He met first with the three Red Section Hurricane pilots earlier to talk about radio signals:

"Now, we will know if the gas is getting sucked into the vents, because there is a red dye marker mixed in with the gas. If you see it going down the vents, we have succeeded. The code word for this is 'Bull's Blood.' The code word for knocking down the wall is 'Sweepstake.' Now these code-words have to be sent back to Intelligence here by radio. If, for some reason, nobody else is able to send, you switch your frequency selector to 'X' and send it. You do this by sending it in Morse using the black key on the set. You have all brushed up on your Morse code, so I hope you don't forget it!" Uncertain laughter from the pilots answered his joke.

The final briefing for the whole squadron had been long and detailed. None of the new pilots were to know the true nature of the attack or the contents of the gas canisters. At the end he roused himself to one more effort of enthusiasm.

"Now Martin and I have one last trick up our sleeves. See this range of mountains here. This is the Harz Mountains. If things get really heavy, Red and Blue Sections will make a run for it. Chart two please!" Martin pulled down a detailed map of the Harz Mountains. "We will fly down this valley here and emerge some time later from this valley here. It's a straight run from there to Berlin. We hope this will lose the Luftwaffe. However, if things are really dicey, or you find yourself selected for special attention, you can make for one of these two valleys marked in blue. Both are valleys that tighten to steep gorges with high bridges. I don't know if we can get through, but we can try, and it might shake any fighters. It might be our only chance. A high-flying Mosquito took these photos a few days ago." Martin pulled down two very large scale black and white photographs. "They show the gorges as they are now, our maps are out of date. Study these photographs carefully. Make copies if you want. Make sure you know where you're going and what you're doing. You may be the only bomber left in the air." This comment met with a hushed silence. "I think that's it. It's Weather now followed by the ack-ack briefing. There will be a navigator's briefing in twenty minutes. We go to dispersal in one hour. You all know your jobs. Good luck!"

Now Richard felt glad of the solitude in his fighter's cockpit. He started to feel more at ease. The two red undercarriage 'locked-up' lights glowed like demon's eyes staring at him, but somehow they were reassuring, perhaps because they indicated the aircraft had already become airborne. At the end of Stradishall's long concrete runway Martin increased the revs of the four engines and Richard slid his canopy closed. Most of Stradishall's other bomber crews had been sent on a training flights that day, and the ground staff and other staff had been gathered together for a briefing in the main canteen. Only a few of the ground crews from the Lysander flight had gathered to watch the strange aircraft take off.

"Time to go, Richie. It's zero hour!" said Martin over the radio.

"Right oh! Starting up now." Richard fired up the Merlin and set it to 1500 revs per minute. The fighter rocked slightly in its cradle while the Short Stirling began to rumble slowly down the long runway.

*This is it!*

Richard regretted that he hadn't been able to tell the crews how unlikely it would be that Michael would get the vents open and that some of them hadn't even met the agent, upon whom the mission depended.

As the end of the runway rumbled closer, Richard began to hold his breath. He remembered his recent accident; his arm still felt sore from the wound.

*Will we get off? Is there too much fuel? Should we have taken out the last two guns?*

He found himself still holding his breath when they reached the end of the long runway and then had only grass underneath the bomber. Its wheels spun freely in air as the aircraft lurched into the afternoon sky. Above the low cumulous clouds, the sky was a clear, pale blue. There was a thin rind of the moon straight ahead.

"We're up!" shouted Martin, jubilantly.

"Yeah and hopefully the rest of them."

"Green Section has just passed on a message. Welcome to the glorious clear blue sky!"

"Tell them; thanks."

Martin's aircraft laboured to ten thousand feet. Over the Norfolk coast he slowed to 180 mph to let the others catch up. Soon there were six Stirlings with their fighter cargoes rumbling over the Channel towards the Netherlands. Five thousand feet above them, distant pin points ahead, were the other six Stirlings of Green Section.

"Five minutes to the Dutch coast. Test guns," Martin called to the other Stirling crews. There was the sound of sporadic machine gun fire.

Richard knew they should sight the American bombers at any moment. He craned his neck to look up at the sky behind them and to the north. Finally, he saw them; little silver stars trailing streamers, glinting in the ethereal blue sky.

"There they are Martin! Right on time. Don't they look *great*?"

"Yep. Sure do. Now we just have to follow them. Red Section Control to all Sections. Yanks above and to the left. Hold present course and speed. Soon they'll be ahead of us." Martin returned his VHF set transmit button to speak to Richard only. "We seem to have a slight problem here, Richard. Fitchell? What's happening?"

Inside the cluttered fuselage of Martin's Stirling his front gunner, Fitchell, struggled to arm his guns. He opened the Fraser-Nash turret doors and leaned back to shout to the Bomb Aimer.

"Pass me a bloody screwdriver. The arming cable's trapped between the duct and the Perspex. I can't pull the ammunition up to the breech!"

The young Bomb Aimer, barely eighteen, took a moment to grasp what was happening. He pressed his intercom transmit button. "Flight! Fitchell needs a screwdriver!"

The Flight Engineer nodded and opened a rolled-up tool kit. "What size?"

"I don't know."

"Here. Take them all. Bring them back."

"Crossing enemy coast!" announced Martin over the intercom. "Get that gun fixed, Fitchell!"

***

Michael Dorfmann nervously sipped his brandy in the main bar of the Esplanade Hotel. He would allow himself only one. He knew the Führer abhorred the smell of alcohol on an officer's breath. He tried to make the brandy last as the second hand on the Hotel clock ticked slowly around the face. He checked his own watch, which ran slightly slower. Time passed so slowly. He felt he had time to fly to London and back before he would be driven to the Chancellery.

Over the last three days his nerves had been stretched to their very limit. The day after he had been told his award ceremony would be on the 20th August, the Chancellery had then told him it had changed to the 21st at 3pm. He tried three times to leave the hotel, to warn British Intelligence through the White Rose drop, but he could no longer escape his tails. He fretted all day wondering what he could do. But in the end, he had only once course of action left. He caught a tram towards Marienstraße, followed by the black sedan and then tried to find a street urchin, some scruffy young kid, to whom he could offer money to run an errand for him. He saw a little boy run down an alley-way and ran after him. Shouts pursued him, and he lost the boy before pulling up. Two plain-clothed Gestapo men, he could tell they were, by their expensive jackets, grabbed him from behind.

"Herr Dorfmann. It's a very dangerous area! You must be drunk. We must take you back to the hotel at once. Come with us!"

Defeated, he meekly let them steer him to the car. But he had not counted on a stroke of luck that day.

Oberleutnant Rudolph Eineger had been troubled by the news of the young German ace Michael Dorfmann escaping from England with the latest prototype Spitfire. Something about it seemed too neat. Something seemed wrong, but Eineger couldn't put his finger on it. Hearing on the Gestapo grapevine that others weren't completely convinced either, and since Dorfmann would be brought to Berlin for the interrogation, Eineger went into action. He pulled every string he could to be that interrogator. He had written to Hitler's personal secretary for orders to do so. Some younger Oberleutnant had been assigned to interrogate Dorfmann, but at the last moment, the letter with his orders had come from the secretary in the Reich Chancellery. Dorfmann had requisitioned the fastest Mercedes and arrived just in time.

During that interview, he had intimated to Dorfmann that the Spitfire probably wasn't a genuine prototype. This remained his view, but he had been unable after six days to substantiate this.

"The damned Luftwaffe!" he had shouted to his adjutant. "They're incompetent. How can it take this long to assess a British prototype when their aircraft are inferior to ours anyway! They must have stripped it to pieces by now!"

Every day since then, he had telephoned the Messerschmitt research establishment, which had the task of assessing the aircraft, and each day the same answer came back:

"We cannot be sure yet, sir. There are features that are new and features that are not. It is often that way with prototypes."

Eineger could wait no longer. In six days Dorfmann would meet with Adolf Hitler personally. Eineger couldn't explain why, but he didn't believe Dorfmann's story and had begun to suspect the young German had something to do with the British Intelligence plot to assassinate the Führer.

He called Hitler's private secretary and dictated a message to be sent directly to Hitler at the Berghoff.

The voice on the other line politely explained that, "I can only bother the Führer with the most important of communiqués and rumours of plots or intelligence reports do not fall into this category." When Eineger insisted that Hitler would want to see this message, the voice replied, "Hm. Well I do send some dispatches once per week. I suppose … I could slip this in."

"Thank you. Thank you very much! I'm sure the Führer will be pleased."

"I hope *so*," the voice replied indignantly.

But the message did not get delivered. Bruno Schtickel had quickly realised that Eineger had tricked him when the source of the Luftwaffe intelligence report had turned out to be false. An old hand at bureaucratic politics, he had moved to cut off Eineger's line of communication. He called in a favour with one of Hitler's under-secretaries. A quick word from this man in the right ear about Eineger's rumoured alcohol abuse and consequent delusions had finally convinced Hitler's personal secretary that Eineger's thinking might not be sound or fit for the Führer's ears.

Another three days passed before Eineger understood that he would not be able to get through to the Führer this way.

In the meantime, Eineger had thought up another tactic to reveal Dorfmann's treachery.

"Send word to Dorfmann that the medal award appointment has changed to the 21st August," he ordered his adjutant.

"But such an order has to come straight from Hitler's personal staff!"

"I know that! It's a ruse. I will take personal responsibility. If he has a contact and *if* he *is* plotting with the British to co-ordinate a bombing attack against the Führerbunker, he will have to contact them to tell them of the change."

"Very well!" his adjutant replied.

The two Gestapo henchmen reported back to Eineger after picking up Dorfmann at Marienstraße and returning him to his hotel.

"Marienstraße, eh? What was he doing there, I wonder?" mused Eineger. "Did you search him? What was he doing?"

"We caught him with a kid in a dark alley."

"Hm … Good! Yes, that's good! Did he have time to speak to this child?" Both men looked sheepishly at each other and nodded hesitantly. "Even better. Ha! Ha! We have him now! I want a full report, addresses, diagrams; descriptions of the child, everything, made out to my adjutant. He will follow up anything as necessary."

Michael Dorfmann felt almost relaxed now after the stresses of the last three days. He had tried everything he could to relay the new date of the 21st to British Intelligence but had failed. He woke that morning to find a note, slipped under his door, written in neat, blue copperplate, which read, simply:

> 'Date for Medal Award Ceremony changed again
> to original date and time: Today, 20th August at
> 5pm. Please be at the Reich Chancellery reception
> at 4pm.
> Private Secretary to Adolf Hitler'

He had almost shouted with delight. He stretched out on the bed, laughing. Whatever fool had tried to trick him had failed miserably. When he finally did descend for breakfast he noticed the two Gestapo henchmen brazenly eating at a table near him. The black sedan had parked right outside the hotel with somebody sitting in the front passenger seat. Michael didn't care anymore. He ordered the most luxurious breakfast on the menu and a copy of Berliner Illustrierte Zeitung to read.

The Esplanade Hotel reeked of opulence. One of Berlin's finest, its giant chandeliers and fireplaces were renowned. There were two glass-covered courtyards, one of which, the Palm Courtyard, had become famous for its tea dances and famous Hollywood visitors before the War.

His tails never lost sight of him all day, except when he returned to his room after lunch to bathe. He didn't even try to leave the hotel. He felt somewhat perplexed that the date had been switched back. After musing in the bath he came to the conclusion that perhaps the Gestapo thought he had passed on a message using the kid in the street.

"Yes. That must be it! Fools! Now I only have to work out how to open the vents. *Only*!"

He went over his ideas in his mind. 'There must be some kind of controls somewhere to operate the vents. However, since they are temporary I bet they aren't too sophisticated. I bet it's some kind of mechanical control, ropes, or pulleys, near to the vents. Perhaps underneath them … . Which means they will be just further back than the main original bunker. I have to look for a room there. Although how I'm going to know where I am is another matter. What did British Intelligence say? Twenty-five metres from the front entrance of the old bunker to the vents. Yes. I will just have to pace it out.'

Rudolph Eineger, sitting in the black sedan outside the Esplanade Hotel could not understand why Dorfmann had not attempted to leave the hotel. If he was a traitor, he had to leave to pass on the new appointment time to his contact. It made no sense. But time was running out. Today seemed the most likely day for the attack; he had heard a rumour that Hitler planned to leave Berlin in a day or two for a tour of the frontline troops somewhere. Perhaps he had missed something? Perhaps Michael Dorfmann wasn't the traitor after all. At 1.16pm he sent a hand-written and coded message in to the two officers watching Dorfmann and then in desperation took a taxi back to his office.

***

Martin spoke into the intercom, "How's Fitchell doing? We will be near the German border soon, and we need those guns!"

The first light flak came up as the squadron of strange aircraft flew over Holland's great inland seas.

Flight Sergeant Fitchell replied, "Yes! It's free. Not long now!" He put back on his gloves. Pulling the ammunition belt up into the breach, he cocked both guns and shouted into the intercom, "All done!" The Bomb Aimer tapped him on the shoulder. Fitchell turned and gave him the thumbs up.

"At last! Test guns!" replied Martin.

Fitchell pressed the gun trigger, and a stream of bullets spat out of his two machine guns, arcing gently down towards the blue seas below.

In his cockpit, Richard finally became too irritated by a faint knocking sound he had been hearing for a while. With so much to think about, he had kept pushing it to the back of his mind; fighters make lots of strange noises. It seemed to be coming from under his seat. He released his harness and reached down to feel underneath. To his surprise, he felt something soft and rubbery suspended by some means.

*What the hell? Doesn't feel like anything technical. Feels like ...*

He yanked at the object which came loose in his gloved hand. He pulled it up to inspect it and laughed.

Donald Duck! Ha! Thanks Anna! And Michael! And whoever put it there! Beattie or Fleiming? It wouldn't be Beattie on his own. He wouldn't dare! Fleiming, you old bastard!

At first, he wasn't sure what to do with the rubber toy, but then decided to attach it to a bracket at the top of his windscreen. The little rubber Donald danced and swung as the Hurricane floated along on top of the Stirling. His radio had been set to automatically receive intercom transmissions from his carrier Stirling when not receiving relayed transmissions.

"Bandits at 7 o'clock high. Making for the main force!" shouted somebody in Martin's Stirling.

By this time, the gaggle of Short Stirlings were slightly behind and well below the main force of Eighth Air Force bombers. They were hampered by the drag of the Hurricanes and could only manage a maximum air speed of 230 mph, whereas the B-17s and Liberators were managing 270 mph. Martin and Richard had planned it this way.

Above them tiny glints of light danced and pirouetted around the main force, enemy Bf 109s and FW 190s picking off vulnerable bombers.

"Only a matter of time before they have a go at us!" Martin announced over the radio.

"15.00 hours. We'll cross into Germany shortly after 15.30 if this crosswind stays like this," announced Martin's navigator.

"Butcher Bird coming in a 6 o'clock," the tail-gunner shouted, breathless. His four machine guns spat orange and yellow flame as a stream of bullets laced with tracer sped towards the incoming hornet-like fighter.

Two bullets ripped through the Hurricane fuselage just behind Richard's head, one hitting the armoured back plate of his headrest.

"Je-esus! I wish I could just take off and attack the bugger! That was close. They've certainly seen us now!"

There came no answer from Martin's Stirling, but a confusion of voices shouting out enemy positions. "Enemy above! Enemy coming in below! We're hit!"

The Stirlings seemed to take an enormous amount of damage to Richard. He thought they were going to fly right through the attack without any casualties when he saw Oakly's Stirling spouting orange flames from one of its engines.

"U-Unicorn to X-Ray Leader: Damaged engine. Am losing height. Activated extinguisher."

Richard watched as the flames ripped back across the wing, but then were subdued by the extinguisher and went out. Still he could see fuel and oil spewing from the damaged wing.

"X-Ray Leader to U-Unicorn. Oakly. Drop your cargo and head for home. Drop your cargo and head … ."

Another voice cut in desperately. "The whole bloody Luftwaffe is coming down on us!"

Richard heard only static from the lead bomber's transmitter, and then he heard Martin's voice on the private channel. "At least twenty 190s Richie. What do you want to do?"

"We have to keep going. Tell all the Hurri pilots to start their engines. It's frustrating! Can't do anything!"

"X-Ray leader to Hurricane pilots. Commander says start your engines!"

"Releasing now!" shouted Oakly over the radio.

Two Focke Wulf 190s went screaming past Martin's Stirling, raking it with cannon fire. At the same time, Grutsberger in the released Hurricane drifted free of the parent Stirling and then throttled up the Merlin, firing ahead at one of the FW 190s. With all eight machine guns firing, Grutsberger scored a few hits on one of the German fighters. It banked around in a wide curve, coming up behind Oakly's Stirling to finish it off. All twenty enemy fighters were now taking turns raking the group of strange aircraft from stern to nose.

Richard looked behind and saw Oakly's Stirling well below, trailing fuel, oil and white smoke.

He's had it!

Richard started his engine.

*This mission may be shorter than we all thought!*

Martin patched Grutsberger through to Richard. "Commander, permission to discard bombs?"

*Damn!*

"Yes. Permission granted!"

Grutsberger's Hurricane had now begun returning fire, and the other crews cheered him on over the radio.

"Shut up! The lot of you. Maintain radio silence!" demanded Martin. "Oakly. Abandon your ship … . You won't make it."

Richard craned his neck and saw Oakly start to bank the Stirling in an attempt to run for home. But a hail of cannon-fire from three of the approaching hornets raked the fuselage and right wing, which burst into a violent red fireball. The bomber began to turn over onto its back and then slipped into an inverted spin. Spewing flames like some wild fire-dancer, it plunged down towards the scattered clouds. After vainly watching for chutes Richard looked away.

"I got one!" shouted Grutsberger. "I tell you this baby handles better than a Focke Wulf 190, without undercarriage! Faster in a turn, roll and climbing! It's great!"

A Focke Wulf with a green spinner flicked, nose over wing, out of control and trailed black smoke. Then the canopy opened, and the tiny figure of the pilot flew out and shot past Richard's Hurricane, falling.

Voices vied with cannon and machine gun fire in the ethereal war symphony of battle. The noise and confusion disorientated Richard. Something suddenly ripped a hole in the side of his cockpit and then pinged against the buckle of his harness. It fell on to his lap and burned through the material of his trousers, stinging him. He flicked off the tiny piece of shrapnel and looked at the matchbox sized hole in the fuselage curiously.

Now all the machine guns of all the remaining Stirlings were blazing at the German fighters.

"Commander to X-Ray leader. Martin, tell the boys to conserve ammunition. There's is a long way to go."

"Right."

Grutsberger could be heard on the radio shouting, "I got another! Whew!"

Martin issued the command, and then the voice of Cloudy came over the radio. "Approaching Osnabrück. Heavy Flak there … ."

"But we're going north of Osnabrück, aren't we?" said Richard.

"They cottoned on to that long ago. They have a lot of flak towers this far north now. Anyway it's better than fighters! They'll leave us alone for a while."

Richard looked around hopefully and saw the truth of Cloudy's words. The enemy fighters were turning for home. One of them waggled his wings as he flew into the setting sun. Ahead, black puffs of smoke began pocking the afternoon sky.

"15.50. Right on time!" added Cloudy jauntily.

***

At 2pm, a knock on Michael Dorfmann's hotel door announced the arrival of his pressed dress uniform. He tipped the concierge and went into the bathroom to shave. He took his time preparing, removing loose hairs from the suit and giving his boots one last polish. He wished he could take his Luger with him, but Hitler never allowed soldiers near him with guns away from the front line.

*I could shoot the bastard. But even if I did, I would be dead within seconds. No. let the RAF boys do it!*

By 2.55pm he felt ready but felt sick with terror at the thought of what he had to do. He sat stiffly on the edge of the bed and waited for the inevitable Mercedes that would take him to the Reich Chancellery.

At the same time, Rudolph Eineger had reached the conclusion that he would find nothing in the file on the man posing as SS-Hauptsturmführer Casper Drall, or indeed the other SS impostor, that offered any clues. He sat at his desk, staring into space. Then he banged his desk.

"There has to be something!" He called for a coffee and stirred it aggressively He waited for some idea to form from the swirl of white cream floating on the black liquid.

"The Report on the capture at Marienstraße!" He suddenly realised he hadn't seen it yet. He asked his adjutant to bring it in.

"I … I haven't finished it yet, sir!"

"Nevermind. Let me see it!" Eineger flicked through the short report; only five loosely typed pages. "Where is the follow-up Report? Who did the house-to-house check?"

"Sir?" Momentarily. Eineger's adjutant felt at a loss. "Ah. Er. There hasn't been time, sir, to organise it. I had the Führer's private secretary to deal with. I meant to do it today, but somebody tipped them off that you changed the date of that Luftwaffe officer's appointment. He probably talked to a reporter. They have been nagging me for an explanation all day!"

"Damn! You idiot. They will have my head for this! How many men do we have available now? We have to go back to Marienstraße and search. It's the only thing we haven't done!" Eineger had already jumped out of his chair and begun putting on his coat as he barked orders.

Within fifteen minutes, two black cars full of flustered Gestapo officers were speeding towards Marienstraße.

***

At 3.16, Adolf Hitler posed for photographers on the steps of the Reich Chancellery. One of the photographers knelt down in front of the Führer for a better shot, but the powerful flash startled Hitler, who had not long been out of bed, and he stumbled over the man beneath him. He fell awkwardly on his elbow and felt his arm crack.

The Führer became apoplectic with rage. SS officers whisked away the unfortunate photographer for interrogation while Hitler screamed, "Traitor. He is part of this plot to kill me! Get the truth out of him and then execute him!"

Hitler knew that the attack on the Chancellery would come on this day, if it would come at all. He cancelled the photography session, only mollified slightly by the fact that none of the public had been there to witness him fall. His issued an order for no journalists to print anything about it and then retired to his office in the building clutching his painful arm. He had no sooner sat down than a secretary handed him a report, indicating that RAF bombers carrying fighters on their back had crossed into Germany and might be heading for Berlin.

"Order a car, now!" he barked to everyone around him. "And tell that Eineger fellow in the Gestapo; I want him personally interrogating that photographer." He glared at his personal secretary. "Eineger was right after all. Order a suite be prepared at the Kaiserhoff Hotel immediately."

His personal secretary hovered around him, pointing to the Führer's damaged arm. "But mein Führer; your arm! It needs treatment. It's probably broken!"

"I know that, you incompetent fool. But that's what the British want. They are going to bomb the hospital. It's so obvious even you should be able to see that! Get that car!"

Within five minutes, one of Hitler's private cars carried him at breakneck speed towards the Kaiserhoff hotel, German swastikas flying on its front wings. It honked trams and other cars out of the way, and where cars wouldn't move Hitler ordered them barged out of the way. Within fifteen minutes, he had been installed in his old suite at his favourite hotel and his personal doctor brought to the lobby.

***

Rudolf Eineger didn't receive the call from Hitler's secretary. He had just arrived at Marienstraße and had organised his men to knock on every door, starting at the western end of the long residential road. They were to briefly interview all inhabitants about anything suspicious they might have seen in the last few weeks. Eineger himself took part in the search. To Eineger it seemed to go on forever, but after only half an hour, a commotion broke out outside the building. He ran outside and stood not far away when a man ran out of the door of number twenty-five waving a piece of paper at him.

"Sir. An old lady … ground floor. Says she saw something. I have it written down … ."

"Alright! Slow down. Let me see. I cannot read your writing. Tell me, man!"

"Says she saw two men over the last month loitering outside number twenty-two, smoking cigarettes. Says she thinks they put something in the letterb … ."

He didn't finish his sentence, because Eineger had already run past him and entered number twenty-five. In the lounge of the ground floor flat, he found a frail old frau with curly white hair, who leaned on the window-sill. She almost jumped out of her skin when Rudolph Eineger stepped into the room.

"I haven't done anything wrong, have I? I'm a *good* German! I *believe* in the Third Reich!" Eineger would have laughed on any other day.

"No. You may do the Führer a very great service if you tell me exactly what you saw. Wait a moment. Is there anybody here who can make you a cup of coffee?"

"Oh, young man, that's no problem at all! I have just boiled the kettle. Why don't you just sit down, and I will make you one. Biscuit?"

She hobbled over to the table and offered Eineger a brown biscuit from an opened tin painted with scenes from the Tiergarten on a white background. Eineger took one out of courtesy, bit into it and sat down. When one of his officers stuck his head around the door, Eineger barked at him, "Out! And close the front door. I don't want to be disturbed until I come out!"

"Yes, sir!"

After what seemed like an age, while Eineger's feet tapped the faded Turkish rug under his feet, the little old lady came back from the kitchen carrying a tray. She placed it on the table and handed Eineger his coffee.

"Now, please … he blurted out. Every second counts. Tell me what you saw?"

"Well about a month ago, no wait, maybe less. Perhaps around the 10$^{th}$ or 12$^{th}$ August, I don't keep notes you know, unlike some of the old battle-axes here … ."

"Yes, please … details."

"Alright young man, no need to shout. I was secretary once to a general. I can give you detail."

Eineger thanked God, silently, for this woman.

"As I was saying, I don't sleep to well and my cat, Oscar, often doesn't come in until late. He jumps up on this window sill at about 11pm most nights, so I wait up for him. This night I saw a man in a nice smart suit standing outside number twenty-two. He was smoking, but then he looked around him. He looked up and down the street, and I thought, 'He looks guilty. What's he doing?' He dropped something in that grey box. I am sure he did! Then I saw him come back another two or three times. And each time he dropped something in that letter box after checking to see he wasn't being watched. Then he stopped coming. I didn't think anything more of it until about six nights ago when *another* man did exactly the same thing! And then I saw him about three nights ago, but this time two men were chasing him. I think they caught him, because I saw three men getting into their black car."

"Good! Yes. I see. What did the man look like?"

"He looked a lot like you; average height, good looking with very short black hair." She winked at Eineger. He took her tiny, frail wrists in his hand and gently squeezed them. "Thank you. You have been very helpful. I will make sure you are rewarded!"

"Come back soon!" she called out as he ran out of the building. Several of his men were already peering into the grey letter box outside number twenty-two.

He ran over to them. "What did you find?"

"Just some matches! Nothing much. They're soggy. No good for anything!"

Eineger knew it didn't matter what the box held, probably a code, but that could wait. He now had proof that Dorfmann was one of the traitors. He had to stop the Luftwaffe officer getting to Hitler.

***

# Chapter Nine

Luftwaffe, Hanover to Berlin HQ:

dytsmhr dufgrwe npznrt xinvublruib sotvtsgy gwlsubf rsdy
dein jrtr

The flak north of Osnabrück had been so heavy that at times Richard could hardly see ahead through the black puffs of smoke which merged into one cloud. The fighters had cut their engines as they approached on Richard's command.

"How is Green Flight doing, Martin?"

"Fine. The Butcher Birds left them alone. They are about five miles ahead of us now."

"And Grutsberger? Can you patch me through to him, or is he too far away?"

"Wait."

"JW. Richard wants a word … ."

"Hello. JW still here!"

"Are you still with us? I thought I told you to head for home. You cannot possibly make Berlin and get back to Holland!"

"I'm coming with you. There are loads of places to put the old girl down. I don't think it makes much difference where I turn."

"Well. Disobeying an order would mean a Courts Martial. Good to have you along."

"Thanks skipper. This flak is not what I'm used to though. I wonder if *any* Hurricane has ever been this far east, on its own!"

"The flak's easing," Richard replied. "I can see blue sky ahead. And the moon!"

In the darkening blue sky above Richard could see the faint rind of the moon. Guessing they were heading for Hanover with the main force, the German fighters stayed on the ground while the biggest flak guns started pounding the bombers approaching the city. By the time 700 Squadron passed to the south of Hanover, the city had been set ablaze, and a great pall of smoke drifted slowly south west with the wind.

"God. Look at that down there! They're taking a real pasting!" Richard commented.

"Yeah. And they're going to be hungry for blood afterwards."

"Yes. But they'll be looking west."

After Hanover, they saw only clear sky apart from the occasional flak battery's puffs of dirty smoke. 700 Squadron had travelled for another ten minutes when Martin called out, "Enemy fighters! Swarms of them. I think this is it. They're on to us!"

Richard craned his neck to see what Martin had seen. Behind he could see nothing.

"9 o'clock!" added Martin.

Richard swung round to peer to his left. Pacing them were a gaggle of two-engined fighters, Me 110s and several squadrons of fighters. They were too far away for the type to be identified.

"Time for plan B," Richard announced. "Cloudy, give us a heading for the mountains."

"Steer 170 magnetic," the Master Navigator replied.

All five Stirlings turned for the Harz Mountains to the south. Green Section flew on to Berlin. Soon after the aircraft turned south twin-engined and single-engined hornets began buzzing around the big pot of honey.

"Head for the deck. 1000!" shouted Martin.

All the bombers started shallow dives, gaining speed to nearly 300 mph.

"Start engines!" Richard commanded.

"Goslar in eight minutes!" Cloud shouted grimly over the intercom.

"Somebody wake up tail-end Charlie," Martin shouted. Each Stirling's machine guns opened fire and unleashed a hail of bullets at the approaching fighters. These were led by red-nosed Focke Wulf 190s. Behind them were Bf 109s and the Bf 110s. Some of the Bf 110s were diving below and ahead of the rest of the fighters.

"He's dead!" the Bomb Aimer replied. "I just went back to check!"

"Great. Fitchell! You are all we have left!"

"Some of those 110s must have Jazz Musik. They are trying to get beneath us!" shouted one of the other Stirling pilots over the radio.

The cockpit of Martin's Stirling filled with cordite smoke as Fitchell emptied his guns into the enemy. Each time a FW 190 made a pass, he had another chance as it sped past and presented a vulnerable tail to him.

"We're hit. Starboard wing!" the Flight Engineer shouted.

With Martin's crew frantically co-ordinating their defence he had forgotten to switch the radio to intercom, so Richard could hear nothing of the crew's struggles. With the bomber diving steeply, he felt terrified that the Hurricane would tear loose from its pylons, because of the increased lift. He cut his engine's revs to 1000 rpm. Then he saw the huge hole in the wing of the Stirling. Fuel gushed out and streamed from the trailing edge of the wing. He feared the worst.

Inside the screaming Stirling fear floated along the fuselage, inhabiting it like the ghostly cordite dust clouds.

"310! 320's the limit!" shouted the Flight Engineer.

Swinging his head around, Richard saw one of the Stirling's in Green Section on fire and another at the rear of Blue Section. He thought it might be Evergreen.

The long, screaming dive continued. Below them two Bf 110s were gradually pulling ahead, and then they let loose with the powerful, obliquely-upward facing cannons, nicknamed Jazz Musik. Two shells went straight through the nose of Martin's Stirling leaving gaping holes in the canopy, nose and belly of the bomber. Then the Bf 110s peeled away.

"Nearly on the floor!" Martin shouted. "We're too low for them!" he added jubilantly.

The fields of Germany, green and lush, sped under the nose like a huge patchwork quilt. Martin deftly used the contours of the hills to make it difficult for the fighters to get a bead on his aircraft. The other bomber pilots followed suit, and then they all heard what they had been desperate to hear.

"Goslar in thirty seconds. On your starboard side!"

Richard still couldn't hear events inside the bomber, but he could see the Harz Mountains rising up ahead of them.

*We're safe! For now!*

***

"We have to find Dorfmann. He's the traitor!" Eineger shouted as his men all climbed in the cars in Marienstraße. "Drive straight to the Hotel!" he ordered his driver.

"But sir, he will have left for the Chancellery. It's 4.20pm!" the driver replied.

"Yes. Damn. Drive to the Chancellery then!"

They reached the government building in fifteen minutes veering in and out of traffic and running across red lights.

Eineger had climbed out of the car and ran halfway up the steps before the black car had stopped.

The SS guard at the main door, to his surprise, smiled and said, "Oberleutnant Eineger? The Führer's private secretary has been searching for you. I had orders to admit you at once and tell you to go straight to his office!"

Eineger didn't wait for the whole message; he burst in the secretary's office moments later. The secretary blushed a deep red.

"Herr Eineger. It seems I owe you a deep apology. The Führer wants you to investigate a new traitor personally … . Immediately."

"What? But I need to find … . Who?"

"A photographer who tripped up the Führer on the steps of the Chancellery."

"Is he alright, I mean the Führer?"

"I said he should go to hospital, but he insisted on going to the Kaiserhoff Hotel!"

"What? Where's Dorfmann? Is the ceremony going ahead?"

"I don't think so. Dorfmann was here, but I sent him on to the Kaiserhoff, just in case."

"Oh no! That's even worse!"

"Why?"

But Eineger was already running back to his car. "Drive!" he shouted to the driver, getting in.

"Where to?"

"The Kaiserhoff! Fast!"

***

In the Kaiserhoff Hotel, Adolf Hitler, after a plate of his favourite cream puffs and pampering from his personal physician, again felt in a rambunctious mood. He now decided that the safest place for him would actually be the Reich Chancellery. His car had been readied to take him back. Before leaving, however, and with his usual fiendishly accurate guesswork, he ordered any available 88mm anti-aircraft guns to be set up at the top and bottom of Wilhelmstraße, in the Tiergarten facing away from the Chancellery. Just for good measure he ordered more 88mm guns to be placed at the Brandenburg Gate end of Unter den Linden, facing east. He also issued a second order for as many SS troops as possible to be made available around the Chancellery within the next half hour. Then he took the car back to the Chancellery himself.

If Rudolph Eineger had taken the normal route to the Kaiserhoff Hotel, he would have seen both the Führer and Dorfmann going the other way. But he was in a desperate hurry and took a short cut. As a consequence, he arrived at 4.45, only to find that they had already gone back to the Chancellery. He cursed himself for not leaving a message with the Führer's private secretary and rushed into the hotel. Grabbing a telephone on the reception desk he called the secretary's number. But he found it engaged.

Furious, he slammed the phone down, scribbled a note and shouted to the concierge, "Call that number, and tell the secretary not to admit one Michael Dorfmann to the Chancellery under any circumstances." He ran out to the car and ordered the driver back to the Chancellery.

He did not hear the concierge calling after him, "But who do I say the message is from?"

* * *

In the shadow of the north-eastern most spur of the Harz Mountains, 700 Squadron flew due south, down the valley and to the west of the highest mountain, the Brocken, which Richard remembered from the map in Whitehall. The town of Goslar at the mouth of the wide valley had been left behind now, and Evergreen's crew had managed to put out the fire in the engine, but they couldn't restart it. With only three engines they could not maintain height and were already dangerously low, trailing well behind the rest of the bombers. A gaggle of keen FW 190s had followed him down into the valley. Only the single Hurricane of Grutsberger could defend Evergreen's Stirling against the Butcher Birds.

Martin led the Gaggle of Stirlings in a gentle curve to the east, around the Brocken Mountain. Richard could do nothing to help and listened to his brother's voice, constantly encouraging and shepherding his beloved bombers through the valleys, on towards the desperate trap they had prepared as a last resort.

"Evergreen! You're too low! Jettison your cargo! Now!"

Evergreen's voice sounded faint, far away. "Will do!"

Moments later, the Hurricane lifted lightly away from the stricken Stirling, but not before the Butcher Birds slammed full belts of ammunition into the bomber and a few into the fighter.

"Bastards! Going to get on their tails if it … ," shouted Grutsberger.

Richard saw, first Grutsberger's Hurricane and then, moments later Blalock's F-Freddie, launched from Evergreen's Stirling, arcing over his head to the left.

*Come on boys. That's the spirit!*

But then he thought of Blalock's bombs. "Martin, get onto Blalock. Tell him he cannot, repeat, cannot drop bombs. Suggest he tags along quietly and lets Grutsberger handle the Butcher Birds."

He soon heard Blalock's dry American response. "Shucks! I was gonna have such good fun!"

"Hasselfelde; two minutes." announced Cloudy, dryly.

"I'm on the tail of one of the buggers!" Grutsberger shouted, out of breath. "Closing in … closer, damn. Missed! He's climbing to get on my … . What the hell … ! More of the blighters. Five of them coming down. Yellow tails!"

Richard felt rather than heard an explosion somewhere behind him. It rocked the two airframes underneath him.

"Grutsy's gone," Blalock commented pithily. "They're coming down on you, Frankie!"

"Mon deut! Nazi scum!"

Suddenly, Richard's Stirling flew over water, a large lake, and then the little town of Hasselfelde passed by. Some of the adult inhabitants stopped and stared at the strange aircraft while children waved and ran after them.

"Right chaps. This is where we part ways," called Martin. "T-Tiger. Evergreen. Are you able to maintain height?"

"Not sure. Not for much longer," came the faint reply.

"Okay. You follow S-Sugar and V-Victor. Go for the second gorge. You know the way. If you don't think you can clear the gorge, keep going south, but it will be straight and flat. Good luck if you go that way. The rest, follow me! Everybody who gets through, remember to form up at Aschesleben."

Martin suddenly banked the Stirling so sharply to port that Richard thought they had been hit by flak. He held on to his seat with his left hand.

*Steady on, old boy!*

He heard the four engines' pitch rising to a screaming wail as his brother pushed the heavy bomber towards a narrow gap in the mountains to their left. They were followed by Amalfi Douglas in Y-Yankee and Dewine in Z-Zebra. Joseph Mitten in S-Sugar and Geoffrey Hutchinson in V-Victor, continued south with Evergreen.

Martin kept the Short Stirling close to the valley floor where a sparkling river reflected the August sun. They skimmed along just above the banks of the river at thirty feet, scattering sheep and cows in all directions. A road on one side of the river showed an occasional car whose headlights sent faint pin pricks into the gloom of the valley ahead.

"Tell 'em, engines on!" Richard transmitted to Martin.

"We've gone over this map, Richard and I, a hundred times. The rest of you just follow my instructions, and we'll be fine. How many Birds followed us?"

"Looks like three, but they're staying up high," Douglas at the rear replied. Richard craned his neck as the bomber twisted this way and that around the turns of the valley. He marveled at the agility of the big aircraft, realising what Martin had always known; that short wings were a big advantage at low altitude. The walls of the gorge rose 600 feet either side of them, sheer in places, steep and rocky in most. Trees gripped the rocky cliffs and covered the top of the hills like a thick green blanket.

"Turn right, ninety degrees … now! Bodetal coming up. Turn left ninety degrees now and then another ninety … now!"

Richard felt sick. Sitting motionless in his cockpit while the whole composite aircraft jinked around felt completely unnatural to him. His helplessness as well as the lurching uncertainty of it all unnerved him.

*God. Please let this be over!*

"Oh oh! Those Jerries have figured out what we're doing. One young fly-boy is coming down to have a go at us!" called out Douglas. "Coming down on my tail … ."

"Where's Grutsberger?" asked Martin

"And no Grutsy to defend us!" Douglas finished.

Richard heard Y-Yankee's rear turret Browning machine guns opening up on the pursuing FW 190.

"Oh. Hold on 'Malfi. Just a few more turns. We'll shake him. Right forty-five. There goes Bodetal. Now left ninety. Okay boys … ."

"Aaah!" The sound of somebody hit by a shell in Douglas's Stirling came over the radio. "We're being plastere- … ."

"Ah! Ha! Forgot about me!" came the familiar sound of Blalock. "Just thought I'd follow you all. Looks like it was a good idea. Down you go, yellow-tail. Ah! He's hit!"

But the Butcher Bird didn't go down.

"This one's two-seventy degrees … all the way round. Everyone careful. And then the bridges!"

Richard felt his stomach lurch into the back of his throat as the Stirling banked steeply to the right. Ahead, only a half a wing-span away, the sheer rock wall of the gorge seemed to be dancing with them tightly. As Martin banked, the aircraft kept the same distance from the wall and then slid closer.

"We're not going to make it!" Richard shouted to nobody but himself in the tight Hurricane cockpit.

The gorge wall crept closer, but Martin increased the engine revs just a touch, and the bomber turned away slightly from the cliff. His voice came, panting over the radio. "No slower than … 230!"

Richard hardly dared look when he saw the valley ahead curve sharply to the left, but it wasn't such a tight turn. And then he saw the first of three bridges. The first stood not far above the water, but the second spanned the water at a height of about 100 feet. Here, the valley narrowed, and the spans of the bridges were not big enough to admit even a fighter. Martin eased up the stick and pushed the boost and revs on the engines to maximum. "Richard! And the rest of you fly boys! Full engine revs now!"

Richard had almost forgotten this part of the plan. He nearly jumped out of his seat, reaching for the throttle and pushing it all the way forward. He wasn't sure if the airframes and pylons would take it.

Sickeningly, like a drunk old man, the Stirling picked its nose up and lurched towards the parapet of the iron bridge. Richard closed his eyes at the last moment and prayed. But they were over in the next instant, and Martin cut the revs. So did Richard as soon as he could breathe. He heard the engines of the other Stirlings behind, straining to climb over the bridge, and then he heard Blalock's voice:

"Kraut's on fire. Don't think he's going to make it! He's trying … ."

Then, a colossal burst of orange and white light came. Richard heard the sound, over the radio, of fifteen men shouting their jubilation.

"Okay boys! We're though. Wonder how the others did?" Let's make for Aschesleben, straight ahead. And keep low. Let's hope those other boys don't like the odds any more.

In the main valley of the Harz Mountains further south, both S-Sugar and V-Victor, with Mitten and Hutchinson at the controls respectively, made for the second gorge, much less twisty that the first. David Evergreen, feeling his aircraft had been too damaged to attempt the gorge, flew on south. Following Hutchinson, Joseph Mitten eased the sickening Stirling around the curves of the steep gorge. "Flying on just three engines now!" he announced. "Rear Gunner's had it."

"I'm with you," shouted Mitten. "They're staying up high. We'll make it."

Until it opened out onto the flat plain beyond the Harz Mountain range, the gorge ran relatively straight. Hutchinson led them on while the Butcher Birds dropped down for only the occasional pot shot. S-Sugar lagged behind.

"This is the last turn, Joey. Get around this, and you're home … ."

"Getting … really heavy … on the … I think something's gone … aileron's sticky."

"You can do it. 180 degrees starting now!"

Hutchinson himself, with all his experience, flying first Ansons, then Hampdens, Wellingtons and Stirlings all over Europe in the most difficult conditions found himself battling with the controls of his bomber to negotiate the tight turn with such a full load. In his Hurricane on top, Razor closed his eyes as the rock walls seemed to roll past just feet away from his cockpit.

"Oh my bloody God!"

But then they were around. Razor craned his neck to watch Mitten's S-Sugar as it started to labour around the tight curve.

"He'll never bloody make it!" But it seemed like the Stirling would make it. Only at the last moment, when the rock wall seemed to be about to run out, did the pilot in the Hurricane on top of S-Sugar, George Lenoit, shut his eyes and said one last prayer before the bomber slid into the rock in a ball of red flames and rending metal. A black pall of smoke rose up as the wreckage crumbled and tumbled down the cliffs into the burbling river on the bottom of the valley.

V-Victor flew on and emerged from the gorge on to the plain beyond the Harz Mountains. Above, the two FW 190s waggled their wings and turned for home.

Martin's voice crackled faintly on the VHF radio. "S-Sugar, V-Victor. Are you reading us?"

"V-Victor here. I'm out of the mountains, five minutes from Aschesleben. S-Sugar has bought it. Sorry."

"Evergreen?"

"I don't know. He continued on south. We saw a couple of Bf 110s circling, looking for business to the south."

"How about the cargo?"

"Gone too."

There came only the sound of crackling on the frequency for a moment. "Understood. We are near Aschesleben now. We will circle just east of it once. Press on at maximum speed."

"Understood."

Richard saw V-Victor to the west emerge from between two hills just as some local farmer took a pot shot at them with a twelve-bore shot-gun. Pellets spattered the fuselage of their Stirling but did no damage.

"Martin" he said quietly after pressing transmit. "We have a problem."

"I know. Only two bombs left. I'm thinking … ."

V-Victor fell in at the rear of the group of four bombers as they continued eastwards out onto the flat plain that led to Berlin. Blalock's Hurricane, the last carrying demolition bombs, tagged along above them keeping an eye on the sky above for enemy fighters.

"What happened to your Focke Wulfs?" Hutchinson asked Martin.

"They turned for home after we made one fly into a bridge. None too happy, I think."

"Probably out of fuel," added Martin's flight engineer dryly.

"Ours did the same. They waggled their wings at us."

"Turn 080 degrees magnetic," Martin relayed to the other bombers. "Berlin in twenty minutes. We've fallen a little behind schedule. Green Section will be approaching Berlin in ten minutes."

Above Wittenburg, half way between the Harz Mountains and Berlin, the moment which Richard had most dreaded occurred. They were spotted by JG26's Focke Wulf 190s flying out of the Capital. Richard recognised them by the gothic 'S' on a white shield painted on the left side of each aircraft's fuselage.

"Start your engines!" Richard ordered.

***

On arrival at the Kaiserhoff Hotel, Michael Dorfmann had been told the award ceremony would take place at the Chancellery, but, to his horror, when he reached the Chancellery for the second time, he found that he would be the only officer available to be awarded his medal. It was 4.45, fifteen minutes too early.

There seemed some confusion while secretaries searched for the right medal. However, after five minutes everything had been made ready. Desperate to stall the ceremony, Michael excused himself and went to the gentlemen's cloakroom, making a great effort to get lost as many times as possible on the way. He knew this would infuriate the Führer, but he had no choice. He counted to six hundred as slowly as he could, estimating that this would take ten minutes. When he reached four hundred and twenty, while pacing up and down, he heard a loud rap on the door.

"Herr Dorfmann. Are you there? The Führer is ready for you. Please hurry!"

"One minute!"

After exactly one minute a red-faced secretary burst in to find Michael wiping his face with a towel.

"I've been sick. I'm sorry. It's an old wound … and the nerves. I didn't sleep too well last night either."

The secretary seemed to be about to lift off the ground by bouncing on the balls of his feet. "I quite understand. But we must hurry. Please!" His hands fluttered as if he wanted to take Michael's shoulders in his hands, wheel him about and march him to the door.

"Alright! I'm coming!" He straightened his jacket collar and opened the door. "Which way?"

The secretary tut-tutted in frustration. "Follow me." He set off at a furious pace and Michael almost had to trot to keep up. Around red-carpeted corridors they sped until they approached two giant doors.

"Wait!" Michael called. He quickly bent down and spat on his hand. "My boots have a smudge." He rubbed the boot and pretended to shine it.

"Come on!" the secretary whispered hoarsely, clearly almost hysterical.

Carven, the great doors reached to the ceiling, thirty feet or so overhead.

The secretary nodded at the doors. "In there!"

"What, now?"

"Yes. Go!"

Michael pulled the giant door knobs, and the doors whispered open. Sweating, Michael stepped though and saw the Führer standing at the end of a long table. Either side of him were several generals and other high-ranking officers. In front were two photographers with large plate cameras and flash sticks on poles.

The little man in the grey flannel suit smiled at him and then swept back his forelock of black hair with that familiar gesture.

Michael marched up to him and saluted.

"Ah. Herr Dorfmann. So glad you could come."

At that moment, a small ornamental clock chimed five o'clock in tiny, tinkling chimes.

"Come on!" said Michael silently to the crews of 700 Squadron.

A moment later sirens started somewhere in Berlin. Adolf Hitler cocked his head slightly and muttered something. An aid behind him passed a small box containing the medal to him, and he beckoned Michael closer.

"Oberleutnant Dorfmann," the old man said, politely. "I hear you have been in England … . What was it like?"

Grateful for the respite Michael began to give a full account.

"Yes. I found the British to be a friendly … ."

Michael was still talking, four minutes later when a mighty boom, following by the sound of crashing masonry somewhere nearby, interrupted the ceremony.

Hitler muttered something and began to walk calmly towards the doors behind his desk at the end of the room. Opening them he turned left and disappeared. Everyone else in the room followed him until only Michael and one aide stood facing each other.

"Come on, Herr Dorfmann. We're going to the bunker. You must come."

Astonished at his luck, Michael followed him.

***

Above them, Green Section of 700 Squadron began delivering their bombs on the Reichtag. Martin had called the lead ship by VHF radio and asked for a delay of five minutes. To the incoming force of five remaining aircraft, this meant flying in a wide loop before coming in on the bomb run. They were at the mercy of some of JG26 which had remained over Berlin to protect the Führer. Two more aircraft were destroyed before they dropped their bombs around the Chancellery at 5.05pm.

"You've done your job!" called Martin over the radio. "Now get the hell out of there! All except O-Oscar. You know what to do."

O-Oscar carried the special cable-cutting bombs and headed for the River Spree. There it turned north and followed the river in to the end of Unter den Linden at five hundred feet. Two Butcher Birds spotted it and attacked it, one from the front and the other tailing it like a hunting dog after a lame deer. The Stirling already had damage from a flak blast, and one engine ran roughly. It sank lower and opened up its bomb doors. The Butcher Bird attacked from in front and emptied its whole remaining load of cannon shells into the oncoming bomber. The Front Gunner's turret had been smashed to pieces, and both the pilot and flight engineer were wounded. The Stirling lurched to the right for a moment but righted itself.

"Bombs going!" the Bomb Aimer called.

A stick of bombs, timed to drop in sequence over a period of almost thirty second fell among the cars and pedestrians still on the street. Vicious columns of smashed tarmac and concrete rose up into the air, and the cable-cutting blades ripped through cables and people alike. At the slight curve in the long road, the bomber came up against a new threat, two 88mm guns facing it from the Brandenburg Gate. Although the guns only managed to fire four shells each before the bomber was upon them one of these slammed into its left wing, shattering the number three engine. Spewing flames from leaking oil and aviation fuel, the stricken bomber limped over the Gate and crashed into the Tiergarten beyond. Only one of Green Section's bombers made it all the way back to Stradishall.

Red and Blue Sections were still struggling north towards Berlin under repeated attack from JG26's main force of Focke Wulfs.

"Passing Wittenburg now, 16.56." Cloudy called out. "Looks like the weather's closing in over Berlin."

Somebody replied, "*That* wasn't in the briefing!"

"As we Yanks say; SNAFU!" Blalock's voice crackled.

Richard's direct line to Martin suddenly crackled into life. "Richie. We can't hold on much longer. You chaps will have to launch soon."

"Just a few more minutes more Martin. Just get us to Eichwalde."

"Yeah. If any of us make it … !"

Above and behind them, Eugene Blalock took pot-shots at any Focke Wulf 190 that came between him and the bombers but soon came under attack himself. Taking the most violent evasive action he could with bombs on board he quickly persuaded the German pilots that easier pray could be had elsewhere.

Richard closed his eyes each time a Butcher Bird attacked Martin's Stirling from the front. It wasn't so much the fear of death as the horror at being unable to do anything that horrified him. Fitchell's two Browning machine guns in the front turret kept blasting away and damaged two of the German fighters. The shells exiting the barrels of his guns became intermittent and then stopped.

"What's wrong Front Gunner?" Martin called over the intercom.

"I'm out of ammo! I'll need some from the rear guns!"

"Well get it! You have five minutes at most. Y-Yankee from X-Ray leader. You have to take over lead. We don't have any guns right now!"

"Right you are, mate. Drop back now. We'll go over the top!"

The two Stirlings swapped places but not before another Butcher Bird attacked from the rear and raked the side of Martin's bomber with cannon shells. Two of them ripped into the pylon holding the Hurricane steady on top.

"Boy. That was close!" Richard said inside his cockpit. The little fighter began shaking slightly. He watched the Butcher Bird as it streaked ahead. It had the number seven painted in white on its fuselage.

Voss?

The four remaining Stirlings of Red Section struggled on watched over by one lone Hurricane. Z-Zebra flew at the back, closely following V-Victor

"How's the ammunition situation?" Martin asked over the intercom. No reply came. Fitchell was still clambering back into the rear of the fuselage. Each time the bomber took evasive action he got slammed against the metal ribs inside the skin of the aircraft.

"Look out Z-Zebra. Here comes another!" called Blalock.

The Focke Wulf, sporting a yellow spinner and radiator ring, came right up to the tail of the Stirling, determined to get a kill. Z-Zebra's tail gunner pumped everything he had into the airspace of the Butcher Bird, which jinked about wildly to avoid being hit. Simultaneously spraying the air all around the Stirling with cannon shells the German pilot scored a lucky hit, damaging the number one engine on the port side. The engine coughed a few times, and then something exploded out of the cowling. Dewine announced in his Scottish brogue that he was, "Feathering number one engine," but his action came too late. Suddenly, the propeller sheared off and carried by its own spinning momentum veered to the right, cutting into the

number two engine. The last transmission from Z-Zebra came;
"Going down!"

"Z-Zebra. Release your cargo. Repeat. Release your cargo,
now!" Martin calmly called over the radio. Richard watched as
the Stirling lurched to the left, dropping its wing. Within
seconds it would spiral into the ground. Then the bolts fired on
its pylons, and the Hurricane with Slick at the controls drifted
away from the plummeting bomber.

It's too late. He won't make it.

Richard held his breath as the Hurricane struggled to right
itself. Richard knew the Stirling was doomed. Its left wing-tip
already brushed the tops of trees, but he prayed his friend
would somehow find a way to keep the fighter airborne. It
looked more and more as if he wouldn't. The Hurricane pilot
had to turn away from the main force at 90 degrees to stay out
of the path of the parent aircraft, all the time losing height until
its wing tips were barely above the furrowed soil of a ploughed
field. But then the wings levelled, and it started to climb away
from the ground. The pilot brought it back towards the main
force where two Butcher Birds pounced on him.

Z-Zebra finally lost its fight to stay airborne. Its left wing
touched the ground, and the rest of the aircraft went into a
violent cartwheel. It trailed red flames like a Catherine Wheel
as it spun in. When Richard looked away, Z-Zebra had become
just a small pile of burning metal in a ploughed field,
somewhere in Germany.

*God rest their souls.*

"Still here! Just!" panted Slick. "Could somebody kindly
get these damned German's off of me!"

All remaining guns of the Squadron were turned on these
two Focke Wulfs, pumping them full of hot cannon shells.
Both German pilots quickly saw their life passing in front of
them and veered away.

"Three left, Richie. Now's the time. If you don't go now,
none of us will make it!" Martin pleaded.

"Eichwalde," stated Cloudy, quietly. "Everyone turn north.
Drop zone."

"Thank God!" Martin added.

Richard pressed 'transmit.' "Martin, patch me through to
the Squadron."

"You're through."

"Okay chaps. Three of you big boys left. Now's the time to launch. While we still can. F-Freddie; we'll provide top cover. You know what to do. We all need your bombs to be on target."

"Roger. Can hardly hear you above the noise. I know what to do."

All three bombers turned north, lining up with the River Spree as it too curved north into eastern Berlin. Its silver band looked almost like a mirror in the dusk. It reflected the moon in places where the water lay calm.

All pylon bolts fired, and the three remaining Hurricanes were free.

"Head for home, Martin. You all deserve a rest. Meet you in The Black Dog in about two weeks-time!"

"Will do, Richie. Just get the job done. V-Victor and Y-Yankee, head for home. The fighters will probably leave you alone. Turn starboard, 200 degrees magnetic, now!"

"This is it!" announced Richard over the radio. "We're going in!"

***

SS Guards led Michael Dorfmann down a steep staircase and then along a corridor, through two sets of doors to a large open door on the left. He felt slightly disorientated but guessed they were now entering the original bunker.

The little group of men passed store rooms and kitchens on the left and then entered a large dining area. Beyond this they entered a large conference room. Above, Michael could hear the dull crump of bombs being dropped. He began to feel the enormity of his task. He thought he must look white with fear to anybody looking closely enough. A drop of sweat trickled down the back of his neck which irritated him for a moment before the collar of his jacket absorbed it. The aide in front of him pointed to a door on his right guarded by a single SS Lieutenant in a black cap armed with only a pistol.

"Please wait in here. The Führer will call for you."

"Surely he's not going to award the medal *down here*!"

"Oh yes. He normally carries on business down here, just as usual. It's quite safe!"

Michael stepped inside the room, closed the door and paced up and down.

'One guard to get past,' he thought. 'Then we'll have you, you petty little man!' He forced himself to sit on one of the luxuriously upholstered chairs in the guest salon and picked up a magazine, so that he could pretend to read if anybody came in. He scoured the room for something he could use as a club. A heavy glass decanter on a sideboard offered an almost ideal weapon.

A distant string of crumps lasting about thirty seconds told Michael that the lone Stirling had just bombed Unter den Linden. He had at the most, five minutes before he had to act. He started counting.

***

"Following you in, Eugene," Richard announced. "We'll cover you. Once you get around the bend, watch out for telegraph poles. There are three main groups. And don't forget there may still be some cables intact."

Three Hurricane's followed behind Eugene Blalock's Hawker Hurricane as it dipped down to just ten feet above the river. They held back, above the rooftops, to ward off the attentions of five Focke Wulfs still trailing them. The rest seemed to have turned for home eager to avoid the intense flak that seemed to be coming up in vicious black puffs from everywhere in Berlin. A black pall of smoke soon smothered the sky underneath the darkening clouds, further bringing down an early sunset upon the City.

Blalock's F-Freddie skimmed over the water, hopped over two low bridges, and then reached the sharp turn opposite the Berliner Castle. Richard held his breath as he watched Blalock lower his flaps and slow to 135 mph. The Hurricane veered right, and then, gunning the engine, Blalock pulled the complaining aircraft around the Berliner Castle's five-storey edifice and into Unter den Linden.

A collective cheer went up from all the other three pilots. "Well done, Eugene!"

Their glee would be short-lived.

"Je-esus! It's Armageddon down here. Cars and bodies … ! My God! You were … right, skip. Watch out for a power line still across just before the bend. And … some poles … . Oh my god, Eighty-Eights!"

"Where?" asked Richard, calmly.

"End of street. At the gate. And facing us. And … light machine guns all over the place. In windows on either side. I am getting hammered!"

Even in the noise of battle the other pilots could hear the unmistakable sound of machine gun rounds bouncing off the metal of Blalock's Hurricane. They watched him, just ahead, and below, as he turned the corner and headed towards the Brandenburg Gate.

Something flashed by on Richard's right. He glanced over just in time to see the emotionless face of a German pilot looking back at him. A moment later the pilot pushed the nimble fighter into a dive to aim his guns at Blalock. A gothic 'S,' on a white shield, had been painted on the side of the Focke Wulf's nose, a black, cat carrying a bomb ahead of it. The aircraft had the number seven on its fuselage.

*Voss! It's him.*

"Watch out, Eugene. You have an ace coming in above you. I'll try and head him off!"

Richard aimed the Hurricane's two guns at the Voss's tail and opened fire. The paltry firepower of the Hurricane did not impress the German, who pressed home an attack that ripped the cloth on the Hurricane's rear fuselage into shreds.

"Another one like that, and I'm a gonna!"

The 88mm gun crews had been warming up since the previous Stirling's bomb run. Now they fired rapidly at the approaching Hurricane accompanied by SS troops using small arms weapons from windows in buildings either side of him. He jinked once to avoid a standing pylon and then twice more to put the 88mm gunners off their aim. He had almost reached the Gate. Voss' Focke Wulf passed overhead and went around for another run.

Blalock, his Hurricane hit by machine gun fire from the top of the Gate, had been taken completely by surprise. One round entered the engine while another entered his cockpit and his leg.

"Agh! I'm hit! Watch out for guns *on top* of the Gate!"

The trailing Hurricane's followed him around as he crossed over the Tiergarten. It seemed as if every flak gun in Germany had gathered in the ancient park. Some of the biggest pounded away ineffectually at a ghost target, thousands of feet above them, but the smaller guns were pointing directly at Blalock's Hurricane as if they had been expecting him. Black smoke gathered over the eastern edge of the park like a long signal fire. Blalock's Hurricane flew into it.

"Damn! This is madness! Nobody said it would be this hot!"

Richard began to seriously consider abandoning the operation. He saw Blalock make his final turn, and then he knew he would not order the operation aborted.

"Nice and steady, Eugene," he heard himself say, calmly.

"Roger. Going in."

There stood the wall. Richard saw it first, and then moments later he saw Blalock's Hurricane emerging from the black smoke.

"I see the wall. Aiming. Bombs gone!"

All eyes in the remaining 700 Squadron eyed the wall in the back garden of the Chancellery. A split second later the ground in front of it erupted. The wall disappeared in a cloud of mud and dust. Richard felt sure it had gone. "Nice work, Eugene!"

Richard, Todd and Slick flew over the cloud of debris and over the Chancellery itself, following Blalock out. No sign could be seen of the Focke Wulf now.

"Back to the River Spree," Richard ordered. "Form on … ."

"Wait! The wall's still there!" shouted Razor, bringing up the rear. "It's still bloody there!"

"What. All of it?" asked Richard.

"No. There are two big holes, about five, maybe ten feet across, but I can't see the vents. I dunno if it's enough, like!"

***

Michael heard the sound he had been waiting nervously for. He had been told the demolition bombs for the wall would sound closer and louder than anything else. There would be three bangs, but he had to move on the first. He heard the first loud and clear.

'Move!' he said to himself. At first his legs didn't want to move. But he forced himself to stand, and then his military training cut in. Suddenly, he could think as clearly as if he were in his beloved 109 over France. He piled cushions on one of the chairs facing away from the door. When the pile rose high enough, he balanced his dress cap on top level with the top of the chair. He walked to the door and admired the affect; it looked as if he still sat in the chair.

He grabbed the decanter, called out, "Hey, guard! I need to speak to somebody!" and hid behind the door. A few moments later, it opened.

"What do y- … . Agh!" Michael had flipped of the soldier's cap and brought down the decanter down his head with his full might. The SS guard fell unconscious to the floor. Michael grabbed the pistol from the man's holster; a Luger.

He peered into the corridor and saw nobody. None of the British Intelligence boffins had any information on the layout of the bunker. He had to guess where to go. He needed to get to the new section. He guessed he needed to continue further in the direction he had been going when they arrived. He turned right and stepped very quietly. He found another door and opened it. It surprised him to find more steps leading down and to the right. He tentatively descended them listening for any sound of movement, turned left and continued. At the bottom, he saw a long hallway, stretching to the left and running the whole width of the old bunker. But now he thought he must be in the new bunker. The smell of fresh plaster, sawn wood, drying concrete and other building aromas filled his nostrils. He could also detect the damp and faintly sickly smell of domestic gas. In the centre of the north side of the hallway, on the opposite side to the staircase, ran another passage with more descending stairs. Michael Dorfmann knew he must now be ten metres or more below ground level.

Another long hallway, as long as the first, stretched to his left. He saw a desk, with a large cupboard behind it, and a chair, pushed away from the desk, near him on the north side of the hallway. On the desk, were loosely ordered piles of papers. In the centre of the corridor's northern side, he saw another very heavy iron door, but it had been left open. Still Michael had seen nobody. He began to think they had all left. Another heavy door, again open, stood at the end of the short corridor, no doubt meant as a blast door, fire door or gas door. Beyond lay some kind of lounge and then another open door beyond that. Michael heard voices and then footsteps. Behind the second gas door, he saw the open entrance to a plant-room.

Inside, pumps were thrumming. He stepped quickly into the room and hid behind one of the machines.

As luck would have it Michael had stumbled upon the ventilator plant. After the footsteps had passed he examined the machinery around him. He had no doubt that the two vertical tubes, each constructed from hoop-frames about three feet in diameter, covered with canvas, went up to the temporary vent towers. But he could see no sign of any controls for the vents there.

He stepped back into the main corridor and turned right. Through another door, he entered a large open space with treadles and wooden planks piled high. Pots of paint and a board with half dried cement sat in the centre of the floor. At the other end a tarpaulin, hanging from hooks near the ceiling, wafted slightly. Michael could feel the cool breath of evening air blowing in around the tarpaulin. Here, then, he had found the limit to the new construction. He walked to the tarpaulin and pulled it aside. Beyond lay a mud bank, reaching up at almost ninety degrees to a row of planks above. A piece of scaffolding tube lying next to him offered a convenient prod. He picked it up and reaching up to poke the wooden planks. They were firmly nailed down. Putting down the tube quietly he turned around to retrace his steps, letting the tarpaulin fall back into place and froze.

A door to his right opened, and a small man in a flannel suit stepped through it. It took a moment for Michael to recognise Adolf Hitler.

The older man turned and glanced at him. A smile passed briefly across that bleak face like the winter sun in a cloudy December sky.

Michael wanted to fire his pistol, but his hand wouldn't move. How could he kill this kindly, defenseless old man? For a moment, he felt hypnotised by that strange power Adolf Hitler held over so many people.

Then the older man turned and re-entered the doorway, shutting the door behind him.

Michael drew his pistol but too late. He went to the door only to hear it being locked from the other side. He had only moments now.

He ran back to the plant room and ducked inside just as he heard a cough in the hallway beyond. The source of the cough didn't move closer. He couldn't hear any footsteps, so he stealthily searched the plant room again for any controls to the ventilators. Looking up at the ceiling he could see that one of the tubes turned a right angle and passed over the main hallway just below ceiling height, disappearing into the wall on the far side. Apart from this detail he could discern nothing more of interest or use in operating the vents. Time was running out! Michael felt desperate. Then he heard a second bang, as loud as the first.

***

Eineger ran the last two blocks to the Chancellery. He had to abandon the car, but his colleagues declined to follow as he scrambled over rubble blasted from the buildings that had once stood next to Wilhelmstraße. Bombs continued falling with a deafening scream amid the wailing of the sirens and the cries of wounded and frightened people. Cars were rammed up against each other and parked at random on the road and the pavement. He arrived at the chancellery only to find almost everyone gone from the ground floor.

A single guard let him when he flashed his identity papers, but after that he found only one secretary, who shouted, "They're all in the bunker. Get out! The bombs are aimed here!" as he scuttled away.

"Where *is* the *Bunker*? I have to get there. The German pilot, Dorfmann, is going to try and kill the Führer."

The man pointed vaguely at an anonymous looking white door. Eineger went through the door and ran down a flight of stairs to the right. He found himself in the same corridor Dorfmann had seen earlier. He went through two sets of doors to the main bunker entrance on the left. A single SS Guard stood at attention there. The moment he saw Eineger, he swung his rifle down from his shoulder, cocked it and aimed it at the Gestapo officer before Eineger could consider drawing his own pistol.

Eineger felt in no mood to argue. He flashed his papers, but the guard shook his head.

"Sorry, Oberleutnant. Nobody is to go past this point, during an air raid." However, the guard placed the butt of the rifle on the floor while he held on to the barrel.

Eineger feigned replacing the papers with one hand while he withdrew a Luger from a holster inside his jacket with the other.

"Sorry, I don't have time to argue." He shot the SS guard in the chest and head with two neatly aimed shots. The SS guard looked perplexed as a single bead of dark red blood ran down his forehead, and then he crumpled in a heap at Eineger's feet.

Eineger had just committed treason, but he would be forgiven if he saved the Führer's life.

Eineger felt as lost as Dorfmann. Wondering at the silence and emptiness of the bunker he cautiously peered into the rooms on either side of the corridor beyond the entrance. Opening all the doors he could find, he soon found the guest lounge where Dorfmann had waited. His keen eyes quickly took in the opened magazine on the table and the displaced chair. Closing the door, he continued until he found the flight of stairs which led down to the new bunker.

***

Two hundred feet above Eineger and a mile to the east, Richard's remaining Hurricanes reformed over the River Spree. Todd would be first to attempt a run in on the Chancellery with the gas canisters. But Blalock's Hurricane misfired badly and trailed puffs of oily black smoke.

"I think my leg's broken," said Blalock over the radio.

"Hang in there, Eugene. Can you cover Todd on his run in?" We need your guns.

"I'll try, but she's not going to hold up much longer. I'll have to put her down."

"In the Tiergarten. That's your best hope. Or the river."

"I'll take the park!"

"Okay follow Todd in. The rest of you stay here and keep out of trouble. If you see any Focke Wulf's, take a shot at 'em."

"But I thought we were all going in, line astern, skip, you first," commented Todd.

"Change of plan. The Wall's still up. We're going to have to make this up as we go along."

The thump of a heavy artillery shell from one of the Tiergarten guns exploding nearby physically knocked

Richard's Hurricane ten feet off course. He struggled to correct it.

"Jesus. I didn't think it would be this bad. That Archie's got a lot to answer for … !"

Todd lined up on the River Spree, flying north. "Starting my run, now."

"Okay Todd. Eugene and I will cover you as far as the Gate. After that, Eugene watch him bomb and then put her down. Alright?"

"Right, mate," The big American replied between gasps.

"Todd. Aim your canisters right at the wall. They have no explosive power, but just the sheer weight of them might knock the rest of the wall over. In any case, you would be very lucky to get even one of them through the gap."

"Seems a bit of a waste of these beauties!"

"Well, we have no choice."

"Right oh."

Todd flew above the river at ten feet, sending a 'V' of spray up into the air behind him, as he sped towards the Berliner Castle.

"Don't forget; fifteen degrees of flaps, 135 and give her full boost," Richard reminded him calmly.

All three Hurricanes veered right just before the Castle and then were forced into a tight left turn by their pilots. Richard and Blalock followed at just below rooftop height.

"Watch out for the poles!" Richard warned.

"Small arms fire coming in on both sides," Todd announced over the radio, "Hey, there's one of those Butcher Birds up there! Where's he come from?"

"Watch him Todd. It's Gunther Voss. He's bad business. I'll try and get a bead on him."

Voss had been tracking the Hurricanes from further north and a few thousand feet up. He felt hungry for at least one kill.

"Hopping over that cable, and … woah! Around one pole, coming up to the bend … . Jesus! It's Hell on Earth down here!" The sound of machine gun shells peppering the Hurricane could be heard over the radio. Richard looked down and saw Todd's aircraft dodging in and out of obstructions; downed poles, crashed buses, twisted cables and fallen masonry, while little sparks flew off his engine cowlings where bullets were hitting it.

*No aircraft can take that!*

Several shells exploded in front or Richard's cockpit, obscuring his view with black cordite puffs for moments. Two machine gun rounds hit his aircraft's cowling making rough holes in the aluminium.

Gunther Voss put his Focke Wulf into a dive and aimed his four cannons and two machine guns at Todd's Hurricane. Richard flicked the nose of his Hurricane up to get off a short burst from his two guns. He pressed the gun-trigger and saw his thin line bullets streaking towards the Butcher Bird. At the same time six lines of lethal fire erupted from the Focke Wulf, many of them slamming into Todd's aircraft.

Todd let out a yell of pain. His Hurricane had now come within the sights of the two 88mm guns, which pounded away at the oncoming fighter.

"Todd? Are you okay?" Richard asked.

No answer came, but the Hurricane flew though the hail of fire, smoke now pouring from its engine and the radiator under the wings. Half of the rudder's fabric trailed like torn stockings from the fighter. Less than two-hundred metres stood between Todd and the Gate, but Voss lined up another burst. Both Richard and Eugene opened up on the German. They saw some hits each, but he pressed home his attack.

A burst of cannon shells penetrated right into the engine of Todd's Hurricane sending bits of metal spraying out from the nose. The propeller's rotation slowed, and the aircraft veered slightly to the left. For a moment Richard thought Todd must already be dead.

Any less experienced fighter pilot would have crashed losing power at ten or twenty feet above the ground. Todd, however, had always flown a Hurricane as if it were part of him. Richard remembered him saying often, "Don't like Spits. I know pilots say they fly like they are strapped onto you, but they don't feel solid like a Hurricane. A damaged Hurricane is more likely to get you home than a damaged Spit."

With a hair-trigger moment, the Hurricane's pilot pulled it up and away from the ground and the street, using speed to gain height and threw Voss off. Richard knew Todd must still be alive. Voss pulled up and veered away north, to watch the stricken fighter. Todd flew right over the gate, wrong-footing those gunners too. With the engine dead he put the Hurricane into a long, shallow glide and made his final turn towards the Chancellery garden.

"Come on Todd. You can do it!" Richard found himself saying out loud.

Even under his skilful control, Todd's Hurricane clipped the tops of trees and barely skimming the ground when it reached the wall. The boyish Australian, who had once charmed Anna with his guileless charm, released the canisters right on target before hauling up the nose of the Hurricane and just edging it over the wall. The canisters hit the brick and concrete construction, blasting multiple cracks in it. But they fell, inert, against the outside of the wall. Richard took in the whole scene as the canisters started spewing red gas. At the same moment Todd's Hurricane slammed into the side of the Chancellery building. It exploded in a ball of red and orange flame as Richard himself cleared the Chancellery roof top.

"Todd!" he whispered.

"Skipper. I am going to have to duck out of this show," Eugene muttered weakly.

Richard twisted to look behind him. He could see Blalock's Hurricane, wreathed in black smoke, veering away west to make a crash-landing in the Tiergarten. Richard could not help but chase after his friend to watch over the landing. He banked right which brought him around behind Blalock and into the path of the flak gun fire in the Tiergarten. He reached there just in time to see the little fighter touch down. Its belly grazed the grass of the park and then cut a long furrow between two lines of guns. It came to a halt after swinging slightly at the last moment and then the pilot wrenched the cockpit canopy open. Richard saw two gloved hands sticking up in surrender, and a number of German gunners running towards the crashed aircraft.

"Eugene's okay. Todd's gone. It's just us three, now. I'm on my way back to the river."

"Boss. What's the point of going down that street? It sounds like murder. Let me try going in over the rooftops?" Razor asked.

"You don't stand a chance. The park is *thick* with guns."

"Do you want to see this thing done or not? Let me try it?"

"Alright Razor. But if it gets really thick, get out of there. I'll follow you and watch out for Voss. Michael told me about him. He is a real killer."

"Going in."

Richard followed Razor as he tore through the air one hundred feet above the rooftops and one hundred feet below Richard. Almost as soon as they reached the eastern end of Unter den Linden great black puffs of smoke filled the air ahead of them in a solid wall as the combined might of the Third Reich's flak guns in the Tiergarten let rip.

"There is no way through that, Razor!"

"Let me try."

Richard's instinct told him to pull away, but he followed Razor on into the dark dungeon of sky-borne metal and smoke. Shrapnel clattered off the aircraft's metal skin, one piece breaking a pane of Perspex in Richard's canopy. The cold air whistled around his face.

"I can't see you, Razor. Where are you?"

"Just a little … . Damn! I'm hit. Tail. Can't … . Turning around."

"Good. See you back at the river." Just as he banked to the right Richard saw a flash of bright metal far above them. "Here comes Voss. Watch out!"

Gunther Voss made one pass on Razor's damaged Hurricane but found himself under fire from one of the Hurricane's and something else, something above him. He felt confused for a moment and drew off to get his bearings.

"Right. Now we do it my way," Richard announced. "The street is the only way in. You both go in together ten seconds apart. I'll follow slightly above you to watch for Voss. How bad's the damage?"

"I dunno. I can't see. Rudder and elevators awfully heavy, like. Can you take a look?"

Richard dropped behind Razor's Hurricane. "Yes. You lost half of both. I'm surprised you are still in the air!"

Razor began his run in, followed by Slick and, higher up, Richard.

All three negotiated the Berliner Castle and headed into the long Unter den Linden, Richard at just below rooftop height. Still no sign of Voss's Focke Wulf could be seen.

Ground-fire peppered all three Hurricanes, but Razor's received the heaviest fire. Both leading pilots expertly jinked their aircraft around the various obstacles in the devastated street, making it difficult for Richard to see the obstacles in time to avoid them himself. He clipped a telegraph pole with a wing-tip and narrowly missed the roof of a school bus.

As soon as they made the turn, the 88s opened up and the concentration of small arms fire from windows of building in the street grew more intense than before. Several bullets passed through Richard's cockpit. One grazed his leg and another cut the oxygen line to his mask. He heard the sound of tiny rips in the canvas of the fuselage behind him and the aircraft rocked from side to side from the blast of 88 shells and partly from the impact of so many bullets. He longed to fire his guns at something.

"Gate approaching. I'll never do this again. Didn't you say it would be easy, skip?" quipped Razor.

"Watch out for the guns on the Gate. They're very good."

Something large flew past Richard's cockpit.

"That's torn it. Lost even more of my rudder now!" answered Razor. "You were right." Seconds later, Slick and then Richard shot across the top of the Gate and Richard caught a brief glimpse of Razor's aircraft through the hail of bullets and smoke. Its rudder had almost completely gone. "Having trouble … ."

Richard watched as Razor's Hurricane appeared again between flak bursts and half rolled to the right before its pilot corrected and took a haphazard course towards the Chancellery garden.

Richard and Slick followed the bucking and weaving Hurricane around to line up on the garden. Bursts of low flak from the park shocked Richard's Hurricane forcing it left and then right, almost out of his control.

"Three, two, one, bombs gone. Damn! Missed! Going around, skip. Need to get this right."

"No, Razor!"

Razor's canisters dropped just short of the wall. One of them bounced and hit the wall, bringing down another five feet of wall. But the wall remained largely intact. Razor quickly banked his Hurricane around to the right as Slick cleared trees at the edge of the garden. Richard saw Razor line up his fighter on the wall. He shut his eyes as his friend's fighter crashed into the wall at 250 mph right below him. The wall and garden erupted in an enormous explosion that seemed to shake the Chancellery building itself.

Richard followed Slick back to the River Spree, saying nothing. Then over the radio, Slick asked, "Why did he have to do that, silly sod?"

"He's gone. Just you and me now Slick. Let's get this thing done and get out of here!" Richard pressed the 'X' button to transmit. Then he used the black button to tap 'Sweepstake' in Morse code.

"Right!"

***

A klaxon blared in the bunker. Michael heard a third bang, much louder than the others, and then a fourth. This nearly deafened him and rocked him on his feet. Accompanied it, a rush of hot air came from somewhere in the bunker. He had expected three demolition bombs before the first of the gas canisters would be dropped.

'No more time!' he thought. He stepped out from the plant room and into the main entrance hallway. To his left an SS guard stood in front of the previously empty chair. The guard saluted and then saw the Luger pointing at him.

"Sir?"

"I have no time. Where are the controls for the vents? If you don't tell me in three seconds, I will shoot you."

"But … ." The SS guard closed his mouth and reflexively, glanced at the cabinet behind him. Then he closed his eyes. Michael shot him cleanly once in the forehead. He ran behind the desk and opened the cabinet door behind the desk. He saw a bank of labelled levers and buttons.

"Don't move, Dorfmann. I have a pistol pointing at the back of your head."

Michael recognised the voice.

Without thinking he said, "There is more than one of us in here."

Eineger hesitated for a moment. "Who? Where?"

Michael saw two red buttons labelled, 'Ventilator One' and 'Ventilator Two.' Both were set to 'Off.'

"You won't know if you shoot me, will you." Gambling, Michael twisted around to face Eineger and aimed his pistol at the Gestapo man's stomach.

He had taken Eineger by surprise.

"Stop! Or I shoot!" yelled the Gestapo officer.

"Don't worry. I have no intention of shooting yet. Where are the controls to the air ventilators?"

"I … I don't know what you mean. Now tell me who's in on this conspiracy with you. I can plead leniency for you. You have a good record."

Michael had become used to facing death but had never before shot a man whose face he could see. Now he might have to do it twice. He looked into Eineger's eyes. He saw fear there but a man prepared to die. He saw the loyalty, loyalty to the Führer in the Gestapo man's eyes. Michael had seen it many times before. It would be his edge.

"One of us will have to shoot."

***

"You go in first, Slick. I need to see how you do."

"Why don't you let me go first, sonny. The flak's getting worse. It will be suicide next time."

"It's suicide *now*, if you ask me."

"Going in."

Both Hurricanes made the turn at the Berliner Castle, but this time the crossfire had moved even further towards the eastern end of the street. Both were under furious attack right from the end of Unter den Linden. A gun position, near the first island of broken telegraph poles, sent up jabbing bolts of fire. Slick gave the gunners a half second burst from his guns just to make him feel better. "Take that, you bastards!"

A hail of bullets arced towards Slick's Hurricane as it reached the bend in the street. And then they were in the sights of the 88s.

"Here we go. Care for a bet that I'll be the one to get the 'Bulls Blood'?"

"Ten shillings."

"You're on. Where's that Voss fellow?"

"Must have gone home for tea, or coffee."

"Ersatz! Blimey. This is rough. Ouch!" The staccato sound of bullets hitting Slick's Hurricane almost drowned out his voice. An 88mm shell exploded right above Richard's Hurricane, completely shattering all the remaining Perspex panels in his cockpit canopy and bending the frame out of shape. It also put a large crack in the bullet-proof glass windscreen. Richard's cheeks were cut to pieces, and one piece of flying Perspex cracked the lens of his goggles. He drew them off and threw them out of the cockpit. He pulled one shard of Perspex from his cheek.

"No canopy, Slick! This is like flying those old Gladiators. Remember them?" But Slick had become completely focused on the upcoming Gate and the lethal guns on top of it.

"Agh!" he screamed as shrapnel ripped open his jacket over his chest. Blood oozed out of a deep wound. "I'm hit!"

"Is it bad?"

"Bad enough. Turning now. Stay with me. Keep right behind me, skip."

"I'm here."

But now Slick came within the sights of the Tiergarten guns which were keen on getting their first kill. Every gun that could lower its elevation to reach the Hurricane blasted everything it had at him. Part of his right wing-tip came off, but he continued on before making the final turn to the garden.

"Voss!" shouted Richard. Barely had he spoken the name when the Focke Wulf 190 blasted ahead of him, diving on Slick. Voss let a five second burst rip into the lead Hurricane which bucked under the impact. Black smoke started belching from ragged holes in the engine fairings. "You bastard, Voss. I'll have you!" Richard whispered to himself.

Slick struggled to line up his aircraft. "Three, two, one, canisters gone!" he shouted. He pulled the stick up, and the Hurricane clawed the sky for height, barely clearing the gutters around the rim of the Chancellery.

The two canisters were dropped right on target. Moments later, two plumes of red gas curled into the air to mix with the smoke and faint red gas clouds remaining after Razor's attack.

"Can you make it back, Slick?"

"Doubt it. Gasoline and coolant all around my feet. Putting her down. The left vent is gone. Blasted away, Richard!"

"Understood."

"I think I was right on the other one. But it's not sucking!"

"Yes. I can see that now." Richard could see the red cloud of gas near the right-hand ventilator, but the gas just dispersed evenly. None of it got sucked into the ventilator. "Damn. Come on, Michael!"

Slick's damaged Hurricane banked to the right and Richard followed him at first but veered to the south as Slick turned again to put the fighter down in the Tiergarten.

Richard watched over his shoulder through the flak bursts as Slick gently guided his aircraft down to the grass in the park. But at the last moment the fighter's wing dipped and then the nose. Richard saw it plough into the ground and then cartwheel. Slick's last moment came in a ball of fire that lit up the darkening sky.

Richard gritted his teeth and set his jaw for the final run. His face became fixed in a look of pure, gritty determination. He banked left and headed back towards the River Spree. A few 88mm shells come up from the north end of Wilhelmstraße and surprised him, but he evaded the black puffs of smoke and shrapnel. The nose of his Hurricane looked more like a sieve than part of an aircraft. Half of one of the engine access plates had peeled back like a fruit skin and flapped in the airflow. This made the aircraft veer to the left. Richard dare not look at his tail, but both wings were pocked with holes. Fuel leaked slightly from his port tank, and he set the pump to transfer any remaining fuel from it into his emergency tank which lay just ahead of the cockpit. The cold blast of air around him chilled his bones, but the adrenaline pumping through his veins numbed him to the discomfort.

Lining up on the northward arc of the River Spree into Berlin, Richard dived for the water one last time. He reached the Berliner Castle and put on 15 degrees of flaps. He slowed to 135 mph and gunned the engine as the Hurricane made the sharp turn one last time.

"I will marry you, if you get me through this, baby," he said to his aircraft. But an image of Anna's smiling face burst into his mind. Her lively range of expressions played across her face, which hung in front of him like a mirage until he saw something black and ugly, bursting from the vision of her mouth.

*Telegraph pole!*

He jerked the control column instinctively, grazing the obstacle with the underneath of the right wing. The Hurricane shook like a rattle.

*Jesus!*

***

In Stradishall, Anna couldn't bear the waiting anymore; a leaden silence hung over the aerodrome. She had the irrational urge to scream, to break it, but instead called for a staff car.

She felt almost surprised when the station adjutant replied, "Right," and minutes later, a black can stopped outside the blockhouse; clearly her association with both Richard and Michael gave her some clout too.

"What do you have there miss?" the well-trained driver asked. "Sorry; security. I have to ask!"

Anna lifted the tea-towel, covering the box, and showed him Jackie, who briefly looked up, curiously.

"I can't take you outside the perimeter; security," the driver added.

"Doesn't matter. I saw some rabbits on the north western perimeter, the other day. Take me there."

"Isn't he the Squadron Leader's?"

"You heard about him?"

"Sure! Everyone knows about the rabbit with the blue scarf, even if… Sorry. Idle talk costs lives an' all that!"

"Wait here… just ten minutes," she instructed, leaving the car.

A gentle breeze lifted the towel corners from the box, but it was still a warm evening. She sat down on a clump of grass, turned the box on its side and rearrange the cushion inside, so that Jackie could sit comfortably on it. She gently untied the miniature blue scarf.

"You won't need that. Off you go Jackie! I think it's time."

But the little rabbit seemed quite content to nibble at the fresh grass by his nose. He stayed in the box.

She looked up at the empty, dark sky and tried to sense if Michael and Richard were both still alive. A recollection of how Michael had told her he had persuaded the mechanics to put Donald into Richard's cockpit jolted her. Did she still love Michael? Yes. Now, more so than ever.

*So confusing! I should have told them. Soon I might have to choose!*

The bitter fear of the decision was instantly followed by the conflicting faint hope that at least one of them would survive. She *knew* both would not.

*Oh God! Is it always a woman's lot to be torn inside and suffer in silence? Jackie?*

She glanced at the box. Jackie had gone.

***

"Dorfmann. Let's be reasonable. You cannot get out alive."

"But you can. Join me. I have learned things about the Führer. Things you suspect are true. Germany will lose the War and Adolf Hitler will be hanged if he is not found to be insane."

"You're a traitor. You're *not* a good German."

"You know what he has been doing? He's been making Jews kill each other for scraps of stale bread. Scraps of bread! He has made almost a whole race live like animals! I may be a bad German, but I *am* a *human being*!"

For just the briefest moment, Eineger glanced away in doubt. Michael fired, and a hole appeared in Eineger's stomach. He lurched, and his gun hand went wildly up to his shoulder. Michael fired again, this time at Eineger's head. But before he pulled the trigger Eineger himself fired. Michael's stomach seemed to explode at the very same moment a neat round hole appeared in Eineger's forehead. Both men fell to the floor, Michael on his knees. He held his stomach, and blood poured around his fingers. He could see Eineger was dead.

Michael twisted round and pressed both red ventilator switches. Somewhere a humming started, its cadence and tone increasing until it became a steady note.

He forced himself to his feet and lurched into the corridor running north. At the far end, he could see the tarpaulin had been set ablaze. Pieces of charred wood and metal were falling on the floor.

'Can't go that way anymore,' he thought.

***

Richard's Hurricane headed along Unter den Linden at barely ten feet. Now the full might of Reich fire seemed aimed solely at him. It felt like flying though a tornado of hot lead. Not an inch of air seemed free of bullets or shrapnel from the flak. However, some of the guns were now pounding the air above him for some reason. He released the safety catch on the bomb-arming switch.

Over the small battery of guns at the island of fallen poles, he hopped, flicked left and then right, around some crashed cars and a bus. He hopped over a length of cable which still hung from the side of a building and then reached the turn in the street. Already he had lost count of the bullets that had passed right through the aircraft. One had grazed his knee and another put a hole in his flying jacket. There seemed no hope of making it to the Gate.

Then he saw the fire from the 88s. He shuddered and wanted to close his eyes.

"Richie! Look above you! We couldn't leave you!"

*What the … !*

He twisted his neck and saw the shadow of something blotting out the moon. Then he made out the unmistakable shape of a Short Stirling; the most blessed sight he had ever seen. "Martin!"

"Fitchell fixed the guns," Martin said, gasping. "We'll cover you."

Fitchell blasted away at the 88s with the front guns of the Stirling. Together, both aircraft flew towards the Brandenburg Gate. Richard flicked his little aircraft left and right. It responded to his every command as if they were telepathically linked. Richard had no time to consider anything. At last, he approached the Gate, and then a shell burst right over the cockpit. A chunk of shrapnel, the size of a hand grenade, punched into Richard's stomach. It knocked him back into the seat and almost wrenched the stick from his hand. He gasped, just managing to avoid crashing into a crashed truck. He flicked the fighter up to the left and watched the blank eyes of the gunners on the Gate as they stared at the miraculous fighter passing them for the last time.

"Fitchell's had it," gasped Martin. "Cloudy and me are the last ones left. I'm not much good I'm afraid, Richie. Don't know any girls who'd want what's left of me. Voss got the rest of us. Cloudy and I have been thinking … . We've come to a decision. Won't be joining you back in Blighty. Remember that French girl, Francine? I didn't tell you. She was in the Resistance. The Nazi's caught her and tortured her. Then they killed her. I owe her one."

Richard knew his brother; there would be little point trying to dissuade him, but he tried. "No Marty." Then, after a pause, "What are you going to do?"

No answer came.

Richard had no time to think. Flak bursts rocked his Hurricane from side to side. He banked the Hurricane into the final turn and lined up on the garden. Easing back on the throttle, he let the Hurricane float down towards the ground, so that it brushed the top of a line of trees. Ahead lay the carnage of the crushed wall and the two Hurricanes of Todd and Razor. Like an obscene firework display burning rounds of ammunition sparked and jumped up into the air. To his right Richard could see the remaining ventilator. He corrected using some right rudder and lined his sight up on the tower. Taking a deep breath, he waited until the cross-hairs of the sight lined up on the tower. He pressed the release button. The canisters dropped away. Instantly, the Hurricane jumped into the air, relieved of their weight. Richard pushed the throttle forward and cleared the roof top. Remembering Martin's Stirling, he banked to the south and searched for it. There it was. But he had to return to the garden to see if the attack had been successful or not. Tearing his eyes away from the tail of the damaged Stirling he continued to bank until he crossed the Tiergarten. He saw the two wrecked Hurricanes of Slick and Blalock in the park. But the gunners were caught out. Not expecting this last chance only a few managed to get off rounds at the Hurricane. Richard lined up one last time on the garden and let the Hurricane float down to just above tree height. He saw the tower:

"There and … ."

He had to screw his eyes up and look again. Yes, it was true. Two plumes of red gas were spiraling around the ventilator tower and then disappearing inside.

"It worked! Yes, we've done it! Yes! Yes! Yes, Michael, yes! Martin! We did it!" A tear formed in his eye but immediately got whisked away by the biting wind.

***

In the Bunker, Michael heard the sound of jackboots coming down the double flight of steps. In one telephone call, Adolf Hitler had informed the commander of his own personal bodyguard that a traitor had got into the Führerbunker. They only took five minutes to arrive.

Michael lurched into the plant room clutching his stomach. There could be only one way out. Another explosion rocked the bunker.

'That has to be the last one,' he thought. 'I have to wait.' He hid behind one of the two vertical tubes. He held his breath as the jackboots ran past the plant room.

Moments later somebody started shouting, "Gas! Gas!"

In his private quarters Adolf Hitler had seen the red gas coming out of the ventilation grating. It took only a moment for him to realise what had happened. He walked to the door and turned the handle. But he had locked it! Reaching into his pocket he cursed himself for pocketing the key, a habit of over-cautiousness. He found the key, but by the time he had unlocked the door, he had already begun coughing from a cloud of faint red gas. Nevertheless, when he regained the main corridor he thought he had been lucky. People were running towards the bunker exit. Somebody shouted, "Gas! Gas!"

Michael waited until he could see red gas curling around the doorway into the plant room. Now he had to go. More jackbooted feet were descending the stairs outside.

He reached inside his trousers for the penknife he carried. A gift in childhood, he never went anywhere without it. He cut a long slit in the canvas tube nearest him from the loop at waist height to the floor. He cut a 'T' at the top and pulled the canvas aside. No gas seeped out from the cut.

'Good,' he thought. 'I'm in luck!'

He slipped inside the tube. Using the hoops as footholds, he clambered up the tube but found it blocked at the top. Frustrated, in immense pain from his wound and out of breath, he clambered back down the tube and slit the other one. Red gas escaped came from the slit. This tube took a right angle and passed over the passageway. Michael didn't know the lethal nature of the gas; at least he knew it would be lethal but not in what doses. Holding his breath would not save him as the gas could penetrate the skin, nostrils, ears and eyes. Nevertheless, he tried to hold his breath long enough to escape through the long tube, but as he scrambled up it and around the bend, he had to take a breath. His skin tingled. The red gas had become concentrated here. He continued on, but each metre took more effort than the last, and then muscle cramp set in. After he had traversed half of the horizontal section of tube he heard shots. Looking behind him, he could see a punctured in the tube, through which red gas escaped. He crawled on. The pain in his chest almost made him faint. He had almost give up, when he reached a ladder. He took another painful breath. He gripped the rails in agony and ascended to the top of another tube. Here, a wooden panel blocked his exit. On either side of him now were open wooden slats. Through the gaps he could see the garden. Smoke and carnage were all around. He saw a latch beside him and guessed it to be a latch for a door. He released it and pushed open the panel-door. The smoke-filled, evening air rushed in around him. He stumbled with relief into the darkness.

***

Richard cleared the Chancellery roof one more time and then headed south to catch his brother's bomber. He saw it in the distance and just above it, two black shapes. Night had fallen over Berlin now but a night without stars.

"Martin! Martin! Two bandits on your tail. Repeat, two bandits on your tail!"

No reply came, but Martin pushed the big bomber over into a steep dive. The two Focke Wulf's followed him. Just above the rooftops they opened up on the bomber. But Martin pulled up on the stick and eased his aircraft into a loop. The two German pilots missed and peeled off, astonished. At the top of the loop Martin's bomber rolled once and then straightened out, so that it flew straight towards Richard. Richard laughed. Then Martin pushed the bomber into another dive He aimed it towards a large building below Richard, not far from Wilhelmstraße.

Richard remembered Martin trying to tell him something on the way to the last meeting in Whitehall. "Richie. I happen to know where Gestapo Headquarters are, Niederkirchnerstraße, further south along Wilhelmstraße … ." but they had been interrupted by a pretty girl asking directions. Martin had never completed the sentence.

"No, Marty! No!"

The 88mm guns in Wilhelmstraße opened fire on the bomber, realising his target to be the Gestapo Headquarters. Just as it looked as if Martin would hit his target an 88mm round entered the right wing of his bomber. It penetrated one of the self-sealing fuel tanks. But sealant couldn't protect against live ammunition. The wing erupted, and then the bomber exploded in a fireball that engulfed the city for several blocks. From out of the fireball red hot bits of metal rained down. Anybody caught below was either killed, badly burned or wounded by shrapnel. But the Gestapo Headquarters remained.

With an unfathomable sadness in his heart Richard heavily hauled the stick on his fighter to bank it slightly to the right and head for home. A thought nagged at the corner of his mind, and then he remembered he had to send the call sign for success. He laughed ironically at the word 'success.' He turned the radio set to 'X,' and began punching the code phrase, 'Bulls Blood.' He reached the first 'o' of the second word when the Morse key jammed.

"Blast." But he no longer cared.

He had been considering whether he should empty the last round of ammunition out of his guns and begun thinking about what he needed to do to get home when he remembered Voss. It was dusk now.

*Surely even that Bastard has gone home!*

A volley of cannon shells ripping into the fuselage behind him gave him the answer.

"Right Voss. Now I can deal with you!"

Search lights criss-crossing the sky gave Richard just the light he needed. He let Voss get closer and then corkscrewed madly. The Hurricane felt as light as a feather under his hand. He knew not even a Spitfire or Focke Wulf 190 could stay with him. But he didn't want to just evade Voss. He wanted to kill him!

Gunther Voss, eager for his third kill that day, flew on steady and straight to line up for his final shot. He guessed he only had a few rounds left in his wing machine guns.

He couldn't see the Hurricane ahead of him clearly all the time. Sometimes a blind spot created by the glare of a search light would blot it out. Suddenly it seemed to disappear completely. He searched the sky ahead eagerly for it.

Richard, guessing that Voss would be flying in a straight line suddenly executed a wide corkscrew with a roll that would bring him on to the tail of Voss if the German's reactions weren't quick enough. The agility of his fighter amazed Richard. Before he could draw breath, he had rolled over the head of Voss and falling back onto his tail.

Voss just saw the Hurricane out of the corner of his eye as it rolled over the top of him. He couldn't believe how fast the fighter was.

'Something is not right, here,' he thought. He had quick reactions and pulled back on his stick to execute an evasive manoeuvre himself, something he rarely had to do. But this time his reactions were too slow.

Richard wasn't sure if he had any ammunition left. He pressed the firing button on his stick and a three second burst leaped from his two Browning machine guns.

*Not enough!*

But his fire *did* prove enough. The burst ripped into Voss's Focke Wulf just ahead of his cockpit and raked back through the cockpit and into the fuselage behind him.

The German fighter started belching flame and smoke. Richard saw the fighter roll on its back and then dive into the ground.

"Good night, Voss. Sweet dreams."

***

Clasping his stomach and drawing the Luger again, Michael lurched to his feet in the Chancellery garden. He weaved in and out of burning aircraft wreckage and bomb craters and headed away from the buildings. He struggled through a line of trees and over a fence before reaching another line of trees. He heard voices behind him. They were coming closer. He felt so numb and tired that he simply wanted to lie down and sleep. But he had to keep going. He pushed through the line of trees and saw the headlamps of a car approaching. He stood beside a road. Beyond that lay the Tiergarten. He hid as the car drove past and then stumbled across the road and into the park. Turning to look back at the road he saw the weak beams of torches beyond the line of trees. He didn't have long.

He stumbled across the neatly mown grass for a hundred metres. There, he found a path running south. He turned onto it and leaned against a statue. He could go no further.

Remembering his Luftwaffe training for shot-down pilots he desperately looked for some way to put his pursuers off his trail. He could see nothing; no water, no friendly face. He drew his pistol.

Michael had thought of climbing into a tree as a last resort. But now he spotted something better for a hiding place. On the path to the left of the trees, he saw the unmistakable outline of a manhole cover. The little globe-lights in the park lit up the pattern on its iron surface. He crawled over to it and used his penknife to lever up the edge, breaking the blade in the process.

With one last gasp of effort he hauled himself into the shaft and pulled the lid closed over the top of him.

Michael's desperate plan worked. The SS guards couldn't understand how Dorfmann had given them the slip. Inside the shaft, Michael reached the bottom, a sewer, and slumped, exhausted and barely conscious. He shook violently.

***

Richard Earlgood now had one last thing to do; he had to reach Holland. He had no ammunition left and almost no fuel left. He could think of nothing he could do to lighten the load and increase his chances of making it, except to lean out the fuel mixture.

*This aircraft must be fifty pounds lighter anyway, from all the lost bits and pieces!*

At treetop height he scudded west, aiming to reach the German border at least. Once out of Berlin he turned slightly south and then west to aim for Hanover. He passed close by the city within thirty minutes, its search lights twinkling to the south in the evening sky. Then, thirty minutes later he passed Osnabrück. He almost passed out from the pain in his stomach several times. Only the constant blast of cold air kept him alert. He knew he had lost a lot of blood, but he would rather die free than as a captive of the Third Reich. Twenty minutes passed, and he knew he must be in Holland and not far from Veluwemeer. He took out the little torch they had all been supplied with for the mission and switched it on. He struggled to hold the map flat on his leg. He had to remove his damaged oxygen mask and put the torch in his mouth to read it. Identifying the coast of Veluwemeer, he turned south for the area of water near Elburg. He had to grit his teeth and pinch his face to stay conscious. Just when he thought he would make it, the Hurricane's Merlin engine coughed, twice.

*Out of fuel. I thought it was too good to last.*

He turned the two wing tank fuel pumps on, hoping there might be one last drop of fuel somewhere. He slipped the tired fighter into a serious of gentle banks, and the Merlin's beat picked up again.

"Come on, darling. You know what I said about marriage!"

The Hurricane's engine coughed twice. Richard flew on, scanning the night sky for any sign of Elburg.

***

Adolf Hitler found himself waiting in the Chancellery garden with Blondi for the return of the SS Guards with the prisoner, Dorfmann. When they returned empty handed he wasn't too disappointed. They would find him eventually. Back in his main office with his secretary he stamped his feet once with jubilation.

"They missed again! Just like in the trenches! The British are so stupid!"

Dorfmann's body wasn't found until 1947, by a drainage inspector.

Back in Whitehall, the incomplete message, "Bulls Blo" had been taken as meaning success. That they could not raise any of 700 Squadron on the radio after this had been taken to mean that no aircraft were still in the air.

Amalfi Douglas, in Y-Yankee crashed near Hanover and Geoffrey Hutchinson's crew had to ditch in the English Channel. They were picked up later by Air Sea Rescue and were the only complete bomber crew from Red Section to get back alive.

By 7am the following morning, with no word from any British airfields or the Dutch Resistance to the contrary, it had to be assumed that all the fighter pilots were now dead. In fact, the CS-6 radio at Elburg had developed a fault and no message could be sent.

Finally getting ready to go home for some sleep, Archibald Gates caught the attention of his boss.

"It will be hard for Anna," he said. "She has lost both men in her life. What shall I tell her?"

"Tell her they died bravely. It's the official line. What else can you tell her?"

"I mean about the raid? What did it achieve?"

"We won't know *that* for some time … ."

"So now you can tell me. What does this gas do? I mean, innocent civilians might have been killed. I would at least like to know what it does."

"Very well. I will tell you what I know, which is not much. And I must emphasise, this is Top Secret. It's a nerve gas. It attacks the central nervous system. If you are exposed to it in sufficient concentration, it can cause death in minutes. If not, early symptoms are shaking, loss of control of arms and legs and stiffness. Later it causes cognitive and behavioural problems and eventually dementia. If you have heard of it, its effect is very similar to that of Parkinson's disease."

"I see. You know Richard once told me that people like us would end up behind bars or writing the Evening Standard crossword puzzle. Maybe he was right. I think people like him are the *real* heroes! It's they that will win the War."

"People need heroes, but they don't win the wars. And anyway Archie, you are quite naïve. There will always be place for us. Winning wars isn't the most important thing … ."

The carnage in the Reich Chancellery had been cleared away within a week and new grass planted. By the spring of 1944, the new Führerbunker had been completed, and no sign remained of the British attack. Adolf Hitler thought he had 'got away with it.'

***

# Biography of Lazlo Ferran

Lazlo Ferran: Exploring the Landscapes of Truth.

Educated near Oxford, during English author Lazlo Ferran's extraordinary life, he has been an aeronautical engineering student, dispatch rider, graphic designer, full-time busker, guitarist and singer, recording two albums. Having grown up in rural Buckinghamshire Lazlo says:

"The beautiful Chiltern Hills offered the ideal playground for a child's mind, in contrast to the ultra-strict education system of Bucks."

Brought up as a Buddhist, he has travelled widely, surviving a student uprising in Athens and living for a while in Cairo, just after Sadat's assassination. Later, he spent some time in Central Asia and was only a few blocks away from gunfire during an attempt to storm the government buildings of Bishkek in 2006. He has a keen interest in theologies and philosophies of the Far East, Middle East, Asia and Eastern Europe.

After a long and successful career within the science industry, Lazlo Ferran left to concentrate on writing, to continue exploring the landscapes of truth.

**From the author:**
Thank you for reading my story and I hope you liked it. I value very much feedback from people and need this if each book is to be better than the last, so if you could take the time to either post a comment on my amazon page or my blog or simply email me, I would appreciate it.

Where to find Lazlo Ferran
Blog: http://www.lazloferran.com
Email: lazloferran@gmail.com

www.ingramcontent.com/pod-product-compliance
Lightning Source LLC
Chambersburg PA
CBHW070440120726
47910CB00003B/872